ROGUES AMONG THE RUINS

ACHALA MOULIK

olive turtle

NIYOGI BOOKS

Published by
NIYOGI BOOKS
Block D, Building No. 77,
Okhla Industrial Area, Phase-I,
New Delhi-110 020, INDIA
Tel: 91-11-26816301, 26818960
Email: niyogibooks@gmail.com
Website: www.niyogibooksindia.com

Editor: Sucharita Ghosh
Cover design: PealiDezine with inputs by the author
Design: Shashi Bhushan Prasad

ISBN: 978-93-89136-69-2
Publication: 2021

All characters and events portrayed in the novel are imaginary. Any resemblance to persons and events is purely coincidental. However, historical figures portrayed in the book are grounded on facts.

Printed at: Niyogi Offset Pvt. Ltd., New Delhi, India

Those who toil under blazing sun and furious rain to feed us

Those who guard our frontiers on land, sea and air to protect us

Those whose tireless labour swells our national wealth

The silent dedicated thousands who keep the machinery of government running

Those artists, musicians, sculptors, writers who keep alive our diverse heritage

The doctors and nurses who endanger their lives for us

Those who love our country without expectation of reward

To them this book is humbly dedicated.

Thy seat is empty today,
Oh brave one, assume thy place

—Rabindranath Tagore (1939)

Sad are the times when
Common decency was called courage

—Evgeny Evtushenko

PART I

LIFE AMONG THE RUINS

September 1939

The great poet Rabindranath Tagore looked sadly at the young man and asked: 'Are you certain that you are following the right path? You will have a solitary struggle if you oppose Gandhiji.'

Subhash Bose looked gravely at Rabindranath Tagore. 'I do not believe in squabbles, *Gurudev*. The liberation of India must not begin with unseemly strategies. We will struggle for freedom with dignity and courage.' Bose bent down to touch Tagore's feet in homage.

Tagore touched Subhash's head in benediction. His vast eyes brimmed with unshed tears. This was the kind of son he had wanted, a man of courage, compassion and stern dignity. Regarding Subhash pensively, Tagore murmured, 'I will compose a few lines for you, my son.'

'May I be worthy of your words, *Gurudev*.'

Rabindranath watched Subhash stride towards the waiting jeep and join his palms in *namashkar* before alighting on the vehicle.

As the jeep drove away the poet glanced at the September sky filled with the last of monsoon clouds. He felt a strange pain stir within him. This pain came in frequent waves now, replacing the effulgent creativity that had attended him even amidst grief and desolation. In his insomniac hours he heard Nazi bombs dropping over the European cities he had seen and admired, where he had been honoured and welcomed. He could not see the Creator amidst the debris of cosmic destruction. Perhaps it was time to leave the world he cherished.

Rabindranath Tagore went inside, sat by his window desk and composed lines for Subhash Bose:

'Thy seat is empty today,
Oh brave one, assume thy place.'

By the Waters of Babylon

My name is Elangovan. Born when British Orientalists were exploring the ancient heritage of India, my father explored temples and epigraphical records which revealed enigmas of our past. This life of idle scholarship was possible because his fertile lands yielded enough rice for our needs and selling the surplus. He came to the notice of Sir Alexander Cunningham, founder of the Archaeological Survey of India; the two men became friends and I, Elangovan, was offered the post of assistant archaeologist in the Archaeological Survey of India.

I worked in the Pallavur Circle of the Archaeological Survey of India (ASI) which then encompassed entire South India. I married a timid maiden who was a contrast to my virago mother. Between their warfare and my archaeological journeys, my wife and I brought five children into the world of which Raman, the eldest, was the most promising. In time I grew to love my work more than anything else in the world.

Life among the ruins had a romance of its own.

The monotony of our lives was dispelled, not by the outbreak of the Second World War, but by consternation in the Archaeological Survey of India. Sir Alistair Mackenzie, director general of the Archaeological Survey, a man who had presided over its destiny for four decades was now returning to his half-forgotten England. Nobody appeared suitable to take his place; some were considered too junior and others not adequately qualified to manage this multi-dimensional organization. When Viceroy Lord Linlithgow was informed of the impending calamity by Archibald Blandford, his civil secretary, he was astounded. Forgetting patrician manners, the King-Emperor's Representative-on-Earth-and-India exploded.

'Need I remind you, Archie, a war is going on? There is desertion from the British Indian Army to the Bloody-Hind-Fauz. The Japs are at our frontiers, the Huns are overrunning Europe, and you dare tell me about the care of ruins! *The whole bloody world is in ruins!*'

The viceroy's civil secretary sighed and wiped his clammy forehead and thought: the pre-monsoon swelter has affected the viceroy who was not *normally* unhinged. Blandford resumed his plea. 'We cannot have a vacuum in the Survey, my Lord. Some very important work is going on there. We require a DG to safeguard the work … and secrecy.'

The granite-faced viceroy regarded his secretary with angry disbelief. He said icily, 'Have you not understood what I said, Archibald Blandford?'

In response to the viceroy's fulminations, Blandford spoke patiently. 'I understand Your Lordship's anxieties about Europe, but in India we have our own problems. We need a suitable person for military reconnoitering in the North-West Frontier Province and also to lead and guide the Survey.'

His Lordship shook his head, exasperated. 'I haven't the foggiest what you are saying, Blandford! But go ahead and get a new director general!' He paused. 'Will it be some woolly-headed don from Oxford?'

Blandford smiled smugly. 'No, my Lord, I have asked Dr Julius Norton to take charge immediately. If he agrees we will fly him out from Mesopotamia. He served in the army as a major and saw action in Belgium in 1940 where he won his spurs. He was discharged after being wounded.'

'A soldier for archaeology?' the viceroy shouted again. 'Has the heat got you, Blandford?'

Blandford smiled wryly. '*I* am accustomed to the heat, my Lord. Military men do a good job at the digs, especially in war-time.' He paused before saying, 'The founder of the Archaeological Survey was General Alexander Cunningham. In Britain, General Augustus Pitt-Rivers initiated new methods for excavations.'

Not bothering to conceal his disgust, the viceroy said, 'That's why we are losing the empire. It seems the army chaps now prefer to dig for broken cups rather than fight the Huns and Japs.'

Archibald Blandford could not resist saying, 'The technical word, my Lord, is potsherds, not broken cups.'

'Go to bloody hell!' His Lordship sputtered and turned to the more urgent task of saving the empire.

***

Dr Julius Norton was directing excavations near Nineveh in Iraq, when he received a telegram from the office of the Viceroy of India, inviting him to be director general of the Archaeological Survey of India. He read the communications with mixed feelings. Archaeology in Mesopotamia had opened new frontiers of historical knowledge. He wanted to make a name here, as his guru, Sir Leonard Woolley, had done decades ago. As a student, Norton joined Sir Leonard in Mesopotamia in 1930. This had led to spectacular discoveries on Sumerian civilization.

Julius Norton remembered the excitement when they excavated forty feet below the ground; they found royal Sumerian tombs, burnt clay tablets with archaic scripts, painted pottery-ware in al'Ubaid. These treasures led to deeper knowledge of ancient Sumer and Babylon which had developed in the lower reaches of the Tigris and Euphrates rivers. Sumeria's main contribution to civilization was the wheel and the cuneiform alphabet. British archaeologists found the capital where ruled the lawgiver King Hammurabi.

Sitting on an undisturbed *tell,* Julius Norton gazed at the mounds that concealed buried cities. He wondered if his dream of excavating these was to be abandoned. But to be director general of the Archaeological Survey of India – who could refuse such an honour? Perhaps in India he would find the remains of another ancient civilization that had ties with Sumeria.

As dusk now fell upon the excavation camp Julius Norton went inside his tent. Familiar scenes, sounds and smells assailed him; of men drawing water from oasis wells, lighting of charcoal stoves, the hiss of goat meat roasting on spits, aroma of Arabica coffee, figs and dates. Attendants sang mournful ancient tunes that remembered images of Hammurabi's raftered halls.

Inside the lamplit tent, Athena Norton scrutinized a cuneiform tablet. She glanced up as her husband entered, and gave him the swift bright smile that had enchanted him when he first met her at her grandfather's 'dig' in Knossos nearly three decades ago. Her grandfather Theodore Milianos was a Greek-Cretan, who had worked with Heinrich Schliemann who found the Troy of Homer at Hisarlik. Then he joined the excavations at Knossos where Norton's father worked. There, the schoolboy Julius heard Cretan legends from Athena, Milianos's orphaned granddaughter, who ran around barefoot in summer, sunburnt and windblown, anxious to find a home in her grandfather's nomadic existence.

After graduating from Oxford, Julius returned to Knossos to work with the famous epigraphist Michael Ventris. There he found seventeen-year-old Athena Milianos, learned and fully formed, like the goddess Athena from the brow of Zeus. When twilight glinted on ancient ruins Julius sat on mimosa and lemon scented hillsides and learned the Minoan script from the precocious Athena. He decided to take her home, as guide and bride. When Theodore bluntly refused, the English archaeologist arranged abduction - not in the style of Paris of Troy - but with assistance from a Greek Orthodox priest. Athena had looked forward to a home; she found that she had exchanged one nomad's life for another as Julius Norton went from one excavation site to another. Amidst these expeditions they produced son Justin and daughter Elena, and several books on the Minoan civilization. Athena was now reconciled to the life of a nomad.

Julius watched her for a few moments before asking, 'Would you like to go to India as wife of director general of archaeology?'

'Why not?' she responded lightly. 'And to Troy as the wife of Hector, and to Amarna as wife of Akhenaton.'

Julius Norton gave her the telegram from the viceroy's office. Athena read it carefully and then looked at him. 'Are we going?' she asked, hoping he would decline the offer.

'Let us go and see if we like it. Who knows what ancient grandeur we may find there?'

The Nortons were excited during the journey from Basra to Bombay. British warships guarded the gulfs of Persia and Oman. The other passengers comprised British army officers going to India for work and those seeking sanctuary in India from Field Marshal Erwin Rommel's swiftly advancing Afrika Korps. German victories under the brilliant Rommel in North Africa and the rapid advance of the Samurais in South East Asia caused deep anxiety in Britain and the British officers on board.

As the small P&O liner steamed through narrow straits towards the monsoon-tossed waters of the Arabian Sea, Julius and Athena read about India. They studied remains of the ancient ports of Dilmun and Magan where Sumerian ships once carried rice, spices and carnelian from Meluhha, perhaps the Sumerian name for west coast of India.

After the ship's dinner, when brandy was served and cigars lit, Julius expanded on his theory of the links between Mesopotamian and Indus Valley civilizations.

'We were planning some maritime explorations along the gulf coast when the war intervened,' Julius told the officers.

'One sunken ship with remains of merchandise tells more about trade than a pile of documents,' Athena added.

The men looked at her with surprise; the faded beauty did not look like a scholar. Women passengers regarded her with reluctant respect. When the P&O liner entered the Arabian Sea, Julius and Athena decided to get acquainted with their new milieu. India was terra incognita to them. It had the charm of the unknown for Athena; for Norton India was a name in school books and later in Oxford an object of vague veneration. It was also a vital part of the British Empire, the well guarded jewel in the crown.

'Can we excavate ancient sites in India?' Athena asked eagerly.

Dr Norton shook his head. 'Excavation, without prior knowledge of a civilization, is like whistling in the wind. We must get to know more about the country where great civilizations have flourished and which are now under foreign rule.'

'Foreign rule can erase identity of a people,' Athena murmured.

'Foreign rule can bring unintended benefits,' Julius replied quietly. 'Two centuries ago East India Company adventurers came to take India's fabled textiles, gold, metals, spice and saltpetre. India's wealth, like Italy's, has been her worst enemy, inviting invaders to traverse formidable mountain passes and sail on uncharted seas. Some invaders plundered and left, others remained to rule, built edifices over razed temples and exulted in the triumph of their divinity. The British had no inclination for iconoclasm. They plumped their purses and swelled their nation's coffers on the riches of the conquered realm – until a strange man headed the empire in India.'

'Who was that strange man?' Athena asked.

'In Freudian psychology, Warren Hastings would be analyzed as a schizophrenic, like a man who violates a woman and then banishes the sordid memory by praising the victim's beauty. Schizophrenia notwithstanding, Hastings also wanted a place in history. He wanted to attain immortality by building a great empire for his native island. With a chilling brilliance, Hastings set about to build an empire that he hoped would rival Rome's far-flung domains. Every weapon and method was used for furthering this purpose. One Indian state after another was annexed to the territories of the East India Company.'

'He sounds more than strange - he sounds sinister,' Athena replied.

Julius Norton smiled. 'And then he fell in love - with Indian metaphysics. Warren Hastings had been in love before – with himself, then with the frail woman who had borne him a son and a daughter, and then with Baron Imhoff's wife whom he married. These attachments did not bring him closer to comprehension of life. Nor had they assuaged the grief of his children's deaths. Neither had it dispersed the grim prospect of inevitable death. Waiting at Benaras to annex the raja's territories, he read the Bhagavad Gita which described how the immutable soul lived on after its liberation from the body.'

Athena listened intently.

'Hastings annexed Benaras and sent its treasury to the East India Company. After that he pondered over the words of the Gita and the spiritual fortitude of a people who had refused to be destroyed. As Ashoka Maurya had built Sanchi in atonement for the carnage at Kalinga, so Hastings established the Asiatic Society soon after the annexation of Benaras to study and to let others study the wellspring of Indian civilization.'

Athena nodded and murmured, 'It was not enough to ravish the body of India; he wanted to understand her soul!'

Julius Norton sighed. 'Will I be able to understand the soul of such a complex entity as India?'

The Norton family arrived in Delhi a week later. The rains had come, ending the blazing heat of Delhi summer. For two brief months, the arid landscape would be lush and green;

birds would come out in large flocks to splash their withered wings on puddles and fountains, the scent of rain-drenched jasmines would add a feminine aroma to this rough city of pomp and power.

One of the oldest cities of India, Delhi is mentioned as Indraprastha in the ancient epic *Mahabharata*. Fleeing from revolutionary Bengal where the East India Company had built a stately capital in Calcutta, the British built their new capital around the Rajput-Moghul remains. The broad, tree-lined boulevards, spacious bungalows with large lawns, and the massive sandstone edifices of the Central Secretariat flanking the viceroy's palace had impressed Julius Norton though he disliked the medley of architectural styles. Monuments, he felt, should capture the spirit of the times and not make half-hearted attempts at diplomacy. Anything false loses its relevance in the crucible of time.

Was the British Raj trying to adopt local styles? Too late for that, he mused.

The Quit India movement had swept away British illusions of the fidelity of Indians – except for a few servile souls who lurked in the corridors of power.

Julius Norton surveyed the scene from the veranda of Eastern Court, a government guest house. Athena came out and joined him, wearing new clothes she had purchased in Connaught Circus. She disliked wearing thin cotton gloves that were intended to conceal her broken nails and darkened fingers. 'I am a *Cretan-Greek archaeologist* and am not expected to look like an English countess!' she mused. Both looked at the street below, with cars, cycle rickshaws, pedestrians carrying umbrellas, Indians in saris, pyjama-kurta, dhotis, and white men and white women in their version of tropical attire.

'Having grown up around ancient sites I never imagined there could be so much sound and movement,' Athena murmured.

Julius Norton nodded. 'Now you will see the world of cities, vehicles, sound and fury.' He paused. 'My personal assistant will take you to see a few houses, and then have the children enrolled in a good school. And I will call on the viceroy's private secretary.' Athena looked at the bustle of the street below. She missed the serenity of the digs in Nimrud and Nineveh, the stark beauty of the windswept, sand-dusted plains, the scent of palms and cedars. Yes, she had grown up on ancient sites and disliked the present world; it made her feel irrelevant.

Archibald Blandford was delighted to meet the archaeologist who was unearthing not only the secrets of Mesopotamia's past but who had also been keeping an eye on movements of Afghans and Turks across the border. Blandford asked, 'Did you get any information about troop movements on the Iraq-Turkish border?'

Julius Norton nodded. 'I went north up to Carchemish, and asked permission of Turkish authorities to visit a few sites across the border. Since I speak German, I posed as a German archaeologist and picked up shreds of information about Turkish plans to assist Rommel's Afrika Korps. If I had stayed on I could have made forays into German camps,' Julius Norton reproached Blandford.

'We need you on the North-West Frontier,' Blandford replied. 'Subhash Bose has made an alliance with Afghan leaders who are aiding Indian rebels. In league with the Germans, they could open an armed front on our doorstep.' He paused. 'After the formalities of taking charge, you are to visit Rawalpindi where you will go ostensibly to explore

Taxila, but we want you to find out what plots the Afghans are hatching with Subhash Bose.'

Julius Norton smiled and said, 'And I thought you wanted me to save Indian monuments.'

'Save *the Empire,* dear chap, and then we will think of Indian monuments,' Blandford said.

Julius Norton looked around him, at the vaulted ceilings, carved doors, wide casements, satin upholstery, ornate Victorian furniture. Turbaned bearers wearing white jackets and red cummarbands glided in and out with red dispatch boxes, while the *petits fonctionnaires* treaded softly as they brought in files and neatly typed letters on silver-plated salvers. Long white ceiling fans whirred wearily overhead. The scene resembled Daniell's paintings of early Raj days.

'How long will your empire last?' he asked.

'What?' Blandford asked, astonished.

'This great empire – fair Britannica, which rules the waves and never *never* shall be slave – how much time do you give her?'

'Heavens! I wonder if I *have made a mistake* in inviting you to take charge as DG, ASI,' Blandford sputtered in rage. 'You can *ask* such questions at a time like this, when the empire is being challenged by Huns and Japs and these misguided Indians!'

Julius Norton inhaled his cigarette and then slowly exhaled, sending rings of smoke drifting above. Blandford waved them away angrily.

'Had you seen ancient cities buried under massive banks of clay, you would understand why I asked about the durability of the British Empire.'

'Philosophy won't run empires!' Blandford retorted. 'Nor will I anticipate the end of the British Empire! We are not here to *do that*!'

'Of course not, Hitler is *doing* that for you,' Julius said mildly. 'But do not break your heart when it happens, as it surely will, one day.'

'And please, God, I am not here then!'

'I wouldn't be too sure of that, Archie. It might be sooner than you think. From the look of it, the Axis powers are triumphing in Africa and the Far East.'

Blandford gave Norton a withering look. 'I expect them to crumble before the might of our empire,' he enunciated coldly.

Julius stubbed out his cigarette. 'We historians are observers and view the impending calamity with equanimity. Ancient Romans believed in the immortality of their empire. Tibullus and Livy sang of the walls of the eternal city. They believed this imperium was desirable for everyone and proceeded to impose it on peaceful Goths and Huns who lived in dense forests until they woke up and decided to plunder the wealth of Rome. Attila's and Alaric's sack of Rome sent shock waves from Palestine to Paris in Anno Domini 410. But nothing could bring it back, not even the pathetic revival in name - Holy Roman Empire ruled by Germanic kings!'

Norton rose and ambled over to the tall windows. 'That,' he said pointing to the northern flank of Lutyens' sandstone edifice, 'may survive longer than Pax Britannica, as the Roman Forums have outlived Pax Romana.' He turned to a subdued Blandford. 'That is why archaeologists try to preserve the physical remains of a civilization.' He paused. 'I am not sure if I want to go to Taxila to spy on the Afghans. If I go, it will be to locate the palace of the Punjabi King Lysander of Taxila who was a protégé of the Greeks.'

'I have conveyed the orders to the military chaps. You are free to do what you wish,' Blandford replied stiffly.

Julius Norton nodded. 'Anyway, thank you, Archie, for this splendid appointment. Even if I can't save the empire from Subhash Bose's intransigence, I shall try to leave behind monuments in a better shape than they were found and tell the natives of our disinterested benevolence.'

Blandford sighed and shook his head. 'Sir Alistair Mackenzie is an autocrat. You sound like an anarchist.' He paused. 'The viceroy is having a tea party in the Moghul Gardens today. He commands you and Mrs Norton to be present.'

'We are honoured and shall obey.' Bowing extravagantly Julius Norton took leave of his friend. 'Shall go now to the office of the Archaeological Survey and take command. Wish me luck, Archie.'

'The best of British luck, Jules,' Blandford said with a wry smile.

A Director General Arrives

The Archaeological Survey of India (ASI) is a venerable institution. It was established in the heyday of the British Raj; its officers traversed the land on horseback under blazing skies to survey and document physical remains of an ancient civilization that had succumbed to British rule through the treachery of Indian kings.

The headquarters of the Archaeological Survey of India stands in the heart of Lutyens' New Delhi, on a road leading to King's Way, later renamed Rajpath. The wags had a joke that the decrepit building should have been declared a ruined protected monument. There were many such down-at-heel, paint-peeling edifices scattered across Lutyens' city; their construction had enriched many civil contractors from North India. These buildings had seen better days – as had the Archaeological Survey. Such buildings humbly endured their shabbiness but the ASI flaunted its cobwebbed decrepitude with pride. The grandeur of the past, declared its daytime denizens, is not dimmed by structural problems of the present. The nocturnal denizens of the building – bats, rats and chowkidars – could not care less.

That afternoon, the high ASI gate was festooned with rosettes; a band burst into the strains of 'God Save the King' as Sir Alistair Mackenzie, the retiring director general, received Dr Norton under the arched entrance. Two Indian officials came forward holding a jasmine garland, and a bouquet of tuberoses. With inscrutable expressions the ASI staff assessed their new director general.

For all his autocratic ways Sir Alistair was a known entity, a known devil, some said, when no one was within earshot. He worked hard and made others work. He had become an institution, identifying himself so completely with the Survey that it was impossible to imagine the Survey without him. He had led his devoted team and opened new frontiers for them to explore, excavate, conserve and restore. And now he was returning to a modest flat in mist-laden London which he had once called home. He was leaving behind Indian friends and comrades, leaving them to a total stranger, a man who had never worked in India. Sir Alistair wore a melancholy smile; no man likes his heir or successor. And this one with his casual elegance and wavy auburn hair did not even look like an archaeologist except for the weathered bronzed face and calloused hands. A long table had been laid in the lawn adjoining the one-storeyed building. Sir Alistair led his successor to the 'high table' for the farewell ceremony. He introduced officers of the Survey stationed at headquarters – the British and Indian directors of the branches: Excavation, Monument, Conservation, Antiquity, Publication, Epigraphy, Chemical Conservation and Survey. Julius Norton noted the names; Sharma, Nizami, Ghosh, Rawat, Kansal; different from Roselli, Milianos, Rashid and Faisal from the Mediterranean and Mesopotamian shores. 'No doubt, I will become familiar with them in time,' he mused. Sir Alistair advised Dr Norton to visit the various 'Circle' offices and make his own assessment of the work to be done. Sighing, Julius Norton asked, 'On what basis can I make an assessment? Conditions in Mesopotamia were quite different. I hope I can consult you and seek your advice.'

The older man shook his head sadly. 'I shall be six thousand miles away, Dr Norton, across seas swarming with warships. But feel free to write to me and I shall give you my frank opinion.' Sir Alistair gave his successor thumbnail sketches of the officers, mentioning their specialization and experience, and told Norton of the projects undertaken. His restrained farewell speech had undercurrents of deep emotions. Officers of the Survey sat with tear-bright eyes as Sir Alistair took leave of an organization that he had brought to its present eminence. Julius Norton wondered how he would fill the place of an illustrious predecessor. Notwithstanding Sir Alistair's reluctance to brief his successor, Julius Norton persuaded him to do so and used the ruse of a tea party with the viceroy to get a briefing. The viceroy's secretary Archibald Blandford grumbled at having to organize a tea party with the *Burra Lat* (Big Lord) for the archaeologists.

'There's a war going on, you know, Julius, old chap,' he said tartly. 'We don't have time now for tea-time chin-wags.'

Julius used another ruse now. Displaying an ill temper he did not feel he said, 'If this is the sort of assistance I can expect from you, Athena and I shall sail back to Iraq. She never wanted to come here anyway.'

'Oh all right, come over then, and drive me to distraction,' an exasperated Blandford replied.

Sir Alistair Mackenzie belonged to that rare species of Englishmen who were unimpressed by the trappings of British Raj power. He looked upon the viceregal palace as a 'concatenation of irreconcilable architectural styles peopled by men who had not a clue of what they were doing or where they were going'. This view had led to his subtle ostracization by the viceroy's set; Sir Alistair was grateful for this but it injured Lady Mackenzie's pride. So he came reluctantly for the viceroy's tea party that sultry afternoon.

The tea party was arranged in a south-facing room of the viceregal palace. The vicereine set everyone at ease with comments on the weather, the garden where she grew camellias and wisteria. The *Burra Lat Saheb,* as the Indians called the viceroy, conferred with his military secretary on the day's war news from the Far East.

Lady Mackenzie was delighted to be invited and gave her wayward husband admonitions about anti-establishment observations. Sir Alistair assured her, 'I shall be on perfect behaviour.' On entering, he gave a slight bow in the direction of the imperial representatives; Lady Mackenzie executed a graceful curtsey she had practised all morning.

The entry of Athena and Julius Norton caused a sudden silence. The viceroy rose and swiftly scrutinized the new director general of archaeology of India. He greeted Julius cordially, surprised to find a man of commanding bearing, who looked more soldier than scholar. Blandford was relieved that his choice had been approved. Lady Linlithgow bestowed a kindly smile on Athena; she did not curtsey but bowed her head before the vicereine who ignored the *lèse-majesté*. Between pleasant chatter, Her Ladyship assessed Athena's suitability as member of the vicereines's select circle of wives who played the role of ladies in waiting. Of course she *wasn't British,* and didn't play tennis and gin-rummy, and had a distracted air that *would not do* in a circle where everyone believed in stiff-upper-lip and chin-up in the face of danger. But then, *her* lord had told her that as Dr Norton was going to do important work on the Indian-Afghan border it was necessary to be polite to *his* wife.

Blandford asked Sir Alistair to brief the viceroy and the new DG of ASI. The military secretary and the ladies listened in cold silence as Sir Alistair narrated his favourite subject – the discovery of India's greatness by Britain.

'The Asiatic Society was the starting point of Britain's discovery of India. British scholars studied Indian culture and metaphysics. Their discovery of India ran parallel to wars of conquest and annexation by the East India Company. Hastings's friends – Sir William Jones, Henry Colebrooke, Charles Wilkins, Nathaniel Halhed – revealed India's civilizational achievements to Britain and the West. He established the Fort William College where young British officers learned about Indian history and art.'

Since the vicereine's ladies set had not a clue as to what 'the old digger' (as Sir Alistair was secretly called) was referring, they discussed the problems of monsoon garden parties. Athena pretended to listen to them but her ears were tuned in to Sir Alistair's words.

'It took fifty years for antiquarianism to evolve into systematic investigation into the past. The initiative in this was taken by James Prinsep who guided archaeology and epigraphy in India. He made momentous discoveries of India's past; by deciphering the forgotten and disused Brahmi and Kharoshti scripts, knowledge of the history and achievements of ancient India expanded.'

The ladies were relieved when the door opened to admit half a dozen scarlet-liveried attendants. They served tea from silver pots, savoury and pastries from three-tiered silver trays. A frowning Lady Mackenzie watched a delighted Sir Alistair ponder over the cornucopia and pile the gilt-edged plate with canapés. In atonement for his gluttony she ate only a watercress sandwich. The other guests plucked out delicacies. The viceroy and vicereine watched them benignly.

Stirring tea, Sir Alistair continued. 'The Archaeological Survey of India was established soon after by a military engineer General Alexander Cunningham who, saddened by the ruins of great Indian monuments, recommended that an organization should be established to survey monuments in India and preserve them as a testimony of Indian civilization.'

Sir Alistair turned to *Burra Lat Saheb*. 'Military men are not given to scholarship, but General Cunningham was fascinated by India's past.'

This remark brought a surge of blood to the cheeks of the viceroy's military secretary who growled, 'Military men should fight, not look for broken pottery! Soldiers in England have set a lamentable tradition!' A ghost of a smile appeared on Julius Norton's face.

Undeterred, Sir Alistair continued: 'The Survey began large-scale explorations in North and Central India. It would be another half a century before Rakhaldas Banerjee would discover what lay beneath the mound – the Indus Valley

Civilization. This discovery and consequent excavations by Sir John Marshall's team transformed perceptions of India's ancient civilizations. The frontiers of history were pushed back thousands of years. Archaeologists attempted to date the Vedic age and explore both its material and cultural achievements.'

'The Aryans *brought civilization* to India,' the viceroy pronounced with papal infallibility.

'There is *no Aryan* race. There are Indo-Iranians and Indo-Europeans,' Athena stated stubbornly. '*Only Hitler* thinks there is an Aryan race.' Dr Norton's eyes sparkled with delight.

In shocked silence the entourage stared at Athena for contradicting the viceroy. Perceptions of India's past greatness agitated *Burra Lat Saheb* and his acolytes. It was one thing to rule a primitive people; it was quite another to dominate a people with superior civilizational pretensions.

Not intimidated by the hostile silence, Sir Alistair continued. 'When it was least expected, the Archaeological Survey of India received strong support from the viceroy Lord George Curzon. A fervent imperialist he also passed the Ancient Monuments Preservation Act in 1904. Imagine, a century earlier Governor-General Lord Bentinck had tried to sell the Taj Mahal, slab by marble slab!'

The patrician guests now appeared uncomfortable. The viceroy thought that it was not such a disaster after all that Sir Alistair was retiring. If he stayed on, the ASI could well become a hotbed of insurgency!

Sir Alistair Mackenzie turned to Dr Julius Norton. 'Have you now got a feel of the organization you are going to administer?'

Julius sighed. 'How shall I take the place of a remarkable and dedicated director general?' He paused and added, 'A war is raging in three continents. Both sides are perpetrating destruction of civilizations.'

'Yes. You have been summoned to save the monuments of India,' Blandford said brusquely.

The viceroy glanced with distaste at his civil secretary and the two wayward archaeologists.

On their way back to Eastern Court through a steady monsoon drizzle, Julius laughed and said, 'We are up against the Empire League!'

The day after taking charge, Julius summoned the director of Monuments branch in order to acquaint himself with monuments that were under the jurisdiction of the Archaeological Survey of India. The director of Monuments brought a leather-bound catalogue of some five thousand monuments in the Indian subcontinent.

'A huge list,' Julius murmured, overwhelmed.

'From Kashmir to Cape Comorin, from the mountain borders of Afghanistan to the forest borders of Burma,' the director pronounced his words slowly.

'And the Survey looks after them all?' Julius asked.

'We try to.'

Julius Norton put away the catalogue. 'Dr Sharma, let us go on tours of inspections of some of the important monuments. Suggest an itinerary. We shall go to the Northern Circle first since the region is closer to Delhi and then we shall take up the Southern, Western and Eastern Circles.' Dr Sharma agreed and suggested that the regional officers would accompany them.

Julius returned to their suite in Eastern Court to find Athena satisfied with her day. 'We have seen several bungalows and there is one which is picturesque with a large garden near the Red Fort.'

Julius was interested but other considerations made him pause. 'That's rather far from the Survey office, isn't it?' he asked.

'Some few miles. You are going to travel by car, not a camel.' Athena paused. 'I thought you would like to be near the great citadel.'

'Well of course I would, but at times like these I think one should be near the place of work and the government offices,' Julius replied.

'I would like to be a little far from them,' she said quietly. 'Justin and Elena liked the house, the trees, a small fountain to splash in and, most importantly, we found good English medium schools nearby.'

Julius sighed. 'All right, if that's what you want, we shall take the house.'

'And the staff who go with it. They served the previous tenant and occupy the quarters at the back. Seemed like very nice people. Although I have no idea what work to give ten people! I am not a memsaheb.'

Julius felt a flicker of irritation at her words. With a hint of rebuke, he said, 'I hope you will get along with the wives of the officers.'

'Certainly, we have *so much* in common,' Athena said sardonically. Now more than ever she missed the silent stillness of the shores she had left behind!

After settling the family in the rambling bungalow and the children enrolled in their respective schools, Julius Norton began his tours.

A Monumental Heritage

It was customary to begin the Archaeological Grand Tour by going to Agra, site of the exquisite Taj Mahal. Julius had read about it, seen photographs and was prepared to be disappointed. After a smart shower it stood luminous like a huge pearl. Julius drew in a sharp breath, overwhelmed. 'Three hundred years old, yet she looks like a bride,' he murmured.

Julius Norton went on a round of inspection. He saw the parts where conservation work had been done so deftly that it was not visible. Chemical treatment was in progress to remove the stains made by desert sand and beehives nestled in the smaller cupolas. Muslim and Hindu craftsmen worked quietly together, as they must have done when the mausoleum was being built. As dusk fell, the muezzin called from a minaret, summoning, it seemed, the spirits of Shah Jahan and Mumtaz Mahal from the crypt where they lay in final union. Deeply moved, Julius mused, 'What survives is not love but memorials to love.'

In contrast to Emperor Akbar's magnificent life his mausoleum at Sikandra was austere. His greatness and achievements, unlike love, survived without exquisite tombs. From the seat of Akbar's death they came to Fatehpur Sikri, the city of his dreams where the great emperor had sought to bind his disparate subjects and their varied creeds into a religion of brotherhood, *the Din Elahi.*

The group drove through the damp night to 'camp' in the abandoned capital. The lodge built by Lord Curzon stood out in silhouette. Attendants in Moghul costume rushed out with lanterns to welcome the new custodian of Indian heritage, and served dinner on the flagged stone terrace. Later, Dr Norton sat on the terrace, and dwelt on Lord Curzon's vision for saving the physical heritage of India.

After a fitful slumber Norton woke at first light sensing the presence of the great emperor. Not for the first time he wondered if the life force of humans is snuffed out by the cessation of the body. After breakfast the officers took their director general to see Akbar's palace fortress of Fatehpur Sikri which became a meeting place of all religions – unique in the age of bigotry.

'This is a very significant monument,' he said. 'It is a monument with a message which India now needs for her unity.'

At Agra the director general boarded a train bound for South India. Two junior archaeologists from headquarters came to Norton's coupe with great trepidation, sat at the edge of the velvet seats, refused refreshments, and told their chief about the unique monuments of the region.

I, Elangovan, met the group in Pallavur. I was now a middle-aged archaeologist. Like many South Indians I inscribed a tilak on my forehead, wore shirt, coat and tie over my dhoti, and sandals, and took pride in speaking correct English. Julius Norton liked Pallavur which was clean and orderly, and people went about their work with Teutonic precision. At Thanjavur he saw the grandeur of the imperial Chola dynasty which sent scholars, sculptors and traders to the Far East.

Before leaving Pallavur, Dr Norton visited the whitewashed St. Mary's Church with its dusty stained-glass windows. Norton was inspired by the life of Sir Tom Munro, one of the greatest Britons who came to India. He sat gazing at the marble statue of Munro Saheb, who gave his life for

Indians. And there Julius Norton made his own promise for serving India – like Tom Munro Saheb.

***

Dr Norton was curious to see the monuments of Deccanabad in the nawab's domain. A British Resident was posted there to keep an eye on the dubious loyalties of the nawab. Hearing of the arrival of the director general the nawab's court lost no time in inviting him for a 'private banquet'. They wanted to investigate Julius Norton's intentions for coming. Dr Norton had heard of the nawab's decadence and indifference to his people; he sent word through the superintending archaeologist that he would prefer to meet the nawab over a cup of tea as 'Banquets are unthinkable when thousands are dying in a war.' Offended but undeterred by this rebuke the courtiers arranged a sumptuous tea in the terrace-garden of the Talaknama Palace. To titillate the insolent Englishman the nawab summoned his favourite concubines to the party.

Norton was treated to a display of gold – cutlery, cups, plates – and bejewelled concubines in glittering costumes. As he tried to absorb the scene, a woman with clouds of auburn hair around an arresting face and a voluptuous, chiffon-sari-clad figure stepped on the terrace. Norton halted in his conversation with the nawab. As she floated towards them, he rose and bowed slightly over an extended pale hand.

Her flashing eyes appraised Norton. As if referring to a prized *objet d'art*, the nawab said, 'Begum Zoya, my fourth and Turkish wife, granddaughter of the last Ottoman emperor.'

Sitting down, Julius Norton said, 'I have just come from that part of the world, Your Royal Highness.'

'She is addressed as "Your Highness". I am also only "Your Highness". That is what the British have ordered,' the nawab snapped.

'That is rather ridiculous, considering your kingdom is larger than Belgium or Holland where the kings are addressed as "Your Majesty",' Norton said.

'Ask your British government the reason,' the nawab retorted.

'You *ought* to be called "Your Majesty",' Norton replied, tongue-in-cheek. Then turning to Princess Zoya he said, 'And you would have been called "Imperial Highness" had the Ottoman Empire still existed.'

Princess Zoya smiled. 'Thank you. I shall mention this to the viceroy when I meet him next. But tell me what were you doing in my native land?'

'I went looking for some ancient sites.' He paused as if in explanation. 'I am an archaeologist.'

The Turkish princess emitted a tinkling laugh and spoke in French. 'And my liege lord thinks you are a spy.'

Norton also wanted to laugh but seeing the nawab's glowering face he said, 'I am a scholar, Your Highness. I look for the past, and not try to shape the future.'

'What did you find?' Zoya asked.

'Ancient sites of the Bronze Age – probably part of the Trojan Empire.'

'Troy – Helen of Troy,' Zoya murmured. 'I wonder what was she like?'

'I have my own theories about the Greeks and Trojans, Homer notwithstanding.'

'Tell me, Dr Norton,' the princess coaxed softly.

By now the beetle-browed nawab scowled at his fourth begum. Norton decided to soothe him. 'One day we will discuss this with my Greek archaeologist wife. She has her theories on the real reason for the Trojan War. Despite being Greek her sympathy is with Trojans.'

The Turkish princess took the hint and said, 'Yes, one day I must listen to both of you on the subject.'

The conversation turned to trivialities since the nawab refused to be drawn into any serious discussion. When Norton said that he was going to see the Golkonda Fort, the nawab asked testily, 'What do you want to see there?'

'The ruins. They are my speciality,' Norton replied and went on, 'I hear there is buried treasure there?'

'Lies!' the nawab snapped.

Zoya spoke in Urdu to her lord. He listened and nodded. Turning to Norton she said, 'Perhaps a few of us can accompany you to Golkonda?'

Frowning he said, 'I climb quickly so you may find it tiring.'

'She will go,' the nawab declared magisterially.

Julius Norton and his party set off next morning to see the medieval fort of Golkonda. Arriving there, Norton looked at the stone hierarchy of towers, bastions and turrets. Despite its disrepair, Golkonda Fort had an overpowering majesty. Whispers of power still echoed here.

Reaching the highest level, Dr Norton and we archaeologists stopped to drink coconut water which the peons had carried. Princess Zoya sat on a stone slab, removed her wide-brimmed hat, took a few sips of coconut water, and gazed down at the citadel below.

'Not quite the view from the Bosphorus, is it?' Norton asked quietly. 'You must miss Constantinople.'

She shook her head sadly, remembering her native imperial city. 'Mustafa Kamal changed the name

Constantinople to Istanbul. Kamal Pasha, the grey-eyed Macedonian, is called Ataturk, the Father of the Turks. What a laugh!'

'To historians it will always be Constantinople. Departing men leave behind their ghosts.'

'Is your Greek wife beautiful?' the princess asked anxiously.

'She is my *only wife*,' Norton said with a wry smile. 'And she has a beauty that is not tarnished by time. It is called beauty of the soul.'

'Did you marry her for her soul then?' Zoya asked with asperity.

'I married her for her learning; she made my search for ancient worlds a reality. She belongs to olive groves, old temples and seaside grottos.'

I coughed and moved away. If Dr Norton wanted to be enticed that was his business. Did he wish to be ensnared as Paris of Troy had been? Uneasy with this disruptive woman, he rose and asked, 'How did you persuade the nawab to let you accompany me?'

'I said that you would be looking for a treasure trove and I would follow your scent. My liege lord tires of concubines but never of his jewels. That is a perennial passion.'

Looking intently at her, Dr Norton asked, 'Why did you come? You must have seen Golkonda Fort a hundred times.'

'I thought you might be Paris – sent to take me to freedom.'

'If you wanted freedom why did you not go to Europe and marry there? Why did you become the nawab's fourth wife?'

'I was commanded by my emperor-uncle to marry either a Hashemite prince or the nawab. I did not want to live in the desert. But I did not know how oppressive it would be here.'

'Was it very different in the Topkapi? Was the Ottoman emperor better than the nawab? At least he lets you roam around – to the Riviera, Ascot. In your homeland wayward begums were drowned in the Bosphorus with cement bags tied to their shoes.'

Her grey eyes glinted. 'For an archaeologist you are very well informed about my movements, Dr Norton. If you *are* an archaeologist, that is.'

Julius Norton laughed. 'I am an archaeologist all right but we make excellent espionage agents. Now shall we begin our descent?'

They began the descent from the highest level of the ruined citadel. When they reached the royal car, the begum told the chauffeur to drive past the Charminar or Four Towers which seemed to be made of lace and ivory. When the car halted at Talaknama Palace, Norton alighted and watched the princess step out and disappear within its portals.

A sense of guilt enveloped him; in fourteen years of marriage he had never craved for another woman. Athena was his comrade and companion, his love and wisdom. They were bound by their quest for the past. He had no bonds with this alluring daughter of the Ottomans yet she had disturbed him enough to want to see her again. Before returning to the ASI guest house Norton went to the famed pearl market of Deccanabad to buy jewellery for Athena. I took him to a known shop where luminescent gems were heaped on tables. To assuage his guilt he purchased two strings of Basra pearls for Athena – Basra pearls he could have purchased at half the price in Baghdad – but never did.

Traversing Ancient India

Arriving in Delhi, Julius Norton received urgent summons from Archibald Blandford, the viceroy's civil secretary, who asked in exasperation, 'Where on earth have you been?'

'I went south to inspect monuments. Isn't that why I am here?' Julius asked to provoke his friend.

'Not at all, old chap. You are here because we want you to go to the North-West Frontier and see what is going on there. So why don't you go ostensibly to inspect monuments there and let us know what is happening?'

'I hope the monuments are there, otherwise it will be obvious that I have not come on archaeological work and that wouldn't do, now, would it?'

'His Lordship is expecting your report in a fortnight,' Blandford replied angrily.

Julius Norton was glad to find Justin and Elena happy in their new schools. Athena had explored and was impressed by the Moghul edifices within Red Fort but deplored the ugly military barracks there. Norton smiled. 'I am glad that you are finding Delhi interesting, Athena.'

'Every place with a past is interesting.' She paused. 'Like a woman.'

He did not meet Athena's perceptive eyes. Nor had he met her eyes when he gave her the pearl necklace from the Charminar shop. Athena had examined it with delight and pronounced it exquisite. Only later Norton realized that the necklace was the only expensive jewellery he had given her in fourteen years.

'I shall wear it at the vicereine's lunch next week,' she had said happily.

'Yes, do that, darling,' Norton murmured, overcome by tenderness for this child of ancient grottos and olive groves.

Athena had glanced up at him in surprise. 'India has made you romantic, Julius,' she said with an enigmatic smile. 'Have you been reading Rabindranath Tagore's poetry?'

Sometimes Norton thought of Begum Zoya; it was not her past but her future that intrigued him.

The viceroy's lunch party was small and select. This is where he discussed affairs of state with his advisers. Today's agenda was Subhash Bose's Azad Hind Fauz. *Burra Lat Saheb* was visibly troubled. 'The man is inciting mutiny in Singapore!' he fumed. 'Don't these deserters know what happened to the mutineers in 1858? We hanged them on gibbets from Patna to Peshawar and blew them from mouths of cannons! And by Jove we shall do it again!'

Despite Blandford's warning look Julius Norton sat forward and said, 'Excellency, things are very different now from what they were in 1858. The Mutiny was an isolated episode concerning army sepoys and disgruntled princes. There is now a national upheaval of which Bose is the armed wing and Gandhi the unarmed wing. The prophet armed and the prophet unarmed, so to speak. We had better formulate strategies other than hanging rebels on gibbets to preserve the British Empire.' Norton paused. 'I doubt if any empire can survive the challenge of an idea whose time has come.'

All that could be heard in the ensuing stunned silence was the sound of raindrops falling on the flagged terrace below. The British king-emperor's envoy flushed a deep scarlet, followed by a deeper scarlet of Blandford and the military secretary. The vicereine fanned herself in agitation while the ladies sat confused, not fully comprehending the import of the director general's words. A smiling Athena waited for the storm to break.

Unaccustomed to such impertinence, the viceroy asked icily, 'Are you telling me, Norton, that we are wasting time fighting the Japs and Huns?'

'Oh no, we have to fight the Germans otherwise they will conquer us. Nine hundred years ago we managed to convert the Norman Conquest of England into a national event but it will be difficult to do that with the Nazi Reich.'

The viceroy stared at Norton in angry disbelief. Unperturbed, Norton continued. 'I fear Time has caught up with us, Excellency. We can stave off national uprisings by a few years, that is all.'

The long silence was broken by a pretty English woman who declared, 'We shall fight to the last drop of our blood, my Lord! We will never give up!'

'Bravo Gladys! That's the spirit!' cried the military secretary to his wife. Blandford followed with 'Hear, hear!'

'Well, Dr Norton,' the viceroy said heavily, 'does that answer your question?'

Julius Norton smiled wryly. 'I have no questions, Excellency, only melancholy observations.'

Despite Norton's contretemps, he was asked to discuss an urgent matter with the officers after lunch. The viceroy settled himself in his favourite armchair with Havana cigar and Turkish coffee; his civil secretary, military secretary and the director general of ASI were in attendance. The viceroy spoke: 'Your real work is about to begin, Norton.'

'I have already started my real work, Excellency. Hasn't Archie told you about my extensive tours in the United Provinces and the Pallavur Presidency? I have been seeing the remains of several great civilizations.'

His Lordship waved his hand dismissively. 'Oh, drop it, Norton. That is for public consumption.'

'Permit me to disagree. I agreed to come to India to look after and care for Indian monuments, leaving behind my fascinating work in Mesopotamia. Anything else is of secondary importance.'

Scowling, His Lordship asked, 'Even the defence of the empire?'

Julius Norton sighed in exasperation. 'What is it you want me to do?'

'We have located a Bengali chappie who used to be with Subhash Bose. He operates from Bodh Gaya – a Buddhist centre where several Japanese agents moonlighting as Buddhist monks are collecting military information.'

'What is my role in this cat-and-mouse game?'

'You will make contact with this chappie at Bodh Gaya and obtain information on Bose's next move.'

Norton laughed and said, 'As if a Japanese agent is going to confide in me, a member of the British establishment!'

'You are talking like a pacifist!' the military secretary thundered.

Norton retorted, 'If I am to go to the place of Lord Buddha's enlightenment, it is appropriate to begin as a pacifist.'

'The empire is doomed with chaps like you,' the viceroy muttered.

Leaving Justin and Elena in the capable care of an Anglo-Indian housekeeper, Julius Norton took Athena with him on his trip to Bihar. They seldom went on exploratory trips together but now he wanted her by his side, as a talisman against Zoya's bewitchment. Their train passed across the Gangetic plains of India and halted at Patna, ancient capital of Emperor Ashoka. After seeing a few ancient edifices they sat by the river Ganga, witness to events, absorber of turmoil and triumphs, as timeless as Time itself.

They set off early in the morning for Nalanda, site of an ancient university which had been devastated by Turkic invaders; the burnt brick edifices of the ancient university were testimony to their vandalism. The local populace had watched helplessly as thousands of books and manuscripts burnt for weeks.

The secret agent, Anand Chowdhury, met Julius and Athena in the quiet environs of Nalanda; they behaved like tourists to dissuade any observer from pursuit. While Athena went off to explore the remains of the ancient university Julius Norton and Anand Chowdhury went to an isolated place. Around them were echoes of past Buddhist sermons on non-violence, compassion and detachment. What a terrible travesty, thought Norton, to meet a double agent here for continuing violence and bloodshed. Suddenly he regretted this assignment; it was better to write compendiums on Mesopotamian history than play these cynical games to continue carnage.

'Subhash Bose has collected an arsenal for his campaign,' the agent informed Norton. 'Thousands of officers and soldiers of the British Indian Army have joined the Indian National Army. From Singapore they are marching west towards Siam, Burma and then India.'

'Are the Japanese actively aiding them?'

'No, Japan wants the Indian National Army to fight its own battle. That serves their purpose better. They plan to come to India in the wake of the INA – something Subhash Bose will try to prevent.'

'What are Japanese chances of occupying Indian territory?'

The agent smiled. 'Who can say? That is written in the stars.'

'British stars or Japanese stars?'

'You, a historian, know that the age of colonialism is ending. It is a matter of time. Why have the Japanese not met with real resistance in South East Asia? Because the people hate European rule. Your government should realize the futility of it all.'

'I was told you were working for the safety of the British Empire,' Norton replied.

'I am giving a correct assessment of your chances. If I wished, I could give information to ensnare the British Army.' He paused. 'I do not want to see blood spilt in a futile campaign – Indian or British blood.'

Norton smiled wryly and nodded. 'I was wrong. I thought it incongruous to meet in Nalanda to discuss war games. But I see it was entirely appropriate. You are a true Buddhist.'

The agent shrugged his shoulders. 'Take it as you will.'

'Come, let us join my wife for tea and then go our way. If there is anything else you wish to tell me – to prevent bloodshed – let me know.'

Later sitting on the tiny veranda of the ASI office-cum-guest house at Nalanda Norton wondered whether the agent Anand Chowdhury was trying to gauge the British situation by pretending to play their game? Seeing Norton's pensive face Athena said, 'Anand Chowdhury saddened me – as if he is being swept along by forces he did not understand.'

Norton nodded. 'Like all of us.'

Athena spread out her slender sunburnt arms. 'Now you are speaking like a Greek.'

Norton smiled. 'I *am* Greek – deep down. That is why I found a soulmate in you.'

Blandford was disappointed by what Norton had to say. 'Surely you could have collected some solid information from our agent!'

'Your agent, as you call him, is not your agent at all. He is a follower of Bose. He is collecting information about your intentions. There are Indian monks at Bodh Gaya who are Japanese agents. They will never serve you against a Buddhist nation.'

'You call the violent Samurais followers of the Buddha?' Blandford fumed.

'Why not, if bloodthirsty crusaders are called devotees of Christ?'

Blandford had not expected his archaeologist protégé to be obdurate and contrary. But he needed him, so he controlled his growing anger.

'I suggest you visit Taxila. The Afghans are hand-in-glove with Bose. There you will definitely get some clues about the Fauz.'

In the Trail of Alexander of Macedon

The road from Delhi to the North-West Frontier is picturesque; invading Persians and Afghans galloped on this route. Since Afghans had defeated the British Army in two ruinous wars, the British feared that Afghans were preparing to assist Subhash Bose's Azad Hind Fauz. It was from here that Subhash Bose escaped from his British adversaries to the welcoming arms of the Pathans in their mountain fastness. It was with their help that he travelled on the ancient overland route to neutral Turkey and onward to Europe to secure weapons for his army.

Norton felt he was travelling backward in time. Remains of old forts merged with the brown hillside. In between green patches small towns cropped up, peopled by descendants of invaders and traders from Iran, Greece and Central Asia.

Rawalpindi had the romance of a garrison town where the British Indian Army kept an alert vigil on the activities in Kabul. So alert was their vigil that Subhash Bose, a quintessential Bengali *bhadrolok*, had eluded his British pursuers disguised as an unkempt Pathan!

Soon after arrival Julius Norton called on the divisional commissioner, a quiet civilian overshadowed by the garrison hierarchy. The commissioner had been informed of Norton's arrival but not of the purpose for his visit. He was told that Norton was a maverick who had to be humoured because he was 'damn useful' for ferreting out facts. The commissioner provided a jeep and escort for Dr Norton.

An hour's drive along the Khyber Pakhtunkhwa brought Norton to Taxila, capital of ancient Gandhara, now Kandahar, situated on the river Tamra-Nala, a tributary of the Indus. This kingdom figured in the four-thousand-year-old epic *Mahabharata*. Norton strolled through the vast site and saw the remains of the three cities of Taxila. When the sun grew strong Norton went to the museum where artefacts of ancient Indian, Bactrian, Parthian and Kushan eras had been assembled and displayed. A bespectacled and bearded middle-aged man sat nearby, watching him. His watchful gaze drew Norton. Going to the man he said, 'You must be the curator of this wonderful museum.'

The man nodded with a smile. 'And you are the famous Julius Norton of the Dilmun expedition.'

'I must be famous if I am known even in far away Takshashila,' responded Norton warmly. 'And may I know your name, Sir?'

'Danyal Khan. I have read your papers on Dilmun. I was surprised when I learnt that you had left your work at Nineveh to take charge at ASI.'

'It was an honour I could not refuse. We all want a little status.'

The curator shook his head. 'Status comes with work – not with a chair.'

Dismayed, Norton murmured, 'I am sorry to have disappointed you.'

'It was important work that you were doing. If you had persevered you might have found the clue to the Indus script. Somewhere there must be a bicodal key – between Sumeria, Assyria, Mohenjo-daro,' Danyal said.

'Perhaps I shall find it here on the banks of the Indus,' Norton replied.

'Perhaps,' Professor Danyal Khan said with a sigh. 'Perhaps you will find that key as James Prinsep deciphered the Brahmi and Kharoshti script.' He paused. 'Now tell me, what brings you here?'

Norton replied, 'I have come to see how this museum is maintained and what sort of excavations are in progress. I know such things take low priority at war-time but then this site will survive long after this war is forgotten.'

'The site will survive if the area does not become a theatre of war – if the Afghans do not take arms against the British.'

'Are they likely to?' Norton asked, slowly lighting a cigarette to gain time.

Danyal Khan gave Julius a sardonic smile. 'Is that not what you have come to find out, Norton Saheb?'

Norton saw no point in denying the fact. 'It is a matter of the gravest concern to all British citizens and Indians – the security of India.'

'The Defence of India Act?' Danyal Khan asked mischievously. 'Why not call it "Defence of the British Empire Act" and be done with?'

'Why not? And don't be so derisive about the British Empire, Professor. You would not be curator of the Taksha-shila Museum if the Afghan warlords were raiding the area.'

Danyal Khan smiled. 'No, I would be a warlord myself.'

Norton laughed. 'And plunder the site?'

'We would not destroy our heritage. We are proud of Taksha-shila, the oldest university of the world. It was established in seventh century BC. Scholars from Greece, Central and West Asia and China met here to study science, mathematics, astronomy, archery, art and philosophy under great teachers. Many races mingled here and created a new civilization. Alexander of Macedon came here in 326 BC. He was aided by King Ambhi of Taxila who inaugurated the Indian tradition of collaboration with a foreign invader in order to defeat a fellow Indian ruler, King Porus of Punjab.'

Julius Norton listened with keen interest. Danyal Khan continued.

'Long before your people came here two centuries ago, *we* were guarding Taksha-shila.' He paused. 'Did you not find the same pride among the people of Iraq and Turkey over their ancient legacy?'

Dr Norton nodded. 'And now let me look around Taksha-shila.'

The professor sighed. 'You won't find what you came to find, Dr Norton. Pathans are taciturn and proceed on secrecy and trust. Once they take up a cause they will not abandon it. They admire Subhash Bose for his nobility and courage. They will not betray him.'

Norton stubbed out the cigarette. 'What makes you think that I came to find out about Subhash Bose?'

Danyal Khan smiled. 'British archaeologists have been excellent espionage agents – Moorcroft, Younghusband,

Aurel Stein. British soldiers at Rawalpindi garrison question Pathans but they listen and gather information. You are at a disadvantage.'

Norton sighed. 'So I see. Anyway, Professor, as a member of British officialdom you may like to pass on information about threats to the security of the realm.'

Danyal Khan nodded. 'There is considerable threat to your realm. Hitler's army has overrun Europe. Ironically only your other enemy – Soviet Union – can save you. Let us see what happens at Stalingrad where the snow is running crimson. And Subhash Bose is marching towards the north-east frontier while the Afghans are sharpening their knives against you to aid Bose from the North-West Frontier. They are calling it the Fourth Afghan war.'

Norton frowned. 'You are quite sure of this? Could I talk to your sources for exact information?'

'Do you expect me to expose my informers to the interrogation of MI5?'

'I will not reveal their identity.' It hurt Norton's pride to plead before the Pathan scholar.

Danyal Khan shook his head. 'You must take it as verified from me.' He paused; the corners of his blue-grey eyes (a legacy, he claimed, from Greek ancestors) creased into a smile. 'As a historian, Dr Norton, can you not read the sign of the times? Why not accept it with a little philosophy?'

'I am not paid to accept the end of our government here with philosophy,' Norton replied sardonically.

The professor laughed and said, 'Tomorrow I will take you deeper into Afghan territory to see things for yourself. Perhaps my friends will tell you what they know.'

Next morning Professor Danyal Khan, draping his body in baggy Pathan clothes with the Pashtun dialect on his tongue, drove up to the ASI guest house where an anxious Julius Norton waited, dressed deliberately in shabby clothes befitting a down-at-heel scholar. He did not know that these disguises no longer deceived Afghans. They had seen such 'scholars' for the last hundred years, usually before the British mounted an offensive on Afghan territory.

They broke journey in mountainous villages to break bread and drink tea at picturesque *musafir-khanas*, where Danyal Khan introduced Norton Saheb as a writer who had come to see the trail of Alexander of Macedon or Iskander Shah as he was known here. The hostility evident in the people's attitude left Norton in no doubt that Afghans would not ally with the British in a war. If he had not come with Danyal he would have been disposed of suitably.

'Are you satisfied now?' Danyal asked Norton as they sat by a bonfire. Norton said nothing.

'Before we return can we see the border with Iran? One day I will take this route and return to Mesopotamia.' Dr Norton gazed at the Hindu Kush ranges spread before him – a strange landscape of serrated hills frosted by snow, pyramidal peaks rising out of the land, and long stretches of arid, desolate scenes.

Danyal nodded with a smile. 'A long journey that will be, *musafir*.'

On the Banks of the Indus

Julius Norton did not want to get involved in political work. With a historian's perspective he saw the skirmishes as a futile attempt to halt the inevitability of history just as Asia had not been able to halt colonial armies four centuries ago. Now the age of European empires was ending. Norton thought it immensely ironic that the age of European supremacy was being terminated not by Asian revolutionaries but by two European powers - Nazi Germany and Soviet Russia - the former by destroying British and French military might, and the latter by an ideology irresistible to a subjugated continent.

He went to the various 'Circle' offices to see how they worked, which monuments needed conservation and how to train the young recruits. He sat with artisans to see methods of conservation - mixing lime and mortar for repairs, adding egg white with honey to simulate the lustre of marble. He squatted with 'diggers' as they patiently scraped away layers of dust to unearth remnants of distant millennia. And from these scattered fragments he had to define the events and achievements of an age.

Dr Narasimhiah, an erudite archaeologist, confided to Dr Norton. 'Indian archaeology bristles with difficulties. There are no steatites or tablets that recorded events of ancient times until Emperor Ashoka began carving edicts on pillars. But what happened before that? Who are the so-called Aryans? Were they migrants from Europe as Max Mueller advocated? Or was there no race of Aryans at all? Was it merely an appellation for the nobility called *arya* in Sanskrit? Did they introduce the caste system or was it there even earlier as a prescribed division of labour?'

Julius listened and then asked, 'When were the Vedas composed? Which was the race that composed these magnificent verses? How did the poetic pantheism of the *Rig Veda* change into the stern intellectuality of the *Upanishads*? How many centuries passed before the oral tradition was transmitted to palm leaves?'

Dr Narasimhiah shook his head. 'These are the mysteries that Indian archaeology must solve.'

'I want to unravel them. I know I will meet opposition from those who find the theory of "Aryan invasion" a convenient manner of justifying racial inequality. But Britain's cultural imperialism could not have flourished without the collaboration of Indian Trojan horses.'

I, Elangovan, heard this singular conversation, and wondered if Julius Norton was an agent provocateur or a genuine admirer of our civilization?

Back in Delhi Julius Norton tried to tackle the nitty-gritty of administration of which he had not the slightest idea. Fortunately, the quiet men trained by Sir Alistair Mackenzie guided him about the procedure of conservation through the Works Code meticulously composed by Sir John Marshall.

Norton listened to Vishnu Rawat, the superintending archaeologist who headed the Antiquity branch, on the manner by which Indian antiquities and artefacts were dated through the style of sculpture, the contours of the body and the headdress. Then, Rawat sat back with a timid smile and placing a sculpture before Dr Norton asked him to analyze. It was difficult at first; the Mesopotamian artefacts with which Norton was familiar were different. Their inner spirit was different. The Assyrian styles were more akin to Achaemenid ones which was later emulated by Greeks. Both had a curious combination of earthiness and necromancy that inspired the Hellenic world.

Excavation reports fascinated Julius Norton; herein lay the mysteries of the past. He pored over the excavation reports of Sarnath, Sanchi, Sravasti and Nalanda which elucidated the new Buddhist ethos blossoming amidst the effulgent Mauryas that gave way to the austere grace of the nomadic Kushans and then the opulence of the imperial Guptas.

Julius Norton was thrilled to read of the greatest discovery of twentieth-century archaeology - of Mohenjo-daro and Harappa - cities of the Indus Valley Civilization. Spanning some thousand miles, it was the largest unitary civilization of ancient times. 'At a single bound,' wrote Sir John Marshall, 'we have taken back our knowledge of Indian civilization some three thousand years earlier and have established the fact that in the third millennium BC people in the Punjab and Sind lived in well-built cities and had a culture with a high standard of art and craftsmanship. They developed pictographic writing.'

Julius Norton and Athena set off to see Harappa, one of the two famous cities of the Indus Valley, site of one of the greatest civilizations of the ancient world. It stood three hundred miles to the south of the Indo-Afghan frontier. They arrived by train as dusk settled over the little town. Two massive mounds rose from the level ground; the grandeur and mystery of the forgotten past overwhelmed them as had Nimrud and Nineveh.

At first light they went to the site. Making their way through rubble and rain-furrowed paths, they saw the remnants of towers and battlements encircling a man-made acropolis. Harappa was a fortified city with a hierarchical character ruled by priests. Then they went to the twin city of Mohenjo-daro where two decades earlier the first excavations of the Indus Valley Civilization had commenced.

John Marshall had exulted: 'This stupendous civilization was entirely indigenous and connected with the Vedic age. The Aryan Invasion theory is unscientific.' This declaration angered the British government.

Julius and Athena read the vivid excavation reports of these sites. These brought to life civilizations and the inspiration of ages gone by. The reports on Mohenjo-daro and Harappa constructed a vanished civilization and revealed a great historical enigma.

A New Schliemann

It was while inspecting Moghul buildings within Red Fort that Tejvir entered our lives. Sometimes portentous incidents occur in our lives without our awareness. Ruddy complexioned and ramrod straight, the landlord from nearby Sonapath made a fantastic claim – that he was a direct descendant of the Pandava brothers of the epic *Mahabharata*. He cursed the Moghuls for trespassing on hallowed grounds when they built the Red Fort because it was there, at Indraprastha, that the Pandavas had built their kingdom.

The British officers in the barracks laughed at his pretensions but not openly because Tejvir was a wealthy landlord who gave generous loans to spendthrift officers. He served Scotch at soirees at his house in Chandni Chowk where nautch girls cavorted with subalterns at a discount. But lately his hospitality had waned; he had become taciturn and resentful.

Now he watched Dr Norton and Athena inspect the historical edifices. Introducing himself, Tejvir said, 'I have heard about you, Norton Saheb. It appears you admire our ancient culture.'

Dr Norton nodded. 'All archaeologists are interested in antiquity. What is your interest in our excavations?'

'My interest is in the revival of our ancient culture. Take Purana Qila where episodes of the *Mahabharata* were enacted. Now it looks like an army camp!' As Norton turned to go Tejvir stopped him. 'I can fund your excavations at Purana Qila,' Tejvir enunciated clearly.

Norton frowned. 'Why?'

'To find the *Mahabharata* site. To let the world know that Indian civilization is as old as Egypt and Mesopotamia. We have lost our self-respect and pride. Your work can revive it. Your excavations can unearth our epic sites.'

Julius Norton gave the landlord an appraising glance. 'Let me think about it,' he said.

There was something in Tejvir that troubled Norton, but hearing of the offer, Athena was enthusiastic. 'This sounds wonderful! With Tejvir's help we don't have to beg Archibald Blandford for funds.'

The new alliance was sealed with dinner at Tejvir's house. Until now the Nortons had not seen the interior of a traditional Indian home; spacious courtyard where wheat was being threshed and tied in bundles, where cows chewed cud with expressions of bored indifference, while dough was thrust into clay stoves to make bread. Then they went to the rectangular hall where Tejvir entertained friends.

Guests sat on the floor and leaned on bolsters. At the centre of the hall sat a man singing ghazals. Beside him sat a young woman strumming melodies on the taanpura. Her fingers slowed down as the Nortons entered and then she smiled as Norton and Athena sat down on the sheet-covered carpet. Athena listened to the unfamiliar music while Julius and the other guests discussed archaeology. Later Rupamati, the young woman, was introduced to the Nortons. She expressed a desire to work with them at the *Mahabharata* sites around Delhi.

Excavations at the *Mahabharata* site evoked excitement as the scene of the world's oldest epic. The *Iliad* and *Odyssey* are about mortal combats between the Greeks and the Trojans, and of voyages across uncharted seas. The Indian epic is set in several kingdoms of North India. It has many themes and many stories culminating in the unforgettable dialogue between Lord Krishna and his disciple Arjun that forms the core of a world religion. While the *Iliad* and *Odyssey* are now read only by the Western literati, the *Mahabharata* is a palpable presence in every Indian home.

Excavations began in the old fort. When the dust and debris was removed the remains of a very old civilization began to appear.

At this stage a young kinsman of Tejvir appeared on the scene. Dhokaram Karma stated he had come to make a fortune in Delhi. Tejvir was relieved that Dr Norton did not know Hindi and would not therefore understand the meaning of the newcomer's name – *Fraudulent Worker*. Dhokaram had a confectionary shop in Chandni Chowk but was keen to learn archaeology. I, Elangovan, thought him a comic figure but Dr Norton fobbed him off as he retrieved dusty pottery shards from the trenches.

'Is archaeology a fool's errand?' Athena asked.

'Only those who set off on journeys of discovery find what they seek, Pallas Athena,' Julius affectionately admonished his wife.

Sthapatis

I, Elangovan of Pallavur Circle of the ASI, suggested to Dr Norton that before resuming work at Mohenjo-daro and

Harappa, and in order to replicate structures of buildings and statuary found during the excavations there, it would be worthwhile to procure the services of Sthapatis from South India who were trained in sculpting statues, temples, friezes and bas reliefs. The director general readily agreed.

I told Dr Norton about Sthapatis. 'In the sacred Vedic texts the word Sthapati meant "chief" or "viceroy". Among these architects and sculptors there is a hierarchy of status: Sthapati, Sutragrahin, Vardhaki and Taksaka. The Sthapati is the chief architect-sculptor while the others survey and take measurements of buildings. The artisans, craftsmen and artists must be born to the Vishwakarma or craftsman caste to qualify as Sthapatis. They are taught ancient texts, especially the *Shilpa Sastra*s, which teach epigraphy, calligraphy, painting, geology, mathematics and acoustics. They learn rules of Hindu architecture; of proportion, auspicious spatial directions and iconography. Before temple construction began, Sthapatis were required to decide whether the site was auspicious and whether it was conducive to meditation.'

I narrated to Dr Norton how the Sthapatis played a special role in India's cultural expansion in East Asia. Without them no sacred or aesthetic structures were undertaken. They accompanied princes and merchants to East Asia in the early years of the first millennium AD. There they built temples to Lord Shiva and Lord Vishnu, sculpted statues of deities, depicted episodes from Hindu epics or contemporary local scenes and inscribed verses from sacred texts.

So now the Sthapatis came from South India, foreheads furrowed by intense concentration, shoulders slumped from bending over objects, and supple hands gnarled by chiselling stones. They disliked Delhi, as I, Elangovan, did, with its harsh summers and severe winters, the enforced diet of roti, dahl, vegetables wrapped in rich gravy instead of a pyramid of rice, sambar, poriyal and curd.

The advent of the Sthapatis did not evoke much interest; they were the accompaniment to any restoration or conservation project. But Dr Norton was fascinated as I, Elangovan, told him of their work.

'I have seen them over the years; of how their fingers followed the trajectory of their eyes and, as if in obedience to a divine command, reproduced what they saw into stone. They could replicate the soaring *shikhara*s of Chola temples, bracket figures of Vijayanagar sculptures, ornate *gopuram*s of Madurai's Meenakshi temple. They fashioned exquisite figurines out of bronze and copper. When old age stiffened their fingers and bleared their eyes they taught the young of their tribe to continue this grand tradition.'

Julius Norton nodded. 'It seems that Sthapatis are the custodians of Indian art.'

I noticed that Dhokaram Karma watched the Sthapatis with acute interest. Little did I know that this would be a portentous encounter between Dhokaram and the Sthapatis.

End of an Era

I, Elangovan, like many Indians, witnessed epochal upheavals in India. Our secret hopes for the success of Subhash Bose's army were dashed at the battle of Kohima when Indians of the British Indian Army killed Indians of the Indian National Army. That put an end to dreams of a war of liberation that would have ended centuries of servitude. Perhaps some of our national leaders secretly rejoiced at Subhash's defeat. Who shall blame them? Manipulative pacifist politicians would have found a serious challenge in a triumphant charismatic Subhash Bose.

We recalled the career of Subhash Bose and realized the futility of nobility. Subhash Bose had graduated with a first class degree from Cambridge University. He was the 'topper' in the Indian Civil Service Examinations of 1921 but shortly afterward resigned from the ICS and joined the freedom struggle. His charisma drew people to him. He was elected president of the Indian National Congress. There was a possibility that the Congress party would split with the younger members joining Subhash Bose. Reluctant to split the party, Subhash Bose did what Giuseppe Garibaldi had done a century earlier in a similar predicament; he left the scene of victory and plaudits of the populace rather than create a schism.

He went on to raise the Indian National Army to liberate India by force of arms. 'Every nation – Bismarck's Germany, Garibaldi's Italy and Ypsilantis's Greece – attained independence through a war of liberation. We shall do the same. We shall raise our army of liberation!'

When Britain was engaged in a mortal combat during the Second World War with Germany it seemed the perfect moment for his plans.

There was a terrible stillness at our ASI office in Red Fort on the day news of the carnage at Kohima reached us – the Red Fort which Subhash Bose made his ultimate destination with the soul-stirring cry of *'Chalo Dilli!'* or 'March to Delhi!' We scanned the English newspapers that reported the deaths of soldiers and officers of the Indian National Army. I tried to shut out the images; the bamboo thickets from where the INA men made their last stand, the banks of the Brahmaputra river where their blood flowed and mingled with the monsoon rain as the British Indian Army tore through their ranks.

As we sat in silence, Julius Norton, a decorated sometime-major of the British Army, entered the office that is located behind the Lahori Gate. On the far side is the *Diwani Aam* from where the Grand Moghuls once dispensed justice. Dr Norton stood at the entrance for a moment in silence, his sapient blue eyes sweeping over us. Then he shook his head and murmured, 'This is a sad day for liberation armies.'

We were silent. Silence is the only defence for a subjugated people.

The chief unarmed prophet, Gandhi, had no intention of being outshone by the man he feared most – Subhash Bose. Those of us who had some fire in our bellies were repelled by the philosophy of passive resistance to foreign rule. It seemed like sophistry and not the expression of valour. Subhash Bose had shown us how to rise and, if necessary, how to die – with heads held high.

Soon after the tragedy of Kohima we heard of the famine in Bengal that carried away three million people.

The Second World War was drawing to an end. Delhi was full of rumours as several exalted envoys of the British government came to negotiate the future of the subcontinent.

Simultaneously Red Fort became the scene of trials of the officers of the Indian National Army. Amidst this, age-old questions surfaced – to whom and what does one profess loyalty – to the paymaster or to one's conscience? Was this question not discussed in the *Mahabharata* many millennia ago at the battlefield of souls in Kurukhshetra? And so on 15 August 1947, India became a sovereign nation after one-hundred-and-ninety years of British rule. While the new tricolour flew on the ramparts of the Red Fort, I remembered

Subhash Bose who had disappeared. Had he died when his plane crashed in Taiwan? Or had he survived and sought sanctuary among friends? Or had he been eliminated by erstwhile comrades with British help?

Along with celebrations for freedom and flowery speeches there were millions who perished in the carnage that followed the Partition of India. Never in a recorded history of five millennia with its turmoil and violence had this country been divided into two hostile nations. The capital of Delhi was a vast refugee camp and Calcutta, the second city of the British Empire, burnt with flames of hatred between Hindus and Muslims.

The sovereign Indian government was formed but vestiges of the British Raj remained. Indian members of the erstwhile Indian Civil Service remained to run the ministries; some of its members formed the skeletal diplomatic service. A strange metamorphosis transformed Indian members of the Raj into steadfast adherents of the new regime. How did they now reconcile their pride to their new paymasters, their conscience to their new commitments?

The viceroy was gone. His secretary Archibald Blandford had left for his English country home but Dr Julius Norton was asked to stay on until a replacement was found. We at the ASI were happy and relieved.

One afternoon when we archaeologists and artisans were waiting for the sun to mellow a Bentley car drove up to the camp. Hearing the commotion, I, Elangovan, came out of the tent and saw Zoya, the Ottoman princess and fourth wife of the nawab of Deccanabad. She wore Western clothes and a straw hat over her red-brown hair cut short. Coming to me she asked imperiously, 'Where is Dr Julius Norton?'

Hearing the commotion Julius Norton came out of our camp-office. He stared at her in astonishment. Then he walked slowly towards her and said, 'What a surprise, Your Highness! What brings you here to this scorched land?'

Her hazel eyes glittered. 'You,' she said.

Embarassment tinged the director general's bronzed face. It was easier for him to encounter skeletons of long gone Sumerian queens than a banished Turkish princess with hunger in her eyes.

'Me?' he asked lightly. 'And in what way can I be of service to you? I have already forwarded my report of the Golkonda Fort to your husband the nawab.'

She waved her jewelled hand in dismissal. 'The nawab!' she snapped. 'He is now a rubber stamp, thanks to the Indian government. Deccanabad is now part of India.' She paused and lowered her voice. 'I heard you were in our realm but you did not come to see me. So *I* have come to see you before you leave for England.'

Julius Norton regarded her gravely. 'I will be here for sometime until the Indian government finds a successor.'

The princess said, 'I am leaving for Europe. I do not intend to waste my life as the old fool's concubine.'

'Europe has been devastated by a world war. What will you do there?' Julius asked.

'I will go to the Riviera where my parents built a villa. I have money in the Bank of England. I shall lead the life I always wanted.' The princess stepped closer and murmured, 'Would you join me? I could fund your excavations in Greece or Anatolia. We could have a wonderful life together, Julius Norton!'

I, Elangovan, stood rooted to the spot. I had never heard a lady speak like this. As I tried to retreat, Dr Norton turned to me swiftly. 'Mr Elangovan, could you arrange tea on the green patch by the river?' He paused before saying, 'Please go to our tent and tell Mrs Norton that I would like her to meet a lady guest.'

I could have wept with relief. The scholar was making it clear that he would not be ensnared by the royal siren. I made a move to go when a mischievous junior archaeologist interjected: 'Madam Athena has a fever since the morning … she is resting.'

'Nevertheless, tell her to come!' Dr Norton commanded.

The princess's eyes glittered in anger. I stole away, afraid of the brewing storm. While tea and biscuits were laid out on cane tables the two sat in silence. Athena Norton arrived shortly. Her cheeks were flushed by fever, and there was a strange look on her chiselled face. She held out her sun-tanned hand to the princess who took it gingerly, as if afraid of dust and mud.

'Have you come to see this epic site? My husband told me you were interested in history.' There was a hint of sarcasm in Athena's voice.

Princess Zoya's jaws tightened. She retaliated by saying, 'I came to see Dr Norton before he left India.'

'Well, have a nice chat over tea. Excuse me for not joining you. I have a slight fever.'

Athena's dignified contempt subdued the princess. Dr Norton told Rupamati to accompany Athena to their tent. A heavy stillness ensued after her departure. Later Rupamati told me that she had warned Athena that the predator princess had come to disrupt Dr Norton's work. With tears trickling down her cheeks Athena murmured, 'When you try to dam a strong current there is turbulence, but if you let it flow untrammelled it spends itself out and forms a quiet pool somewhere.' She paused. 'And now, Rupamati, let me sleep so that I can work tomorrow. Don't wake me up for dinner.'

Princess Zoya left at dusk. The hostile atmosphere did not halt her pursuit. Next day she came again and stayed for several days in our camp, professing keen interest in the current restoration project. Too busy counting and selling his treasures to nouveau riche buyers, the nawab was indifferent to his concubines. The princess shared a tent with a hostile Rupamati. Athena remained aloof. One day Dr Norton took Princess Zoya across the river Jamuna to see old monuments. They returned at twilight as the river turned into molten gold.

I noticed that Julius Norton was not his genial self; he seemed preoccupied and taciturn. His eyes sometimes rested mid-distance on some invisible horizon. I had never seen him fluctuate between rapture and gloom. Athena's fever got worse; unaware of the true malaise our camp doctor diagnosed it as malaria.

Having failed to get herself abducted by Dr Norton, Princess Zoya left as suddenly as she had arrived. Julius went back to his equable self. Athena recovered – from malaria – and resumed work in one of the *Mahabharata* sites.

We returned to Delhi. Julius Norton called us to his office one sultry September morning that heralds the end of the monsoon. He was wearing a light grey suit, his auburn hair plastered down, smoking one of his interminable cigarettes.

'Sit down, gentlemen,' he said in his usual courteous manner.

We directors and superintendents of archaeology sat down and waited for the orderly to serve tea and leave.

'It has been a long tenure of British director generals since 1861,' he said without preamble. 'Now it is time for you gentlemen to take charge of your heritage.' He paused and shook his head. 'Ah, but I stand corrected. You have already taken charge and are already custodians of your heritage. But it is time you had an Indian director general to head this venerable organization.'

'You are not leaving, Sir?' the senior most director asked in deep dismay.

Dr Norton nodded. 'I have asked your prime minister's office to select a new DG. I am no longer needed here – to snoop around for secret agents in the North-West Frontier. What the Survey requires is a chief who knows the history of this land, and how to reconstruct the unknown eras through excavations and epigraphy. There are so many of you to choose from.'

I had not known until that moment how much I admired and loved this English scholar who had enclosed us in warm camaraderie. My heart sank. 'Where will you go now, Sir?' I asked, bereft already.

Dr Norton sighed. 'Where all archaeologists go – to mounds and tells and graves – from where present mortals have fled and where they return as future gods.' He paused. 'No, it is not as bad as that. We will return to Nineveh and complete our excavations there. We shall pore over timeless steatites and try to find a bicodal text that may give us a clue to the Indus Valley script. And after that is accomplished I shall swim across the Arabian Sea to land up in Mohenjo-daro or Harappa and reveal the secret of your ancient civilization – with your help.'

'Mohenjo-daro and Harappa are now in Pakistan,' I reminded him gloomily. 'We cannot go there any more.'

'Civilizations do not recognize frontiers made by politicians. We will all meet there – by the banks of the Indus.

How is that for a plan?' He paused. 'And while Athena and I are by the banks of the Tigris you gentlemen should complete the programme we have drawn up for the next two years. You can show me no greater affection than to do that.'

I, Elangovan, stayed awake all night, gazing at the ruins of Purana Qila, recalling discussions about ancient civilizations. With what dedication Julius and Athena did their work! No, it was more than dedication; it was a passion that consumed them. In five years Julius Norton had thoroughly acquainted himself with the work of the ASI and had become one of us. He was a true scholar. What mattered to him was the quest for truth, for facts, for evidence of civilizations. It mattered not whether their discoveries suited political ideologies. Like true historians they sought answers about Time, about events, about the progress and regress of Man. Archaeology was their handmaiden for this quest.

How we were going to miss them! A traitorous thought invaded me. With the close of British Raj would the glorious traditions of the Archaeological Survey of India also end? Would that incandescent determination to explore and investigate flicker out?

So came the time to say goodbye. It was a glorious spring day when even untamed flowers and broken statues in the ASI headquarters gardens looked picturesque. Tables were spread out, laden with tea and cakes. Wearing a sari, Athena looked like a Greek goddess. Julius regarded her with a strange sadness. We remembered the sultry monsoon afternoon when Julius Norton 'took over' from Sir Alistair Mackenzie, of how we had regarded the new chief with suspicion and reservation. Sir Alistair had been with us for two decades; we both feared and venerated him. In five years

Julius Norton had won our hearts and captured our minds with a vision of history shorn of all prejudices.

Dr Norton concluded his farewell speech by saying: 'The benefit of working on ancient sites is that one gets a measure of Time, the importance of events, and an idea of the insignificance of our own existence. This accomplished, we can see all things - happy and sad - in their perspective. We can then console ourselves with Lord Krishna's admonition to Arjuna - "And this too shall pass."'

Interlude to a Dark Dawn

It was at this juncture that a momentous event took place. Dhokaram Karma (Fraudulent Worker) abandoned the occupation of making ghee-dripping sweets and savouries and opened a curio shop near Chandni Chowk in old Delhi. He was joined by his cousin Besharam Karma (Shameless Worker).

I, Elangovan, could not understand the reason for this. The confectionary shop gave him a steady income whereas the curio shop catered to travellers who wanted to carry back souvenirs. There were not many travellers now; the turmoil of the Partition kept all but the bravest away from India. Now only scholars and academics came to study Indian conditions. The other foreigners were officers and staff of the various embassies that were being established in New Delhi in recognition of our new sovereign status.

The new director general of Archaeology - an Indian - was a man of sterling virtues and wide learning. He had been trained by Alistair Mackenzie and belonged to the classical school of archaeology. Now with a nascent pride in India's heritage there was also a growing demand for preservation of heritage. This preservation became a problem because heritage had to compete with the imperatives of economic development. Some five thousand edifices scattered over India needed urgent attention. Our resources were meagre. While vows were made to save India's culture, the Indian government did not have adequate funds to preserve the myriad monuments. Guided by Marshall's Works Code we worked late into the night with our new director general to select the monuments which required urgent conservation and which were of historic-cultural importance.

Important excavation projects were undertaken in the first decade of Independence – at Mathura, Kalibangan, Burzahoam, and Indus Valley sites such as Rajgarhia. To assist in these extensive excavations, numerous young men (whose enthusiasm was greater than their skill) were recruited by the new director general. Rasam Pagrawal and Kalo Gunacha were symbolic of this new class. They were recruited to the ASI as there was a shortage of trained personnel after the departure of British archaeologists.

An archaeological team was sent by the director general to excavate the ancient port of Tamralipta on the coast of Bengal. It was an old Buddhist site from where ships had sailed for East Asia. On a rainy day the archaeologists were digging trenches when they found a cluster of statuettes, and an exquisite figurine of a *yakshi* or celestial dancer. This *yakshi* was taken, as customary, to the excavation camp, to be cleaned, labelled, provenance recorded. Other members of the excavation team never saw the statue again.

During an excavation trip a colleague narrated what had happened. The sounds of digging and the subdued drone of intense discussion was around us. Cautiously, I asked, 'What happened to the *yakshi*?'

My colleague remained silent for a while. Then he said, 'The figurine was smuggled abroad, sold to an Indian collector of antiques based in London who in turn sold it to Sotheby's. They became suspicious when the antiquity collector could not provide provenance for the sculpture. Sotheby's informed the Indian government that a valuable antiquity had been sold to them by an Indian collector. They sent a photo and description of the figurine. Enquiries by the Central Bureau of Investigation revealed that two venerable archaeologists of the ASI, Babu Pal and Dalu Hasmukh, were involved in its removal from India. The British antiquity collector who bought the statue had regular dealings with them.'

Rasam Pagrawal soon became their cat's paw.

Babu Pal went on to excavate the *Ramayana* sites – places that were associated with the life of King Rama of Ayodhya. Inspired by Schliemann's discovery of Homer's Troy we wanted to find these. *Ramayana* is more than a poetic legend; it is the very breath of life for Indians. So Babu Pal thought he would do for *Ramayana* what Schliemann had done for the *Iliad*. Substantial funds were allotted for these excavations. The archaeologists returned from these excavations but the reports were not written for three decades. Had reports on those sites been timely written by the excavators, we would have knowledge about the material civilization of those distant times, about the episodes mentioned in the great epics that were the touchstone of Indian civilization.

The celebrated archaeologist Mortimer Wheeler had declared 'The failure to write excavation reports is more than a lapse in administrative procedure. It is an unforgivable act of destruction of historical evidence. Archaeology is not an end in itself; it is the handmaiden of historical research.'

I, Elangovan, kept asking myself, why did my senior colleagues not write the excavation reports? It is not that they lacked information, training or even reporting skill. They had been trained in these fundamentals by great mentors. Was it indolence or was it something more insidious? I would come to know a decade later, not through archaeological introspections but through the boldness of a civil servant.

Rasam Pagrawal took charge of crucial branches of the ASI. The director general trusted him; the affair of the *yakshi* at Tamralipta had not yet surfaced. Some archaeologists are not only skilled in *digging up the past;* they are also adept at *burying the past.* Besides, the DG required senior trained officers and could not afford to be too fastidious. Rasam Pagrawal joined the chorus; we needed more trained personnel. Ad hoc interviews were arranged to recruit such personnel.

I, Elangovan, was perturbed by Rupamati's proximity to Pagrawal. It is professional camaraderie, I told myself but I could see signs of something more. My fears were justified when Rupamati applied for the post of assistant archaeologist. She had no background of history, even less of archaeology, and yet she aspired to hold a position of responsibility in our venerable organization! She had long planned this by cultivating friendship with the naïve Athena Norton who gave her entrée to the ASI.

The day of the interview arrived. Pagrawal was tasked with examining the candidates for Epigraphy. I was the co-examiner. Candidate after candidate came and went; none of them knew how to read the ancient Brahmi and Kharoshti scripts. And then came a confident Rupamati. Pagrawal handed her a parchment and commanded brusquely: 'Read!' Rupamati frowned and began reading. I was astonished to see her holding the Kharoshti script scroll upside down.

Obviously she could not read the script but the manner in which she rattled off the words made it clear that someone had tutored her to recite it. Completing her memorized part she gave us a smug smile. I, enraged by this effrontery, glared at Pagrawal. He fixed me with a baleful glare and said, 'She is a promising student. We will select her.'

The soul of the great epigraphist James Prinsep, who had deciphered the ancient Brahmi and Kharoshti scripts, must have cried out in heaven at this infraction. But I, more earthbound than Prinsep, could see what men like Rasam Pagrawal and K. Gunacha were unleashing on our venerable organization.

Dhokaram Karma now joined this influential group. Instead of samosas and jilebis he now sold stone and clay figurines at his new curio shop. Selling these objects gave him great pleasure; the sales were accompanied by foreign currency notes. Overruling my protests Kuppuswamy the Sthapati had been appointed chief designer of Dhokaram's The Cultural Curio Shop in old Delhi's Chandni Chowk.

'What are they asking you to do?' I asked Kuppuswamy in Tamil.

Kuppuswamy shook his head. '*Ayya* [sir], why are you badgering me? Did you not ask me to come here, leaving my home and rice fields in Mamallapuram, my weekly puja at Kanchi temple? And now, because I am not working for you, you bother me!'

'So what does the jilebi maker ask you to do?' I asked with foreboding.

Kuppuswamy beamed. 'He shows me photos of famous statues and asks me to sculpt them in sandstone. Easy job, really – very much what I did in my shed at Mamallapuram. But Dhokaram gives me twice the price. Once I have made enough money for my two daughters' dowries I am going back to my native.'

I persisted with questions. 'Can you tell me what sort of statues you have sculpted since you joined The Cultural Curio Shop?'

Kuppuswamy's face was suffused with pride. 'I made a replica of Lord Ishwara of Brihadishwara temple, the Divine Flutist at Thanjavur, and Nataraja of Chidambaram temple.'

I heard my heart thudding against my chest. 'The most famous statues of South India,' I murmured. 'The great Ernest Havell, Percy Brown and Ananda Coomaraswamy made them known to the world.'

Kuppuswamy nodded vigorously. 'These will be sold to foreigners who will see our glorious traditions.' I felt my guts tighten in dread.

'Will that be all?' a pleased Kuppuswamy asked.

'For the time being,' I replied. 'But let me know what you are doing, all the same.' I tried to put The Cultural Curio Shop out of my mind. Perhaps I was imagining things, I told myself. And then came another round of recruitment where Pagrawal and Gunacha presided and where I also interviewed the candidates. I quarrelled with them at the interview because we could not agree on the candidates. Having made friends with the establishment Pagrawal had more clout than me and had his way.

I opposed the recruitment of Besharam Karma (Shameless Worker), a loutish fellow who tried to affect westernized airs. If his English made me wince, it would have mortified an Englishman. His knowledge of ancient Indian history was shaky. The other candidates were far superior to him but Pagrawal was adamant. Mysteriously and recently Besharam had acquired a Ph.D. from a mythical university. He was selected along with other candidates. I gave my dissenting note on Besharam to be forwarded to the ministry. Many months later an official of the culture ministry told me that no dissenting note, as is mandatory, had accompanied the list of selected candidates. Besharam Karma was appointed assistant archaeologist in the Antiquities wing where he would be trained by the scholarly Kashinath Rawat.

I often had afternoon tea with Kashinath who was a leaf out of legends. He had merely to glance at a piece of old statuary and say from whence it came and its age. His sensitive hands glided over the statue, reliquary or ornament with a lover's caress, a half smile on his ruddy lined face as he indicated the provenance of the piece. 'Look at the head-dress,' he instructed the young recruits. 'That's half the secret. Then examine the feet, folds of the dress. That will tell you a great deal because every age leaves its signature on art.'

Kashinath paused and quoted the great English art historian Havell on how to judge a classical statue, through its balance and proportion, folds of garments and facial expression which would indicate the evolution of art in various civilizations.

It gladdened me to hear Kashinath Rawat speak because he embodied the concept of '*vidya*' or learning, in all its bounty. He would not be able to write books like Percy Brown, Havell or Ananda Coomaraswamy but he would pass on the knowledge and skill that he had acquired to a younger generation and enable them to decipher and classify the art treasures of our land. Had he possessed an enterprising temperament he would have become curator of a famous Western museum and author of several books. But like many of his generation he was content to sit at his desk and perform his tasks with devotion. Men like him have preserved our heritage and learning. He knew more about stones and metals than anyone else I knew and guided the arrogant Sthapatis. Many young archaeologists learnt about art and sculpture at Kashinath's feet. Some continued the great traditions. Others used the sacred knowledge like Kachh, the celestial spy, to betray their mentor.

An unerring instinct prompted me to see how my bête noire Besharam was undergoing training. Surprisingly, Kashinath found the young man compliant and eager to learn. When his obsequiousness annoyed me I told myself that I was getting crusty with advancing years. Perhaps Besharam meant no harm.

Six months passed. Rasam Pagrawal declared Besharam had become quite an expert in this and should be posted as assistant superintending archaeologist on customs duty.

'Is he that good?' I was impelled to ask.

'He can identify antiquities – that is the skill required for the post. He has to ensure that the objects of art sent abroad are not antiquities. Besharam will handle the task well. He is polite, tactful but firm.'

I was tempted to observe that he was too obsequious to be firm but restrained myself.

Instinct again took me to visit Kuppuswamy who lived behind The Cultural Curio Shop near Delhi's Juma Masjid where Dhokaram Karma's sweet shop was now run by a kinsman. The Hindu Sthapati felt uncomfortable in the Muslim locality where rich aromas hung in the air; garlic-marinated goat meat sizzled in tandoor stoves, many layered onion parathas grilled on live coals, and iced kulfis sprinkled with rosewater. Sometimes this austere sculptor went up to the *barsati*, pent-room, of the narrow tenement, to watch veiled giggling girls walk with jingling anklets to the local brothel.

In the evening he heard the cry of the muezzin summon the faithful to prayer. If Kuppuswamy longed for the temple bells by the river Kaveri, as I did, he never expressed himself. In time he was introduced to a fancy woman of the doss house so that her caresses softened the rigours of his alien sojourn.

Kuppuswamy was busy chiselling a figurine that was a replica of a bracket figure at the Belur temple in Karnataka. His skilled fingers moulded the heavy breasts and hips, and fashioned tendrils of hair on her rounded neck. The sandstone obeyed the command of his hands and became malleable as human flesh.

'You seem to be sculpting figures for a high-class museum,' I observed.

He shrugged. 'I do what Besharam Karma tells me.'

'I had no idea he had such high-class tastes,' I said to provoke the Sthapati who once more shrugged and replied, 'He doesn't; it is Rasam Pagrawal who culls out photos of these figures from the ASI photo library.'

Alerted, I asked, 'Why would he be interested in replicas of images and figurines of the photo library?'

'He is your colleague. Suppose you ask him?' Kuppuswamy replied testily.

As he was speaking, Pagrawal came to the tarpaulin-covered *barsati* to assess Kuppuswamy's work. He was accompanied by a chirping Rupamati. Their chatter halted upon seeing me. But Pagrawal swiftly composed himself and said, 'You know, Elangovan, you could be of great help to me in my new project.'

I forbore to ask questions. Brahmins never ask questions; they elicit answers by their very silence.

'I am organizing an exhibition of Hoysala art and sculpture. After that I hope to take the exhibition to England

and Austria. You could guide me in this. You are as good as Ananda Coomaraswamy. Would you like to write a few lines on each figure?' He paused to infuse warmth in his clammy voice. 'Visitors to museums will value these lines on Indian art.'

'Havell, Coomaraswamy and Brown have already done that – with vast erudition and at great length,' I retorted. 'I would not dare to compete with them.'

'No!' came the impassioned retort. 'I want interpretations of Indian art from our point of view – not the foreigners' opinion!'

'If I compose captions for Kuppuswamy's statues I will be guided by these great men,' I replied stubbornly.

Rupamati glanced apprehensively at her mentor-lover and then at me. I returned her glance with a malicious smile and asked, 'How is the epigraphy going?'

She had the grace to blush. Her reading the Kharoshti scroll upside down had done the rounds in the ASI accompanied by derisive laughter. I returned home feeling uneasy. Something was going terribly wrong. Epigraphists who could not read ancient scripts; self-conferred Ph.D. degrees by archaeologists; sweet vendors posing as antiquarians.

The exhibition of Hoysala art was arranged by Rasam Pagrawal at the National Museum in Delhi. As customary on such occasions, art historians and artists attended in large numbers while Pagrawal acting as the master of ceremonies showered fulsome praise on them. Going around the exhibition I was assailed once more by that uneasy sensation but could not put my finger on the cause.

And then I saw the sculpture of a Hoysala courtesan. I closed my eyes and saw Sthapati Kuppuswamy moulding her out of sandstone. Each artist, like each criminal, leaves his signature on his work. In his zeal to gild the lily, Kuppuswamy had touched the statue with his own vanity. He had given his statue an ethereal quality absent in the earthy original. Stunned by my discovery I went to see the other exhibits. They were perfect Hoysala period pieces but my startling discovery now gave me new insight. I could pick out the telltale differences and the subtle divergence from the carnal allure of Hoysala art. Interspersed between these exquisite imitations were a few original sculptures to confuse the art historians. While rage gathered within me, I circumambulated the exhibits like a pilgrim possessed.

My first impulse was to start screaming to the assembled experts that they were participating in a huge fraud but second thoughts followed swiftly – thoughts of revenge and possible rectification. I had to think this through calmly. And possibly take Kuppuswamy into confidence. Casting a glance around the illumined exhibition hall and the enraptured faces of the experts, I rushed out and hailed an auto-rickshaw to old Delhi where Kuppuswamy and his *confreres* lived. My furious banging on the door brought no response. A shopkeeper who provided Kuppuswamy and Co. with parathas informed me that the Sthapatis had left a few days earlier for Pallavur. So, they had been packed off to prevent any speculation or worse, any discovery of what had happened! I decided to go to Pallavur – ostensibly to inspect progress of conservation works while I gleaned information from Kuppuswamy.

Arriving in Pallavur I went immediately to the seaside town of Mamallapuram from where ships laden with merchants, priests and Sthapatis had set sail for East Asia two millennia ago. Kuppuswamy and his tribe now pursued their profession here.

Kuppuswamy and company had left Mamallapuram. Their families were informed that they had boarded a ship for England to attend a conference. Cheques were enclosed to enable the families to live comfortably for a few months. Stunned and furious I returned to Delhi.

It was with a perverse delight and smouldering anger that I sought out Pagrawal, like a cuckolded husband catching his wife in flagrante delicto. He both repelled and fascinated me. I pretended to be an ally instead of arousing his suspicion. I told him that I would be happy to draft brief introductory notes for his brochure for the exhibition.

'From an Indian point of view. In your own words,' he reiterated again. 'Not a regurgitation of Havell or Brown!' I wondered why he insisted on 'an Indian perspective of Indian art'. I was soon to know.

Preparations for the foreign exhibitions continued. Brochures were printed. Applications were sent to the ministry of culture for permission to take the sculptures abroad, especially if the sculptures and antiquities were rare and came under the 'A' category in the Acquisition List. Pagrawal summoned Besharam Karma, now deputy superintendent of archaeology (customs) to prepare the necessary documents that enabled the ASI to take antiquities outside India.

'Check every item!' he commanded his subordinate imperiously. 'Get Jhutha-bhai [Liar Brother], the Xerox clerk [instead of the concerned photographer], to take proper photos. You must observe the same drill when the items are returned. You understand?'

Besharam was the embodiment of obedience as he said, 'Of course, respected, Sir! That is our sacred duty!'

And then came the momentous day when Pagrawal, Rupamati and a few trusted acolytes set off for the exhibition abroad. The team returned after a fortnight, radiant with the success of the exhibition; some newspapers lauded them for displaying the grandeur of medieval Indian art.

Experts were called in to verify that the antiquities had returned home safely. I was present at the meeting and noted that the 'experts' were a new and unknown lot on whom Pagrawal had bestowed his generous patronage. Thus the antiquities that came back from abroad were certified 'as verified to be the same sent abroad'. They were then returned to the museums from whence they purportedly came.

Pagrawal went off to Goa with Rupamati for a well-deserved holiday. Taking advantage of his absence from headquarters I made a tour programme to inspect conservation works in some areas. My real itinerary was to visit those museums from where the exhibited sculptures originated. With the brochure in hand I began inspection of the sculptures.

My worst fears were confirmed. While some of the originals had been returned, others were replicas – innocently fashioned by the Sthapatis. I booked a trunk call to the ASI Pallavur office to ascertain if Kuppuswamy and company had returned. They had. I went to Pallavur on official work and found the Sthapatis.

I confronted them with their crime. Kuppuswamy was astonished. 'But I committed no crime! I was told by Pagrawal and Gunacha *Ayyas* that all three of you wanted some replicas for an exhibition abroad. You were doing the write-ups. So I did it! After all, do we not make replicas all the time? Did not our forefathers carry models of the great sculptures of Cholanadu and Pallavanadu to the lands across the eastern seas to build temples and palaces?'

'I never asked you to do anything! How dare Pagrawal involve me?' my voice rose.

'You suddenly became friendly with him, Elangovan-*Saar*,' Kuppuswamy replied sullenly. 'Since you seemed part of their group I assumed it was regular. How was I to know Pagrawal's game?'

'I wanted to get at the bottom of their game. I have – but the crime has been committed.'

'For a Brahmin,' Kuppuswamy sneered, 'you are not very bright. Perhaps the northern Brahmins whom you despise are cleverer.' Tying his lungi tighter he rose and lit a bidi. 'What are you going to do about it?'

'I shall report the entire matter to the culture ministry. Pagrawal will hang.'

When I confronted Rasam Pagrawal with the fraud he smiled. 'Come, Elangovan, don't act so high and mighty. You knew all about it. You helped me locate the Sthapatis in your home state. You even helped me with the brochures; your words – so different from Brown and Havell – describe the replicas.' He paused to spit out a mouthful of paan-juice and offered me an evil taunting smile I shall never forget. 'You have been handsomely rewarded; I deposited thirty thousand rupees in an account made in your name in Bombay.'

Stunned, I could not speak.

Pagrawal continued. 'If you collaborate with me I will not refer to the matter again. If you do not, I shall inform the government of your bank account.'

I found my voice and said, 'I will tell them the entire story. You cannot foist such fraud on me.'

Pagrawal chewed paan-leaf thoughtfully. 'But I can and will,' he said silkily and spat out some more paan-juice. 'I have a letter from you outlining the project – the fraud as you call it. I even have your signature. Besharam Karma does a nice job copying signatures. The Sthapatis will not testify against me because they have been paid well. Neither will Rupamati because she is my mistress and Besharam is my disciple. So stop playing the Tamil film hero and join the new fraternity.'

Trembling with impotent rage I shouted: 'You have sold our heritage to foreign museums. Can you live with that?'

'Men have lived with more serious transgressions,' Pagrawal said dismissively. 'They sell wives and daughters. I have sold deteriorating stone images that some crazy foreigner wants to buy. And we have put beautiful new ones in their place.' He paused and emptied his mouth of all paan-juice. 'There are men who do not even replace stolen goods. Take that high-placed bureaucrat from the Bihar Terai. After he became a powerful civil servant he removed, over a decade, some seventy odd statues from various archaeological museums in his home state. I know it is grand larceny but why should I buy trouble? His clan is powerful and will finish off my family.'

'Gateway to India! That is what all of you are! You are the breed that betrayed your masters and let in the Turco-Afghan hordes! You have collaborated with them, cohabited with them and have become whores!' I stepped forward, with an intense desire to kill the man.

Rasam Pagrawal laughed, immensely amused. 'That is why we are strong and innovative. It is easy to be chaste when you live in sheltered southern kingdoms.'

I turned away, afraid I might strangle him in my great rage. I had lost a big battle. It did not seem worthwhile to live any longer. Truth, honesty, virtue – had all been trampled underfoot. I should have killed Pagrawal and then announced to the world why. I should have called his bluff right away and denounced him to the authorities – but fear – the greatest enemy of Indians – held me back. Fear that my action would bring disaster to my family checked my first honourable impulse. Fear would go on checking all our honourable impulses until we were castrated, shorn of pride and courage and the very purpose of life.

What legacy would I hand over to my son Raman around whom I had built my dreams?

Woe to the land where liars
And slaves surround the throne

—Alexander Pushkin (1836)

Rise as high as honour permits

—anon

PART II

ROMANCE AMONG THE RUINS

Civitate Dei – City of God

City of God was envisaged by the theologian St. Augustine fifteen centuries ago. He believed that such a city could be founded on divine knowledge, that it would be of both flesh and spirit, symbolizing the unity of human existence. The divine spirit would dwell there in timelessness. The ruler would be the representative of God.

Delhi could have been such a city. This city had seen invasions and massacres: patricides, fratricides and betrayals: drunken stupors and gargantuan orgies: infernal arsons and decimating epidemics. It was mentioned by another name – Indraprastha – in *Mahabharata*, one of the greatest epics of the world.

When the Pandava princes were banished by their Kaurava cousins, they built a splendid city named Indraprastha. Archaeologists believe it to be the site of modern Delhi.

Delhi was the capital of Prithviraj's powerful kingdom. His treacherous cousin Jaychand encouraged Mohammed of Ghor to invade the kingdom. Thus began five centuries of sporadic invasions from India's north-west frontiers. In the interregnum of plunder and pillage the Turco-Afghans built mausoleums to commemorate their fleeting presence on an ancient land. Then a family from far Ferghana built a magnificent Moghul India, whose contribution to architecture, administration, music and courtliness is a living heritage.

Three centuries of Moghul rule passed like a splendid somnambulist dream. Opulent Moghul Delhi fascinated European traders. They pleased the grand Moghuls, obtained trading rights or firmans that gave them access to India's lucrative global commerce. The golden calm was disrupted; the wounded empire fell apart. Britain established its empire here. An upheaval tried to dislodge them but the rebellion was quelled. A stunned populace settled down to silent servitude.

The British moved from revolutionary Calcutta and made Delhi their new capital. They tried to transform this imperial capital with official quarters, wide avenues, sandstone government houses and a palace for their viceroy. Edward Lutyens built a capital intended to endure for a thousand years. It lasted twenty years - because the Second World War and Indian nationalism made short work of imperial progress.

There were men who abandoned promising careers and affluent homes to follow the revolutionary beacon. They filled the jails or mounted the gallows, without fear or regrets, and with an inextinguishable belief in their cause. Delhi became capital of independent India, ruled by men who professed non-violence. For a brief interlude the capital was imbued with lofty ideals. Their ideal was Rama, the self-effacing king who had annihilated his own happiness in order to please his subjects. No slogan of the French or Russian revolutions had aspired so high. For a while people believed it was possible. For a while the world looked on, curious to see how the new *Civitate Dei* would function.

In a land that was ancient with anguish the new *Civitate Dei* began to take shape like a celestial dream. It was not conceived by disembodied angels, but by men and women who had striven for freedom and self-respect. Humble folk came from remote parts of the vast republic, trudging across dusty highways and unquiet waters to see their *Civitate Dei*. It was assembled by the hopes and tears of a people who believed in goodness even when they were being plundered and massacred.

At this dawn of a new age we believed this City of God would be a unique experiment in governance.

City of Dreams

It was to this city of dreams that I, Raman, son of Elangovan the archaeologist, came as a young probationer of the Indian Administrative Service. Spring flowers flaunted brilliant hues along the Rajpath. Flocks of birds pirouetted and splashed their wings on flat circular fountains. White Ambassador cars came down Raisina Hill and headed for the squat modern buildings that housed the burgeoning ministries. A balmy spring breeze brushed our heads, as if in benediction.

We were inspired by unsung men and women who had brought us freedom, who had unbound the shackles of a millennium, who had given India an honourable place in the comity of nations. We were determined to repay these debts of history, achieve great deeds for our country, and leave our names in the annals of administrative history - and in the City of God.

Exulted, I stood before the grand vista of Rashtrapati Bhavan, the previous viceregal palace, flanked on two sides by massive coral-hued edifices. I had come a long way from the southern temple town where I had been raised in a humble family. When the days of privilege ended gifted young men and women of humble birth entered the administrative service on the criterion of merit.

Standing next to me was a fellow probationer, Subhash Chowdhury, of a privileged but troubled background. His father Anand had joined Subhash Bose's Indian National Army in 1941 and had been tried for sedition at the infamous Red Fort trials. My father Elangovan had seen the proceedings. The intersection of the lives of Anand Chowdhury and S. Elangovan made their sons friends.

After joining the administrative service, we probationers reported at Metcalfe House, where the intrepid Theodore Metcalfe was Resident of Delhi during the great uprising of 1857. The rambling house stood on the banks of the blue Jamuna which had been the backdrop for Lord Krishna's frolics and legends of events over many millennia.

Sitting by the banks of the Jamuna, Subhash and I, Raman, mused that India who is poor can offer no guidance on power and success but she could transmit the message of goodness and of the victory of good over evil. We felt responsible for our compatriots who had withstood sorrow, violence and humiliation. We had no sacred book but many books. Trapped in this cosmic confusion we possessed an immense humility before the Almighty. We did not have the effrontery to define Him or attribute to Him virtues that were not ours to know.

And we young lions who thought ourselves to be immortal would depart one day, and hopefully would become part of the sacred river's memory. This sense of belonging to a pageant greater than our present existence stirred us to a fierce patriotism. We vowed we would serve this country with selfless dedication.

The Collector's Garden

We received administrative training at the National Academy of Administration. In the *'koi hai'* atmosphere of the academy, we, clad in jodhpur breeches and solar topees rode on horses, attended formal dinners wearing closed-collared *achkans* and discussed hypothetical administrative crises. For me, the academy was an exotic interlude. Apart from learning to be a saheb, I became infatuated with one of the women probationers who enticed me with the lure of a 'double income' and a 'dynamic partnership'.

When the training ended we paused for a few days in the capital before going to the states where we had been allotted to serve and where we had to complete the second half of our probation. District training required a complete change of outlook. Getting back to my home state was a return to reality and a reminder of my responsibility to my family, my caste and community.

The clamorous and curious denizens of our temple town crowded into our little house to see how *'nammapulei'* (our boy) had been transformed. They hurled a volley of questions and opinions at me and were disappointed that I was still 'the same old Raman' instead of a snooty IAS officer who would make them proud. I waited impatiently for the visitor who did not appear – my college-mate, Vidyavati.

In the uneventful twenty-three years until I entered the administrative service, Vidya had been the only excitement. Pretty yet demure, accomplished but modest, with dark wistful eyes, she and I used to return home from college on our bicycles, and discuss our studies. She gave me her notes and did better than me in the university examinations but despite my entreaties she declined to sit for the civil service examinations. I daydreamed of us both joining the IAS and becoming an 'IAS couple' – a glamorous rarity those days. Her father was dead, so she had to be the breadwinner without delay in order to support her mother and three siblings. Vidya obtained a junior lecturer's post in the local college. I went now to the small house where she stayed with her family.

In the one year that I had been away, Vidya had grown thin, her olive complexion had darkened, and the eyes had lost their wistfulness. She greeted me with the formal courtesy with which one greets an important acquaintance rather than a person with whom one had shared one's dreams.

'I wondered if you had left this town,' I said with asperity. 'You did not come to see me.'

'You did not invite me to visit you,' she murmured without reproach.

I laughed. 'Since when have you become so formal?' I asked, remembering how we used to walk by the river Kaveri when it was in spate, or sit on the temple *mantapa* as arati, evening ceremony, was performed. When the devotees departed we exchanged brief embraces.

In silence Vidya gazed at the twilight outside. I wondered if she had forgotten the tender pledges we had exchanged under the shadow of the *dhwaja-stambha,* outside the temple.

'To which district have you been posted?' she asked in the same even tone. I mentioned the district. She nodded. I was puzzled by her attitude and wondered why she was aloof. I had expected a rapturous welcome and words of emotion. So I took leave of her, hoping that on our next meeting she would be once more the blithe spirit I had known.

As the nine days of 'joining time' was drawing to a close, I noticed but ignored the whispered confabulations among the family members. Then they formed a brigade, with Paati, or grandmother, leading the charge. She donned her battledress; a gleaming Kanchivaram sari, diamond nose-rings and earrings. My father, Elangovan, now a sparrow of a man, fidgeted in his cane chair while my mother hovered nearby, intimidated by her mother-in-law.

'Raman,' the dowager announced in her gravelly voice, 'we have found her!'

'Who is *her*?' I asked.

'The girl you are to marry!' Paati replied triumphantly.

I looked at them and thought of Vidya whom I had vowed to marry after completing my probationary period.

Grandmother tapped my chest with a gnarled forefinger. 'She is rich beyond our expectations; a mansion in Pallavur, fifty acres of wetland in Kaveri basin and a lakh of rupees in cash.' Grandmother paused for breath. 'She is well connected. Her grandfather was deputy secretary in the public works department of the old presidency. He made his money there.'

I laughed and then retorted, 'So this is your idea of lineage – a dishonest deputy secretary in the PWD as grandfather! But I do not wish to marry now. I want to complete my field training.'

Coming forward my mother murmured apologetically, 'The ... er ... dowry ... would help your sisters to get married. We could not save for their dowries ... we have offers for them from a bank officer and junior engineers.'

My three sisters looked at me pleadingly with bovine hazel eyes (legacy from a white adventurer in the nineteenth century who had taken his siesta with our ancestress). I was angry that they had taken for granted that I would comply with their mercenary plans. I looked into grandmother's hawk-eyes and announced, 'I cannot marry your heiress. I love another girl.'

She snarled, like a bird of prey. 'And which hussy would that be? The one who used to go cycling with you and lure you to the temple?'

Anger swelled within me. I shouted, 'Don't you dare speak of her in that manner!' My parents were visibly distressed but the dowager was undeterred.

'*Ai-ai-yo*! So she has bewitched you! The scheming hussy!' Paati now turned her fury on my mother. 'So, this is how you raised your precious son, eh? Useless woman that you are!'

My father made no attempt to defend his timid wife against his virago mother. So I commanded grandmother: 'Don't insult my mother because I will marry where I choose!'

The prospect of dowry money gone, my sisters ran into the courtyard, howling in misery. My younger brother, an unemployed mathematics graduate, laughed maliciously. 'Wise man,' he said. 'The girl is no beauty.'

I too laughed. 'Really? Is that why you have not yet showed me her photo?'

My sisters rushed in with several photographs. I stared at the face. The promised bride looked nondescript except for the throat, ears and nose glittering with diamonds. I tossed the photos back to my sisters who returned to the courtyard to resume their howling. Grandmother stood her ground. 'So what reply do we give to the prospective bride's party? That you want to marry some out-of-caste-dowry-less hussy, sever ties with your family and community?'

'Give whatever reply you wish. I am not going to marry for money. I will not be purchased. I will marry a woman I can respect and love,' I replied loftily.

In reply my grandmother collected a mouthful of saliva and spat on the red-oxide floor. That was her opinion of men who married for love rather than for money. Then with another snarl she said, 'I have warned that fast hussy that you are already spoken for! If she has shame – which I doubt – she will not bother you!'

Now I understood why Vidyavati was polite and aloof. I seethed in rage against Paati. I wanted to rush to Vidya and make amends for Paati's ways but did not. Other thoughts clamoured within me.

Fortunately, the district where I was posted for field training was some distance away from our temple town where I would not be pursued by the family. And since I had announced that I would send half my meagre salary to them, their anger subsided. I wanted to lead a carefree existence before I was fettered into domesticity.

The district headquarters offered sparse excitement. There was a cinema house which screened salubrious films and a place (quaintly called Hindu Military Hotel) where I could surreptitiously devour forbidden meat curries. However I remained under the nose of the collector, who could be relied upon to interfere and find fault.

The assistant commissioner of police occupied a small house adjacent to the collector's bungalow. I was invited to share the premises. He had two police orderlies who performed chores, fetched and carried.

The district had traces of history with a medieval era fort where Robert Clive and William Bentinck had received their baptism of fire. The moat with floating water hyacinths looked entrancing from a distance. Set amidst arid plains the British Raj collectorate was imposing. Beyond this area farmers waged a losing battle against drought and dust. The greenest part of the district headquarter was the collector's garden.

The administrative head of the district, or collector, T.N. Bhasham, commanded fear. His aggressive ways concealed his lack of assurance because he was a promotee from the provincial service and not through the competitive examinations which conferred a special distinction like the 'heaven born' officers of the British Raj.

Collector Bhasham had dyed his sparse hair to a translucent purple that encircled his scalp like a tonsure. Subcutaneous fat had thickened his vulpine features. His outer geniality could not conceal his cold nature.

The collector's wife Ratna reminded me of Vidya; they had the same wistful eyes and gentle smile. The flush of youth had been replaced by a mellow ripeness. When the collector invited me and the assistant commissioner of police to his house for dinner and drinks (provided secretly by excise contractors) I stole furtive glances at her alluring form that launched me on lascivious daydreams. The police officer, I noted, never spoke about her.

I learned from the district gossip circuit that though Bhasham could have chosen from a menu of rich maidens, he married the impecunious Ratna to compensate for his unattractive appearance. In gratitude she had brought a spurious dignity to his life. She was not arrogant as were some of the collectors' ladies; she amiably presided over charity bazaars, school prize days and 'variety programmes'. But if watched closely, one saw her restlessness and distaste for those who fawned on her and the collector.

An Indian Administrative Service probationer's training is fairly rigorous. I was fortunate to have an elderly and competent assistant commissioner, Mr Arcot, who took me on tours of the district to *taluk* headquarters, taught me to decipher land revenue documents like *pahani patra* and *jamabandhi*. As the 'green revolution' had just been inaugurated, frequent inspection of cultivation of hybrid crops was necessary. At night we camped by narrow rivers, or on the ramparts of ruined forts and ate unleavened *jowar* bread and curried country fowl.

I memorized the laws and manuals on which we would be examined in a few months. On passing that we would get a salary increment. While studying these laws on the roof of our quarters, I saw the collector's lady sitting on the veranda of the rambling house, a book on her lap, staring at the flowers and spreading trees where an elderly gardener worked silently.

One monsoon afternoon, I was astounded to see my house-mate, the assistant commissioner of police, walk over to the fence which separated the collector's residence from our lawn. He stood there motionless until the collector's lady turned to look at him. He smiled, and slowly she smiled back. He stood there gazing at her raptly and then abruptly returned to the house.

A few days later I surreptitiously ferreted from his desk a poem he had composed. It read: 'Come to the edge of the garden where I may gaze upon your divine countenance and increase my life force.' I stayed in the house to watch developments and was not disappointed; I spied him going out and hand the folded paper to the collector's gardener who went inside to deliver it to the collector's lady.

The police officer waited by the fence until Ratna appeared. They conversed – separated by the fence. She was obviously impressed by his dash and nerve. It was if a monsoon shower soothed the parched summer of her marriage.

It was the beginning of many encounters – innocent and intriguing. The young police officer told her of his exploits, his pursuit of dacoits and smugglers; when he could not meet her, he laid verses at her feet in homage like troubadours of medieval Europe. I saw Ratna read these with a beatific smile.

For a while the epistolary flirtation continued. Though a novice in amorous matters, I guessed that she yearned for more than epistolary homage as an escape from her sterile marriage. The gardener who had created verdant beauty in this arid place, carried the messages to and fro, the little notes tied with strings of jasmine. I advised the police officer to be careful but he did not heed my words. I was afraid of getting involved; the collector's displeasure and an adverse Annual Confidential Report (ACR) could prolong my probationary period and smudge my future career.

The collector's residence is not a private place. Between the gazetted assistant, the *sherestedar*, *munshi*, *daffedar*s, *mazdoor*s, and gardeners, a daily Gazeteer could have been published. They all watched the collector's wife with interest. Reports of her arborial dalliance eventually reached the sovereign of the district.

When Collector Bhasham toured the district, details of his tour programme was circulated to all officials. One day he returned earlier than expected in order to catch his wife and the police officer in flagrante delicto. He was surprised to find his wife playing mahjong at the district club with wives of district officers. He sent an orderly to the house which I shared with the assistant commissioner of police to enquire of my friend's whereabouts. I informed the emissary that my police friend was away on inspection of rural police stations.

I rose from my table and went to the window from where I could see without being seen by the collector. He stood in his garden, looking at the scene before him – the imposing bungalow set amidst a rolling lawn and stately trees, and the paling which separated his august precincts from our humbler abode. Both gardens had the same flowers and shrubs. Unaware of my presence he said audibly and angrily, 'So the whore replicates my garden in his, and meets him here!' He emitted a snort of rage.

The sound woke the gardener, dozing under a tree. The wizened man hastily scrambled to his feet and bowed in obeisance to the lord of the district. In his hurry, he dropped the folded note in which Ratna had quoted a verse from the mystic poet Thiruvallavur. The collector saw the scrap of paper pirouette and fall to the ground like a leaf. The gardener made a desperate bid to retrieve the slip of paper. The collector lunged forward and picked it, unfolded it and read it with inflamed eyes. Turning to the jeep driver and *daffedar* he ordered them to leave. Then slowly, he advanced towards the little man who stood trembling with folded hands.

'Forgive me, *Ayya*,' the gardener whispered, terror writ in his hollow eyes.

'Forgive you for what?' the collector asked menacingly. The gardener's Adam's apple quivered as he swallowed saliva. 'So you carried messages to and fro, is that it?' the collector asked.

The gardener nodded.

'Did they arrange meetings through you, eh? Did they fornicate in his house?'

My blood turned to water in panic. Would I be dragged into this squalid mess? Would the collector also accuse me of cohabiting with his wife? What would happen to my Annual Confidential Report? No, I decided, I would tell him of my repeated warnings to the police officer.

My frenzied thoughts were interrupted by the gardener. He shook his head and said, 'No, *Dorai,* lord. They never ... did anything improper ... the police officer stood on his side of the gate and recited poems while the *Dosani,* esteemed lady, listened from here.'

With one hairy paw, Collector Bhasham hurled the frail gardener on to the ground, where he lay sprawled and stunned. Next clutching a fistful of hair Bhasham raised him and struck the little man; the gardener became a bloody pulp on the grass. Then wiping bloodied hands on the leaves of a frangipani bush, T.N. Bhasham drove to the collectorate, to address himself to the task of improving the district.

Petrified, I watched the scene, my conscience screaming to intercede for the gardener and ward off assault on the puny man – but I dared not. When the collector's van was out of sight I went out and with the help of the police orderlies, attended to his wounds. Later, under cover of darkness we took him to a private doctor for treatment.

When Ratna returned from the club that evening, there was a furious quarrel. For the first time I heard her low voice raised in anger. And during that exchange of abuses I realized the squalor of their marriage. Late at night I saw her go out into the garden, stand by the gate and sob brokenly.

The assistant commissioner of police returned a few days later and heard all that had transpired from the district superintendent of police who in accordance with established protocol hated the district collector. Going to the collector's house the furious police officer gave the collector a few smart slaps while abusing him with words I seldom heard: impotent bastard, erectile dysfunctional eunuch. The diatribe ceased only when the collector rushed to take refuge in his bathroom. Next day the police officer applied for long leave and without waiting for sanction of leave, left for his home town in an adjoining state.

I stayed on in that little bungalow, without the luxury of police orderlies attending to me, but determined now to complete my probation and go elsewhere. Though I avoided the garden, my eyes always went where glassy-eyed Ratna swayed to and fro on the swing.

One afternoon when the collector had gone to the state capital on some urgent work, Ratna called out to me and asked me to have coffee with her. I went in fear and dread. She told me about the gardener. Ratna secretly sent food to the mud hut where he lived with his three motherless children. His son, Selva, took care of them. Ratna also sent an ayurvedic expert to massage him daily, so that the twisted limbs could return to some semblance of normalcy. After a while the gardener was able to hobble around in crutches but he could never bend or squat to plant his beloved flowers and saplings and watch them grow in verdant splendour. The man who loved earth, water, grass and trees, now sat like a mendicant on a bench by the dusty roadside.

Whenever the collector passed the gardener in his official van he used to glare at the hapless man. He who had fled in fear from the amorous police officer felt he had avenged his honour by punishing the gardener-messenger.

I immersed myself in work and prepared for the departmental examinations, pushing out thoughts of the collector, his lady and the police officer. But on starlit nights when I camped in village *daak* bungalows I pondered on the nature of love and the havoc it brought on people. Could Vidyavati dishonour me one day with another man, I asked myself. She was pretty and winsome like Ratna. Would it not be wiser to marry a woman with whom there would be mutuality of interests rather than an unreasoning passion? I had convinced myself so. Half a century later I realized it was sophistry. What I wanted was to marry for gain.

I wrote to Vidyavati, explaining my predicament and family responsibilities, the necessity of recompensing my parents for the 'sacrifices' they had made for me, and the dire need to get those bovine sisters married. I begged her forgiveness and expressed my undying love and hinted that we could still be friends. She wrote back; a polite letter wishing me luck and informing me that she was moving from the little temple town to another city where she had obtained a senior lecturer's post in a leading college. She gave no forwarding address and had obviously instructed her family not to divulge the new address to me because when I wanted to send her my wedding invitation, they refused to disclose her address.

My probation successfully completed, I was promoted as assistant commissioner and sub-division magistrate. What astonished me was that the collector sent a special request to the state revenue secretary that I should be posted to the headquarters sub-division. Apparently he had appreciated my discretion over the gardener affair. I was mortified to see Mr Arcot transferred to another sub-division, to make room for me. His family could not join him there as there were no good schools but the collector assured me that 'old Arcot' would manage as they were accustomed to rural life.

Satyabhama and I were married amidst pomp and ceremony in Pallavur. My family was ecstatic. A handsome marriage settlement had preceded the nuptials. There would be enough money to get *all three* of my sisters married, to build a modest house for my parents (and grandmother), and grander things for the two of us. Satyabhama was not unattractive, I consoled myself. She had nice eyes and a lovely smile. My malicious brother taunted me: 'A huge dowry hides a multiplicity of flaws.'

I returned to the district headquarters with Satya and began our married life. I hoped that my wife and the collector's lady would get along well and that Satya might learn refined manners from Ratna.

I was surprised to find that the collector's lady kept her distance from my wife; when they met at district functions, she was civil but aloof. I saw that Ratna had become a shadow of her blithe self, and something of a recluse. The collector made no secret of his disdain for her. Alone and helpless she had nowhere to go.

A year passed. I was busy with official work and supervising construction of a small house for my parents, building a large one for us in Pallavur, getting my sisters married, and welcoming the birth of our daughter, made sadly in the image of my hawk-nosed grandmother. Her birth was an event in the district headquarters. Our bungalow was flooded with gifts from all those who wished to please me, the assistant collector. The collector was transferred to Pallavur. I was unhappy that Ratna did not visit to say goodbye. One day I expressed my unhappiness to the gazetted assistant.

The elderly gentleman looked at me with a strange expression before saying, 'You have not heard that she is … living in Pallavur?'

'I know she has left the district,' I replied.

He nodded, betel leaf-stained lips pursed in disapproval. He glanced around to check if others had left. Then leaning forward, chewing paan-leaf, shaking his head he spoke: 'The lady is now … the chief minister's *keep*.'

Having passed on this vital information the gentleman nodded with satisfaction. I was astonished and exclaimed, 'Surely ... surely you cannot be serious!'

The gazetted assistant nodded. 'How is it you have not heard of the matter?' He lowered his voice. 'They met at an *arengetram,* dance debut, where Ratna-madam was the announcer. The chief minister was also there. He took a fancy to her and invited her to a party. That was the beginning.'

'And the collector?' I asked in a whisper. 'Has he not ... objected?'

The elderly official looked at me with contempt. Then he informed me that the collector sought transfer to Pallavur, to a post which had many perquisites, especially that most treasured of all perks in those austere socialistic days – foreign travel. I was curious to know more about the strange affair but no one dared to talk. When I next went to Pallavur, I decided to call on the lady.

If the house built by my father-in-law for me and Satya was impressive, Ratna's seaside villa was beautiful. The garden had an exotic and yet a strangely familiar look. When the wind blew through the jasmines and frangipanis it whispered about another garden. A turbaned guard stood at the gate and led me to the house. Another turbaned retainer ushered me into an opulent drawing room where the upholstery and drapes were of pale brocade, flanked by carved rosewood tables. Seeing a bronze Chola Parvati, an ivory Nataraja, and a sandalwood Krishna playing the flute, I wished that Satyabhama had such refined taste in interior decoration.

Ratna entered, wearing her customary Kanchivaram sari, with little jewellery and a large diamond pendant nestled in the hollow of her throat. She wore no *mangal-sutra,* the de rigueur necklace for a married woman. This gesture announced her flouting of propriety. I hurriedly rose to greet her. She looked at me for a long moment, remembering perhaps my reckless police colleague, and then waved me to my seat.

'Visiting Pallavur?' she asked.

'Yes,' I replied, tongue tied and embarrassed.

'Still in the sub-division?'

'Yes. I expect to get my promotion soon and be collector.'

'Collector,' she echoed, with a sardonic smile. 'What an exalted position!'

I looked down at the gleaming marble floor. Did she have to be derisive about collectors because her husband had been a weird one? Defensively I said, 'I hope to be a good one.'

Abruptly her sardonic expression changed. She gazed at the beach where fishermen were bringing in their hauls on catamarans. 'I am sure you will be a good one … if you remember to be a little brave.'

'I … am not … a coward,' I retorted.

Ratna shook her head angrily. 'It was in your power to save the gardener. You could have told your collector that nothing improper had happened. But you remained inside and let a poor message bearer be mutilated.'

'Yes,' I replied. 'I failed.'

My admission of guilt disarmed her. 'Never mind,' she said, 'you are young and a little timid. It is safer that way.' She paused. 'I was timid once … but now I am … bold and brassy.' She looked at me with defiance. 'Do they gossip about me in the district?'

'It hardly matters what "they" say. If "they" malign you, it is out of jealousy.'

'You are still innocent, Raman,' she said softly, her eyes on the twilit sea. She looked lovely and I felt excited by her nearness. Sensing my sympathy she spoke freely. 'I am not respectable any more. But I chose this path because the straight path was full of thorns.'

'I know. You suffered.' I hoped to win her over with sympathy. All women succumb to sympathy, especially those fallen from grace.

'Yes, I did. For a long time – even before the police officer came into the scene. After that episode, the collector became worse and abused me. I had nowhere else to go so I endured it all. And then I met … the chief minister. When he asked me to join his dinner party I felt a surge of shame. Did I look like a tart, I asked myself. I was about to give a rude refusal when one word screamed in my ears. Revenge! I remembered the young officer who had laid poems at my feet, saying that I was like "moonlight that cannot be touched but only seen." I remembered how he left, and never saw me again. I remembered the poor gardener. I saw myself, living like a shadow, afraid and abused. Here was the chance to teach the collector a lesson and to escape from him.'

She paused and drew a deep breath. 'I accepted the invitation, not only for the dinner, but for the night which was the prelude to many more nights.' She paused. 'The chief minister has had flings with *devadasi*s, starlets, dancers and singers – but he wanted me to be his … mistress … to live in one of his houses and spend time with him … away from his domestic and official world.' She gave a little laugh. 'He even told me that he loved me.' Tears gathered in her eyes.

'I can believe that,' I murmured, wishing she was my mistress.

'I cannot return his love … I still long for the dashing young police officer … but I am a good companion. We discuss books and films. I occasionally sing for him. We go discreetly on foreign trips together. He is kind and considerate.'

I listened fascinated. I had never met a 'mistress' in all my twenty-seven years.

Ratna frowned and continued. 'In fact I was enjoying my new life when my husband turned up, asking for an interview with the chief. I advised the chief not to meet him but he was afraid. "The man can make a scene and create a scandal. Besides he is an officer of this state. How can I refuse?" He had paused and asked, "Suppose your husband asks for a divorce? What shall I say?"'

Ratna now spoke grimly. 'I realized then that such a liaison as I had with the chief minister was built on shifting sands.'

'What happened?' I asked, afraid for her.

Ratna emitted a laugh of pure mirth which had captivated the chief. 'The ex-collector asked the chief for a better post, where he could have a car *for me* to move around, an extra allowance so that *I* could have some pocket money, visits abroad where *I* could shop. The ex-collector said it would be wiser if he is posted at Pallavur so that people wouldn't gossip about me and the chief minister. All nice and respectable, you know.'

I was astonished that any man could be so shameless.

Ratna shook her head. 'The chief could not endure it and agreed to whatever the man asked. As he gave a sign for the ex-collector to leave, he bent low in obeisance and thanked the chief minister for the kindness shown *to us*.'

We sat in silence for a while. Then two white-uniformed, red-turbaned peons came in with a wrought-iron tea trolley filled with a bone-china tea set, pastries and sandwiches. I watched Ratna pour out tea. A bluish solitaire glittered on her right hand. After tea and pastries I felt emboldened enough to ask, 'Does … my former boss… live here?'

Ratna shook her head. 'He lives in the centre of town. I do not meet him except when I have to play hostess at one of his parties. For form's sake, you know. And I do it more for the chief's position than my reputation. After that I drive back here, to scrub myself clean, breathe clean air and gaze at the mocking stars.'

Somehow, I felt Ratna had not told me everything. I sensed that she was holding back something. But I dared not probe further. I rose to take leave. When she came with me to the portico, I bowed a little and said, 'I am glad to see you are happy, Ma'am. Please let me know if I can be of any service to you.'

She regarded me with a whimsical smile. 'You know, Raman, if you were ten years older and if we had met when we were younger I would have been happy with a man like you.'

I felt my pulse racing. Before I could utter a word she said, 'But there, you had to marry for dowry, not for love. Not that dowry-less marriages fare better, as I should know. Maybe payment of a dowry imposes on the bridegroom an obligation for good behaviour.'

Stung and angry, I was about to retort when a white Ambassador car drove up to the circular portico. A tall sturdy man, wearing spotless white dhoti and silk shirt with a small red tilak on his forehead, stepped out. His thick curly hair was more salt than pepper.

When he removed his sunglasses I saw his astute humorous eyes. I made a deep bow to the chief minister who glanced at Ratna in enquiry.

'Our former probationer and a dedicated officer,' she said sardonically. 'He is due for promotion as a collector shortly.'

The chief minister smiled and nodded. 'We must then send him to a good district.' Overwhelmed, I bowed again. The chief minister went inside.

'You have not come in vain,' she said with a gently sarcastic smile and disappeared into the imposing villa.

I drove back to town, bewildered. I had genuinely come to see her, in her new position. I had no intention of asking for favours. Obviously she regarded all visitors as supplicants on whom she bestowed favours. Maybe that gave her a sense of power. How different she was from the shy and serene woman I had seen a few years ago in the collector's garden!

During my subsequent meetings with Ratna I sensed that she felt no qualms about her new lifestyle. Indeed she enjoyed all that she was able to wrench from this new existence. The most enjoyable part of it was the power she now exercised over her husband.

The chief minister lost a legislative assembly election; with quiet dignity he faded from the political scene and Ratna's life but gifted her the villa where she continued to stay. Two gardeners worked to landscape the lawns while competent servants did their work. In the evenings interesting, cheerful guests flowed into the house. The former collector, now a sick and aging man, implored her to let him stay in her house. She gave him a corner room and told him to remain invisible. He endured this existence and then suffered a stroke. While he lay helpless on the hospital bed, Ratna remained strangely serene and said, 'You are in good hands. Doctor Selvanayagam is a very capable neurologist.'

Ratna's husband sighed, awaiting his saviour.

The neurologist entered, smiling at Ratna. He was not handsome but there was something distinctive in him, as if he had traversed many paths before arriving at his goal. The former collector found him strangely familiar but could not remember where they had met. As he tried to remember he was surprised to find the neurologist well acquainted with Ratna. They exchanged news, laughed and sometimes gazed at each other with inexplicable expressions. After examining the old collector, the neurologist left.

Old Bhasham asked Ratna about the doctor. She stared at him for a long time, then spoke with a cold contempt he had never heard before. 'I met the young Selva soon after his father became a cripple. He dreamt of becoming a doctor so that he could cure his father.' Ratna paused, her eyes blazing with anger.

'When I became the chief minister's mistress I decided that the youth would become a doctor. I secured a seat in a medical college for him. He worked hard and did well in college. We made arrangements for him to study abroad. He chose to be a neurologist – so that he could cure his father.' Ratna paused, her eyes now softening with pride. 'Selva has helped his father to recover; who is now able to walk slowly and do things for himself.'

Old Bhasham shivered; he guessed the identity of the neurologist.

Ratna's smile was cruel. 'Do you remember the gardener in your district, the one you maimed for carrying innocent messages between me and the assistant commissioner of police?'

The former collector looked as if he would die from fear.

'Doctor Selva-nayagam is that gardener's son … and my lover,' Ratna said softly. 'But don't be afraid. He will not harm a helpless old cripple. He is a gentleman.'

The Eavesdropping Orderly

Since Subhash Chowdhury and I were posted in adjoining districts we used to meet whenever there was a string of holidays. Many officers followed this tradition - ostensibly to continue the camaraderie of the National Academy of Administration but actually to gauge each other's potential in the administration scenario. Sometimes mortal combats simmered beneath fraternal bonhomie. He was born to privilege and I to a struggling youth. While I counted my paisas, Subhash was reckless with his purse. But more than that, he had a self assurance which was mistaken for pride, and a mind which I recognized was superior to mine. Though high-born damsels were offered to him as brides, he declined these offers and married a refined young woman whose family had neither wealth nor powerful connections. Secretly, I wanted to be like him and would have hated him had he not been affable, generous and genuinely concerned for others.

Subhash invited me for a long weekend to celebrate our promotion to the senior scale of pay. It was indeed a cause for celebration, especially for those who had opted for early matrimony. Our pay-bills leapt from a meagre four-hundred-and-fifty rupees to nine hundred, in addition to the comforts of being the deputy commissioner or collector of a district. We lived in large old houses, had numerous free servitors, free petrol when using the ugly district van or *junga*, and grew vegetables in the extensive grounds attached to the deputy commissioner/collector's residences. Orderlies tended to milk-providing cows and egg-giving chicken.

I had expected a leisurely weekend when Subhash and I could take long walks through the picturesque Deccan plateau, try our hand at fishing on the nearby river or try to shoot some unoffending deer romping on the table-topped hills. These were attempts to build macho images for ourselves – an invaluable asset when commanding other men.

Subhash was from West Bengal; by a few marks in the final selection seniority list he had missed obtaining allotment to his home state. It was rumoured that Mr Nehru's adherents had ensured Subhash did not get his home state because his father was a fervent follower of Subhash Chandra Bose whose charisma continued to haunt Prime Minister Nehru. After a brief bout of melancholy, Subhash settled down to his allotted state in the Deccan. He was now deputy commissioner in the dusty district of Kempadurga or 'Red Fort' in the local language. Though we laughed at the name that languid weekend, the district lived up to its dramatic name.

The weekend turned out to be a defining moment in modern Indian history. Mr Appajappa, the chief minister of Dakhinstan, was from Kempadurga. He was a politician with concern for the welfare of his people, inhibited by ethical principles, and possessed patrician distaste for demagoguery. He owned a large tract of land where the hardy 'ragi' crop grew or shrivelled on its stalk, depending on the vagaries of monsoon. The unpretentious ancestral house was comfortable. Unhurried visitors came and went, after receiving rustic hospitality and patient hearings of their troubles and demands.

The major domo of the household was Shafi, a young man whose Arab ancestors had crossed the Arabian Sea and carried coffee seeds and their monotheism. Appajappa had a special fondness for Shafi whose speciality was preparation of tea whose aroma and flavour was unique. One would expect a descendant of coffee traders to specialize in that beverage but Shafi concentrated on the preparation of tea. No one knew the magic ingredients of his amber-coloured fragrant tea, laced with cardamom and ginger.

Shafi's day began by bringing in a tray on which reposed a porcelain teapot containing the elixir, arrowroot biscuits and a vernacular paper which summed up the momentous events of the region. Shafi woke Appajappa with a gentle nudge and then poured out tea into a cup. Appa sipped each drop appreciatively, his eyes twinkling with pleasure.

One day after drinking a cup of a particularly delicious tea, Appa-ji observed, 'Shafi, had you been a woman attender in a royal household, you would have won a prince's heart by serving such tea.'

Shafi blinked and asked, 'And what good would that have been?'

'What good?' Appajappa asked, laughing. 'What a muff you are, Shafi! Why, you would be rich and powerful. Think of it – a palace, cars, servants, jewels, honour in society. In short everything one can wish for.'

Glancing at Appajappa, Shafi nodded and mused: What a muff my master is! Could I, an orderly of this household, ever dream of such things!

'Now I must get ready. Some members of parliament are coming to see me.' Shafi bent and slid the ministerial feet into slippers. Appajappa said, 'Ah Shafi, you were made for the harem. Your gentle care is unusual in a man.' He sighed. 'What would I do without you?'

Shafi beamed with pleasure. But as he went round his duties during the day, one thought shoved aside all others.

I could have, in other circumstances, pleased a royal master. But where is the royal court in this arid land?

A few years earlier, Prime Minister Nehru died, and the mantle of democracy had passed to a dedicated politician, Lal Bahadur Shastri. It seemed like a turning point in Indian politics. He was confronted with famine in parts of North India followed soon after by a war with Pakistan. His slogan – *jai jawan, jai kishan* – victory to the soldier, victory to the peasant – won the heart of the country. In the eighteen months of his governance, sycophancy disappeared, extravagance was checked, and development projects were taken up in right earnest. Shastri's untimely death in Moscow after negotiating peace with Pakistan sealed the fate of Indian democracy. He died penurious, and left behind a widow and sons who nursed no dreams of power. Appajappa and his close colleagues, who were now the kingmakers, bestowed the throne of India on Nehru's daughter, Indira, through the ritual of dynastic democracy. They felt that the amateur Indira would serve their purpose well. They would keep the pretty puppet happy with praise and pampering.

Three years had passed since then. Indira had behaved as they had anticipated. She listened to them with her large lidded eyes, simpered and smiled in acquiescence, and did what they said. Appajappa and the elder statesmen were delighted – as much by her as by their own astuteness. What a joy it was to have Indira under their tutelege! They were even beginning to be a little infatuated by their pretty puppet. Some even dreamt of dalliance with the beautiful widow. Then they saw disquieting signs. Indira took to tapping her feet in impatience. Appajappa and his friends saw no danger at first. They were rudely awakened one day by an eerie silence following the tapping of feet.

'I have decided to nationalize some banks,' she announced to her 'advisers' who had been summoned to the republic's capital.

The assembled kingmakers gasped and cried in unison. 'Nationalize banks? But that is illegal! That is against rights guaranteed in our Constitution! There will be a hue and cry over this!'

Indira's eyes swept over the older men without annoyance or anxiety. 'I have decided. I expect you gentlemen to work out the details,' she commanded.

It was Appajappa, the upholder of rules, who spoke out firmly. 'That will not be possible, Madam. We cannot implement irregular acts!'

Indira's eyes glinted with a hint of anger. 'Appa-ji,' she said without raising her tonal decibel. 'I hope *you* understand. *I* have decided. What *you* are required to do is to formulate the details of this scheme.'

'Such decisions have to be taken collectively, not arbitrarily. That was our understanding when *we* elected *you* to head the republic,' Appajappa protested vehemently.

Indira rose, a thin smile on her face. 'In three years I have learnt my work. I am grateful for your earlier guidance.'

The six men of the syndicate rose as she glided out of the room. Then they stared at each other in disbelief. 'The puppet, it seems, has strings of her own,' one of them muttered. The enraged men nodded. They left the capital and adjourned to Appajappa's domain to plan their strategy. They were not going to let that novice, *their creature,* become insolent and authoritarian! They would show the puppet her place!

I, Raman, and Subhash came to hear of the brewing tension. Subhash was concerned. Underneath his hauteur there lodged a kind heart. 'I hope Appa-ji will not be dethroned. He has ruled this state fairly and justly. Neither he nor his relatives plunder the state treasury.' Subhash paused, before adding: 'But Appajappa belongs to the past. He does not have a future in these times.'

'Aren't you being a little harsh?' I asked Subhash.

My idealistic colleague regarded me pensively. 'Have you not read the sign of the times?'

While we planned a leisurely weekend, there were signs of hectic activity in Appajappa's residence in Kempadurga. Summoning his tea-boy Shafi, Chief Minister Appajappa said, 'We are holding a secret conclave today. No one is to enter while we discourse. *I repeat, no one*. You are the only one who shall come and go with the refreshments.'

Shafi blinked. 'Not even your personal assistant?'

Appajappa shook his head. 'Only you can come because you are my most trusted retainer.' Appajappa refrained from adding 'and my stupidest retainer'.

Shafi *salaamed* in appreciation and went off to make preparations for the forthcoming tea party.

The tea party at Kempadurga was as portentous as the one at Boston two centuries ago. Both tea parties changed the fate of their nations.

Our fishing trip was cancelled when deputy commissioner Subhash was urgently summoned by Chief Minister Appajappa and told that an important meeting would be held at the chief minister's ancestral house and that police *bandobast* (arrangements) should ensure that they were not disturbed. Though the chief minister did not wish it his request for quiet was the best way of ensuring attention. The arrival of the kingmakers would have gone unnoticed but the clumsy arrangements drew attention. It was soon known that Appajappa and comrades were confabulating at his ancestral house.

Shortly the grim-faced determined kingmakers arrived from different parts of India. As per protocol Subhash welcomed them. As they entered Appajappa's sitting room he heard their opening remarks.

'The milksop dares to misbehave with us! She dares to be peremptory with us who set her on the throne! Well, we will teach her a lesson!'

Subhash left hurriedly; he had no wish to be caught in the crossfire between the chief minister and the prime minister. What transpired in any case would soon be known.

'Indira grows more powerful each day,' Appajappa warned his political colleagues at the commencement of the plenary session. 'We are not here for personal advancement. You may like to suggest how we check her authoritarianism. It is our duty to do so because her actions will eventually undermine democracy.'

'Well?' asked the powerful sugar lobby chief. 'What are we to do?'

An eerie silence fell upon the conspirators as they scanned each other's faces to verify sincerity and the possibility of treachery. It was braveheart Appajappa who crossed the Rubicon.

'We have to checkmate Indira by a quick opinion poll amongst our party chiefs to see if they stand by her agenda.'

'She already has many adherents,' cautioned the colliery lobby chief. 'Make no mistake. The younger people are backing her. They see her as a Joan of Arc against us older politicians.' He prided himself on knowledge of European history. 'Of course we know what happened to Joan of Arc.'

As the kingmakers laughed, Appajappa turned to Shafi who was standing at the door, listening wide-eyed to the conversation. 'Bring us some refreshments, Shafi,' he said. 'We need sustenance to fortify our resolve.'

Shafi bowed, arranged the white gold-rimmed turban on his head and went to the kitchen where Mrs Appajappa had prepared crisp *dosai*s folded with a puree of potatoes and coriander. There were cries of delight as Shafi brought these in six plates on a huge tray. As the kingmakers took first bites of the *dosai* there were sounds of appreciation that a courtesan might hear after coupling. When the crescendo of belches had subsided, Appajappa nodded to Shafi who went out and swept in again, to lay out with flourish, six china cups filled with his special tea.

'Fine tea,' sugar lobby kingmaker pronounced. 'What is the trade name?'

Appajappa beamed. 'It's called "Shafi's Blend". Only he knows how to mix all the ingredients. In fact,' Appajappa chuckled, 'I once told Shafi that if he were a woman in some royal court, he might have shared the throne with a king by concocting such fine tea.'

There was the sound of uproarous laughter. Several kingmakers turned to glance at Shafi who suddenly became very pensive.

One kingmaker said, 'Why don't we plant this fellow in Indira's suite when she comes to Sandalore next week, and get him to tell us all that transpires?' Robust laughter greeted this suggestion.

Shafi did not laugh; he brooded on their words and impossible dreams.

The powerful politicians decided that Indira would be 'advised' to go slow on radical methods, that the plebians should not be courted overtly because the plebs had a habit of forgetting their station in life. Besides the West should not take fright at clamping down of private enterprise.

'And suppose she is not in a mood to listen?' Appajappa asked his confederates.

'Then, we will have her ousted from the party by convening an emergency meeting of the executive committee which comprises us six. Indira will cease to head the government.'

There was a long moment of silence. Then Appajappa said: 'We have crossed the Rubicon – all of us. There is no going back.'

They rose and adjourned for dinner; Shafi served and listened. It was time, he mused, for him to cross the Rubicon, as his master had done.

The weekend turned out to be more exciting than anticipated; Subhash and I huddled together to discuss the events at the chief minister's residence. Our wives sulked; to embarrass us they went swimming in the river and emerged with wet saris clinging to their bodies. It was with some reluctance that I, Raman, left for my district on Monday morning. Subhash promised to keep me informed of developments.

Hearing of the conclave of her former mentors at Kempadurga, Indira made an excuse to visit the state capital; the inauguration of a police housing colony. She decided that the best way to hunt for the fox was not to go on horseback with the hounds and bugles but to creep up to the foxhole with a rod.

So came the enigmatic woman whose brooding eyes and wintry smile barely concealed her hauteur. Indira's arrival caused a flurry in the chief minister's official residence.

Appajappa's wife, daughters and daughters-in-law stood at the entrance to greet her with garlands and earthen lamps. They experienced a vicarious pleasure on seeing a woman who possessed the power and authority that they lacked and envied.

Shafi beheld her with mesmerized eyes. He had never seen a woman with short hair, lissome figure and flashing eyes. Shafi served her his special blend. When he bowed deeply and raised his hand to his forehead, she reciprocated with a murmured '*adaab*'. So she knows I am of another faith. My sovereign, my goddess, he thought inwardly. In his ecstasy Shafi forgot that his religion allowed no goddess.

Then he remembered his master's words: 'With your tea, you could have won the heart of royalty and become a court favourite.'

'A favourite in a royal household, rewarded … not for making tea … but for treachery … and betrayal of my dear lord, who has cared for me since I was an orphan child,' mused Shafi with an involuntary shudder.

While Appajappa's household was busy entertaining their liege lady, Shafi went about his work like a somnambulist, in a kind of frenzy, trying to piece together the information he had heard at Kempadurga and the conspiracy to depose Indira before she deposed them. Speed, he thought. I must do quickly what I must … if my information is to be of any value.

Indira was staying in the state guest house at Sandalore, which once belonged to a family who had betrayed Tipu Sultan of Mysore to Arthur Wellesley, thus facilitating British conquest of South India. To enact another betrayal Shafi took faltering steps from Appajappa's official residence to the guest house next door.

Indira was sorting out documents before visitors and supplicants poured into her room. But the place was almost empty; as if aware of a pending storm the people kept away. They expected her imminent ouster. Shafi's appearance aroused her curiosity. With her acute memory for faces Indira remembered him serving tea at Appajappa's house. Why had Appajappa sent him to her? To poison her? Or to spy on her?

'Yes?' she asked coldly.

Shafi *salaamed* but could not find his voice.

'Have you come to serve tea? I've finished my breakfast. Take the tray away,' she commanded. 'The chief minister should be here soon.'

In that moment of dread Shafi's eyes almost burst from their sockets. He knew that if Appajappa found him here, it would be the end of everything - even his position as the chief minister's orderly. Fear and hope coalesced, not to make him retreat but to plunge into action.

Sinking to his knees, Shafi joined his palms in entreaty. 'Do not trust Appajappa or anyone of his group,' Shafi muttered hoarsely. 'They plan to depose you. They have joined together, all six of them, and will force you to quit. They will select a man of their choice to supplant you. One of them will come to Sandalore to present you with a decision of the central executive committee ... and ask you to step down.'

Indira heard Shafi in silence. Anger hardened her eyes into black ice. 'How do you know all this?' she asked tonelessly.

In a quavering voice Shafi revealed the discussions at the Kempadurga tea party.

'Why are you reporting this? Are you not a retainer of respected Appajappa?'

Shafi had anticipated this. Women – no matter how powerful or beautiful – had fixed notions about 'loyalty'. Running his tongue over cracked lips, Shafi said, 'I am his retainer, as my ancestors have been for centuries. But you are said to be a champion of the poor and have offered hope to wretches like me who toil night and day. They say you will make life bearable for us. Please, great goddess, stay in power – for our sake! We need you!' Tears flowed from Shafi's eyes in sheer exhaustion. He also begged pardon from Allah for using a kaffir word – 'goddess'.

Hearing him, the ice in Indira's eyes thawed slightly. She mused, 'So the humble people are behind me. They want me to guide their destinies. Appajappa and his tribe do not reflect the temper of the people.' Aloud she said, 'I will remember your service. Take an appointment with my office and see me in the capital – when all this is over.'

Scrambling to his feet Shafi held his palms together. 'You will take care, goddess? You will deal with them?'

'Do not concern yourself with what I do. Give me the names and dates of the proposed meeting of my advisers.'

Shafi took out a slip of paper tucked within his grimy vest. Grimacing, Indira took the paper with thumb and forefinger and quickly scanned the information. A strange smile lit her face. Glancing at Shafi she said, 'You can go now.' Bewildered and exhausted, Shafi bowed himself out.

Indira kept a close vigil on the activities of the six men for the next few days; their meetings, discussions and negotiations. Shafi's information proved correct. She swiftly gathered her adherents and with the silent swiftness for which she was famous, nominated them to important party posts to neutralize the power of the kingmakers. Their scheduled confrontation was aborted. Indira divested them of their party posts for 'anti-party activities'. She grew in power and became the unchallenged ruler of the Republic of India. People, and even some opponents, began to revere her as a goddess.

In a last gesture of defiance Appajappa formed a splinter group that became a history of splinters.

But power is built on shifting sands. One day Indira's head would also bend to the dust. However that is to anticipate.

I, Raman, rejoiced when Indira triumphed over the 'forces of reaction' and powerful vested interests. My humble background aroused sympathy for the exploited and the unprivileged. I saw in Indira a champion of the oppressed, a solitary woman who could take on and defeat a cabal of powerful men. Perhaps it helped that she was elegant and attractive, and that she carried a grand name. I doubt if we would have been quite as enchanted if she had been called Hidimba Baltiwalla. I was disappointed when Subhash failed to share my enthusiasm.

'The lady,' he said, 'has encouraged disloyalty on the personal level. This instigates indiscipline and intrigues. She has broken faith on policy matters. She has autocratic tendencies that bode ill for the country.'

As for Shafi, no story of the *Arabian Nights* was as incredible as his rise to eminence. Indira never forgot to reward loyalty to herself – especially if it meant disloyalty to her foes. He rose like a meteor; from Member of Parliament to a Union minister with property and influence. Prime ministers treated him carefully because he had support of a powerful religious group and could alter electoral psephology. Shafi never looked back; he banished his past. It was of no use any more.

A decade later Indira was defeated in a general election. The old kingmakers returned to overturn her policies. Shafi was afraid of their retaliation because he had betrayed them. To protect his power and possessions Shafi planned alone and defected alone. No one knew of his change of loyalty until he joined the opponents because he carried one lesson from the past with him. When he discussed his defection with a kingmaker at a meeting, he ordered flasks of tea and coffee to be left on a side table.

He was afraid of orderlies who eavesdropped on their masters' conversations.

The Failed Seminarian

After checkmating the kingmakers, Indira became all-powerful. She was called 'the Empress' by her sarcastic critics and referred to as 'our Mother' by her devotees. Even after a victorious war of liberation waged for Bangladesh and a landslide victory in the elections, certitude continued to elude Indira. She knew that the 'vested interests' were her adversaries who strove to undermine her policies and authority. Adept at intrigue, she knew of its danger to herself as well. It was this sense of insecurity that impelled Indira to place pliant men on provincial thrones. She had been surprised to find Chief Minister Appajappa whom she regarded as a simple and courtly man leading the rebellion against her. Thereafter she selected her chief ministers with care; she wanted men who would assist her in governance without aspiring for her throne. This feudal federalism worked to her satisfaction for a few years, while the populace was still enamoured of her. Then, as her position weakened, the provincial satraps cast covetous eyes on her throne. This is not a new phenomenon. Roman Caesars always kept ambitious aspirants to their thrones engaged in warfare in the outposts of the empire. Moghul *badshahs* did the same with their ambitious sons.

After the Kempadurga tea party and the ensuing general elections, Indira selected Delonius as successor to Appajappa. He had once served Appa but later leapt into Indira's bandwagon. As Delonius appeared to be a naïve rustic Indira believed that he would be tractable. After assuming office, Delonius wanted as his private secretary, a civil servant who would be both competent and pliable. Subhash informed me that a panel of names had been prepared in which he figured. Notwithstanding Subhash's immaculate record (or perhaps because of it), Delonius selected Iago de Sanctis, a civil servant who reminded the chief of the bygone colonial era.

Sandalore is now a hub of various technologies. It was different half a century ago; a picturesque little town not unduly burdened by history. There was a fort built by Tipu Sultan, a palace which attempted to imitate Windsor Castle, spacious bungalows, parks with flowering trees and roads canopied by verdant arcades, 'Canarese restaurants' where one ate off glistening banana leaves. The winters and summers were mild and monsoon rain made the town look like misty merry England. Some retired people from merry England had refused to return to their foggy island and stayed behind even after 'the natives took over'.

Decades earlier, seeing in me, Raman, some promise, a grand-uncle living in Sandalore financed my education at a Jesuit school there. He felt that a Western patina on my rustic form would serve me well in the future. I spent two happy years at St. Athanasius School where I met Iago. The name Iago de Sanctis is a heavy burden for a boy in a 'native' society where Anglo-Saxon prejudices are rampant. Iago's father was from Macao; in him the blood of a Chinese noodle-maker mingled with a Portuguese stevedore. Iago attended school in well-ironed uniform, woolly hair brushed into an irrepressible plume while hairless arms and legs lent him girlish grace. Unlike us heathens he was a Catholic but we emulated Iago's spiritual rituals to please our Jesuit teachers. However Iago once confessed to me, 'I dream of glory and success, when I should be thinking of martyrdom.'

I wanted to laugh but dared not offend Iago. He was frightened at the thought of losing martyrdom.

Iago lived in a bungalow in the European or cantonment area where inhabitants had occidental names and habits. Their women wore 'frocks', baked cakes and played piano, their men organized dances on Saturday evenings when they got tipsy in a good-natured way and then went to church on Sunday morning to confess imaginary transgressions against their deity. Later, nubile youths and maidens went to the church compound purportedly to discuss religion but to conduct flirtations. Iago once invited me to these dos when I danced and flirted with the damsels. On the way home he murmured disdainfully about the life of the flesh.

'One day we shall all be corpses. But our souls will be happy in heaven if we are good.'

The thought of being a corpse made me shudder. 'You are quite certain of this?' I asked sceptically because my father, a votary of Vedantic doctrines, had more complex theories about the future of the soul.

His narrow eyes with glints of cruelty regarded me contemptuously. 'Of course, I am sure. If I was not, would I give my life in the service of the church?'

'You … are … going to be a padre …?' I asked in astonishment.

Iago nodded, gazing mid-distance. 'I want to be like Francis Xavier or Ignatius Loyola ... go to distant lands to preach and win souls for the true faith ... and become ... a leader of men.' He looked so far gone that I dared not interrupt his eloquence. 'It is finally power over the minds of men which give real power.'

Iago entered a seminary for training priests, fervently prepared for religious life and nurtured dreams to become a bishop or even pope. Morris West's book *The Shoes of the Fisherman* had just been published posing an interesting possibility; if a Russian could become a pope why not an Indian? I once saw him reading the breviary, dressed in white robes and rope sandals. It seemed as if he had transcended this world and was hurrying towards the angels.

I muddled through college, entered the civil service, fell in love with and jilted Vidyavati, then married a young woman with a handsome dowry.

What a shock it was to find Iago posted in the border district next to mine as a probationer in the administrative service! I was still a sub-division officer, serving under a sadistic collector, whereas Iago was under the guidance of the eminent Son of the Soil, Suresh Chandra. No one in the adjoining district was surprised by Iago's presence because no one knew about his earlier commitment to the spiritual life. On my next visit to Sandalore I snooped around and pieced together a singular story.

While preparing for ecclesiastical life Iago visited local strumpets in the hope of winning them over to *his vision* of the good life. The strumpets found the young seminarian a bore. So they won him over to *their vision* of life; a vision filled with lascivious oblivion. Iago forgot his dreams of being pope or cardinal. After hearing of these bacchanalian interludes, the seminary chief admonished Iago who did not mend his ways. It became evident that Iago had no inclination for a life in cloisters, poverty or chastity. With a sense of defeat, the pious abbot asked Iago to leave. Iago left – not without regrets because he did nurse visions of being the first Indian pope and all that such a position implied.

God's loss was the gain of man, especially of Chief Minister Delonius.

I knew Iago would prosper. The training of a seminary is not wasted. Yosef Stalin was trained at a seminary. Look how high he rose though his ideological adversary Leon Trotsky called him 'the failed seminarian of Tbilisi'.

Sanctimoniously, Iago and Suresh Chandra raided houses of pleasure and gambling dens. They were said to be cleansing the district. In time the failed seminarian married a pretty young woman, who played the piano and chattered with incessant merriment. Accompanied by linen, crockery, cutlery and a man who called himself 'botler' (butler) Filomena started a new life with Iago de Sanctis.

They were a model pair; he of mournful solemnity and she of garrulous gaiety. Iago began to regret relinquishing dreams of being a pope for the dreary life of a householder. He mused on how to retrieve the power and glory which he had renounced.

His dreams were to be realized when Iago was selected as private secretary to Chief Minister Delonius.

Indira wanted to unite the republic under her orb and sceptre and to do a great many things for the people of the republic. But she also wanted unquestioned power. There were many who wanted to acquire power for themselves and others had ideological differences with her. Since Delonius was immune to ideologies he became one of Indira's powerful satraps. Even when Indira knew that Delonius's avarice was passing the threshold of decency, she turned a Nelson's eye.

As a small-time farmer, Delonius had toiled on his few scrubby acres. Sophisticated politicians had snubbed him, had laughed at his rustic manners, and sneered at his intellectual deficiencies. Now as his power and amassed wealth grew, Delonius extracted the homage of all below him.

I met Iago on one of my brief visits to Sandalore. Images of childhood are usually seared in our minds. My inner eye carried the image of Iago de Sanctis as the boy who had a craving for spiritual life and thirst for martyrdom. Unreasonably I had expected Iago to uphold spiritual values over temporal ones. How different it turned out to be!

In his sporadic letters, my batchmate Subhash described the new mood of the state and the administration. I was surprised by the undertone of disapproval. But there was progress in the three years that followed. Despite earlier predictions of doom, Indira was proving to be a brilliant ruler. She had stormed the citadel of vested interests, had won a war against an adversarial Pakistan, which enhanced her image both in India and abroad. Above all she had embarked on poverty alleviation programmes. She realized that a poor country was vulnerable, and at the mercy of strong nations. Further, being the ruler of a weak nation would make her a puppet of the West. In this quest for making both her country and herself strong, she relied on political colleagues both in the Union government and in the states.

Delonius implemented his liege lady's programmes; improvement of the condition of the backward classes, land reforms, expansion of industries. He wanted a core group that would assist him to implement Indira's ambitious agenda. Unfortunately he asked Iago to suggest names.

Early ideas of poverty, chastity and self-abnegation now seemed repugnant to Iago. He had kindred souls in two senior colleagues: Chief Secretary G. Venkrish Pao and Industry Secretary Suresh Chandra.

As could be expected, the fastidious Subhash did not feel comfortable in the new order. Without any provocation the upstart Venkrish Pao told Subhash: 'We don't want outsiders here who know nothing of the greatness of the state. This is frontier country. We don't want public school manners here. This is an age of democracy, we don't want elitism here.'

They feared talent and favoured mediocrity.

In his next letter Subhash wrote: 'Parochial bureaucrats like Pao will subvert the idea of an integrated India. Or is the very idea of India a mirage?'

I, Raman, experienced a shiver of satisfaction at the plight of my batchmate-friend. Perhaps underneath the camaraderie, I had always envied Subhash from our academy days. And this colleague – whom I expected would take Sandalore by storm – was discontented and derided!

I cooked up official work to visit Sandalore to meet my sometime classmate, Iago de Sanctis, the boy who had wanted to follow in the footsteps of Saints Xavier and Loyola and acquire power over the minds of men.

Iago was sitting in a small, spare anteroom, adjoining the chief minister's imposing and opulent office. In contrast he looked thin and austere in shabby clothes. A mountain of files from supplicants lay atop his table. Celebrities, power brokers, adventurous women, supplicants and rogues, all had to pass through his modest room before they entered the 'Throne Room'. Iago greeted me with cold civility. Despite the snub I decided to flatter him. I told him of the reason for my visit; the improvement of public sector industries in which Dakhinstan had once led the way.

'I hear new industries are mushrooming in your state, and that your chief minister is regarded as a really modern person.'

Accepting the compliment to his master Iago slightly inclined his head. I glanced around at the visitors, leaned forward over the table and said obsequiously, 'But I believe it is *you* who are the prime mover in these matters and that the chief relies on you.'

Spots of pink stained Iago's yellow cheeks. He sighed and shrugged his shoulders. Even in that ambience of male power, his manners had an effeminate coyness. 'I only place *my views* before the chief.'

'Obviously very sound views,' I replied smarmily. 'The big man is no fool. In fact,' I said, raising my voice, 'they are already speculating that he might be Indira's successor for the throne of Delhi.'

There was a murmur of surprise from the waiting visitors. Iago was delighted. His narrow eyes gleamed and a thin smile smeared his face. 'Really? Is that what they say?' His query was pregnant with hope.

I laughed inwardly; no person is immune to flattery and impossible dreams. 'Come, you must be aware of this.' I sighed. 'Well, I had better get my work done before you go off to the capital as the next prime minister's *éminence grise*, as Richelieu was to a French king.' I paused to savour the effect of my nauseating flattery; those obsidian eyes flared into life. I let my voice rise so that the other visitors could hear. 'You know, Iago, if a bureaucrat like you is in the PMO to guide and advise, you can do so much good all round. I know your temperament. Austere and detached. No personal agenda. Total dedication to your task. How many of us can be like you?'

Iago glanced around to ascertain that every visitor had heard my words. Though he tried to suppress a smile, I knew that my tribute was warmly received. Just then a turbaned peon came running and said that 'the ruler' was calling him. Iago rose and said cordially. 'Drop in anytime tomorrow, Ramu, and I'll tell you whom to meet for your project.'

I nodded back and held out my hand to his clammy hand. Stifling distaste, I said, 'I hope your chief knows how lucky he is to have you.' I paused and continued. 'Can you imagine the chief's problems if that maverick Subhash had been selected as the private secretary?'

A delighted Iago smiled gleefully. 'Difficult chap, isn't he? Square peg in a round hole. Carries his British university tag.' Iago hated 'class' and lineage because he had neither.

'Quite, quite,' I agreed and went out into the crowded corridor where people stood to meet the chief minister's private secretary. Looking at them, bowing with joined palms, who would have thought this was a twentieth-century democracy?

When Subhash invited me for dinner that evening I felt ashamed about the disparaging remarks I had made about him to Iago. They stayed in a small and well-scrubbed government quarter. His wife Radha had cooked a delicious meal. Subhash told me about Gunnar Myrdal's provocative book *Asian Drama* on development economics of Asia. I listened, reluctantly acknowledging his powers of analysis, his well-informed mind. This man, I thought with a stab of jealousy, is going to head the World Bank. He has the necessary intellectual equipment. I no longer felt bad for sniping about him to Iago de Sanctis.

'I met your bête noire today,' I told Subhash, deliberately to rile him. 'He seemed in fine fettle.'

Subhash poured me a glass of beer. 'He should be. He is the power behind the throne. The chief minister adores him.'

'Really?' I asked, feigning innocence.

Subhash nodded, amused. 'Let me tell you the latest joke overheard in the corridors. My former boss Appajappa has, even now, quite a few adherents and they occasionally indulge in naughty stories.'

'Please, don't repeat them,' Radha entreated with a nervous smile. 'This is how you get into trouble.'

Subhash frowned. 'Raman is a friend. Surely we can share a joke!'

Radha's lambent eyes burrowed into my mind. She shook her head as Subhash began to speak.

'Iago was overheard calling the chief minister "Sire". The chief asked him why he was calling him that. Iago replied that ordinary superiors are called "sir" but rulers are called "sire". Iago informed him that the custom began from the time of the Caesars. The chief asked what *scissors* had to do with it. So Iago informed him that *Caesars*, not scissors, were rulers of imperial Rome.'

When I asked Subhash to repeat more jokes, a frowning Radha announced that dinner was ready.

Radha's disapproval did not prevent Subhash from describing the state of affairs in the state. He told me how Iago, aided by G. Venkrish Pao and Suresh Chandra, were becoming the centres of power and authority. 'This is what happens when men are selected to positions of authority for which they neither have aptitude nor capacity. Indira wants viceroys who would rule as she wants them to rule, without questions. She turns a blind eye to their transgressions when adherents amass wealth and rely on amoral civil servants to achieve these ends.'

'Are the civil servants obliging him without getting anything in return?' I asked.

'Oh yes, each one is getting what he wants. You see, Iago has convinced Delonius that the throne of Delhi is waiting for him but to attain it he must be rich enough to manipulate people, to exact obedience of power brokers. He constantly repeats how Appajappa lost to Indira because he had no money power. So where does the money come from? Licences are given to aspiring entrepreneurs for establishing industries, even though the infrastructure - water, electricity, roads and transport - are absent. Permits are sanctioned to excise barons even if they kill the poor with cheap methanol spirit. Contracts for building are given to unqualified builders resulting in edifices that collapse in heavy downpour. Iago directs the operations. Revenues flow in.'

Subhash paused. For the first time I sensed a palpable anger in my genial batchmate. 'They posted me to the commercial tax department. When I slapped a notice for recovery of sales tax on one of Delonius's excise baron friends, Iago warned me of "serious consequences". I was sent off to a backwater job. When a young officer, serving as land acquisition officer, awarded a just and fair solatium to farmers who were to be dispossessed of their ancestral land so that an industrial tycoon could build a polyester factory in those fertile lands, Chief Secretary Venkrish Pao transferred the officer overnight, to oblige the industrialist who could well afford to pay the solatium and who would be making a fortune by setting up his polyester unit on the farmers' land. Their land was taken and the small farmers were relocated in an arid place with inadequate compensation. They are now landless labourers.'

'What about Suresh Chandra? Why has he joined them?' I asked.

Subhash nodded. 'His need is the greatest. He has married his niece – to keep the pineapple and coconut groves within the family. Unfortunately the progeny are frail and sickly. So he has a compulsion to provide for them. He believes that if he obliges business houses, they will provide permanent employment to his offspring. So he is on a licensing binge. He is a weird character.'

Subhash continued gravely. 'The state citadel has a dark side. Lucullan feasts and bacchanalias are arranged where deals are transacted.'

I tried to be pragmatic. 'Is that a bad thing if at the end of it they rule well?' I asked.

Subhash cried derisively. 'Rule well? Those three have changed the administrative ethos of this state. It was not like this when I came here fifteen years ago. Officers could state their views before the chief minister; he appreciated their honesty. But now ...'

'What happens now?'

'Those close to Iago are exempt from all rules. When an officer raped a woman clerk in the cellar of the treasury, and was facing dismissal from service, Iago, the former seminarian and upholder of chastity, came to his rescue.'

I was shocked but said nothing. Subhash was quite capable of quoting me before Iago. Instead I offered advice. 'One must be a little tolerant of people's failings, Subhash. Everyone cannot be saintly.'

Subhash regarded me grimly. 'I think it is something more than being good or bad. If Iago wanted only flattery and homage it would be understandable. But Iago tries to break the spirit of the proud. He wants unbridled power over the minds of his colleagues.'

On the journey back to Pallavur I recalled all that Subhash had related about Iago de Sanctis. The train of thought led me back to the past when I had known the boy Iago. Those hidden fires I had glimpsed were not for martyrdom but for dominion over others. He had believed that service to the church would offer such authority. But he preferred political power.

In his position of power Iago's deepest craving for unbridled power was satisfied. He could extract the homage he had yearned as a youth. He could darken the destiny of gifted men and bring proud women to their knees. Since on his benevolence depended their future, even the rich and the consequential were humble. Iago enjoyed their fear and humility. He felt omnipotent and omniscient.

Is it a sense of one's insignificance that makes people seek power? Did Iago seek power because he recognized his irrelevance in this vast universe? Had Iago the failed seminarian succeeded at last?

In Praise of Poverty

Having completed the mandatory district service followed by a stint in the state capital, I decided it was time to move to the nation's capital that is the centre of excitement.

The prime minister had declared Internal Emergency. She declared that forces were attempting to disrupt the nation's stability and security. Intellectuals and liberals protested against muzzling of the press, and curtailment of civil liberties. They called her a tyrant who wanted to preserve her power. Indira Gandhi was not to be blamed entirely for paranoia.

Fearing her invincible position the antagonistic Old Guard began weaving webs of intrigue and decided it was time to strike. The moneyed classes, blackmarketeers and traders cooperated fully with their programme; essential commodities became scarce through systematic hoarding leading to price rise and resentment. An idealistic but irresponsible politician gave a call to the police and armed services to rise against the national government and stage a mutiny. A crippling railway strike disrupted the nation's transport, travel and telephone services. Agitations spread. It was a classic scenario for rebellion.

Declaration of Emergency brought all this to a halt. Suddenly chaos and indiscipline vanished, at least from the surface. Trains and planes ran on schedule, indolent telephone operators promptly connected callers, postal staff stopped being rude. People attended office on time. Presumably they worked harder. Everywhere we saw the admonition pasted on buses and hoardings – 'More work, less talk' which some wags interpreted as 'more work-less talk'. Agitations stopped; but at a price. Indira imprisoned numerous political opponents. It was no secret that her able but authoritarian son loomed behind as the real centre of power. It was clear that she was preparing the people for dynastic democracy as her father had once paved the way for her anointment to the throne.

Indira counteracted her opponents by once more winning popular support. In her flirtation with the siren of Socialism, she followed the Russian Narodniks who 'went to the people'. Indira called for the removal of poverty with renewed intensity. Her words – *Garibi hatao* – remove poverty – won universal support.

Since I, Raman, was neither a politician nor an intellectual, the Emergency did not bother me. The national capital beckoned to me as a place where my career, stagnating in the state government, could blossom. The memory of the first sight of the capital fifteen years ago flashed before me as I timorously made my way to the small office room in the ministry of rural development. Gone was the heady idealism of the twenty-three-year-old IAS probationer. Now I was pragmatic and knew ground realities. Knowledge of this was necessary if I was to advance in the labyrinths of bureaucracy.

When we join the premiere civil service, we bear in mind where our multifaceted and multifarious (never to be confused with nefarious) talents would be best utilized. The department of economic affairs is a coveted target where one can contribute towards improving the economic status of the nation by collaboration with international agencies. Commerce was also in demand by those who had mercantile blood in their veins, especially during the years of 'licence raj'. There is a great deal of preparatory activities for procuring these posts. Much hair is lost and both diastolic/systolic blood pressures are raised; even a few myocardial infarctions take place while trying to enter the portals of these gorgeous ministries. Not to mention the bad blood between ambitious consorts of the aspiring officers.

There were joint secretaries, additional secretaries and finally *The Secretary* above me – a mere director. I knew I was not important in the hierarchy though a fellow director informed me that since proposals commenced from the director's humble desk that is also where patronage commenced. Over tea he told me that the secretary was stern and smart, and the additional secretary with whom I would work, stood in mortal awe of the secretary who was close to the 'crown prince' – the prime minister's formidable son.

I began to study the specific tasks assigned to me by C. Dhenuswamy, the additional secretary. He belonged to a community that had three millennia's experience in overseas commerce and trade. He looked upon me with the natural suspicion of a Mudaliar for a Brahmin because we had an aptitude for intrigue. Everyone had a propensity for it but we gave it a finesse that others envied.

C. Dhenu had responded ecstatically to the clarion call of the prime minister for removal of poverty. He had found his mission in poverty; heart-rending, tear-jerking poverty. He felt that poverty had not really been exploited in the country. Europeans had a head start in that field. They had glorified it in their monastic orders with the motto of chastity and poverty. However I had seen a Benedictine monastery in an Italian village, where the poverty practised by the cherubic friars tempted me to annul my marriage and join their Order.

Dhenu realized early that he did not have the requisite attributes for economic or commercial ministries. He lacked the *savoir faire* and *sangfroid* required for skating on the thin ice of these ministries. Besides, one had to have a godfather, or a guilt-ridden natural father, a financier, or an industrialist to assist advancement. Or one needed a senior colleague who had a moist eye for one's wife's cleavage. Dhenu was of the rustic gentry and was his father's legal son; he had no natural father nursing a guilt complex. His wife had brought him bounty not in a deep cleavage but in the form of paddy fields that would not moisten a senior's eye. He therefore cast around for other ministries for advancement.

He had laid the grounds for his central deputation early. He selected his field of specialization so that his expertise would be at the service of the poor. By the time he came to the capital he was a reputed crusader for the poor.

After the first departmental meeting in his room, Dhenu told me with that mournful mien: 'I am so glad you have come to this ministry, Raman. One can do so much good here.'

'Actually, Sir,' I replied, in a burst of candour, 'I would have preferred tourism or aviation. In fact I tried very hard but the establishment officer had his own candidate for the jobs.'

Dhenuswamy frowned. 'Tourism? Aviation? They are for the rich. You cannot serve the poor there!'

I itched to, but dared not reply that I had come to Delhi to advance my career, not serve the poor. Dhenu continued. 'The prime minister is committed to the removal of poverty. I could have joined the ministry of finance or defence production but my heart was not there.'

I wanted to say, 'Bullshit,' but did not. Instead I observed, 'Poverty alleviation has become a global preoccupation, hasn't it?'

His opaque eyes scrutinized me. 'Has it? It seems to me that the developed world is indifferent to the plight of the developing nations. That is why our prime minister is averse to external aid. They have too many strings attached.' He paused, a trifle uneasy. What if the prime minister had suddenly become pro-Western? Then he smiled benignly and continued. 'Anyway, you are young and have a long way to go. You will eventually understand the predicaments.'

After two weeks, I was summoned by the secretary of the ministry. Anxiously I went to make my obeisance before the formidable man.

Sunit Khosla sat on a swivel chair, talking quietly on the telephone when his private secretary ushered me in. He did not even glance at me as I stood before him, my hands joined in a respectful *namashkar*. With his right index finger he pointed to a chair opposite him on whose edge I sat down, ready to leap up and bow. As he continued the murmured conversation, I looked around the tidy room. A few books and journals on the coffee table, a vase of flowers, and the mandatory photo of Mahatma Gandhi on the wall offered no hints about its occupant. When the conversation ended the secretary lit a cigarette and looked at me. 'You are the new director,' he said, informing me of my status in case I was stupid enough not to know that.

'Yes, Sir,' I replied. 'I joined two weeks ago.'

'Rural development is very important,' he said. 'In fact rural development holds the key to the country's progress. Your joint secretary will assign you specific tasks. I want you to tour widely – in the villages, in remote places, in fact, and bring me reports of what is happening and what needs to be done. Understood?'

'Yes, Sir.'

'Good. I shall see you in a fortnight's time.' He glanced down at his papers to indicate that the audience was over.

I walked back to my small room through the neon-lit corridor, wondering about my tenure in the capital. To make it at least comfortable, I began the hunt for appropriate government accommodation. In this city of inflexible hierarchy I was entitled to a moderate-sized D-II flat in a nice area, with one servant quarter, and a reasonable distance from a good school for my children. My wife and children arrived shortly and by the time we were settled in, the first breath of summer was upon us.

The Poverty Alleviation Programme was Dhenu's primary concern. It had an urgency that other programmes lacked. What could be more fundamental to human existence than food and shelter? And who knows the pangs of hunger more than those who have experienced it? Dhenu displayed such mournful empathy that I thought he had experienced the sting of hunger, though his burgeoning paunch obviously had no recollection of such trauma.

However there was an argument against this intense involvement. Our training emphasized the virtue of detachment when dealing with problems and the need to maintain distance from the actual arena of warfare. I surmised that this must be the reason why our colleagues frequently flew to calmer shores where these predicaments can be resolved through a dispassionate outlook. It was advisable to cogitate on national problems outside the confines of one's national boundaries.

That summer the blazing sun was frying our capital. Dogs, cats and cattle withered in the heat but the rulers and mandarins of sterner epidermis bore the summer with stoicism. Concern for the poor raged through the capital as wildly as the hot desert air that rendered ineffective our desert coolers. Fear of a severe drought provoked a flurry of activity in political and bureaucratic circles to formulate relief measures for the poor, the ignorant, the sick and the disabled.

C. Dhenu was appointed to head the country's delegation to a seminar to be held at the seaside resort of Rapallo. When news of the proposed crusade for '*les miserables*' in the seaside resort was circulated, bureaucrats from different ministries burst into our additional secretary's visitors' room. Esha recited her achievements in social welfare; Neha declared her contribution to the field of rehabilitation of the disabled.

While I sat there, trying to take down instructions regarding travel and stay in Rapallo, a harassed Dhenu closed his eyes before this white heat of commitment. He weighed the pros and cons of taking the two women officers. They both had powerful 'protectors' who had promoted their ascent on the career-ladder. Both were adept at weaving the twin miseries of physical pain and economic distress into a strategy that would require many visits to Washington and Paris. Dhenu included both women in the delegation.

After the ladies left, Dhenu said sadly, 'I was planning a week's leave to take my venerable mother on a pilgrimage to Haridwar.' He sighed. 'Alas! The well laid plans of mice and men.' I wanted to say that I would not mind being a mouse if I could go to the Italian resort.

It was late when I went home. My consort Satyabhama fretted because the air cooler in the drawing room was not functioning due to the blistering heat. She was also annoyed that our Nepali cook had gone home to avoid the Delhi heat. 'So I have made *their sadam*.'

The dish of spiced curd and rice added to my frustration. 'That's fine,' I said coldly. 'I can work better on an empty stomach. I have to get notes ready for my A.S.'s foreign tour.'

Satya instantly looked up. 'Foreign trip? Where?'

'To Rapallo.'

'Are you going?'

'Of course not,' I snapped. 'The additional secretary is going with three joint secretaries from various ministries.'

'You *must* go. *Other* directors go. Mrs Goyal told me that her husband is going on a foreign trip. And he is also a director.'

'Maybe he is smarter than me,' I replied angrily.

'One can learn the ropes,' she admonished. 'You should try to go.'

I considered the matter. Would Dhenu snub me if I offered my services for the tour?

'And you? You do not mind staying in this heat?' I asked.

Satyabhama smiled. 'I will go on a foreign tour with you when you are an additional secretary. I believe Air India gives a complimentary ticket for companions to additional secretaries and secretaries.' The spirit of self effacement passed as she said briskly, 'I will make the shopping list if you get yourself included for the jaunt.'

I was the junior-most member of the delegation to attend an international seminar on Integrated Human Resource Development. I was included at the last hour because Dhenu saw my utility as a man Friday; getting financial sanction and visa notes approved, pursuing *note verbale,* unofficial notes, from the foreign ministry, and getting the sumptuary allowance (for entertainment of foreign colleagues) released in time.

I returned home in time to pack my clothes and papers. The children had gone to bed, leaving for me a list of things they wanted from abroad. Under a hot starless sky, standing on the square patch of green fronting our flat, Satyabhama waved to me. I rushed off to the airport to await the arrival of Mr C. Dhenu, leader of the delegation.

A joyous alchemy transforms us bureaucrats as we are whisked through the airline counter, customs and immigration by efficient private secretaries and into the VIP departure lounge and soon after to the waiting Air India jumbo jet. Chilled champagne is served by sinuous sari-clad air hostesses. As a morning raga plays on the music system we bid adieu to the singeing heat of the capital. I worked on the agenda notes and glanced up once to see Dhenu gently snoring in his spacious first-class seat. Lack of sleep made my eyes burn but the thrill of attending the international seminar kept me awake.

Pale sunlight gleamed upon Rapallo. A crisp breeze blew in from the sea. Mesdames Neha and Esha wrapped their shawls closer and murmured, 'Oh, for our blue skies!'

for the benefit of the Milanese gentleman from the reception committee who had come to receive us. The ladies wanted to inform him that they were unimpressed by foreign climates, landscapes and faces. The Milanese gentleman could not know that one week earlier they were readying to gouge out Dhenu's eyes if he did not include them in the team.

The organizations funding the conference had booked the delegates at a picturesque mansion hemmed between sea and hills. The bedrooms had roughly hewn wooden furniture and woollen draperies; the lounge flaunted parquet floors, Lisle tapestry and a vast fireplace ordered by Catherine de Medici who had halted here before going to France to become its dauphine.

Joint Secretary Esha was in an apoplectic rage when she saw the room assigned to her. Flashing small close-set eyes Esha asked Dhenu, 'Is this the dump where we are going to stay? Why are we not booked at a five-star hotel?' She spun round to see the Renaissance fireplace. 'And no central heating! The white buggers obviously like to freeze their arses.'

The courteous Milanese came to Dhenu's rescue by promising to take the ladies into town since they preferred a five-star hotel. 'But the vista from Madame's window is beautiful!'

'F*** the vista,' Madame replied.

Dhenu turned purple with shame. I was stunned. Unfazed, the suave Milanese said, '*Va bene,* we will find for you a vista that cannot be f****d.'

The champion of the underprivileged scouted around for a five-star hotel more appropriate to her exalted status.

Dhenu summoned Ms Neha and me to a secluded part of the hotel lounge where we could prepare for the next day's conference. For both, as I was later to realize, the conference was not just a conference; it had portents for the future.

For a decade Neha had explored the roads to El Dorado. She had found it finally in the pain of the mentally challenged. She could have collaborated with industrialists or liquor barons, as her unimaginative colleagues did. But that would have the miasma of commerce at which her fastidious blood curdled. Her El Dorado was draped in idealism and selfless service. It was now waiting to be actualized into a career of noble commitment accompanied by the trimmings of foreign travel, international networking, secret foreign accounts, and promise of post-retirement consultancies paid in hard currency from the steadily depleting funds of international agencies. For Dhenu, his anguish for poverty, ignorance and disability gave him ideological advantage over colleagues with commercial agendas.

The Seminar for Integrated Human Development began in all sobriety. An immense chandelier coruscated above us in the conference hall. Various fragrances were pervasive. Tall windows admitted pale sunlight. Rapallo did not possess the glamour of a French Riviera resort. Its grey skies had a subdued sparkle, soaring pines and conifers replaced orange and olive orchards. Visitors were quiet and discreet, as if in search of anonymity. It was more suitable for secret assignations rather than international seminars requiring global attention. But it had its advantages; easy proximity to Switzerland and Luxemburg and unnamed bank accounts.

We delegates rose as the chairman of the seminar came on the dais. Tall, blond hair turning silver, blue eyes behind gold-rimmed spectacles, wearing a suit of costly elegance, he gave us a smile of hesitant camaraderie. Then gravely, he inaugurated the seminar with words of both caution and comfort for suffering humanity. Several members of important agencies delivered their speeches.

The delegates paused for coffee and tea, accompanied by *pasticini,* the renowned pastries of north Italy. Murmuring delegates discussed the chairman's speech. Dhenu effusively congratulated the gentleman. Neha flashed him an alluring smile. Esha listened not at all. Her small eyes darted here and there, scrutinizing the garments worn by the women participants. She looked satisfied; the garments brought from her workshop (where destitute women worked) were of similar designs.

Dhenu was the last speaker at the morning session. His portly Saville Row suited figure made its way to the podium. The chairman smiled encouragingly at the representative of the nation which was engaged in a valiant fight against poverty and its attendant evils. Dhenu stood motionless for a moment, his expression mournful, as if seeing in the delegates visions of toiling humanity. Echoing the Chicago address of Swami Vivekananda, the great social reformer of India, Dhenu began his address with: 'Brothers and Sisters of the Third World and friends from the West!'

The thunderous applause that had greeted Vivekananda failed to materialize for Dhenu. The audience felt a trifle embarrassed by the homely greeting. An undaunted Dhenuswamy proceeded. He donned his Ray-Ban spectacles and scanned the notes before him. This was superfluous because he had fully memorized his speech. 'Kalidasa, the great poet of ancient India, said, "Poverty is the greatest vice. It destroys a thousand virtues." We have seen that poverty provokes crime, disease, discord. It is poverty which we must fight as our greatest foe.' Dhenu's voice quavered with emotion, as the well-fed, well-dressed audience applauded enthusiastically.

Dhenu continued. 'Who has seen the ravages of poverty when the monsoon fails and crops wither on their stalks? Hunger and malnutrition bring disease. Epidemics break out because the hungry are weak. Men turn lawless. Morality is forgotten. Goodness is scorned. Violence becomes the order of the day. Criminals and tyrants take over society. Wars begin in the midst of chaos.'

Dhenu paused, waiting for the eloquent words to penetrate everyone's consciousness. People now listened intently hoping to pick up ideas.

'The strategy we must evolve in this august gathering is how to alleviate poverty. All other benefits then follow – health, education, culture, industry and commerce. But what is the starting point? Our Mother Earth – who gives us food and allows agriculture, the oldest and wisest occupation. We begin with the good earth. Vasundhara as Indians call her, Circe to the West.'

The delegates applauded. I felt a surge of admiration for my additional secretary. Neha, his adversary in idealism, glared at him. Encouraged, Dhenu succinctly outlined the Integrated Development Programme. They listened, impressed by his ardour. By the end of the speech, Dhenu had won numerous followers who were equally determined to eradicate poverty.

The delegates paused for lunch. The sea breeze wafted in with the aroma of North Italian cuisine. The sight was as good as the smell; tureens of chilled or hot soup, *pesce pescatore* (fisherman's catch), *pollo cacciatore* (hunter's chicken), *scaloppe de vitella de latte* (steak of suckling calf), asparagus in aspic and sautéd artichoke. Bottles of Orvieto, Riesling, Beaujolais were spread out on another table. I went to one corner of the dining hall to gulp down a glass of Riesling before my additional secretary could see me. Esha was piling food on her plate as if she was a victim of malnutrition though her bulk belied such misfortune. Neha was sipping Beaujolais, murder in her eyes. She summoned me with a scrawny hand.

'Your wily additional secretary is encroaching on my terrain,' she hissed. 'How dare he tread on *my turf* of "attending evils" of poverty – ignorance and physical pain?'

I had to defend the officer who wrote my Annual Confidential Report. So, I replied meekly, 'The additional secretary was trying to give an integrated picture which …'

'Shut up, you stupid prick,' she hissed.

Despite the double-barrelled insult I was glad to comply. Neha turned away to contemplate Dhenu's ruin.

Next day, after some lobbying, accompanied by frequent slipping of sari over a tempting torso, Neha secured ten minutes to speak and plunged into an attack on Dhenu. 'There is nothing degrading about poverty!' she thundered. A few people in the audience snickered softly. Dhenu looked stunned; why was she challenging the leader of the Indian delegation? He would be the one to report on the seminar to the Union government. Neha resumed her homage to poverty and sacrifice. Western delegates wore sardonic smiles. Delegates from African nations who knew poverty regarded her with hostile faces.

Flushed and agitated, she resumed solemnly. 'Eradication of poverty will not eradicate crippling of minds and bodies. For that a special effort is needed, and the evolving of a whole new strategy for the rehabilitation of the mentally and physically challenged.'

Some of the participants looked up, alerted by her words. Recently, the theme of poverty alleviation had been wearing thin in international circles after the new wind of globalization had blown in with emphasis on privatization. Social activists in search of well-funded holier grails applauded noisily.

Debates and discourses continued for two more days as resolutions and strategies were formulated. Representatives vied with each other to record for posterity their particular contribution towards the eradication of poverty. One delegate volunteered to have a look at the famine raging in Ethiopia and present a 'case study' to the newly formed executive committee that would monitor the follow-up action on the resolutions.

Having sat through the perfumed and flower-decked ambience and sessions for four days, I felt need for fresh air, a stroll round the town and a look at the shops where I could pick up souvenirs for the family. I went to explore the seaside town where history had been made and then unmade by the Treaty of Rapallo.

It was at the shopping arcade that I saw Madam Esha. She was conversing with a stylish pant-suit clad woman and a scruffy man in jeans. They were carrying the two suitcases of garments she had brought with her. Beaming, she waddled away towards a waiting taxi. I wondered how many Euros she had made from the sale of the apparel. I suppressed a wild longing to follow and question her but I was afraid of her formidable 'protector' in the citadel. Instead I bought a few things for my family and hurried back for the valedictory dinner.

On return, I learnt that Dhenu had been made chairman of the executive committee as he had the necessary qualifications for that task; theoretical knowledge as well as 'hands on' experience. In fact he had formulated twenty-seven indexes as poverty indicators and was trying to round it off to thirty indexes. Given time, a ballooning population and (hopefully) a few droughts in India, he would formulate other indexes on poverty.

It was resolved that the executive committee would commence its work after participant nation-states responded to the resolutions. Sub-committees would be constituted to focus on the 'special needs areas'. They had decided to hold the next meeting at Casablanca, Morocco, far fom the affluent West. Morocco – half feudal, half futuristic, where Islamic austerity and sultanate luxury met face to face – would provide the setting for a soul-searching session for the Integrated Human Development Programme. I could not help admire the finesse with which Dhenu had procured sponsorship from a well-funded international agency for these meetings and case studies. In return officials of that agency would act as consultants to study poverty alleviation in India and suggest future programmes. They felt that the developing nations needed to copy Western models for progress if they were to enter the twenty-first century as modern communities.

Cocktails were served in the raftered hall of the villa. As I milled around, in an attempt to 'circulate', the 'observer' from an international agency joined me. Ebullient, with pomaded hair, eyes moistened by champagne-cocktail, he said, 'Since I proposed Dhenu's name tell him that I want my trip to Ethiopia sponsored by the executive committee.' He paused to take a long sip. 'I have a yen to see the pyramids at Gizah and Luxor. There's a boat ride down the Nile. Quite romantic, if I can get a pretty secretary to accompany me. I'll need that trip *after seeing the famine deaths in Ethiopia.*'

I was stunned by his effrontery. Nodding, he smiled insouciantly. 'Young man, come join me on this expedition. I promise you it will be fun – group sex on the Blue Nile.' Taking a long gulp of the wine, I fled from the roué.

The valedictory dinner was superb. Wines from Germany, France, Italy, Spain and Portugal, liquers from Slavonic countries, Caspian Sea caviar, Norwegian salmon, pâté de foie gras, and a variety of cheese, were displayed on crystal trays. Delegates adjourned to the terrace for a *millefoglie* pastry, cognac and liquers. As mist rose from the sea, stars peeped from a hazy sky. Discussions continued late into the night on the various aspects of world poverty which made such seminars necessary.

Our hearts were brimming over with compassion and gratitude for the poor of the world who provided us with this opportunity to remove poverty.

And in the secret chambers of our hearts we praised poverty.

Administrative Acrobatics

I was enjoying working in the national capital that was the arena of action. The state of Emergency recently imposed on the country had reduced the autonomy of state chief ministers. The prime minister had introduced the 'Twenty-Point Program' in which the development programmes received attention and encouragement. Many of us junior bureaucrats felt that intellectual dissent was a luxury for those who did not have to struggle for basic needs of daily life. There was a sense of order and stability, direction and discipline. We felt that India was forging ahead.

Just when it seemed that Indira was omnipotent, her regime came down like a house of cards. With incredulity we heard the results of the parliamentary elections. She asked herself why the people had turned against her, the people for whom she (like Elizabeth Tudor) had put her soul in perdition. She had brought order from chaos, commanded respect for herself and for Indians. In her country's interest she had outwitted Tricky Dick Nixon, that most unscrupulous of politicians. India was now a nation to be reckoned with. The Third World nations looked up to Indira as a model. The Communist world had lauded her arrogant neutrality. Indira personified the spirit of resurgent India.

And now on this balmy spring day she faced a devastating defeat!

The shock was not hers alone. Indira's defeat affected the bureaucracy, particularly those who had been close to her in ideology and policies. From positions of eminence, they found themselves as persona non grata, suspected and derided for the very dynamism that had brought them to the notice of the formidable prime minister.

The change of regime in any country produces the kind of drama that can be described as tragic-comedy. From close quarters I saw the tragic aspect of such a situation in the capital. Sunit Khosla, secretary of the rural development ministry, had been a keen protagonist of the prime minister's Twenty-Point Program which sought to raise agricultural production, encourage reforestation, expedite irrigation, and provide low-income-group-housing and protection to the 'vulnerable' classes. The prime minister's hard-headed son realized that a brake was necessary on the 'right to reproduce the human species'. The people who believed that their irresponsible copulation was 'God's will' were warned not to 'go forth and multiply'. The resources of the nation were limited. As the benefits of development were being neutralized by population explosion, its control was imperative.

To make the Family Planning Program a viable reality, Sunit had fought to raise funds for this, monitored it closely, visited the states to see its progress and bottlenecks. This intense scrutiny from Delhi made the state governments effectively implement the Family Planning Program. There was no 'high-handedness' in Sunit's enthusiasm. But there were those who would have preferred to take matters easy, and who resented the Union secretary's admonition for not achieving the targets.

'Target' became an obscene word. Target was synonymous with dictatorship and smelled of coercion in a society that tolerated indifference. Accountability and explanation for poor performance was derided. So when Indira was defeated in the parliamentary elections, her 'development programmes' became a casualty. And its protagonists now became Targets for vendettas.

The thirst for vendetta came from those politicians whom Indira had imprisoned for alleged sedition. Some of her opponents were men of worth and honour, such as Subhash's former chief minister, Appajappa. Some of the opponents had murky antecedents. Or the incomparable Vajonius, orator and free lover, whose career in patriotism commenced as an agent provocateur for the British police. And the irresponsible Ramprakash who had called on the defence services to rise in mutiny in a country recovering from a war against Pakistan. These opponents now came to power and demanded retribution. The new government established the Shah Commission to enquire into Emergency excesses and inflict appropriate punishment.

Sunit Khosla was one of the first senior officers to be summoned before the Shah Commission. Accusations and charges were heaped on him for 'coercion' of development programmes. On the day of his 'inquisition' (as he wryly called it) he looked dapper in a grey suit and a blue silk tie. We, his subordinates, were also summoned by the commission. As we furtively entered the Shah Commission premises to watch the proceedings, I was amazed by our secretary's composure. In fact, he looked impatient, as if his time was being wasted on flummeries.

I trembled – not only for his sake but also for my safety. What if 'they' dragged me in as well? After all, to earn his approval and a good confidential report, I had toured the country (when I was not accompanying Dhenu abroad on crusades for the poor) and monitored the development programmes. Having sent stern letters to poor-performing state governments, I was also a hated 'Target-Setter'. I inserted two fingers in my shirt pocket to touch the copper cameo of Lord Venkateshwara that my terrified mother had sent for my protection. My neurotic wife had inscribed three horizontal red lines on my forehead, invoking Lord Shiva. She insisted that I wear a slightly frayed shirt and trouser and open sandals instead of my prized brogues. 'Look submissive!' she had exhorted. Then, fearing I might be jailed, she had burst into tears.

I watched the proceedings in dread. A senior bureaucrat who was being harangued by the commission members for 'overstepping the bounds of authority' was becoming a nervous wreck. Next to be called was our secretary. He rose, slowly stubbed out his cigarette and made his way to the podium where the 'judges' were sitting. As I looked around, I saw Subhash sitting with senior officers from Dakhinstan. He had come to witness Chief Secretary Venkrish Pao's execution.

The commission officers blasted Sunit Khosla. Through a haze of terror I heard the dreaded words 'arbitrary', 'authoritarian', 'dictatorship', and finally 'tyranny'. My throat went dry. I once again touched the medallion of Lord Venkateshwara and the lines on my forehead in homage to Lord Shiva. Like all eclectic believers I was hedging my bets.

Khosla Saheb heard them in impassive silence. Showing neither anger nor fear he let them exhaust themselves with abuses. When asked to reply he said wearily, 'Yes, I pursued the Twenty-Point Program vigorously. I recognized the urgent need for population control because our poor are multiplying. If our people, especially the rural and urban poor, are to lead lives of modicum decency, the government must vigorously pursue the programme.'

After moments of deafening silence a commission member shrieked, 'Even if it leads to high-handedness?'

'How was *I* high-handed?' Khosla asked imperiously.

'You issued peremptory letters to the state governments!' another member screamed.

'We are not paid to exchange love letters,' Khosla said coldly. There was a ripple of suppressed snickers that infuriated one interrogator. Khosla waited for the snickering to subside. 'The inefficient have to be chastised, yes.'

The enraged judge continued. 'You said our poor are multiplying. Did you support the forced sterilization programme advocated by the former prime minister's son?'

Now, I thought, with cold fear, *now we are stepping on the landmines*. The Shah Commission had been constituted not so much to look into genuine cases of miscarriage of justice but to damn the former prime minister and her son, so that they could never again come to power.

Khosla nodded and said, 'Yes, our poor *are* multiplying. They have no sense of responsibility. They are indifferent to the consequences of their unbridled procreative propensity.

The world has called it a population explosion, something this poverty-stricken nation can ill afford. I support any measure that will be a deterrent to this population growth. Many countries in the non-Western world, even Muslim ones, have successfully adopted such measures: Malaysia, Indonesia, Egypt and China.'

There was a stunned silence in the Shah Commission's main hall.

Recovering swiftly the commission's chief interrogator asked menacingly: 'What about forced sterilization?'

Sunit Khosla met the interrogator's eyes with derision. 'The Family Planning Program has poured money to control population. FAO and WHO have provided assistance. But our rural folk do not care or are unaware of how to control birth. If a man is old and has ten children, or if he is diseased and has ten children, or if he is poor and cannot feed and clothe them, *he should not be allowed to procreate* – by draconian measures if necessary.'

There was another stunned silence in the hall. I could not take my eyes off my secretary. *Now*, I thought, *we are doomed*!

The chairman of the commission essayed a sinister smile and murmured, 'That is what ruthless dictators say.'

For the first time Khosla Saheb smiled and replied, 'And what does a woman say when she has been bled white by numerous childbirths forced upon her by an improvident man? What does she say when she, with a frail body wracked by hunger and exhaustion, has to work in the field or in a factory soon after a delivery, to feed her numerous, under-nourished, illiterate children? Is her pathetic plight to be ignored so that a worthless man can go on procreating?'

The officers of the commission were shamed into silence. In that dreadful silence Khosla's now angry glance swept over the interrogators of the commission. Then the presiding officer confabulated with other members of the commission. They were visibly uneasy.

One of them said, 'You were acting no doubt under instructions from higher authorities. If that is so, please inform us *if you were coerced*. We do not wish to prosecute you if you were under pressure to do certain things. Further, we would not like to blame you for what your subordinates did.'

My heart began to hammer against my sweaty shirt. Had there been complaints against me or a joint secretary? Or maybe Dhenu had ratted on me? He knew how to skip over landmines without detonating any.

Khosla glanced at them derisively. 'I blame no one – neither "higher authorities" nor my subordinates. I am in full possession of my cerebral faculties and take full responsibility for the actions I took in the best interest of our nation.' Pausing, he added with quiet defiance, 'I would do them all over again.'

Khosla Saheb had beaten them at their game. Standing proud and unbowed before them, he forced them to turn to another case of alleged high-handedness. We filed out behind him, silent but with suppressed excitement. He accepted our congratulations with a laconic 'Anyway, that's over.' He did not go over the proceedings nor expressed his opinion about the victors and the vanquished. It was all in a day's work.

In the evening as I and other directors piled into the department pool car to go home, we saw Khosla Saheb drive away in his own car with an attractive woman of uncertain years, whom we knew was not his wife. He had the same air of calm detachment. Whether arraigned before a court of enquiry, or questioning his subordinates, or out on a tryst, he appeared the same. I wondered if this serenity was what our sacred Bhagavad Gita taught. Was our courageous, energetic, *bon vivant* secretary at heart a detached karma yogi?

Relieved that the commission had 'acquitted' our secretary and ourselves, I had quite forgotten my friend Subhash who was also attending the hearings of the Shah Commission. G. Venkrish Pao, the chief secretary of his state, had been summoned to defend himself. It was the first time that I found Subhash gloating over another person's tribulation. 'Venkrish Pao is going to face the music now,' he said. 'He will have to answer for his arbitrary conduct during the Emergency.'

'Did he do anything of that nature?' I asked my colleague.

'He did spiteful, petty and cruel things, not out of any ideological compulsion, but to please the chief minister and to settle his own little scores,' Subhash replied bitterly.

'What can they do to him?' I speculated.

'They can force him to retire as he forced so many people to retire prematurely. Small people, who may have slighted him in their previous incarnations, and who had no one to defend them. What happened to your secretary?'

'Khosla Saheb was superbly unruffled, a trifle contemptuous.'

'So I saw. Anyway he is a different breed from Venkrish Pao. Want to see the commission make mincemeat out of Pao Saheb?'

G. Venkrish Pao's 'trial' had a Kafkaesque touch. He began by apologizing for what he had done in good faith and because as an obedient civil servant he had to obey orders. 'We are all part of a chain of command. It is not possible for us to question every instruction. Administration would then come to a halt.'

'Whose orders?' the chairman of the commission asked.

Venkrish Pao paused, essayed a sideways smirk and said, 'Do I have to give the names? I'd rather not.'

The officers of the commission were alerted by the seductive treachery in Pao's voice. 'We would like to know who instructed you to carry out these arbitrary acts against the bureaucracy – premature retirements, suspensions, dismissals? Who ordered you to order the arrest and imprisonment of some of the Opposition politicians?'

Pao's saturnine face was a study in tragic submission. 'The prime minister,' he enunciated clearly.

The presiding officer of the commission nodded, satisfied. Now they were getting somewhere but loose ends had to be tied up. 'How was the prime minister interested in minor and middle-level officials?'

'They were the relatives or supporters of her opponents. They gave shelter to the opponents.'

'And the arrests? Why did you allow those to take place?'

Venkrish Pao took a deep breath. Shaking his head he said, 'The chief minister asked me to issue the orders. I had no option. He would have sacked me if I had refused.'

'Would not that have been more honourable?'

Pao shook his head miserably. Humbly, penitently, he said, 'I did not choose honour, Sir. Yes, I could have taken the easy way out and allowed the chief minister to sack me. But what would have happened to those who needed my protection? Remaining in my seat I could mitigate the cruelties, help those in trouble, put up mild notes.'

'Were there cruelties?'

Pao essayed a one-sided smile and shook his head in painful remembrance. Then he delivered a tirade against authoritarianism ending with these entirely forgettable words: 'When I joined the civil service, I wanted to serve according to my conscience. I have seen the steady erosion of values and finally the spectacle of the Emergency.' He paused, allowed his shoulders to slouch, and murmured loud enough for everyone to hear, 'Maybe I have outlived my time.'

Unlike the stillness of the courtroom after Khosla's deposition, there was a little flutter now. Venkrish Pao had given the commission the weapons it had sought. He testified against the prime minister and the chief minister whose devoted lackey he had been until the day the electoral results were announced. His testimony would be used against the two people.

I laughed at the travesty of justice. Trying to hide his bitterness at the turn of events, Subhash said angrily, 'One cannot defeat a man like Venkrish Pao who has neither shame nor pride – weapons for survival and success. Do you know what all this reminds me of?'

'Kafka?' I suggested.

'No,' he snapped, impatiently, 'nothing so abstract. These depositions before the commission by men like Venkrish Pao, who profess to have no knowledge of the excesses of the Emergency while they were abusing their power under the draconian rules, are like important Nazis who claimed at the Nuremberg trials that they had no knowledge of Hitler's brutality, and that they were only doing their duty. As the American prosecutor said in exasperation, "It seems that during Hitler's rule, all the Germans had left the country and had been replaced by Eskimos who are now nowhere to be found."'

A week later, we read in the newspaper that Venkrish Pao had been appointed secretary to the Government of India in reward for his cooperation. He had never served as joint or additional secretary because he had never been considered good enough. But now the golden gates had opened for him; he now had a larger arena for practising his brand of administrative acrobatics.

Oddly enough, while men like Venkrish Pao were being rewarded, officers who had done their work were being hounded. It was a time of 'mass deportations' as our secretary referred to the large number of officers who were being 'reverted' to their state cadres before their central deputation tenure was completed. They were 'accomplices' of the previous regime and had to be punished for their complicity in unnamed and unverified crimes.

The ancient Greeks taught their youth gymnastics and acrobatics in the belief that a good mind blossoms in a strong body. But mental acrobatics produced minds that were beyond repair; minds that settled for expediency.

After long years of administrative acrobatics, these civil servants could no longer distinguish the difference between ethics and evil.

The Novice and the Nihilist

After his initial disappointment at Venkrish Pao's rehabilitation by the Shah Commission, Subhash continued to be a supporter of the new regime. He disliked dynastic rule and Indira's efforts to rewrite history by ignoring the contribution made by other people in the freedom struggle. Subhash also resented the manner in which Indira had silenced dissent. He declared that the new government would reinstate the moral values that Indira had violated.

'She wanted to end the last vestiges of feudalism,' I told him angrily. 'The parasites who have fed on the poor must learn to work like everybody else.'

'What about the men who have amassed wealth in Indira's regime and filled the vaults of the Swiss banks?' Subhash retorted. 'Aren't they also parasites?'

'Probably they are. But I am not rooting for them. You, my friend, are seeing events with the prejudices of your own class.'

'Not at all,' Subhash replied with some intensity. 'I admire Fadnis. He is not of my class.'

Subhash's hero was Nikhil Fadnis, a fiery socialist who had opposed Indira, and called her a tyrant for gagging the press. It was rumoured that he had planned to blow up a train in which prominent Congress leaders were travelling. Indira's government imprisoned him for inciting rebellion. He fought the elections from prison and won by a huge majority. Now he entered the national scene, wild eyed, tousled haired, wearing khadi clothes and scuffed sandals, to proclaim his ideals before an adoring public. He called for vendetta against Indira and her second son. Others joined the chorus. As a socialist he wanted workers to have a substantial share in the profits of industries. He despised multinational companies and sent a few packing. Indigenization was his motto. In a country where most people lived in shabby austerity, Nikhil Fadnis's ideals made him an adored hero.

In the teeth of opposition of the big industrial houses and in obedience to popular demand, the new prime minister, who was a champion of capitalism, made Fadnis minister of industries.

Subhash said with passion: 'The new prime minister shows a tolerance that Madam Indira never possessed. This is the mark of a great leader.' Subhash paused and said, 'Mr Fadnis reminds me of the Nihilist Bazarov in a Turgenev novel.'

I hoped I would soon meet the fascinating Nihilist.

Turgenev's Bazarov fell in love with a woman different from his own class. Fadnis had married an unlikely maiden from the upper bourgeoisie. I could never understand this particular equation; perhaps the disciplined maiden was infatuated with Fadnis's anarchism. We began to see Anjali Fadnis at government functions. Her adulation of him was visible; she watched indulgently as officers and politicians crowded around him at these official gatherings.

The Republic Day reception at Rashtrapati Bhavan (former Viceroy's House built by Edward Lutyens) provides an opportunity for women to don silken plumage that is not possible in warmer seasons. The men wore the '*gala-bandh*' or closed-collar tunics that made the lean ones look like commissars and the portly ones like restaurant waiters. Fadnis surprised everyone by appearing in the prescribed dress code. He walked around and then came over to the area where the wives of bureaucrats stood in a cluster, away from the canopied area where the High and the Mighty received homage of lesser mortals. He greeted them courteously, asked about their husbands, joked about the discomfort of the dress code, gave them his best wishes. Before returning to the canopied area where the prime minister and the president (who was Indira's candidate) sat glaring at each other in hostile silence, the austere Nihilist cast a delinquent glance on the luminous Radha.

A few days later, Subhash burst into my small office room, flushed with excitement. 'You will never guess what has happened!' he cried, throwing himself on to a chair and waving a piece of paper in the air.

'I can't guess. But judging by your joy, Venkrish Pao must have croaked.'

Subhash laughed. 'Yes, that would be nice but this is even better!' He smiled wickedly. 'And who knows, from this position I might even be able to fix Venkrish Pao!'

'What position?' I asked, suppressing that familiar tremor of envy upon hearing that a colleague has landed a fine job.

Subhash was jubilant. 'Nikhil Fadnis has asked the department of personnel to post me as his officer on special duty!'

Instantly I remembered my wife saying after the Republic Day reception, 'The industry minister came over to talk to us. He looked admiringly at Radha.'

I had laughed. 'I would have thought he would look at you. You looked more dazzling in your diamonds.'

She had looked at me with a strange smile before saying, 'Would it not be interesting if he had looked at me instead?'

I was now torn between two impulses – to warn my colleague Subhash, or to see what happened in such a piquant situation. My malevolence proved stronger than my sense of propriety. 'Well,' I said feigning goodwill, 'that is quite an honour! You will now have a ringside seat to watch power politics.'

Subhash frowned. 'You really think that is all? That there is no desire and commitment to make life better for our people?'

'Oh no,' I hastened to reply. If Subhash was going to be near the seat of power, I wanted *his* goodwill. 'What I meant was that you will be able to see the functioning of government at close quarters.'

'And help Mr Fadnis achieve his goal – to make India a land of true socialism, where every worker will get a reasonable share in profit, and thereby raise productivity, where there will not be such disparity in wealth.'

Subhash spoke with a breathless intensity. I wondered how a member of the Bengali intelligentsia which had ushered in the Indian Renaissance could admire Nikhil Fadnis's anarchist ideals. I hoped my batchmate would secure for me a cozy post in one of the better public sector enterprises which would provide a car for my use instead of a dilapidated 'pool car' for the conveyance of six officers, a little travel, and a moderate expense account. I would wait for an opportune moment to make my request.

Familiarity does not always breed contempt. Working in close proximity with Fadnis only increased Subhash's infatuation with his fiery minister. I listened as he extolled Fadnis's austere habits, his obsession with freedom and equality. Subhash was excited about the forthcoming tour of the prime minister and industries minister to the Wicked West where they would study the nature of capitalism and how to barricade the evils of that system in our economy.

A few days later came my wife's announcement over dinner. 'Radha rang up to tell me that the industry minister had requested that she be permitted to go to Europe as an escort for Mrs Fadnis. Air India would pay the fares.'

I stopped eating and met her eyes. 'That is very unusual,' I murmured.

Sighing wistfully Satyabhama said, 'What a lovely time she will have!' Smiling beatifically, she asked, 'Why don't you get *your* minister to invite *you* to travel with him and *me* to escort *his* wife?'

Subhash's glamorous posting, his refined wife, his travels around the country and now visit to Europe in luxurious style stirred the suppressed dissatisfaction in me – and the unacknowledged impatience with Satyabhama also surfaced. I had begun to think of Vidya more frequently. But then I consoled myself that Subhash had not acquired substantial property as I had done. And my minister had not turned his delinquent eye on my wife!

When their school closed Satyabhama and our children went to visit her parents in Pallavur. I remained in Delhi. There seemed no point in exchanging the dry heat of the capital for the humid heat of Pallavur, though I was longing for the beautiful seaside villa which Satyabhama's father had built for family holidays. Sitting at my desk, staring at the large Automobile Association world map, my eyes traced Subhash's journey across Europe. And with a malevolence I did not know I possessed, I wondered if Subhash had relinquished Radha to his minister in the tradition of *droit de seigneur,* privilege of the lord.

There was an eerie quality in the capital that summer. During Prime Minister Indira's regime, we had sensed authority and discipline. There was a feeling that everyone was being watched and assessed which necessitated good conduct by both the timid and the bold. Now that atmosphere had been replaced by a burst of boisterous behaviour. People talked more openly, drank more freely, drove faster in celebration of freedom regained. Taking advantage of the departure of order, lawless elements from other states of our republic converged on Delhi. They robbed, raped and killed with impunity. These incidents were not a phenomenon of the suburbs or the unguarded countryside. The incidents took place in the heart of Lutyens' bureaucratic Delhi.

In a gruesome episode, a son and daughter of a senior army officer were murdered; the boy for trying to save his sister from the brutal rapists, the girl for threatening to reveal their identity. It was whispered that the son of a very important minister was the chief culprit. The police, once accused of 'emergency excesses', now feared to investigate. So the high-placed culprits vanished without a trace.

We stopped evening walks in Moti Bagh park. Morning strolls with other walkers were safer. We restricted our evening outings. If we had to attend a party several couples went together in one car, with a thick iron bar at the back, for use in emergency. I eyed our servant from the Garhwal hills with suspicion, wondering if he had been one of the thugs who had murdered the brother and sister.

Subhash returned to Delhi after two weeks, missing the worst of the June inferno. He did not phone me nor did he appear for the dawn-time walks in Moti Bagh. I sighted him at the ministry of industry building as he was entering a pool car instead of one of the white Ambassador cars attached to the office of the industry minister. I wondered if Subhash, like other officers on special duty to ministers, had become pompous. Piqued, I made no attempt to contact him; when finally I did, his personal assistant informed me that Subhash had gone on leave to his home state.

Concern and curiosity swirled around me. So! The son of an officer of Netaji's Indian National Army, a family that was proud of its cultural traditions, had capitulated to a fiery politician and bartered his wife in the process. And having done so, he could not stand the strain of working for the man who had cuckolded him. Well, I consoled myself, though I could not land such a glamorous post, at least my honour was intact. Not that it was ever endangered by Satyabhama's homely ways.

One evening when the first rains lashed the parched city, Subhash appeared at my door. He looked thinner and sunburnt. We sat in our small drawing room and exchanged pleasantries.

'Where have you been all this time?' I asked cautiously.

'I went to our ancestral home near Shantiniketan. I haven't been there for a long time. I saw our lands, worked with the tenant farmers, drew water from the well, swum in the new irrigation canal and visited the homes of our poets and mystics – Tagore, Jayadev, Chandidas. I returned to my roots.'

'After a sojourn abroad?' I asked with an unintended leer.

Looking at me with an even gaze he said, 'Yes. It is necessary to return to one's roots in order to understand oneself better, to put life in its proper perspective.'

I was unable to comprehend his state of mind.

Subhash sighed. 'I am returning to my state cadre.'

'To Dakhinstan?' I asked, surprised.

Subhash nodded.

Astonished, I asked, 'You are going to leave the office of the minister of industry?'

A swift flush appeared on his bronzed cheeks. He looked out of the windows, watching the rain for a few moments before replying. 'It is *because of him* that I am leaving Delhi long before my central deputation tenure ends.'

I dared not ask the dreaded question. Had Subhash been dishonoured? Had Radha become Fadnis's mistress? I heard the rain fall softly on the last of the gulmohurs in our garden – with unease.

'You are not your usual snoopy self, Raman,' Subhash said drily.

'I ... am afraid ... to ask,' I mumbled, suddenly afraid, not only because I feared for my reckless colleague but because of the clouds of power looming over our lives.

Subhash drew in a deep breath. 'Let me tell you then. We went to Europe. It was interesting, negotiating with the French and German governments on industrial collaboration. And Radha was having a wonderful time sightseeing with Mrs Fadnis who is a very fine person. And then, just before leaving for Switzerland, Mrs Fadnis left for home. The couple had a row, a fairly big one, I gather. Radha prepared to accompany Mrs Fadnis back to India but the minister said that he did not want to spoil *her* holiday because of *his wife's* decision to return home.'

Subhash lit a cigarette, and stared at the tiny fiery point before saying, 'The next day he asked me to stay behind in Paris to meet a certain person who would be a liaison officer for the negotiations. I could join them later in Bern.'

'Did you?' I asked breathlessly.

Subhash shook his head. 'Of course not! I told Nikhil Fadnis that I had admired him during the Emergency and had defended him when others called him a cynical opportunist. But now, I said, I no longer wished to work with him.'

'Good God,' I muttered. 'That was suicide!'

For the first time that evening, Subhash smiled, the merry smile he had at the academy. 'No, Raman, it was resurrection. I felt better after the showdown. Radha and I packed immediately, leaving a note with the minister's secretary that as one of our parents had taken ill, we had to rush back home.' He let out a long-drawn sigh. 'On return, I sent a letter to the department of personnel, asking to be relieved of my post because I wanted to return to the state cadre as my children's health was deteriorating in Delhi.'

We were silent for a long time, wondering what the future would bring for Subhash. Had he doomed himself and ruined his career? He brought out a bottle of Glenfiddich whisky from a duty-free shop bag. 'This is the only purchase I made abroad at the duty-free shop.' Then with a catch in his voice he said, 'Let us drink to our future and may we remain true to our code.'

Unexpectedly it turned out to be a hilarious evening. Subhash described humorous episodes of the Grand Tour. We laughed like schoolboys. The Glenfiddich and the cooling rain outside brightened our spirits. I could see that Subhash was relieved that he could tell someone about his ordeal. He had not spoken of the episode to anyone after his return.

I could not help asking, 'Have you discovered that the men who rant and rave about freedom and democracy can be cynical?'

Subhash looked at me with a strange sadness. 'I still admire Nikhil Fadnis. I wish I could have stayed with him. One day he might make a fine prime minister. He is brilliant, dedicated and efficient.'

I looked at him bewildered.

'A man cannot be condemned if he is briefly bewitched by a comely woman.' Subhash paused. 'But I wish it had not been my wife. I had to defend our honour.'

Subhash rose as dawn was breaking. He opened our wicker gate, waved, and went towards his D-I quarters. Watching him I wondered if I would have relinquished a coveted post for an outdated code.

We expected Minister Fadnis to damn Subhash in the Annual Confidential Report. To our astonishment the fiery Nihilist recorded: 'Subhash Chowdhury is a gifted officer of absolute integrity and immense efficiency. The country is safe in the hands of such civil servants.'

Perhaps the Nihilist found in the Novice what he was once.

A Harvest of Pineapples

Subhash felt no enthusiasm returning to the state cadre. A bureaucratic saying was: 'As inevitable as death and as gloomy as reversion to the state cadre.' The national capital was a place of excitement and innovation, intrigues and conspiracies, and wonderful opportunities for advancement. Service in the state was comfortable and predictable. But after his showdown with a powerful Union minister, Subhash did not want to serve in Delhi.

'Reversion to the state' as it is inaccurately called (as if it was a disgrace and demotion), can be painful after a showdown, especially if the party in power in the Union government is the same as the party ruling the state. An officer is then kept on 'compulsory waiting' and harassed in other ways. The government in power in Dakhinstan was in opposition to the central one. But Chief Minister Delonius and his *éminence grise* Iago de Sanctis were not likely to champion a 'maverick' officer like Subhash. Some politicians are united by a common dislike of a strong-willed officer, and if the officer is also honest, he is dreaded like the bubonic plague.

Subhash was posted to Kurtum, an arid district near Sandalore whose only appeal was its pineapples alleged to be superior to those of Hawaii. As Kurtum is drought prone, cultivation of rice and coconut had been replaced by pineapple. At harvest time the highway between Kurtum and Sandalore is dotted with farmers offering pyramids of spiky pineapples that travellers stop to buy.

The deputy commissioner's residence, 'Dobb's Bungalow', was a dilapidated relic of the British Raj and took its name from a stern British officer of the Mutiny days, whose ghost was said to appear now and then and abuse wrongdoers in the local language.

'If we fall short of suitable acquaintances here, we can always rely on ghosts of British deputy commissioners to amuse us,' Subhash wrote to me. 'The assistant commissioners are competent young men so I have satisfactory assistance on the official front. Their wives like Radha and we meet once a month at district headquarters to review development projects.'

When he described his bailiwick, I wondered if Subhash was trying to console himself or whether he was indeed a different breed from officers like me. He described the parched landscape; fields of hardy jowar, dried irrigation tanks that resembled craters and of wolves foraging for human flesh.

Subhash, I consoled myself, has been banished to a dreary place and will soon be forgotten. He has missed the tide and has proved that he is that most dreaded of civil servants – an idealistic maverick. He will stay in Kurtum until he is promoted, and then be shifted to some other nondescript post in Sandalore. Learn the lesson, I told myself, whenever I had a feeble urge to revolt.

But Subhash did not complain. Perhaps after storms in the capital, he found peace in dreary Kurtum. I soon learnt that he had once more taken on wielders of power.

While leading a posse of police to track down the marauding wolves, Subhash came across the estate of Suresh Chandra, the bureaucrat who was an honoured Son of the Soil of Dakhinstan. The old house looked neglected but the nearby fields of yellow pineapples grew in eerie profusion.

The visit of a deputy commissioner (collector or district magistrate) to a village is always a great event. During the British Raj, such visitations were recorded in village chronicles.

Subhash, the lithe young man, with tawny skin and brilliant eyes, was a novelty worthy of investigation. Driven by an inexplicable urge Subhash went to the old house and asked if they could buy green coconut water for himself and his thirsty officers. The manager of the estate readily invited the deputy commissioner's party to the house. A cluster of green coconuts were produced, their tops deftly lopped off, and their clear milk poured into steel 'tumblers'. A servant pared off the white coconut flesh and served it with molasses.

Invitation for lunch was also issued. Subhash readily agreed though his *tahsildar* demurred, saying that a mutton biryani lunch had been arranged at the *taluk* inspection bungalow. A vegetarian meal was produced, concluded by freshly plucked pineapples. Subhash complimented the host on their unusual flavour. The manager essayed a brief smile.

'Your estate is doing well, even in the midst of this year's drought,' Subhash observed. The manager nodded, reluctant to discuss agriculture.

After lunch the officials accompanying Subhash sought shady patches in the garden to smoke cigarettes or doze. They would have preferred the non-vegetarian lunch of mutton biryani at the inspection bungalow followed by siesta on proper beds instead of sitting under trees like agricultural labourers.

After sometime, a restless Subhash went to inspect the pineapple fields. Huge ripening pineapples flavoured the air with tangy aroma. Subhash looked around, wondering why he had a strange sensation; then he saw a man come out of a barn-like house at the adjoining farm. The man wore a dhoti folded up to his bony knees with a frayed towel slung over one shoulder.

'Has the *hejmaan-avaru,* landlord, not come?' he asked truculently.

'Who *is* the *hejmaan*?' Subhash asked.

The man scowled. 'Have you landed from the moon?'

Subhash laughed and replied, 'I have come recently. I am the new deputy commissioner.'

The man looked at Subhash with bleary eyes. Then he shook his head and sighed. 'So many have come and gone but no one has done anything.'

'What is it you wish to be done? Tell me. Perhaps I can help,' Subhash replied.

'Provide for the boy. He is almost fourteen. Should he not enjoy benefits of the legal sons? His grandfather is to be blamed for this mess but he is dead. And the father cares not at all. I too may die one of these days and then the boy will be hounded out of here. But what is the use – none of you will help because you officers stick together.'

A troubled Subhash asked, 'Who is this boy?'

The man's laugh sounded like cracking of twigs. 'Yes, you are new. Otherwise you would have known the story. So, Suresh *Avaru* has managed to bury the past.'

Subhash was taken aback at the mention of the revered Son of the Soil Suresh Chandra. 'Tell me if there is anything I can do.'

'Come, Sir, let us sit down. I cannot stand too long on these unsteady legs.'

As the sunlight slanted westwards and shadows lengthened, Chikkayda, the small farmer, narrated the event that had taken place fourteen years ago.

Suresh Chandra, the great brown hope of Dakhinstan cadre, was betrothed to his niece when he was sixteen and she was aged ten. His family owned large tracts of lands but after the marriage of sons the lands had become fragmented and had passed on to other families. It was decided that thereafter the eldest sons and heirs would marry their nieces so that the lands would not be further fragmented. Suresh grew to manhood, aware of his matrimonial destiny. He watched his niece's evolution from a gawky girl into a gauche woman. A young uncle and little niece growing up in the same neighbourhood probably impeded erotic desires but the commitment to the land kept them steadfast to their betrothal. As soon as Suresh entered the civil service a grand wedding was planned. The niece was still a schoolgirl, innocent of all carnal knowledge, while he brooded on sin, pleasure and rebellion. These inner skirmishes were overruled by external pressure; Suresh wed his niece – for the greater glory of the pineapple groves.

Soon after Suresh went for a refresher course at a British university to learn counter-revolutionary tactics that could postpone land reforms that were threatening rich landlords. Distressed to find Harold Macmillan's Britain indifferent to the menace of revolutionary socialism, Suresh returned home from the fool's errand.

However one benefit accrued from this journey across the seas. He was mesmerized by the uninhibited exchange between men and women. There was no coquetry in their frank expression of physical pleasure. He stared at the undergraduates as they joked, flirted and kissed in college lounges and cafeterias. Sometimes watching their amorous antics in the college refectory he forgot to eat his nut cutlet – the only vegetarian fare in the college refectory.

'Come on, *maitey*,' a student once said jocularly, 'find yourself a lass so that you don't ogle mine.'

The girl student had chuckled. 'No dearth of them here, luv.'

Suresh thought over the matter as he took the tube to his digs at Kensal Green. 'Get a girl,' he mumbled to himself, as he stared at the women who passed by in mini skirts, drainpipe pants and tight sweaters. 'How alluring they must be in bed! I will never know the joy of such delights! I had to marry my niece!'

Nevertheless he approached a peroxide blonde who had a long expanse of legs and generous bosom. She responded with a toneless, 'Cost you ten bob, ducky.' Despite foreign exchange restrictions he agreed; the experience gave him a thirst for carnal delights.

He returned home to his niece-wife. She was what one calls 'a good soul'; she conversed with a frenetic excitement and gave her views with the rapidity of an AK-47 firing. Suresh watched her with suppressed impatience. At night, after performance of matrimonial duties, he lay awake wondering what it would be to have a wife who was a total stranger. Such marriages, he accepted, offered no illusions, no in-law interference, no social adjustments. This made life peaceful and predictable.

While Suresh was busy building his career, his niece-wife fulfilled the dynastic obligations. In time she produced a son. He was frail and weak. Suresh wondered whether the famous pineapple estate would be in safe hands. They tried again. The second son was not stronger or brighter than his sibling. When Suresh once expressed disappointment with his offspring, his relatives reminded him that his marriage would keep their estate unfragmented. To console himself he often went to his estate. It was there that Suresh felt carnal hunger; he watched the robust women toil in the fields, saris hitched up to sinewy thighs, *choli*s taut against thrusting breasts in perpetual invitation. He thought bitterly: I have bartered away all physical delights and made cohabitation a nightmare – and for what? Two sickly heirs.

One monsoon morning he saw a young woman working in the pineapple fields; her innocent face contrasted oddly with her sensual body. Her long rough hair flew in the wind. Encountering Suresh's scrutiny, she turned abruptly and walked across the fields to the fence that separated Suresh's family estate from its neighbour. The next day the peasants did not come to work as an incessant drizzle flung a misty veil over the fields. Suresh enquired from his estate *gumastha,* clerk, about the identity of the young woman he had seen. He was told that she was the daughter of the man who had bought a tiny holding adjoining Suresh's estate but wanted to sell it now.

'Perhaps I can make him an offer,' he said quietly.

On the pretext of commencing negotiations and heedless of the steady rain, Suresh walked across to the adjacent holding where the young woman lived. The owner welcomed him inside the barn-like house and commanded his daughter to bring tea. When she did not appear, he called her again in a peremptory tone. She came reluctantly, holding two glasses of tea, and cast a hostile glance at landlord Suresh Chandra. He made offers to improve cultivation to the small farmer and asked him if his daughter, Anju-bai, would show him the water tanks. The pleased farmer told his daughter to fetch the jute capes that were used by peasants in the rainy season and accompany the big landlord.

'But, Father, it is raining! I will get wet! Can he not see the tanks another day?' There was entreaty in her voice.

'A little rain will not hurt a sturdy creature like you. Now go and show the *hejmaan,* master, the tanks,' the father retorted.

Sullenly, Anju accompanied Suresh to the edge of their holding and pointed out the two small tanks which were beginning to fill up with rain water. He stared at them with unseeing eyes. What he saw was the young woman, jute cape over her head, wet clothes outlining the contours of her body. She flushed at his scrutiny; then seized by sudden fury, she flung the jute cape aside and began running over the sodden fields. Suresh walked back to the barn to make another offer.

That evening, sitting in the barn, the small landowner and the powerful one reached an agreement about de-silting of the tanks and sharing of water. Anju was then summoned and told that she would seal the pact by becoming the 'estate wife' of the big landlord.

'No!' she screamed, 'I will be no such thing! I am going to be *the wife, the only wife* of Chikkayda, a proud and poor farmer!'

The father rose, slapped her soundly and shouted, 'You fool, have you no sense? You will live in comfort as the estate wife of an important man! Everyone in Kurtum will bow before you. Isn't that good enough or do you want to die of hard work like your mother?'

'I want to die of hard work as the wife of a man I love rather than be the whore of this aging landlord!' she screamed again.

'If that is your decision I will drown you tonight in the well!'

As the father came menacingly towards her, Anju looked around for an escape but the creaking door was shut and guarded by a farmhand. She then clambered up the bamboo ladder to the hayloft and hid there. Suresh Chandra followed her in breathless anticipation. Destruction of Anju's little dreams was accompanied by her screams.

The liaison continued for a year. Suresh was exhilarated by his union with the robust and barely literate Anju; her vitality rejuvenated him. His delicate educated wife seemed a pale shadow compared to this rustic Circe. He now came often to his estate. If his niece-wife suspected anything she did not express these thoughts – until Anju produced, despite every precaution, a sturdy little boy whose existence soon became known. Anju's father pressed Suresh to fulfil his commitment. Suresh stopped visiting the estate for fear of being confronted with the illegitimate son. On legal advice, he disclaimed paternity of the child as Anju could have taken other lovers. Furious with such perfidy, Anju slashed her wrists, and was found unconscious on the pineapple fields. Anju's once-betrothed, Chikkayda, removed her to his little home. The attempted suicide was hushed up with the aid of the local police. To silence any criticism Suresh mournfully informed the police that Anju was of unsound mind and given to hallucinations. With a dry laugh he told the sub-inspector of police, 'The poor girl imagines that she is my wife.'

The sub-inspector stuck out his tongue and touched his earlobes in a ritual gesture of outrage and said, '*Ai-ai-yo*! How can that be? To utter such wickedness about such a noble man!'

'Yes,' sighed Suresh, 'this wretched girl has brought much sorrow to my wife. I fear *my wife* will commit suicide one of these days.'

'*Ai-ai-yo*!' Once more the sub-inspector lamented and hid his amusement, this time omitting to touch the earlobes or stick out his tongue. Landlords and sub-inspectors had their fun, and must therefore support each other. He was persuaded through a nice gift, to have Anju-bai declared unbalanced and committed to a distant ashram from where she could not cast aspersions on the honour of an exemplary landlord.

Anju's father died soon after, leaving his lands and the little boy to the care of Chikkayda, who was betrothed to Anju before she became an 'estate wife'.

Subhash was silent as Chikkayda finished narrating. The stillness of the hot afternoon was punctuated by a beetle buzzing over the bougainvilleas. Subhash gazed at the barn-like house and then the old mansion belonging to Suresh's family. How could he, Subhash, undo the events of the past? The sane Anju-bai, banished to a far ashram, now showed signs of acute melancholia. Subhash could not help Anju's son to get rights denied by his very birth. For a brief bucolic dalliance, Suresh Chandra had wrecked havoc on three lives.

As Subhash pondered over this, a boy came out of the barn and brought two steel glasses of cardamom tea. 'Here, Father,' the boy said affectionately, 'here is your tea. I hope the commissioner *sahebru* likes it.'

Chikkayda introduced his foster son, Anju's son by Suresh. The boy joined his hands in *namashkar*. Subhash smiled and returned the salutation. He could see the boy's resemblance to his senior colleague Suresh Chandra – but there was something else in the youth's bearing; strength, pride and fortitude which the natural father never possessed. Those traits, Subhash mused, must have come from Anju.

'You should study and go on to college,' Subhash advised the fourteen-year-old boy.

'Oh I do! After working in the field, I attend the evening adult literacy classes held in the village hall. I study at night and will surely pass the school final exams next year.'

'And after that?' Subhash asked and wondered if the boy had ambitions of joining the civil service in the footsteps of his illustrious natural father.

The boy replied seriously, 'I will study agriculture and develop this farm into a modern one. Chikkappa and I are saving up to do this. We get bore-well water for our crops and good prices for our products.' He paused and essayed a malicious smile. 'I may even have to take charge of the big estate if the *hejmaan*'s sickly sons die.'

'Don't talk like that!' Chikkayda rebuked the boy. 'You keep what is yours and they will keep theirs. You are strong, and manage your studies well. You can progress through your own efforts.'

The boy laughed and returned to the house.

When Subhash was transferred from Kurtum district two years later, Chikkayda invited him to celebrate the boy's joining a renowned agricultural college in Kurtum. They were piling pineapples on to a truck when Subhash arrived. 'We should be able to buy a tractor this year and extend our house,' the boy told Subhash with excitement. He had grown taller and had the shadow of a moustache. When the five truckloads of pineapples had been sold and dispatched, the three men went inside to have a festive lunch of *obattu* pancakes and *puliogerey* rice grown on the farm.

Shortly they saw Suresh Chandra inspecting his pineapple fields. Accompanying him were his frail, wraith-like sons and heirs.

Sensing their presence, Suresh turned and saw Subhash, Chikkayda and his robust illegitimate son who was a contrast to his sickly heirs. Suresh Chandra's obsidian eyes flared briefly with impotent rage; he realized all he had was a blighted harvest of pineapples.

Subhash raised his eyes to the summer sky to make a wish that Anju's son would become an excellent young man, and that his farm would be blessed with bounty, and that Anju would return one day to see that she had not suffered in vain.

Roses and Ashes

After a few years Subhash and I, Raman, returned to serve the Union government in Delhi. The dark drama of the Emergency was receding in peoples' memories. Indira Gandhi was returned to power by a nation that was weary of the incompetence of her adversaries. Squabbling amongst themselves, blackmailing each other, the People's party did not incite the antagonism that Indira and her cohorts had done; they provoked disgust and derision. Returning to power with an affirmative mandate, she promised to stabilize the economy, bring back order and restore our lost national pride.

The imperious matriarch who received the acclaim of the masses changed after the death of her favourite son in a strange plane crash. The relentless rumour mills of the capital whispered innuendoes on the cause of the accident. The once formidable prime minister stood devastated at the funeral, weeping for her son. But with steely grace she carried on, dealing with separatists, intrigues and subversions that are the privileges of power.

For us a few pleasant years went by. Subhash worked in the ministry of energy as joint secretary and I was posted in the ministry of agriculture. These were important ministries in the development sector. The ministry of energy played a decisive role in sanctioning new hydroelectric and thermal projects and was making tentative efforts to encourage nuclear power projects as well. The latter had geopolitical and international implications. The disaster at Chernobyl three years later would cure our infatuation for nuclear stations.

Subhash frequently visited new power stations in the country. He once told me: 'For all our blasé modernity there is something awe-inspiring in seeing the elemental harnessed to the ephemeral, of a great mass of water contained and channelled by concrete. The magnificent dams make one ponder on man's insolence – that puny man had acquired power over the elements and had changed the dry wastelands into fertile fields. It is there in those project areas, watching engineers, mechanics, draughtsman and workers, that an uncomfortable feeling of guilt crept unbidden to me.'

'Why should you feel guilty?' I asked him.

Subhash replied, 'These are the people who are doing the actual work of building dams and hydroelectric stations under a blazing sun or torrential rain while we pontificate from our comfortable offices. I feel even more uncomfortable watching the curious dramas enacted in scientific circles, where location of a nuclear power station was not considered on geological and ecological feasibility but on political grounds, where mediocrity was preferred to brilliance for the simple reason that mediocrity was more manageable. Bureaucratic intrigues seem amateurish compared to intricacies of scientific conspiracy backed by nuclear physics.'

My work in the agriculture ministry was, literally, more earthbound. The innovations of the Green Revolution had transformed farming practices and material. There was considerable enthusiasm for the hardy hybrid crops that could withstand scanty rainfall and destructive insects.

Then everything changed one October morning. Prime Minister Indira Gandhi was assassinated by her bodyguard as she walked across her garden for a television interview next door. I vividly remember that morning when the news of her murder spread like wildfire. That her own bodyguard had shot her seventeen times made the killing a horrifying betrayal. Even before the offices closed and the flag was lowered to half mast, we knew she was dead but heard the confirmation only when her surviving son returned from tour to announce the news. By then the city had exploded in a frenzy of grief and violence. As the assassin was a Sikh the community became the target for mindless vendetta.

Next morning Subhash, and I, with numerous colleagues went to the mansion that was the residence of commanders in chief during British rule. It seemed appropriate that this fearless woman who had led her nation to victory and had helped liberate a sister nation from oppression, should lie in state, surrounded by the spirits of other commanders. Pushed forward by a swelling grieving crowd I stood by the body for a brief moment to gaze at the motionless form, her red sari concealing a fragile body riddled by bullets. I was ashamed, as were millions of my countrymen, that this woman who had made our country proud and strong, should die at the hands of a trusted bodyguard. There was now an outpouring of collective grief. The nation forgave her the excesses of the Emergency, the populist gimmicks, the authoritarian traits, as it plunged into a grief-stricken mourning. They remembered her courage, her patriotism, her commitment to the poor and her eerily precognitive declaration made a day before her death – that she would defend India's unity with the last drop of her blood.

She had done just that.

The vulpine elders, who had been drooling for decades over dreams of the throne, now rejoiced and each made secret preparations to succeed her. But a surprise awaited them. For all her much-flaunted socialism, Indira like her father, was an unrepentant dynast. She had laid the ground for her surviving son to succeed her. Though there were several more experienced men who could have succeeded Indira, the shattered Congress party offered the throne of India to Indira's son Rajiv. It would be reparation for his mother's murder. The funeral was attended by numerous heads of states who came to offer homage to an extraordinary woman.

Rajiv promised a new era. Selecting a group of young men who were his kindred spirits, Rajiv wanted to modernize the republic. His mentor was a cousin who drew up the agenda of administrative reforms, emphasis on efficiency, preference for merit and talent. The young rulers were outward looking, educated, professional men. For a year or so, we looked ahead with optimism. The capital took on the mood of its young ruling elite; there was an air of commitment and hope.

The nation waited – once more – for a new dawn.

Liberation Day

Like all national capitals Delhi has a large number of embassies and high commissions. Some are surrounded by formidable walls and gates in and around Chanakyapuri. Each embassy vies with the other in architectural grandeur, landscape gardening, interior embellishments, and creation of an impressive ambience.

There is the Russian (former Soviet) embassy with its solid grandeur, reflecting its formidable presence in the theatre of history. Competing with this is the American embassy; a veritable fortress with Doric columns and Moghul *jaali* works, barbed wire fencing all around to declare its power. Bricks of the British High Commission echo power and glory as successive national movements have eroded its former eminence. The Scandinavian embassies are noted for their elan and elegance. Embassies of East Asia are designed with exquisite taste; words are whispered in the stillness here; one can hear water dripping from fountains in the miniature courtyards.

Denizens of the capital do not know what happens behind these diplomatic sanctuaries. Senior Indian officers meet senior foreign diplomats at official functions, at signing of Memoranda of Understanding and sometimes in the foreign ministry when a crisis is brewing. In the precincts of South Block one may see the foreign diplomats walk with measured tread and speak with a hushed sobriety that quells any attempt at chauvinistic gaucheries. The mood changes on the glittering occasions when the embassies celebrate their national or liberation day.

And thereby hangs a tale.

Indira Gandhi had seen dismantling of old colonial powers in the wake of Indian independence. Indian foreign policy was aimed at keeping aloof from superpower rivalries. Rajiv Gandhi ushered in an era of economic expansion, and tried to free himself from his mother's suspicion of the West. Rajiv could not afford to display xenophobia; his wife was foreign and until now she had made no attempt to be otherwise. In this atmosphere, foreign embassies became a favoured destination of the rich, the powerful and the social climbers of the capital. Bureaucrats from ministries of trade and commerce, defence production, agriculture, rural development and culture were feted; their cooperation could open the doors for markets, materials and arms deals.

Embassies sparkled on their national or liberation days. And no embassy reception or the *Vin de Honeur* was more gorgeous than the one held by the ambassador of Zaretania on their liberation day. Zaretania had been a proud member of a vast empire in the Middle Ages. When that empire crumbled, Zaretania was invaded by an aggressive nascent empire. Decades later the arms of a superpower liberated her. The ungrateful Zaretanians forgot the birthday of their Emperor Udal the Unready, who had brought them glory in the fourteenth century; they now celebrated the day a superpower freed them.

Recognizing new realities, the Zaretanian ambassador established trade links and economic cooperation with India, and offered lavish hospitality to bureaucrats who could be useful to his projects. That is how I, Raman, was invited to the liberation day celebrations one year.

As the cars of the invitees drove up the circular driveway, two uniformed Zaretanian officers checked the invitation cards, nodded and bowed. Guests disembarked at the portico, were guided through a rectangular hall where paintings of Caravaggio and Rubens hung on silk-covered walls. A massive Antwerp chandelier hung from the gilded ceiling. Tall glass doors at the end of the hall opened into a garden now lit by tiny lights and where food and drink were spread out in Lucullan bounty. In the lilac-hued evening, my wife Satyabhama and I stood for sometime looking at the other guests flowing into the garden.

For connoisseurs of feminine beauty, it was both a visual feast and sensual frustration. Women of every colour, shape and costume stood with their escorts, to be seen and admired. There were svelte Nordic blondes, voluptuous ones from Africa, fragile beauties of the Far East, and languid ones belonging to the Latin world. They exuded glamour from their perfumed silk-clad bodies. Their menfolk in elegant suits, uniforms and epaulettes, looked drab next to them.

I felt lost in this exotic setting. Satyabhama looked around, gazing with interest at the guests. Seeing no one of my peer group I walked on the lawn until I sighted Dhanvir, a budding young politician who came from a place known for its bandits. I did not care for his company – but in this crowd of unfamiliar people it was a relief to find even the conceited Dhanvir. He greeted me with condescension: he was member of a proud tribe, served in various committees and was casting round for a ministerial berth. We stood with drinks in hand, making trivial conversation. Satyabhama disappeared to strike up conversation with a Zaretanian lady.

Dressed in military regalia the ambassador of Zaretania conversed politely with guests, while his pale eyes darted now and then to the entrance awaiting the chief guest. The ambassador's sophisticated wife in a silver Lamé dress, circulated in the lawn, talking to guests in a velvety murmur, on the latest concerts and fashion shows. She never strayed to national or international events, for fear of provoking a controversy. Instead she encouraged people to talk while she listened intently. We learnt later that when the guests had departed, it was her habit to sit in her study late into night and consign her reflections to a leather-bound diary. She wanted to be the Lady Mary Montague of the twentieth century. Lady Montague's memoirs provided the first intimate glimpses of the eighteenth-century Ottoman court, where her husband was ambassador. These well-guarded and serious aspirations of our hostess became known much later when an article on her was published in a national daily.

Presently there was a flurry of activity; the ambassador strode briskly to the chandeliered entrance where the chief guest was disgorged from his car, attended by his entourage. The ambassador led the chief guest to the reception hall. The band played the national anthems of Zaretania and our republic; guests stood stiffly to attention though some found it difficult as their spines were weakned by disuse. The chief guest stood stoically through this ordeal. Anthems over, guests rushed to replenish glasses and plates. The chief guest was led to the lawn where, seated on a brocaded sofa, he smiled benignly at everyone.

The aspiring politician Dhanvir of Bandit County watched the guests moving around the manicured lawns. His eyes, puffed by imported champagne, ogled the women moving with sinuous grace in the lamplit lawn.

Gulping champagne and munching canapés, Dhanvir confided in a low growl: 'You know, *yaar*, I would like to kiss the petal cheeks of those dames.' And then, as the ambassador's wife approached us, Dhanvir's gooseberry eyes were transfixed on her shimmering figure. He had seen her before at receptions and now he sprang forward to shake her hand; she gave him her hand and passed on, to sit with the chief guest. She crossed her shapely legs in an arabesque and spoke in a husky voice. No one guessed then that she was that formidable combination – a blue stocking with beauty.

'What a dame! Come, let's go and sit with her,' Dhanvir suggested.

'You can't join the chief guest and Her Excellency unless they invite you!' I admonished Dhanvir.

'Hey, you bureaucratic jerk, are you teaching me etiquette? I am going to join them! Gad, what a *chanes* to sit close to that *gudia!'*

Before I could formulate a fitting riposte Dhanvir moved swiftly in their direction. I refilled my glass and watched from a hearing distance.

Dhanvir of Bandit County had many commendable qualities that had helped him to garner coveted posts and amass an impressive but not-so-secret fortune. In a bygone age he would have been employed as an escalador by a warlord for scaling walls with the help of claws. After a few non-committal responses from Her Excellency, Dhanvir decided to be more expansive; he did not suffer from lack of self-confidence.

When the Zaretanian lady rose, Dhanvir sprang up at once, and began following the ambassador's lady to the peach satin and white lace drawing room where she went to fetch a cigarillo. She turned sharply as a grinning Dhanvir entered.

'Yes?' the lady asked tonelessly as she ignited a cigarillo with a silver lighter.

'I have come,' he said.

'So I see,' she replied, in an astringent manner that would have made other men shrivel. Dhanvir, you must remember, was made of less porous material.

'I have been waiting to meet you - alone - ever since I met you at another party,' he said heavily.

The lady frowned and spoke tersely, 'I do not remember meeting you.'

The descendant of bandits laughed. 'You must be meeting many guys, huh?'

The ambassador's lady emitted tiny rings of smoke from glossy lips. A strange smile lit her grey eyes. 'Oh yes,' she murmured.

A heavily breathing Dhanvir came closer and asked, 'When can we meet alone?'

The lady's grey eyes narrowed. 'Why not tonight?' she asked.

'Tonight?' Dhanvir repeated, voice quivering with excitement.

The lady consulted her diamond-studded Rolex chronometer. 'Come,' she said. 'I will show you the little room where we can have our rendezvous. But first you must take a shower and get into a comfortable robe while I go and change into a … negligee.'

Dhanvir chuckled with glee. 'Just like that, huh? I can see you have practice.' He chucked her under the chin.

The lady fought off a wave of nausea as the odour of garlic and asafetida emanated from him.

'Just like that,' she managed to echo. 'Now hurry up and have a shower.'

The ambassador's wife led him up the carpeted stairs to a well-appointed little room where she wrote her diary after diplomatic revels ended. A well-equipped bathroom was attached to it. 'Voilà! You can freshen yourself here. I shall return soon,' she said and drifted out, after giving Dhanvir an alluring smile.

Flinging off his clothes, Dhanvir entered the bathroom. Chortling with the triumph of a Don Juan, he told the mirror, 'I think the bimbo likes me.'

The ambassador's wife waited near the door for sounds of the shower to start. Accompanying the sound of water was the sound of Dhanvir bawling the film song '*Piyar milaneke jana*' – my beloved I must meet. Moving swiftly she locked the bathroom door, switched off the lights and fan of the bathroom whose controls were outside. As Dhanvir's serenade climaxed into howls of terror, the lady shrugged and, closing the doors of her little study, went downstairs to resume her diplomatic and patriotic duties for liberation day.

Shut in a humid and dark bathroom for hours, Dhanvir of Bandit County passed out in the bathtub. When he regained consciousness after midnight, the party was truly over. Retainers heard the noise and came up to see what had happened. Dhanvir was liberated from the embassy bathroom the day after Zaretanian Liberation Day. The ambassador apologized profusely for the enforced incarceration of an honoured guest in the bathroom while his consort ascribed the mishap to a faulty locking system.

A few days after this incident, Dhanvir was commanded to disappear for a while not because of this faux pax but because his seniors felt that he had diminished the honour of his countrymen by this incident.

'And that, for a woman who looks like an uncooked macaroni!' they fumed.

After returning from temporary bucolic exile he never again attended *Vin de Honeurs* and liberation day receptions.

It is not as if all my colleagues made spectacles of themselves at embassy receptions and *Vin de Honeurs;* quite the contrary. These events usually offer splendid opportunities for cross-fertilization of cultures.

Having described these personages, I must narrate an unforgettable liberation day. By this I also intend to absolve myself of any charges of criticism of my compatriots. Grand and futile gestures need not be the monopoly of any one nation as I shall shortly narrate.

I came to know a young diplomat from Lusitania, Enriques de Pombeiro, descendant of a duke who four centuries ago had been viceroy in Gomantak on India's west coast. Though Gomantak had been liberated from lazy Lusitanian oppression by our republican army some decades back, unpatriotic Indians continued to flock there to eat sea food and drink Matteo Rose. Since they were already tanned, they did not care much for sunbathing on the picturesque beaches of Gomantak.

Enriques's family fortune had declined over the centuries; he had inherited a ramshackle castle near Lisbon and the disused title of Marquis. But Enriques was proud of his legacy of family glories. Sadly, it was the reminder of the past which shaped his personality and destiny.

Diplomatic life in Delhi brought him pain; Enriques's country had lost its eminence while America, Russia, Japan and China were now the major powers. I was in a ministry which proposed a joint venture for making *Vinho Rosso*, red wine. I met Enriques at his ambassador's party. It was obvious Enriques's interest in *Vinho Rosso* was negligible. He bored everyone by discoursing on his hero Luis de Camoens, who had been banished to India in the sixteenth century and who authored the epic *The Lusiads*.

He had immense nostalgia for the era when his country was a world power and when his family carried the imperial tradition. It became increasingly apparent to his colleagues that Enriques de Pombeiro was living in the past; issuing visas and distributing commercial brochures was distasteful.

So when the embassy set up a commercial office in Gomantak, former Lusitanian colony, the ambassador sent Enriques there in the hope that he would blossom in the atmosphere of Lusitanian heritage. While processing the collaborative wine project, Enriques also visited palaces and churches built by his ancestors. When he saw the portrait of his ancestor – Duke Affonso de Pombeiro y Castenheda, viceroy of Gomantak – hung from the wall of the town's museum, pride swelled in the young aristocrat. 'Next time,' he vowed, 'at national day parties I will not allow diplomats from upstart nations to patronize me! I will tell them about my ancestor who is still revered in a city of India!'

He was pleasantly surprised to find that the Gomantak elite did not resent Lusitanian rule. Rather, they remembered it with nostalgia, especially after the Marquis de Pombeiro (Enriques's ancestor), prime minister of Lusitania, curtailed the power of the Jesuits, and abolished the Inquisition. Some schizophrenic locals who cherished their Lusitanian heritage also claimed to be of blue Brahmin blood. A local heritage activist encouraged him to participate in events to commemorate the day that another ancestor had landed in the city to conquer Gomantak.

A historical seminar was organized. The theme was renaissance of Lusitanian architecture, art and a museum that would commemorate Lusitanian victories in India. How gratifying that the Gomantaks wanted to honour the legacy of their Lusitanian captivity!

This is how he would snub diplomats from Moscow, Washington, Beijing and Tokyo. Enriques mused, 'Surely this will be the most substantial diplomatic victory since our last colonial war two centuries ago.' Enriques went ahead with the plans, encouraged by a swelling crowd of local *fidalgo*s.

Enriques did not inform his ambassador; the idea was to impress His Excellency with an event that would rekindle national pride in his native land. 'What an honour it will be for my family, my fiancée and for my country!' Enriques exulted.

These sentiments reached a feverish pitch on the day preceding Lusitanian Liberation Day. Enriques recalled how his distant ancestor had taken the salute as governor of this beautiful oriental colony. Alas! Those days had faded into the penumbra of history. But now, he, Enriques de Pombeiro, of the house of Castenheda, would make one grand gesture.

Enriques took his stand as had his forefathers on diverse battlefields around the world. The small consular-commercial office was filled with his friends who goaded and supported him. Celebratory champagne was drunk and toasts made to the glory of Lusitania. Enriques went out into the warm starlit night and saw his national flag waving in the breeze. This flag, he mused sadly, which had flown over distant lands from Brazil to Macao, was now enclosed within a small consulate. The pathos of it all enraged him.

Young Enriques went to the flag post and brought down the flag. Folding the flag, he leapt into his waiting car and instructed the chauffeur to drive to the town's central square. Numerous cars filled with cheering Gomantaks followed. They drove swiftly through silent streets until they came to the main square. The podium where our republic's flag flew during the day was empty now. It was here that native activists had been shot decades ago by the Lusitanian gendermarie during the anti-colonial riots.

Flag in hand, Enriques alighted from his car and stood for a moment before the flagpole. His diplomatic training struggled futilely against his national and dynastic pride. He hoisted the Lusitanian flag in the main square of Gomantak. As it fluttered in the breeze, Enriques stood stiffly to attention and saluted, brimming over with pride and joy. The glory of his country and family was revived in that grand gesture.

In a previous age, Marquis Enriques de Pombeiro y Castenheda, would have received the Order of the Golden Fleece from his sovereign. In this age of petty nationalism he was humiliated. The local newspapers printed accounts of this outrageous neo-imperialism. News of this unpardonable conduct travelled to Delhi faster than the speed of light.

The Lusitanian ambassador was summoned to the ministry of foreign affairs and asked to explain such insolence. This sagacious ambassador, who had tried to erase antagonism between Lusitania and India, pleaded that Enriques, like the Lusitanian poet Camoens, had been so hurt by his betrothed that he had lost his head and had drowned his sorrow with Matteo Rose. Unfortunately the Indian diplomat at the Lusitanian desk had no idea who was Camoens, so the analogy left him cold. 'Ask for his abject apology!' the diplomat commanded. The desolate ambassador summoned Enriques to Delhi and asked him to plead temporary insanity from a broken heart, as murderers claim immunity by pleading insanity.

Enriques was indignant. 'But I am not suffering from a broken heart! My beloved fiancée is coming to India shortly. We are to be married in the little chapel adjoining Bom Jesú that my ancestor commissioned! And most certainly I am not insane!' With smouldering eyes he glared at the ambassador. 'I did what I did for the glory of my country! I thought you would support me!'

The ambassador sighed and shook his grey head. 'If you plead insanity and a broken heart, I can retrieve the situation. Otherwise, you will be declared persona non grata by the Indian government.'

'So be it! My ancestors have suffered much more for their land!' Enriques replied grimly.

Enriques de Pombeiro y Castenheda was transferred by the embarassed Lusitanian government to Sarajevo. They could not risk jeopardizing the *Vinho Rosso* project for this unrepentant reincarnation of Luis de Camoens. Posting him to Sarajevo, they felt, would placate outraged Indian sentiments.

Further, the Lusitanian government knew that amidst the gunfire and bomb blasts of Sarajevo even Enriques would not be tempted to make grand gestures on liberation day.

Culchar-Vulchar

India's vast and varied culture has nourished her soul over millennia of pain and degradation. Even when invaders trampled over fertile valleys, villages and towns, they could not extinguish the musician's flute, the poet's voice, the sculptor's hand and the painter's eye. These lived on to keep the feeble flame glowing amidst defeat and destruction. Tucked away in remote villages or forgotten in self-imposed obscurity the descendants of these resilient artists continue to enrich the inner life of the land, because for them creativity runs parallel to existence itself. They neither seek nor receive reward or recognition. The recognition that is their due is enjoyed instead by the glitterati-chatterati who purloin the artists' work for the greater glory for themselves.

One such fraudulent custodian of heritage was an officer whom I shall call Tsarevich because he never attained the status of Tsardom despite his protean talents. Tsarevich was a habitué of many cultural clubs as his godfather headed the ministry of artistic pretensions. He could invariably be found at seminars and workshops in foreign capitals where he engaged in verbal aerobics with the cultural chatterati and where he could discourse on his specialized topic – himself.

Cultural counsellors of various embassies pampered him because they needed his approval for cultural exchange programmes. In the evenings Tsarevich visited embassy national day parties where, between swilling Glenfiddich and Napoleon brandy, he propounded his theories of art and literature using favoured clichés. The foreign diplomats pretended to listen with rapt attention. The diplomat Tsarevich pursued most vigorously was the Swedish Lief Ericsson, whose grand-uncle had once served in the Nobel Committee. Tsarevich believed that Counsellor Ericsson could recommend him for the Nobel Prize.

In the wake of Tsarevich came his deputy secretary who played Sancho Panza to Tsarevich's Don Quixote. He was a puny fellow with a large head studded by a pair of eyes that looked in two different directions like the god Janus. Apparently this diverse vision gave him the aptitude to monitor happenings in both the home and foreign ministries. Before his deputation to the ministry of artistic pretensions, Janus had distinguished himself looking after military stores and location of latrines for non-commissioned officers in the Cantonment Service. In these onerous tasks he had honed his skills in mendacity and intrigue. From the task of locating latrines, he now took charge of cultural exchange that took him to the glittering capitals of the world.

Foreign diplomats who had been un-intimidated by assignments in Kabul, Saigon, Mogadishu and Sarajevo were so unnerved by Tsarevich and Janus that they agreed to their terms for cultural exchange programmes. The duo became a terror to the cultural counsellors of embassies. Outer Mongolia first felt the onslaught of our two cultural emissaries. Its ambassador Ogden Bayor requested Indian archaeological assistance for restoring the Bogda Khan

Palace at Ulan Bator. Janus was intent on this because he, a vegetarian diabetic, had heard that raw reindeer meat could cure his malady. A proud descendant of Gengis Khan, Ogden Bayor asked his government for transfer to the frozen tundra of Verkhoyansk rather than deal with a former locator of latrines.

After Mongolia, came Sweden's turn to entertain Tsarevich who felt that a visit to Stockholm was necessary for furthering his career. Cutural Counsellor Lief Ericsson of Viking lineage, quailed at his advent but arranged a poetry recital for Tsarevich at a Stockholm theatre. There, Tsarevich stood on the stage of the brightly lit hall, and recited his poems. A photographer took pictures of Tsarevich but not of the empty auditorium.

Back in India, the media reported his poetry recital as 'a dress rehearsal in Stockholm of great things to come'.

When Tsarevich's patron, the Hereditary Thief of Turhat, fell out with the prime minister, Tsarevich arranged collaborations with the new secretary in the ministry of artistic pretensions whom we named Tombstone because when he smiled his tombstone-like teeth flashed brightly. Tombstone reinforced my belief in astrology because nothing but the configuration of planets could explain his success. Tombstone bloomed as secretary in the ministry of artistic pretensions. Together with Tsarevich they hatched plots for artistic recognition. They appointed people to selection committees who in turn recommended the duo for literary prizes.

Subhash and I, Raman, attended the dual prize-giving ceremony at Delhi's Kamani Theatre. Distinguished literary figures sat stony-faced through the proceedings but Subhash and I laughed all through.

Freedom from Hunger

Rajiv's dawn was luminous for two years.

Men of talent and merit received opportunities. New frontiers of hope opened before the nation. But no new age begins abruptly and no old age dies without leaving behind the debris of the past. One event leads to another forming the tapestry of a nation's destiny.

The euphoric dawn was darkened by clouds. News of an arms deal was whispered in the corridors of power. The whispers then formed a deafening roar, drowning the defences put forward by the prime minister and his team. A compatriot of his foreign wife was implicated and questions arose about the honesty of Caesar's wife. The astute older cousin who understood the strategy of power had been dismissed at the behest of the prime minister's wife. An honest comrade had resigned from the cabinet ostensibly due to the arms scandal. Fortunately, Rajiv had an excellent administrative adviser in the cabinet secretary who guided him in governance.

He began with good intentions but the Furies were against him. The Bhopal gas catastrophe darkened his reign. There was criticism that the offending company Union Carbide literally got away with mass murder without paying even a modicum of compensation for the maimed and relatives of the dead. Once more there were whispers that though Union Carbide wanted to pay a larger sum as compensation for the dead and the mutilated, the rulers declined the amount. Why did they show clemency to Union Carbide?

On the heels of this calamity came what was called the great drought of the century. By mid-August of 1987, it was reported by *The Times of India* that,

The Indian farmer is in the grip of a drought of exceptional severity. So far the field reports do not appear encouraging – farmers with access to tubewell irrigation are reportedly unable to cope with the drought…Any forecast of the output this year would have to be tentative.

Discussions on the economic consequences of the current drought have emphasized the colossal damage to khariff (winter) crops, loss of agricultural incomes, fall in the water table, and consequent shrinkage of even ground water supplies for drinking and irrigation purposes in the affected regions, power shortages due to decline in the generation of power at hydel plants, deceleration of industrial growth rate and a steep drop in the overall growth rate of the economy to around 1.5 % from the normal 5 % achieved over the past seven years. Estimates about shortfall in agriculture vary but about the magnitude of the damage to the economy caused by the drought, there is hardly any difference of opinion.

However the article went on to say:

Amidst all this pervading gloom there is one important bright spot that needs to be highlighted. That is the current food situation, which if not exactly comfortable, is reassuring. Even after meeting the demands of the public distribution system we should be left with a reserve stock of 12 to 13 million tons at the end of the current agricultural year, that is June 1988. This is well above the prescribed 10 million tons of food for reserved stocks to be maintained for the eventuality of food security.

The prospects of adequate food production were bleak. A poor monsoon for the fourth successive year resulted in a sharp decline in agricultural production. Prime Minister Rajiv Gandhi conferred with the Union food secretary and the managing director of the Food Corporation of India (FCI). The latter informed the anxious prime minister and cabinet secretary that soon after taking charge at FCI he had organized procurement of huge quantities of foodgrains from August 1986 onwards. Resultantly, there was an impressive buffer stock of rice and wheat. He assured the prime minister that foodgrains would reach every person in the country, and that there would be no starvation deaths.

It was a promise this officer kept.

All aspects of food distribution, transport, storage and preservation were monitored. Special trains were sequestered to transport foodgrains direct from procurement areas to consumer areas and from surplus areas to deficit areas in anticipation of shortages and hunger. As anticipated, there was a huge spurt in demand for foodgrains, especially from the areas where crops had failed. Buffer stocks built up in the previous year now were pumped into the vast network of the public distribution system of the country.

Anticipating apocalypse, commission agents of the grain dealers of Chicago, Bangkok and Sydney descended on the FCI chief. Under the threat of an all-country famine, the foreign grain dealers expected the Indian officials to panic and buy substandard grain at fancy prices. The gleam in their eyes died when they discovered that there was a substantial buffer stock that could be moved fast. They left disappointed.

The difference between 1943, the year of the devastating famine, and 1987 was that buffer stocks had been built up and were moved in time. Experts said that if this had not been done starvation deaths would have been ten times the number of 1943. India had developed this capacity because of large-scale procurement in the surplus states of Punjab, Haryana and Andhra who are strong believers in canal irrigation and agricultural credit that made the Green Revolution.

The Economic Survey of the Government of India commended the achievement of the government, the Food Corporation of India and its chief. It said, '*This is how food security was created in the great drought of the century by the far-sight and dedication of one civil servant.*'

A decade later a new age had been ushered in by the protagonists of Nefaralization. Such is the strength of these movements that even when the heralds of Nefaralization had passed into eternity their heirs continued the good work. The power of globalization could not be resisted. Food shortage brought in the grain merchants who had been kept at safe distance a decade ago. There were other foreign merchants as well – for sugar at double the local market price, for fertilizers that never landed on Indian shores but which were dearly bought at the expense of the poor taxpayer.

I, Raman, met the civil servant who had performed magnificently during the great drought. Though he had retired from the Indian Administrative Service, he urged the Nefaralizers to build up buffer stocks for providing food security. The Nefaralizers said that the stocks were a liability. The precious foodgrains were allowed to rot by railway stations and on roadsides. So fetid was their fragrance that only rats suffering from malnutrition made forays into the disintegrating gunny bags that had contained them for transferring to other parts of India.

Newspaper articles, denunciations from former bureaucrats who had created food security, and angry questions in parliament left the new rulers unmoved. They retorted: 'It is disgraceful that such huge buffer stocks have been created! Were there no plans on this, no systematic thinking? Did the FCI just go on procuring in this irresponsible manner? Where was the need when there is so much food available in the open market?'

The truth is that *there was a shortage of foodgrains* in the open market due to meagre harvests. But the FCI was told not to distribute 'old foodgrains'. Hunger raised its terrifying head in India.

Learning about the grim details, the Food and Agriculural Organization observed:

> *There is no other country where a large percent of the population suffer from chronic hunger and malnutrition. The under-nourished condition of their women has wider implications; their children are born under-weight; their foetal under-nourishment manifests itself into poor physical and cognitive ability. They grow into adults with impaired abilities that impede their economic progress and sets off a spiral of hunger and deprivation.*

Some of our new-age civil servants derided the established theory that the remedy for malnutrition and hunger is creation of food security. The twentieth century has seen very often how political upheavals in less-developed nations have led to famines because the public distribution system has broken down. The grim spectre of hunger often attends genocides and ethnic cleansings. The public distribution system was the principal shock absorber against food scarcity. Buffer stocks were an indispensable ingredient for food security.

During a brief stint in the finance ministry, Subhash had friction with the fervent Nefaralizer economist Mohit Wallia who spent millions of rupees on foreign tours to discuss economic reforms. He insisted that twenty-five rupees per day was enough for one Indian family. Since he never drank milk (because he preferred champagne) he did not know that twenty-five rupees was the price for a litre of milk. He declared that poor people must not be given subsidized food because this encourages indolence and impedes initiative of the poor. This votary of laissez-faire said support price for foodgrains to farmers was an anachronism. Farmers must accept the vagaries of weather and capricious monsoons. Resilience makes them tough and the fittest survive. Many misfortunes have befallen our benighted land but the Almighty saved us from having Mohit as our finance minister. Though he was a protagonist of reforms, there was something about him that reminded us of the *Ancien Régime* of eighteenth-century France.

The new-age economists advocated reduction of investment in the agricultural sector. To make farmers self-reliant, subsidized seeds, fertilizers, agricultural implements and rural credit to farmers were discontinued. Farmers borrowed heavily to obtain these. Without the rural support system farmers felt helpless. When food production declined, food prices soared high. Middlemen made a killing by hoarding and speculation. Those living below the poverty line grappled with the spectre of hunger. Farmers waited in vain for the FCI trucks to trundle into their villages to procure their grains. In despair they sold their foodgrain stocks for a song to middlemen; even the prosperous farmers were impoverished. The marginal farmers vanished. They could not repay the loans they had taken to tide them over disaster. The Nefaralizing policymakers declared that agricultural loans must be repaid, no matter what the cost. They fervently believed that the implementation of Malthusian theory – that over-population and poverty would eventually wipe out the poor – was the solution for India.

Simultaneously, and in their effort to augment the industrial infrastructure, Nefaralizers hastily waived off astronomical debts of industrial and aviation tycoons like Vijay Mallya. Pilots who flew his airline planes went without salaries for months. Some of them committed suicide. Before these tycoons could be arrested their Nefaralizing friends assisted their escape to foreign shores where they survived with stored immense wealth.

Faced with the prospect of certain death the farmers made one last attempt to survive. They migrated to towns now swollen with migrant labour and nightmarish slums where the denizens drank water from sewers. In the wake of undeclared famine came disease, crime and exodus from the villages. Villages were abandoned.

In despair, thousands of farmers committed suicide all over India, especially where irrigation was absent. Thousands continue to do so now. Farmers whose fields and homes have been swept away in floods are asked to repay loans or be prepared to go to jail. Even Louis XVI and Marie Antoinette would have been horrified by this.

The civil servant who headed the Food Corporation of India during the worst drought of the twentieth century wrote:

> *As a subdivision officer in the sixties, I used to see the remains of once flourishing tribal villages which had been deserted in famines. Large numbers of tribals had died; others had moved to cities and swelled the ranks of the homeless. They lived and died without a roof over their heads or lived in the squalor of*

city slums. They never returned. Their villages were marked in the revenue survey maps as 'becharak' which means villages without light.

And Old Men Shall Dream Dreams

The annual curse of summer lay over Delhi.

Two years earlier Rajiv Gandhi had been defeated in general elections. But a year and half of incompetent governments made the country turn to Rajiv who had matured in the political wilderness and promised to usher in better times. He was on the comeback trail to power.

One May night news of Rajiv's assassination spread across the country. We were stunned; the country had yet to recover from the shock of his mother's brutal assassination. And now instead of the victory celebrations, people went to pay their respect to his splintered remains.

We hoped that out of the tragedy of Rajiv's assassination and chaos of an election, a person of competence and vision would emerge. In the past, amidst despair, men of strength and wisdom had always emerged to guide our hapless country. Or so our sacred Bhagavad Gita assured us.

Out of the tragedy emerged Nedonius, a figure of chalk and dust, to sit on the throne of India. Not quite what the Bhagavad Gita predicted.

Nedonius was the product of a brief dalliance between his father, a zamindar, and a peasant girl. Nedonius grew up slighted by legitimate siblings who took precedence over him. But when Nedonius's horoscope predicted dazzling destiny, the legitimate progeny were silenced. After completing formal education Nedonius went to the state capital to embark on a political career.

When the British Empire suffered the onslaught of Hitler's Wehrmacht the Indian Independence movement gathered momentum. Nedonius joined the freedom struggle. During a demonstration of the Quit India Movement, Nedonius and other bruised freedom fighters were pummelled by the police and thrust into prison for a few days.

Emerging from jail he met Vajonius, a well-dressed man who took him to a brothel and asked him if he would act as an informer in the service of the British. To persuade him of the benefits of such service, a buxom denizen of the doss house, Zenobia, spent the night with him. Between the intimacy of sheets Nedonius learned that Vajonius provided information to the police about freedom fighters for a tidy sum. Fearing that he had stepped into a snare, Nedonius stole out of the brothel. He was disgusted that an Indian worked for the British while he and his compatriots were squandering their youths for India's freedom.

Indian Independence opened numerous opportunities in politics; educated men were in demand for formulating and implementing new economic policies initiated by the central government. Now married with numerous progeny, Nedonius joined state politics and gained reputation as an intellectual idealist but not as a man of action. He read extensively on history and philosophy, and recorded his views on current events. When these were found after his passing, people realized that he was a deeply reflective man.

If only he had combined qualities of character with qualities of mind he would have been a true philosopher king and built a *Civitate Dei*!

Nedonius's career progressed; he impressed the imperious Indira Gandhi by his modesty and hard work. Seeing in him a reliable adherent with no great ambition she summoned him to the capital. His thrill was tempered by fear of working with Indira. The very qualities that swept men off their feet – Indira's intensity and energy, her alternate fire and ice – Nedonius found unnerving. But if Indira excelled in the art of dissimulation, Nedonius was grand master of deception. His subdued exterior, his air of compliance and propriety, appealed to Indira's residual priggishness. She trusted, relied, confided, and entrusted him with important ministries, certain of his inability to pose any challenge to her authority. But the ambience of power, glory and destruction, ensnared even the pedantic Nedonius.

In spring, when the parks and gardens are redolent with flowers, when peacocks call out hoarsely, dreams of men take on urgency. And so it did with Nedonius.

But he had a rival in the astute Probius, the political confidant Indira trusted more than anyone else. It was assumed that this favourite would succeed her. On that fateful autumn morning when Probius heard of Indira's assassination, he made a fatal mistake. For all his astuteness and ability, he could not curb his impulsiveness. He met Nedonius and proposed an alliance. If Nedonius supported Probius's bid for the throne, Nedonius would be made the deputy prime minister. The devious Nedonius nodded in assent. When Indira's son Rajiv returned to riot-torn Delhi that evening, Nedonius told him that Probius was planning to take over as prime minister.

'Indeed?' Rajiv asked coldly. The family had made sacrifices for India by giving two prime ministers to India. Dynastic democracy demanded that Rajiv should rule next.

'There are other men with more just claims,' Nedonius murmured timidly, hoping Rajiv would understand that he, Nedonius, was the man of the hour. This veiled allusion infuriated Rajiv further. He turned his back on Nedonius, and proceeded to the presidential palace to inform the president that *he,* Rajiv, was taking charge as prime minister. Surely the nation *owed him* that, in view of his family's sacrifices to the nation.

Another nation would have been astonished that this young man, untried and inexperienced in governance, should become their prime minister. But the compassionate people of India accepted him because he was the son of the woman who lay in state, draped in a sari drenched in blood. When Rajiv lost the next election three years later, there followed a chaotic year when governments were ushered in and ushered out with the levity of a comic opera. When another election was declared, we knew that Rajiv would return to power. Magazines that had maligned him now displayed his photos with headlines screaming 'On the comeback trail.'

Probius was not allowed to contest the elections because he was under the new buzz phrase – 'threat perception'. Nedonius, who had betrayed Probius, was also not allowed to contest the election. Rajiv rightly felt the old men had outlived their time. India needed a new vision and direction.

Dejected, but nursing astrological dreams that refused to die, Nedonius now sought Chinna-swamy who allegedly possessed supernatural powers through tantrik rites. Like Grigory Rasputin of Russia, Chinna-swamy had long hair parted at the centre, wore a necklace of basil beads, *rudraksha,* around his fat neck. While Rasputin had wild, mesmeric eyes, Chinna's porcine eyes were watchful. Rasputin controlled the tsarina through his powers of healing her ailing son. Chinna-swamy controlled political aspirations with astrology and intrigues.

When Nedonius came to the tantrik's mansion one stifling hot night, the caretaker prime minister was also present, to seek reassurance about *his* future. The caretaker prime minister had been the tantrik's benefactor, and had enabled Chinna-swamy to amass wealth, through international connections; bankers, espionage agents, arms manufacturers. It was in the tantrik's interest that the caretaker prime minister should continue.

The tantrik was irritated by the sight of Nedonius. He was not interested in people whose sun had set. But Nedonius had helped him in the past with armament dealers and defence contracts, so he could not deny Nedonius the usual courtesies.

Nedonius sighed. 'I came to ask for your help. Is there hope for me?'

Regarding the old man with impatience the tantrik mused: Why did politicians never accept reality? Why must they always be reassured about their future? And then he laughed inwardly. Isn't that why they all come to me, to analyze the planets and foresee the future? And I go on reassuring them with lies!

'Have you brought your *janma-kundali*?' the tantrik asked brusquely. He wanted to quickly dispose off the tiresome old man so that he could concentrate on the caretaker prime minister's fate. From the folds of his shawl Nedonius drew out the silk scroll containing his natal horoscope.

Silly old fool, the tantrik scoffed inwardly. As if I can change the future!

'Great things were predicted by our family astrologer,' Nedonius murmured miserably.

Again irritated, the tantrik thought: Never satisfied, always wanting more. Aloud he said, 'Great things *have* happened, haven't they? You *have been* a Union cabinet minister for many years. Did you even dream of such a fate?'

Nedonius bowed his head in abject dejection. So this is the end of the road, he thought. Even astrologers don't want to waste their time on me.

The tantrik shook the scroll off imaginary dust and unrolled it on a table. He was preparing to give the stock answers of his trade: 'Wait for a year, things will change, wear a yellow sapphire ring, eat yellow rice on Thursdays to please Jupiter, recite *navagraha-strota* [liturgy for nine planets] after bath, fast on Saturdays to placate Saturn.'

Instead the tantrik stiffened in surprise. He scrutinized the horoscope again, snatched up his writing pad, made some calculations, pulled out the astrological almanac. He could hardly breathe; his eyes stared at his client who sat silently, bald head bent, unaware of the dazzling conjunction of the planets hovering over him.

Slowly, gravely, the tantrik enunciated: 'If the timing of your horoscope is correct, then a great destiny awaits you.'

Nedonius stared at the tantrik with eyes ready to leap from their sockets.

'You will become very powerful within a month,' the tantrik whispered hoarsely.

Miserably, Nedonius shook his head. 'How can that be? Rajiv has denied me a ticket to contest the elections. I am returning to my home state.'

'No, you will *not be going home*. You will *remain here*, exalted and powerful!' the tantrik cried out, relieved that he had not sent Nedonius away unceremoniously as he had contemplated ten minutes earlier.

Weeping, Nedonius rose and reached for the tantrik's hand who grasped it. The old man began to dream once more.

His mind awhirl with plots, the tantrik watched him go. Then having taken a momentous decision he went to the room where the caretaker prime minister sat impatiently.

The tantrik quietly told the caretaker prime minister: 'You will remain in power if Rajiv can be removed from the scene. I know people who do not want Rajiv to become prime minister again. We know which agency paid Indira's Sikh bodyguard to kill her and then silenced him with a bullet. Just as the Warren Commission declared that a communist conspiracy killed John F. Kennedy, to conceal the vicious conspiracy of J. Edgar Hoover. A similar act of vendetta-assassination can be arranged.'

'It is madness,' the caretaker prime minister whispered.

'It is the cosmic will,' the tantrik replied.

So the plans were drawn up. Well-laid ones, not of mice, but of ruthless men. Rajiv, the would-be prime minister, was assassinated – by a girl from Sri Lanka whose family had allegedly suffered at the hands of the Indian Peace Keeping Force. Very plausible, but too obvious – like the murder of his mother at the hands of a Sikh bodyguard.

Nedonius was preparing to leave for his hometown when he received the summons to sit on the throne.

There was a tragic irony in all this; the young Rajiv, who was to rule, died, and the old man ready to depart, was exalted. Greatness was thrust on Nedonius through the conspiracy of malign stars.

I, Raman, a South Indian Brahmin (or Tam-Brahm as the North Indians call us), was secretly happy. It was the first time that a South Indian had been selected to be prime minister of India. The domination of North India had been broken.

Every good South Indian rejoiced. Nedonius's victory was our victory.

Nedonius was overwhelmed by the grandeur of his new position. As the prime minister's office staff led him to the sanctum sanctorum he circumambulated the premier's table where several outstanding people had once sat. Then he too sat down and glanced around him. With a smile of triumph and bitter glee, he thought: so, I am now exalted above all others. If only I had attained power when I was younger … but I shall make up for lost time!

Those who had once regarded Nedonius as a man of no consequence, unworthy of mention in their dispatches now rushed for interviews, calling him 'wise and mature', 'a versatile linguist', 'a philosopher king'. Once a grey figure made of chalk and dust, he felt power quicken his blood. He now dressed with style. His bleary eyes, witness to numerous unfinished symphonies, now brooded on symphonies which he thought would never be composed.

Even the family astrologer had never predicted this splendid finale!

The media people flocked to ask the new prime minister: 'Do you have a vision for India? Do you want to make changes? What are your plans to revitalize our economy, bring order and stability, make peace with our neighbours?'

Nedonius nodded, grave and unsmiling, impervious to flattery and enthusiasm, because he remembered how some of them ignored him when he had travelled with Rajiv to New York for attending sessions at the United Nations. Like a humble sage of yore, he said, 'Yes, I would like to make India strong and prosperous.' He paused. 'As all of you know, our nation has gone through tragedies, scandals and chaos. We will require time to set things right. Pray that I have time.'

Nights at the Round Table

The nation now expected order and peace, a respite from the chaos, violence and the near economic collapse that the previous 'cash and carry regime' had ushered in.

Nedonius was considered wise and mature, not given to drama and flamboyance. He had read widely and was once inspired by a treatise on ethical governance written fifteen hundred years ago by the Bishop of Hippo who came to be known as Saint Augustine. His composition *Civitate Dei* enunciated the principles of government that every ruler should obey. When Nedonius set off for Delhi he took the old leather-bound copy of *Civitate Dei*. 'May I rule in God's name,' he murmured, leafing through the brittle old pages for guidance.

He had acquired another guide. Vajonius, once pro-British, now a fiery rightist who believed in free love and adopted children. The wags in the capital wondered whether Vajonius had also 'adopted' India. The bachelor Vajonius and the widower Nedonius often spent evenings together discussing their unfulfilled dreams and unfulfilled desires.

We had come (once more) to the threshold of a new age. We had an erudite prime minister who visualized a new republic, resembling Plato's *Republic* or Augustine's *City of God*. Dynastic democracy was to be replaced by a new system of governance.

My batchmate Subhash Chowdhury remained posted in the Cabinet Secretariat, eluding the usual pogrom of officers with the change of regimes. Rajiv had found him hard-working; his successors were busy saving their thrones to bother about officers. I could not help envy him; he sat where

I would love to have been. He proceeded to tell me about events at the citadel.

'I ought not to talk like this but there is unease about the secretary to the prime minister, Anastas Virus.'

'The man from the ministry of tricky trade,' I murmured, anxious to sound cynical before Subhash's tiresome *naïveté*.

Anastas Virus of fleshy grandeur and courtly criminality was a retired bureaucrat who had risen high but could not become cabinet secretary. Like many retired bureaucrats he refused to retire – like a corpse that defies his funeral and stalks the land as a ghoul.

Subhash narrated what Mr Virus said at a meeting: 'There are too many impediments to change. The fatuous philosophy of Gandhi and his disciples have to be forgotten. Dreams and memories, ideals and principles are the debris of the past, smothering all initiative and innovation.'

Nedonius had listened in bewilderment as Anastas Virus expanded his ideas on the new order. Then he murmured apologetically, 'The founding fathers had wanted an ideal state. Should we not pursue that dream?'

His secretary had replied: 'While the world forges ahead, we insist on flaunting our virginal qualities before a scoffing world. Let us free ourselves from the shackles of the past! Let us liberalize our economics and politics so that we can innovate, experiment and create a new epoch! Let us shape our morals to our needs! We should no longer shelter in old dogmas and outdated values that have crippled our progress. Globalization is in the air; anybody's business is everybody's business.' Misquoting the great English poet John Donne, Virus said, 'The bells are tolling for the debris of the past.'

The new age began with a financial crisis caused by a banking scandal in which millions of rupees disappeared.

The subterranean looting was termed a 'system failure'. Since this liberalization was accompanied by some unavoidable nefarious transactions, Nedonius announced that the new policy would henceforth be called *Nefaralization,* the conjunction of nefarious and liberalization.

The sluggish Indian economy discarded inertia, productivity increased, and profits flowed into entrepreneurial pockets. Profit was no longer considered obscene as in the bad old days. In fact as the rich grew richer poverty came to be regarded as a dirty word. Indian entrepreneurs were seized by an aggressive capitalist mood. Freed from restrictions of imports, the industrial urban sector surged ahead. Landless labour from the impoverished rural sector began to pour into towns and cities. These men and women carried in their tattered bundles perishable parathas and imperishable dreams of a better future. Some of them went further. Sensing the new mood of discontent and resentment some of these dispossessed embarked on political careers to seize power in the name of the poor. While screaming for social justice and equality they became rich and influential and made their own equations with the powers that be.

Seeing the enormity of the problems before him Nedonius increasingly turned to political philosophers for guidance. In the early hours of the afternoon when peons doze in the corridors, humble officials pause to have meagre meals and less humble officials enjoy 'working lunches' at five-star hotels, Nedonius retreated to his sitting room to reflect on existence. To fortify his fragile ethical beliefs he began to read St. Augustine's *Civitate Dei* and Roman Emperor Marcus Aurelius's *Meditations.*

When Secretary Anastas Virus saw those books on the premier's desk, he decided that the time had come to take the ruler in hand. By now Anastas Virus's protean gifts had already cast a sulfuric haze over the citadel. He wanted to guide the premier to evolve a new code for the new realm. Towards this end Anastas constituted a panel called 'Guardians of Public Immorality'.

Premier Nedonius and Mr Virus's innovative foray began with the civil service. He emphasized novel criteria in selection of important civil servants. For all her radicalism, Indira chose to adhere to the staid old formula for selecting civil servants to important posts. Her son Rajiv proved no more original. While they flirted with dangerous ideas they wanted the security of the country in the hands of sober civil servants.

In that balmy Nefaralizing spring when the last of the sober chiefs was to retire, Nedonius sat with his Guardians of Public Immorality to deliberate on the choosing of the chief bureaucrat. To assist him were his two protégés: Niki Sting and his cousin Nishi Sting. Both were renowned for versatile gifts; larceny and perjury. Such men would serve the needs of establishing a new world order. Both had wide connections with the progressive underworld, armament dealers, and antique smugglers.

I, Raman, was serving in our republic's capital when the citadel was selecting its next chief bureaucrat. There was the usual excitement and speculation among government officers.

In earlier eras the chief was required to have experience in various fields in order to preside over the nation's civil service. He was also expected to be a man of honour, who offered objective advice. When the republic evolved over the years, these criteria were abandoned; new virtues were required of a chief bureaucrat.

As soon as news reached of the impending selection for the post of chief bureaucrat, the hopefuls poured into Anastas Virus's chambers for recommendation; scrutinizing the aspirants he realized that they would challenge his Grand Design. But laughing inwardly he mused: Let the prime minister choose whom he wants as his chief bureaucrat but I will be the unseen power behind the throne! With my acolytes we will control the bureaucrats and events!

So Nedonius the Nefaralizer ushered in a new age with these men. But it was not without regret. He had truly hoped to build a *Civitate Dei,* City of God.

One night, St. Augustine, author of *Civitate Dei,* left Elysium to awaken Nedonius who was having troubled sleep. Hearing sounds of the other world, Nedonius sat up and saw his once mentor standing by the windows, watching the construction of a new city.

'Why have you betrayed my teachings?' demanded St. Augustine.

'I believed in your precepts, saintly one, but times are changing. You will not understand our compulsions. We will call this ancient capital the City of God for fastidious souls while we build a satellite town to suit modern times. We will pay homage to you and Shri Rama who also believed in the ideal ruler. But we have to formulate new policies.'

'You are wrong, Nedonius,' Augustine replied sternly. 'Passage of time does not change the nature of human existence. People of that age had the same predicaments of power, the same hunger and lust, the same suffering, and the same aspirations. In fact people of your time are better off. They live longer on earth due to advanced medicine, they travel more safely. You have not seen invaders destroy cities, burn stately edifices, take hapless citizens as slaves.'

'We too have had our share of traitors,' Nedonius replied defensively.

'But the greatest traitors are those *within* the citadel, who mortgage their souls for Swiss bank accounts, who heap misery on the poor in the name of progress. You are doing just that, Nedonius.'

Nedonius felt a surge of anger against his former mentor. 'Did you not have monsters like Nero and Caligula, eh?'

'Of course, there were impious men who had not read my *City of God* whereas you pored over the pages of my book. You had vowed that if you gained supreme power in India you would follow my precepts.'

Humbled and ashamed, Nedonius bowed before St. Augustine. 'I cannot follow your precepts because times have changed. But I will honour you in our innermost hearts. Is that not enough tribute?'

St. Augustine shook his head. 'The pity of it all, Nedonius,' he said. 'Time was ripe for building the City of God. But all of you have destroyed that dream.'

No Need for a Foreign Trip, Really!

Indians have always been avid travellers. Though we had no Fa Hiens, Ibn Batutas, Marco Polos, Afnasy Nikitins and Manuccis, we pious Indians used to set out valiantly either for the Himalayan mountains or the banks of the river Ganga to offer oblations to the deities who reside in the life-giving rivers and the Himalayas whose melting snows in spring replenish our rivers and irrigate paddy and wheat fields. Pilgrims chant mantras at the icy Himalayan caves where Lord Shiva presides over the awesome forces of nature that He created.

When the British built railways for imperial purpose doors for travel also opened. Nineteenth-century innovative Bengalis were the first to set out on travels, especially during the autumn festival of Goddess Durga. I remember those travels of my boyhood when we visited sacred shrines, stayed in circuit houses, ate delicious chicken curries (forbidden at home), and sat on the sun-warmed veranda at night listening to local folklore. Now we go on pilgrimages to sacred foreign shores.

I, Raman, have already narrated the important trips which many of us are obliged to undertake for performing patriotic duties. These patriotic compulsions are more pronounced for officers serving in the republic's capital but similar duties are also imposed on those in the provinces. People have an impression that these official foreign trips are fun. They know nothing of procedures one endures on these official trips!

First comes the proposal of a scheduled meeting abroad. Then the task of preparing notes to propose the foreign trip. The note involves expertise on various aspects of the conference to be attended. When foreign exchange resources were scarce, robust justification for attending the conference was an absolute necessity because the proposal could encounter numerous objections from the finance ministry or sadistic accountants. Once objections are resolved, the prospective traveller must obtain clearances by various ministries. The foreign ministry ascertains that the prospective official traveller will not jeopardize the safety of the republic's diplomatic (sometimes delicate) relations with the country to be visited. The defence ministry ensures that classified matters such as nuclear programmes, armed neutrality and martial conflicts are not discussed at a foreign capital. Then the home ministry scrutinizes the antecedents of the official; is he likely to defect, or is he likely to compromise the sovereignty of his country by lapse in speech or conduct. Once these hurdles are cleared, there is the visit to the foreign embassies for obtaining visa.

We know foreigners are in awe of our republic - not because of our power and prosperity but the immense moral stature we occupy in the comity of nations. Since Western nations recognize our role in dismantling mighty empires, they are apprehensive when our officials apply for visas to their countries. The Far Eastern group eyes us with a subtler antagonism born out of a sense of cultural indebtedness. They fear that we can once again transform or influence their socio-cultural life.

There is a sense of exhilaration after visa clearance is obtained! Officials rush to the airlines office, preferably a foreign one, to purchase the tickets. And then a dash to the bank for that very precious commodity - foreign exchange! Dreamily we pack, make shopping lists and announce our proposed journey to anyone willing to listen! Our status is immediately enhanced by foreign tours.

Apart from those who undertake foreign travel to attend meetings and seminars abroad, there are those few but tiresome petty officials who conceive the extraordinary notion that they must receive medical treatment abroad either for themselves or their family members.

I remember an episode of this kind and the feathers it ruffled.

Paresh Nath was an under secretary who had risen in the Secretariat Service by hard work and fanatical devotion to duty. After lights of the ministry building were switched off, neon lights burned in Paresh's little cubicle. He would be clearing the accumulated files of the day with an earnestness that bordered on megalomania. Hard work often is an expression of intense ego-centricity. It is exhibited by men who believe that the sun cannot rise the next day unless they have done their work. So on condition that he carried the burden of drudgery, Paresh was allowed to indulge in the fantasy that on him rested the fate of his ministry. He was a perennial figure in that ministry, what T.S. Eliot called a fixed point in transient time.

Paresh's obsession in ministry matters was suddenly disrupted by the discovery that his wife, a quiet colourless woman, was afflicted with a dreaded carcinoma of bone marrow. These discoveries are usually associated with beautiful heroines who hurry towards extinction with tragic drama. Mrs Paresh Nath was far from being such a romantic figure. Sensible and self-effacing, thin and prematurely grey, one did not expect such a mundane person to acquire such a rare malady. Paresh reacted most unexpectedly. It was as if an immense tidal wave of guilt and remorse washed over him – for the years of neglect he had shown to the quiet, sparrow-like woman who cleaned and tidied his home, fed him and his children, trudged on foot lugging shopping bags to the third floor flat where they lived in the apartments reserved for middle echelons of government officials.

Forgetting a life of discipline and decorum, and innate reverence for hierarchy, the middle-aged, bespectacled Paresh did not even bother to button his shirt properly when he burst upon the exalted office of the chief bureaucrat that summer morning.

The chief bureaucrat, Birendra Blink (or Bunny as his anglicized friends called him), had just then laid aside his Mont Blanc pen after the arduous task of affixing his hieroglyphic signature to documents typed by his private secretary Chibber. Scrutinizing the documents before signing them had exhausted Bunny. He asked an orderly to fetch cold coffee from the kitchen of the adjoining presidential palace. In the meantime he waited for the premier's approval to go to London to search for additional space for the Indian High Commission. While waiting, Bunny drummed manicured fingers on the green baize of his table. As a pink phone began to ring, Bunny plucked it wearily from its cradle.

'Soufflé?' There was an anxious query at the other end from his wife who called him soufflé because his mind had the ethereal quality of that dessert.

'Yes, Honey?' Bunny replied. *Honey* was his abbreviation for the wife's name *Hriday-priya* or beloved of the heart.

'Has the permission come from the old fellow?' Honey asked.

'Not yet. As you can see, I am waiting in this intolerable heat.'

'Poor darling. When will the old crone let us know?' Honey believed that a premier who held up approval of tour programmes deserved these honorifics.

'Anyone's guess. He has the note in front of him.' Bunny was getting impatient for the cold coffee. He wondered if a few drops of Chivas Regal in the coffee would enhance his vigour.

'You did mention, I hope, that I have contacts with real estate people in London?' Honey asked again, anxiously. 'That should help.'

'Oh yes,' responded her world-weary spouse.

'Let's hope the old goat will do the needful,' Honey said, referring to the premier.

'Suppose he doesn't?' Bunny asked cautiously, afraid to upset his bright, adventurous wife who had so set her heart on going to England to see the tennis match at Wimbledon.

'Well,' Honey said slowly, 'you have purchased your ticket, haven't you?'

'Yes, it should be coming shortly. Why?'

'So, if the old goon doesn't accord sanction I can quietly slip away on your ticket.'

A profound stillness fell over the telephone lines. It is at times like this that Bunny realized how his long-spent passion for Honey was tested. 'Suppose so, provided no one comes to know,' he replied.

'Oh just say you returned the ticket – or that it got lost,' Honey advised. It was this nonchalance in Honey, this Bourbon-like disregard for consequences, which had drawn the sober Bunny to the hoyden Honey.

'The old crone should clear my note soon,' the chief bureaucrat told his consort. 'There's no reason why he should not. After all, he also has an interest in real estate in London.' Bunny smiled, and sipped the cold coffee brought in by the liveried bearer from the adjoining presidential palace.

'The real estate *bania* in London has offered to pay for my tickets if we let him into the transaction,' said Honey, smacked her lips to indicate a kiss and rang off.

Bunny's low I.Q. sometimes irritated Honey. All through their married life she had to do the plotting and scheming while purring and simpering before the world. To cover her tracks she had often announced that she was 'quite crazy'. No one believed her to be anything but astute but she kept up the theatricals as diversionary tactics.

Bunny sipped cold coffee, and stared out of the crystal windows into the president's gardens. He had sent all files away to his additional secretaries and joint secretaries in the event of having to depart at once. Yes, this was happiness; being chief bureaucrat, reveling in the chocolate peels making their way to his epiglottis and waiting for the premier to approve his costly, unnecessary trip abroad. He thought of the trip ahead; the luxurious first class in foreign airlines, the chilled champagne as the aircraft took off, then cold caviar with single malt to follow, and then a mellow Rhine wine with honey-basted duck. He would see risqué films that would stir him to pornographic musings which Honey would never divine. And then London! The shopping at Bond Street which the *bania*-bhais would provide, and front-row seat tickets at Wimbledon where apart from the tennis, the tart strawberries had a sensual tang.

Maybe he could even manage an 'intro' to the Duke and Duchess of Kent? Someone had observed that he, Birendra Blink, chief bureaucrat of the republic, bore a vague resemblance to the Duke. It was a compliment. Perhaps his granny had managed to have an affair with Georgie Five during the Durbar in 1911. What a splendid thought! That would make him, Birendra Blink, a sub-rosa second cousin to the Queen of England!

'You can't go in!'

'Oh yes I can!'

A startled Bunny stirred from his semi-supine position to behold his distraught secretary Chibber trying to block an unkempt man from entering the room.

'I say, Chibby, what's going on?' Bunny asked his private secretary, frightened by the threatened embroglio.

'Sir … this … under secretary has gone mad … it's the heat … he demands to meet you and explain his case!' Chibber was beside himself in anger.

Bunny blinked at the dishevelled intruder whose wild-eyed stare intimidated him. Brimming with fear and therefore forgetful of hierarchy he said, 'I say, *yaar*, this is too bad … I can't be disturbed like this!' Nervously, he placed his Mont Blanc pen in a desk drawer for fear that the mad under secretary might try to stab him with the costly pen.

Chibber nodded his head. 'I told him he can't see the chief bureaucrat … but … he …'

The intruder stood before the chief bureaucrat in an attitude of despair. Joining his palms together, under secretary Paresh Nath spoke with frenzied despair. 'Sir, I've failed at every level … hence forgive this intrusion.'

A bewildered Bunny murmured 'mmm'. Paresh was relieved that he was not being thrown out. He resumed with the same frenzy. 'My wife is suffering from bone marrow cancer … there is possibility of cure if I can send her abroad … but approval of government is necessary for reimbursement of expenses … I've located a hospital in London for bone marrow transplant … I don't have a house to sell and raise the amount … I have spent most of my Provident Fund for my wife's treatment. Please help me, Sir!' Paresh could not continue. He bit his lip to choke back unmanly tears.

Bunny was not an unkind man. Indeed, if you caught him before glasses of Moet champagne dulled his mind, he would respond like any normal mortal. But Paresh's intensity unnerved him. Emotions of any form were anathema to him. His partiality for Honey was because she was quite devoid of emotions. 'However, let me see what can be done,' he said politely, afraid of altercations with subordinates because they knew of their senior officers' peccadillos.

'Oh Sir!' Paresh cried, 'One word from you and the concerned ministry will approve the expenditure on foreign exchange!' His voice broke. 'My wife is still young, Sir, and our children are small … I can't contemplate our life if she … dies!'

Bunny was sympathetic but sceptical. Life goes on, he wanted to tell the over-wrought man, even if a wife dies. But would he, Bunny, get an extension as chief bureaucrat if Honey died? Who then would perform those acts of skullduggery with an air of innocence?

'I'll see what can be done.' He gave a wan smile of dismissal as he glanced at the cold coffee ruined in the heat.

Paresh stood in silence, unable now to check fugitive tears. 'Please, Sir, just one word from you …'

Bunny pressed the bell. Paresh had no choice but to leave as a liveried attendant came in response to the bell and said, '*Chalo, Sa'ab*.'

Next day - though it seemed a century - Premier Nedonius gave his approval for Birendra Blink's trip abroad. The premier feigned ignorance about what exalted secretaries of ministries did on these flights. Bunny was given full authority to 'look around' for suitable premises for a new trade office for our republic. The premier also asked him to locate a nice pied-à-terre for the premier where he could retire in the event of a coup d'état by Anastas Virus.

'God is great,' Bunny murmured, gazing at the approved note. 'He knew of my innermost desire to see the tennis match at Wimbledon … and eat strawberries. Oh how happy Honey will be!' Impulsively Chief Bureaucrat Bunny picked up the pink phone connected to his residence. He reported all developments to Honey so that she could orchestrate future strategy.

Honey was elated. Her ticket sponsored by the London-based businessman had also come. 'So we leave tomorrow. All packed?' Bunny began to feel alive again.

'Of course! My tailor has yet to bring my organza and chiffon salwar kameez. White and pink for Wimbledon, black and white for Ascot,' Honey purred dreamily. She sounded sensual and tender when describing clothes or jewellery. These made her ecstatic; their allure lasted longer than the intrusive caresses of powerful lovers who had to be pampered for gaining bureaucratic success for Bunny.

Next morning under secretary Paresh was waiting at the gates of 32 Prithviraj Road, the chief bureaucrat's residence, to present an aide memoir. The security staff told Bunny that a wild-eyed under secretary had come to see him and was waiting in the 'loggia'.

'What's this about?' Honey shouted irately.

'Some chappie wants permission to take his *bibi* abroad for bone marrow transplant,' Bunny said moodily. 'I said I'd help.'

'Oh, you poor dear! Don't they ever stop harassing you? Now, don't forget to tell Chibber to ring up the real estate people in London for seeing some flats,' Honey said, lowering her voice. '*Bania*-bhai will arrange for the money to reach the real estate guys.'

Bunny emitted a long sigh of relief. Honey beamed. 'I must get my hair set … or maybe I'll have it done in London at Raymond's. We must leave for the airport at eleven.' Honey pirouetted and disappeared into the cool interior of their luxurious official residence, humming a tune from a Hindi musical about love in London.

In that hour of happiness Bunny decided to be magnanimous. He asked his personal security officer to call the wild-eyed under secretary who came running, his shirt drenched in sweat.

'Ah … Paresh,' Bunny said pleasantly, almost kindly. 'I shall speak to the concerned secretary this morning about the foreign exchange ... but it may be difficult ... you see, we're awfully short on foreign exchange reserves ... after a huge import of fertilizers from abroad which was necessary for our farmers.' Bunny did not think it was necessary to enlighten Paresh of how not an ounce of the fertilizer had reached the country. 'You do understand?'

'Sir ...' Paresh cried hoarsely, 'it is not much ... five thousand dollars – a lakh and half rupees!'

Bunny suppressed the insurgent thought that his and Honey's air tickets and stay in London would cost seven times more. Why did this sweaty fellow have to darken his mood today of all days? He sighed deeply. 'Well, I'll try, Paresh. Truly I will. My private secretary will be in touch with you if permission comes.' Bunny paused; it was necessary for the sake of official discipline and decorum to administer a mild rebuke.

'But you know, Paresh, your wife's treatment could be done here as well. There's no need for a foreign trip – really.'

Honey and Bunny returned from London that summer to announce their satisfaction with the trip and how, sitting in the front rows of Wimbledon they ate curaçao-marinated strawberries.

As it happened, the chief bureaucrat forgot to speak to the concerned ministry to accord permission for Paresh's wife's cancer treatment abroad. I later heard that the under secretary's wife succumbed to bone marrow cancer.

Burying the Past

Our republic was once convulsed by an event that could happen only in India.

Seeds of this crisis were sown four centuries ago when Babur, an Uzbek prince from Ferghana, came swooping down to the Indo-Gangetic valley and established a very great empire. But as the conqueror-poet missed the mountains, streams and musk melons of Ferghana, he abandoned his Hindustan Empire and returned home. His memoirs do not mention destruction of sacred edifices. Iconoclastic followers of Babur built a mosque over a sacred temple.

It is astonishing that Ayodhyans did not resist this sacrilege. Many of us were tempted to ask: 'What were the bravehearts of Hindustan doing when this vandalism was perpetrated by a handful of marauders in a venerated shrine?' It took four centuries for Hindu descendants to agitate against demolition of a venerated shrine. Descendants of the marauders retaliated against the desecration of the mosque by fervent Hindus through a series of bomb blasts. A battle royal began.

Dr N. Sauhrab made his appearance soon after. He had taught archaeology at a European university and then came to Delhi. I, Raman, would not have known of his advent had it not been for my archaeologist father, Elangovan, who remained in contact with the Archaeological Survey of India where he assisted at antiquity meetings and interviews. Father came home one evening in a state of excitement.

'There is a new officer in the ASI,' he said. 'An impressive man but different from the usual archaeologists.'

'In what way, Appa?' I asked, feigning interest to please my father.

'In so many ways,' replied my sire, running his hand through his white hair. 'And yet there is something strangely familiar about him … his way of speaking, his gestures.'

'All you have to do is to ask, "Sir, have I met you before?"'

'*Sir* indeed!' Appa retorted. 'He is probably your age – about forty-five! Why should I humble myself before a stranger?' He paused before saying, 'The man is very competent. He knows his subject all right.'

Father's agitation stirred my curiosity. 'Why has he suddenly appeared at the ASI?'

Father essayed a sly smile. 'He applied for the post of director of Antiquity which fell vacant recently. He is an expert on what we call Indo-Saracenic architecture. It is a misnomer of course because medieval Islamic architecture embraces Persian, Ottoman, Moghul and Spanish-Moorish.' Elangovan paused. 'I think that our Union government requires a scapegoat for dealing with the Ram-temple-Babri-masjid imbroglio. This man with his scientific training and political cluelessness might be the answer to their prayers.'

'That is rather nasty, isn't it?' I asked in one of my moods of nobility. 'And what is his religion?'

'The newcomer, Dr N. Sauhrab, calls himself a Zoroastrian.'

I replied, 'If so he will hardly serve the purpose of the government.'

We brooded on the thought that while dealing with the temple-masjid dispute there might be spilling of innocent Zoroastrian blood.

Dr N. Sauhrab was more of a historian than an archaeologist. Father said that when Dr Sauhrab spoke of events it was like being at the ringside of these events. His knowledge was not limited to ancient Indian history. Dr N. Sauhrab had studied diverse periods of human endeavour and could leap from the Assyrians to the Aztecs without pause. He was a votary of the great historian Arnold Toynbee and viewed Indian history as a series of challenges and responses that wove the nation's tapestry.

Once father mused: 'When listening to Dr Sauhrab I hear echoes of the past – as if I have heard this kind of historical analysis before.'

At first his ASI colleagues found Dr N. Sauhrab refreshing. What was less endearing was his insatiable curiosity. His interest in excavations and their reports irked both the present director general and his worthy predecessors. Sauhrab had the effrontery, they noted, to visit the ancient sites 'to see things for myself'.

He tried to be discreet. But Mathura, Kalibangan, the *Ramayana* sites are not in remote areas; they are public places and visits of a senior officer of the Archaeological Survey of India or ASI cannot go unobserved. Sauhrab's enquiries about reports and location of the 'finds' from major excavations began to raise archaeological hackles. Who was this intrusive upstart to question the competence of venerable elders? Who was he to interpret Indus Valley culture?

Soon after taking charge as director of Antiquities, Dr Sauhrab and other archaeologists were summoned by the home minister of India. They were asked if there were any documents to prove that Babri masjid was built on the ruins of a temple. Sauhrab replied that excavation reports of the *Ramayana* sites would elucidate the birthplace of Shri Rama. The home minister of India ordered the excavation reports to be placed before him within a fortnight. To his astonishment, Dr Sauhrab discovered that the excavation reports of these sites had not been written. He reported the matter to the home secretary.

The home secretary thundered: 'Not available with the ASI! This is scandalous! Ask the archaeologists who excavated the sites to prepare them immediately.'

'That will take time, Sir. Composing excavation reports is a long-drawn process,' Sauhrab replied. 'But I shall see what we can do.'

When my father Elangovan finally invited Dr Sauhrab over for tea at our C-II graded government quarter in Ravindra Nagar, the newcomer gave his views on the present state of affairs.

'After Indian Independence, senior archaeologists had a splendid opportunity to address themselves to various historical enigmas. One of them was the Aryan Invasion Theory which had been propounded mainly by Max Mueller as an apologia – in order to divest indigenous Indians of their achievements in the Vedic age. It was expected the senior archaeologists would address themselves to the elucidation of these enigmas.'

My father knit his brows as if trying to remember something, then shook his head and said, 'Tread carefully, young man, for you tread on many egos.'

Sauhrab tried to analyze reasons for the failure of senior archaeologists to write excavation reports. Were they pressed for time? Had they forgotten to record details of their discoveries and could not later recall these? Did they not know how to marshal all these facts and commit them to paper? Perhaps they were field men, expert at the 'digs' but not much good at writing reports.

While visiting an Indus Valley site, Dr Sauhrab found out from an old mason that many antiquities had been removed from the site but no one knew where. After this revelation Sauhrab began visiting other important excavation sites.

After a week Sauhrab returned to tell my father: 'Very few archaeological specimens were found at Kalibangan. Decades of monsoon rain has made short work of trenches. Remains have been sucked into the slush of the trenches. An excavation report would have given us the chronology of Kalibangan's existence, the details of its material civilization; its ethnicity, its flora and fauna through dendo-chronology.' Sauhrab found that the excavation at Mathura suffered the same fate. It is a matter of speculation how a vast amount of Mathura sculpture of the Kushan era found their way to foreign museums.

My father often said in private (since public declarations invite reprisals), 'Had officers in charge of these major excavations written their reports, the country would have known much more about its past civilizations from Harappan, Vedantic and Kushan times to the present age.'

As an assistant to the venerable archaeologists my father had seen much of what had transpired. Since he had shown a disinclination to participate in archaeological frauds, his career had suffered.

After a few weeks Sauhrab returned with an air of excitement. 'I was able to trace some artefacts from an ancient site at a London museum. My archaeologist colleague in London thinks it is probably from Kalibangan.'

'What sort of artefacts?' my father asked, excited.

'Sophisticated sculptures … that have striking resemblance to those I have seen in Ur and Chaldea. It might just be possible that these two civilizations were linguistically and ethnically connected around third millennium BC. I might stumble across a bicodal script. Just think of that! It has always been my dream to follow in the footsteps of James Prinsep, who deciphered the Brahmi script.'

Sauhrab's enthusiasm was replaced by gravity as he said grimly: 'It seems there were reasons, after all, for not writing excavation reports. It was neither apathy nor lethargy, nor even loss of memory. It was a conspiracy of silence, to bury the past without revealing it, to remove physical reminders of civilizations without recording it so that the "finds" could find their way to foreign museums and art collectors. The failure to write excavation reports is more than a lapse in administrative procedure. It is an unforgiveable act of destruction of historical evidence.'

The reaction of the former director generals was exactly what my father had anticipated. They were furious. After all these years of selfless, unsung, un-rewarded labour in the cause of their country's heritage they had to defend themselves! They began a campaign to evict the intruder.

In the meantime both Hindu and Muslim fundamentalists took the temple-mosque dispute to the Supreme Court of India. When material from the area had been collected, classified and estampage of epigraphy taken by the directors of Antiquity and Epigraphy, Dr Sauhrab, the coordinator, wrote a detailed report to the attorney general about the findings. The attorney general had a difficult task – to resolve a potentially explosive situation and to defend government action without inciting further turmoil. He was very satisfied with Dr Sauhrab's report that was a masterpiece of obfuscation. There was no denial that there was a temple below the mosque but no conclusion about the timing of the event and the manner in which it took place. The attorney general's praise of Dr Sauhrab's competence and his demand for excavation reports agitated the Five Horsemen - the former director generals. They sharpened their knives to question Dr Sauhrab's creed, his honesty and impartiality.

A Sanskrit mantra says *veero bhagya vasundhara* – the brave shall inherit the world. But Fortune does not favour the brave – not in the short run anyway. Sauhrab's candour and his refusal to play anyone's game brought him trouble. His enquiries about excavation reports, his correspondence with foreign museums about Indian antiquities and their provenance, his refusal to use archaeology for political agendas and intrigues laid the grounds for his near destruction.

The Treasure Hunt

The five retired director generals secretly met the prime minister's joint secretary Nishi Sting who engaged in secret collection of antiquities. He readily agreed to oust Dr Sauhrab who was making trouble for him and his cousin Niki Sting over stolen antiquities.

'This Sauhrab fellow is in the pay of foreigners who want to subvert our history,' the old archaeologists told the PM's confidant. The Five Horsemen of the Apocalypse (as my father called the retired DGs) then approached the poetaster secretary of the ministry who eagerly offered help with a flash of tombstone teeth. Their final port of call was a trade union hooligan who was assigned the task of harassing Sauhrab's wife and son when they went on evening walks.

The homeland of the Sting cousins was once a hallowed region where the greatest son of India, Lord Gautam Buddha, was born twenty-six centuries ago. The Stings did not embellish the landscape then: their eminence began when a far-sighted Sting became a civil servant of the British Raj. Long before Indians realized the value of antiquities, the far-sighted (or F.S.) Sting saw its immense potential. When the Independence movement disrupted the British Raj, F.S. Sting took advantage of the troubled times. While inspecting heritage in his bailiwick F.S. Sting sent trusted minions to photograph sculptures, manuscripts and scrolls in various museums. The minions photographed some seventy-eight statues and figurines dating from the fifth century AD to the nineteenth.

When the horrific Partition convulsed the Indian subcontinent into violence and despair as Muslims and Hindus fled from their traditional homelands, Far-Sighted Sting took advantage of the chaos; he now sent those minions to the museums – this time not to photograph and catalogue but to wrench the antiquities from their pedestals and secretly transport them to his ancestral village. And there they remained for many decades, securely locked and wrapped in swaddling cloth while Far-Sighted Sting went to the capital to build a career in grand larceny.

In the meantime dedicated Indian archaeologists and scholars in the government passed a slew of legislations to safeguard physical heritage; archaeologists formulated detailed rules for legally sending artefacts abroad for exhibitions.

These legislations thwarted F.S. Sting's plans to send these sculptures abroad for surreptitious sales. And Time also tricked him; he was taken to the netherworld before the seventy-eight pieces of sculpture could be sold abroad.

Twenty years later when they were at the citadel of power, the Sting cousins saw the opportunity to export their precious loot. Dr Sauhrab was then 'in charge' director of Antiquities as the earlier director had retired. The Sting cousins had no doubts that the greenhorn Dr Sauhrab would oblige, especially if they dangled before him the carrot of permanent absorption in the ASI. They sent one Anish Kumar, a clumsy frontman, to request registration of these antiques with photographs of the antiques. Readily agreeing to help, Sauhrab asked the applicant to provide (as per ASI legislation) necessary information as a pre-requisite to registration; provenance of the objects. This was to ensure that the origins and sources of the objects were identified. Thereby no stolen objects could be registered.

Predictably, Anish was agitated. How could he provide provenance for stolen objects? He tried to breeze through by explaining to the naïve (so they thought) Sauhrab that these sculptures had accumulated in the family over a time and no one kept record of the acquisition.

'How does a family acquire sculptures in the fifth century AD?' Sauhrab asked feigning innocence.

'You know how it is, doctor saheb,' Anish purred. 'Some ancestor must have picked them up from fields while sowing seeds.'

Sauhrab scrutinized the photos through a magnifying glass. 'These are in good condition. They have been cared for and do not bear signs of being in fields.'

Smiling, Anish murmured, 'We treasure our valuables.'

Raising his eyes from the photographs Sauhrab said, 'I would like to see the originals.'

Anish broke into sweat. 'They are in our ancestral home in the Terai.'

'Fetch them.' Sauhrab's low voice became imperious.

Rivulets of sweat trickled from Anish's forehead to his chest. Sauhrab cocked his head to one side. A few drops of imperial blood spurred him to torment the oily Anish. 'It is possible that these are copies and not originals. In that case the sculptures do not require registration. For that I have to verify the objects.'

Anish almost wept from relief. 'Oh yes, doctor saheb! I shall arrange to bring them from my storehouse in Sundar Nagar tomorrow.'

Sauhrab frowned. Sundar Nagar – the area where antiquity dealers of Delhi transacted covert operations? But Anish had earlier mentioned that the sculptures were stored in the distant Terai mansion. To forestall Anish's panic, Sauhrab smiled benignly and nodded. 'Yes, do that. We can settle the matter without further investigations.'

Anish was too relieved to notice his faux pas and hurried away. Dr Sauhrab went to discuss the matter with Vishnu Rawat, the perennial mainstay of the Antiquity section of the ASI. Hearing about Anish's proposal, Rawat said, 'These people have sent feelers earlier for registration but never so strongly as now.' He frowned. 'I wonder why?'

'Perhaps they feel that I, a newcomer, may not know the rules.'

'They are not so foolish,' Rawat replied sombrely.

Wearing an oily smile Anish returned next day with a few sculptures 'for you to sample, Sir'.

With inscrutable expressions, Rawat and Sauhrab scrutinized the samples. 'We have to see the others to make a correct assessment of their age,' Sauhrab said. 'As I said before, if they are modern copies, the ASI has no role to play.'

Anish returned next day, not with more samples but with a black eye which had been gifted by one of the cousins for bumbling. 'Our patience is running out! Get the registration done! Otherwise your shop in Sundar Nagar will be closed,' Niki Sting had threatened. Then he pondered over a strategy. 'Tell this upstart Sauhrab that my cousin in the prime minister's office can get him absorbed in ASI as a director – if he cooperates. Tell him also that I am getting impatient with his inane queries.'

The cards were laid on the table. Anish conveyed Sting's ominous message to Dr N. Sauhrab. As I have mentioned, drops of imperial blood made Sauhrab react stubbornly. 'I want *all the photographs* of *all the sculptures*,' he enunciated icily. 'We must be certain that these are indeed your family possessions from many years and not …'

'Not what?' Anish asked menacingly.

Dr Sauhrab removed his spectacles and regarded Anish with narrowed eyes. 'We have to ensure that these priceless objects, as they appear to be, have not been purloined from museums over a period of time.'

Anish's head whirled in panic.

Sauhrab continued. 'I understand your reluctance to show us the originals. But the photographs reveal damaged feet of the statues. They appear to have been wrenched from pedestals. Only statues in museums and temples are kept on pedestals. And is it a mere coincidence that all the seventy-eight pieces of sculpture have their origin in the home state of the illustrious Sting families who have sent you as their frontman?'

He pushed the photographs and the file in Rawat's direction. 'Mr Rawat, we adhere to our stand. No details of provenance, no registration. I am not participating in grand larceny of Indian heritage.'

Anish rose, trembling in fear. The failure of his mission would invite punishment from the powerful Sting trio. This time round they would give him two black eyes and a broken nose-bridge. Yet the cousins seemed less dangerous than this arrogant archaeologist.

'You will suffer for this,' Anish muttered before leaving Sauhrab's office.

Sighing, Sauhrab replied, 'I dare say. Our Lord Zoroaster said we come to this world to suffer.'

The powerful cousins in the citadel decided to teach the upstart N. Sauhrab a lesson. Under their instructions, a note was initiated by Miki Sting, now a secretary in the ministry of artistic pretensions, proposing termination of Dr Sauhrab's deputation to the Archaeological Survey of India.

In these egalitarian days we deride 'class' but there is something to be said in favour of this indefinable factor called 'class'. It has nothing to do with birth because rich people can be obscene. It does not require high education because the educated are sometimes vulgar. *Class* is that quality of dignity and grace gifted by the stars and may be possessed by anyone. The Stings had acquired wealth and power, purloined treasures, obtained university degrees. But they had no *class.*

Miki Sting, secretary in the ministry of artistic pretensions, resented Sauhrab's effortless scholarship, his self-assurance and a quiet obduracy which only men and women of inflexible virtue possess. Miki was further pained when during departmental meetings, his falsetto contrasted with the deep timbre of Sauhrab's voice. Finally came the day when Secretary Miki Sting ordered Dr N. Sauhrab to 'process the file for registration of some sculptures'.

Sauhrab knew that his response to the direction would affect his career in the ASI. He pondered over the matter for a day or two. Being a permanent director in the Archaeological Survey of India was not to be trifled. Though archaeologists had made momentous discoveries, he knew from experience that the scaffolding of an eminent institution provides facilities and access to sites and information not readily available to scholars working on their own.

Sauhrab wondered if it was dedication to India's heritage that made him balk or whether it was a refusal to acquiesce before thieves in high places. He had heard from his archaeologist father of excavations and rich civilizational remains, of how they were classified and sent to museums. He had never seen purloined antiques in his father's home. So he sent a terse note to Secretary Miki Sting: 'Registration cannot be done unless details of provenance are provided. The origins of the antiquities must be revealed.'

Miki Sting ordered Sauhrab's residence telephone to be disconnected. His trusted personal assistant was transferred elsewhere. Files were not sent to him. Intimidated archaeological colleagues avoided him. Miki Sting raised queries of his tours and attempts were made to foist fictitious charges on him. All failed.

Finally it was not official harassment or humiliation (which multiplied with the days) that unnerved Sauhrab. It was the sight of his young son screaming that he would track down and kill the hooligans who had insulted his mother when she was walking in Lodi Gardens. Sauhrab calmed them both and said hooligans were like the many-headed hydra of Greek legends. 'You kill one and another grows.'

His wife murmured, 'We have to move – to safer sites.'

'There are no safe havens for those who defy evil,' Sauhrab replied sombrely.

Two weeks later Dr Sauhrab came to say goodbye to my father Elangovan. He announced that he had sent his wife and son to England where they would live with his foster parents while he took up an assignment at the Institute of Archaeology in London.

'Foster parents?' my father asked, distressed by the implication that Sauhrab had no parents. 'Have you no parents of your own?'

I looked up from the government file which was boring me to death. There was something strange about that moment as Sauhrab shrugged and smiled. 'My mother was widowed after my birth. She remarried and soon after was dying of tuberculosis. She handed me over to foster parents who loved and educated me.'

My father and I exchanged confused glances. 'Well, come back soon,' my father murmured. 'Don't run away from the battlefield.'

Sauhrab shook his head sadly. 'It is not for my sake that I am leaving this venerable organization.'

Distressed, my father Elangovan said, 'It no longer pays to ask questions. In our young days we were encouraged to doubt, question and debate. That has changed. Political freedom has not brought intellectual freedom.'

Sauhrab said, 'At the institute I will research my theory – that the Indus Valley Civilization was the material counterpart of the Vedic intellectual civilization.'

'You will have many opponents on that – in Europe and the secular theoreticians here,' father warned Sauhrab.

'I have no doubt about that. But don't you see how it could transform our understanding of Indian history? Is it possible for a great material culture such as we find in Mohenjo-daro and Harappa not to have an accompanying intellectual heritage? And could the splendid authors of the Vedas have been primitive men living in rude huts? There must have been one sophisticated unitary civilization spanning Southern Russia, Asia Minor, Iran, Afghanistan, India and Central Asia. Look at the linguistic similarities between old Avestan, Sanskrit, old Slavonic, Dari!'

I, the bureaucrat, listened intently to the scholar.

Father stared at Sauhrab with a rapt expression. 'Yes,' he said, 'it is entirely possible.' He paused. 'There was a British director general in ASI whose wife had a similar theory. She too had your obsession for finding a bicodal text to help unravel the mystery. Unfortunately that great director general returned to Mesopotamia after Independence.' Father sighed and shook his head. 'I used to write to him and then I became so immersed in my work and the life of a householder that I lost touch with that wonderful man.'

There was a strange stillness in the room. Late afternoon shadows danced around us. Sauhrab smiled and said, 'But that wonderful man remembers you.'

'You know Dr Julius Norton?' father cried out, happy and excited at once.

Sauhrab nodded. 'He is my natural father … my foster father as I call him.'

Speechless, father stared at Sauhrab while I, Raman, was bewildered. So I asked, 'But how can he, an Englishman, be your father?'

'As I told you, my mother Zoya's husband, the nawab, died soon after my birth. She next married a man who was a racing car driver. They lived in Monte Carlo as she had always wanted to. He ran through her fortune and left her to die of tuberculosis. Mother never informed Dr Norton that she had borne him a son. So like Tahmina, the Turani princess of the *Shah-nama*, she called me Sohrab, the son who did not know his father. The letter "N" for "Norton" was inserted as prefix, in South Indian style. I modified the name to Sauhrab when I came to India.'

Father and I listened in astonishment.

'Faced with death and fear that I, aged five, would be placed in an orphanage, Mama wrote to Dr Norton pleading with him to take care of me. Then my mother told me that my real father was Dr Julius Norton. My father came with Athena to Monte Carlo and took charge of me. I went to live with them and their two grown children in England.' Sauhrab paused and spoke in a slightly quavering voice, 'They are the only family I know. They gave me the only home I had – until I married.'

Father rose unsteadily to his feet and went to Sauhrab who also rose. Father gathered Sauhrab in a tight embrace and emitted sounds that were half sobs and half laughter.

'I knew it!' he exclaimed. 'From the moment I saw you I knew that there was something familiar about you! Oh Sohrab, my dear boy, I am so glad to have found you!' Trembling with excitement father wiped his tears and adjusted his spectacles. 'I am going to England with you! Yes, finally, I am going to make that long awaited, long postponed trip – to meet Dr Julius Norton, my guru and that wonderful lady, Athena madam! Will you take me? Will your parents welcome me?'

'With all their hearts,' Sauhrab replied, deeply moved.

'Together, we – Dr Norton, Athena madam, you and I – will work on your theory about the Vedic culture and Indus Valley Civilization! We will find an answer!'

The evening was rounded off with celebrations. My wife happily cooked an impromptu feast. Telephone calls were made to London; my father Elangovan and Julius Norton spoke to each other. When at last everyone settled down for the night – Sauhrab on the sofa – I heard my father and my wife Satyabhama chatting quietly in the adjoining balcony.

He said, 'I remember that evening long ago when Athena Norton went to her tent, leaving her husband alone with Zoya. Rupamati accompanied her, telling Athena it was not wise to leave them alone. Athena had said: "It is wise to let a turbulent stream run its course untrammelled until it forms a placid pool somewhere." Did Julius Norton's brief passion for Princess Zoya form a quiet pool?'

'Well,' said my pragmatic wife, 'Julius Norton returned to Athena, didn't he? They have grown old together while Zoya lies buried in a grave in Monte Carlo.'

'How do you think Athena felt when confronted with the five-year-old Sohrab?' father asked Satyabhama.

To our discomfiture Sauhrab rose from the sofa and joined them on the balcony. 'Athena was shaken at first but she recovered and was very kind to me. Strangely, my half-brother Justin and half-sister Elena had no interest in archaeology. Maybe they were weary of excavation sites and wanted settled existences. But I grew up soaking it all in. That was what drew me close to my father and Athena.' Sauhrab smiled. 'Blood is said to be thicker than water ... but water is purer and life giving.'

Dr Sauhrab returned to sleep on the drawing room sofa. Father and Satyabhama remained on the balcony. After a while I heard my father say: 'Satya, do not ever make that mistake of letting turbulent streams run their course in my son's case.'

Satyabhama replied with a laugh. 'Your son has been forewarned, Appa. If he is unfaithful I shall file a case for the return of my substantial dowry – something he can ill afford.'

I lay awake, engulfed by a strange sadness, that I would never experience romantic passion because I lacked the courage to pursue its demands.

Shwindler's List

When men became social beings they were honoured for their valour and service to their country. The origins of these honours are diverse.

In ancient India the title *Senapati* was given to the leader of soldiers or *sena.* Among ancient Iran-Sarmatian tribes engaged in warfare there were *Cataphracts* which described the role of arms and strategy of warfare. Ancient Romans gave the title of *Senatore* to members of the Senate which means 'assembly of elders' from the Latin word *senex* denoting 'old'.

Fall of the Roman Empire and the attending chaos necessitated formation of militias that defended fiefdoms and princely territories. The inspiration for military orders sprang from the Iranian cataphracts which Emperor Charlemagne came to know through the ambassadors he sent to West Asia. The cataphracts were precursors of medieval knight-chivalry.

The leaders and officers of European armies were offered titles and honours as inducement for serving the liege lord. Warriors mounted on horses and forming the cavalry were called knights. Paradoxically the word *knight* had a humble etymological origin. It came from the English *cniht* and the German *knecht* which meant servant. In time these mounted warriors or *chevaliers* (from the French word *cheval* or horse) claimed titles from feudal lords for their heroism and fidelity. To discipline wayward warriors a new code of conduct was evolved - the chivalric code that enjoined knights 'to protect the weak, defenseless and helpless, and fight for the general welfare of all'. Out of this grew the ideals of knighthood and chivalry.

When the concept of chivalry began to wane in the intellectual tumult of the Renaissance, litterateurs such as

Castiglione, Malory and Cervantes idealized knights-errant through their writings. To reward knights for their services, numerous orders and titles were established. These were Knights Hospitallier, Knight Templars, Teutonic Knights, the Order of Aviz, Order of Santiago and Alcantara, Order of St. George, Order of the Garter. More modern orders were Légion d'Honneur of France, Order of the White Eagle of Poland and Order of the Rising Sun of Japan. The Soviet Union established numerous military and social orders to reward courage, sacrifice, dedication, intellectual and artistic achievements, and extraordinary deeds. Many of these have been continued by the Russian Federation.

In the aftermath of Independence, the Republic of India established a gradation of honours to reward the noble, the brave and the brilliant. These ranged from titles given to defence personnel to civilians. Many of the defence honours are richly deserved even if they are tragically posthumous. Civilian honours ... well, let me tell you about a few of which, I, Raman, have come to know.

Our country established the Tuberose Awards for contribution to the nation; these were given to deserving men and women in the early years after Independence. Standards began to decline when politicians wanted to reward those who served *them* loyally rather than the country. Knowing that loyalty declined with time and usage, Nedonius the Nefaralizer gave his adherents privileges but never honours; conferring titles and honours on the unworthy would strain the credibility of the public. His principal secretary Anastas Virus once suggested that he should be given a high Tuberose Award whose floral fragrance would remove the malodour of his activities.

Nedonius was an erudite man. He had read how Roman Emperor Commodus rode into the sacred precincts of the

Roman Senate. When the enraged senators protested, the defiant emperor immediately conferred the status of senator to his horse. The powerful senators were outraged but Roman citizens laughed. Nedonius related this episode to Anastas with a sly smile. Anastas made no more suggestions about honours.

Nedonius's successor Gadonius had no such qualms. He bequeathed awards to anyone who helped him. There was one particular favourite, Keyse Freddy, a numbskull engineer of the department of public works which is the King Solomon's Mine of every state government. During his tenure as head of power projects Freddy failed to stabilize power generation in the state. The public was shocked when Gadonius conferred a state award on Keyse Freddy for his non-contribution to the power sector. Keyse was succeeded by a brilliant civil servant who changed the power scenario of the state. Power projects that had languished for years were completed during his three-year tenure. He put an end to severe load shedding and frequent electricity tripping which had crippled both public and private sectors. Small and big industrialists, householders and students were relieved and lauded his work. Decades after he left the Power Corporation, his officers remembered his magnificent achievements. However since he had refused to plump ministerial purses with contracts he was given no awards.

There was Sevi who was awarded a Tuberose Award for her purported selfless devotion to the welfare of the poor. Her husband was rich and politically connected. She wanted to enter the political arena which she could not do by teaching or by presiding over her husband's business. A votary of the school of 'in praise of poverty', Sevi flung herself into social welfare.

To identify herself with the oppressed, she shunned sartorial elegance and wore brittle sandals. But her ears glittered with blue Jaeger diamonds. Confronted with this contradictory image, I, Raman, gave Sevi the benefit of doubt. Perhaps I was being uncharitable to a dedicated social worker. She was fanatic in her devotion to fallen women. Her intensity made me ashamed for not sharing her commitment. With passing of time, Sevi's passion for abused women intensified. She could be seen at workshops and seminars all over the world where participants evolved strategies for the future – always for the future – never for the present. Through her husband's political connections, she secured handsome funds for non-government organizations devoted to worthy causes but who did not provide accounts of expenditure for years. Sevi ensured that these organizations arranged her stay at five-star hotels while other committee members were lodged in government guest houses. At five-star hotels, Sevi satiated her addiction for free shampoo, conditioners and shower caps. She accumulated enough of these to run a beauty parlour. These details never formed part of the proceedings of the committee meetings which recorded her 'insightful observations', her 'self-effacing commitment for the deprived'.

Eventually, and goaded by her husband, the minister of welfare nominated Sevi for a high Tuberose Award. She called a press conference where she announced to astounded ministry officials that she had received more satisfaction working for the deprived than by receiving this great honour – fudged travelling expenses and free toilet accessories notwithstanding.

Then there was Zina, wife of Mohit Wallia, a noted economist and votary of Darwin and laissez-faire who was a perennial participant at seminars on development. Zina did not participate in these debates. What she actually did was a mystery; it became a deeper enigma when we found her name in the Tuberose list on Republic Day. There were innuendoes about her position in the premier's life. When innuendoes reached Premier Sardonius he was indignant. He asked, had not European kings and emperors made their fancy women into countesses and marquesses? Why should brown-skinned Indian rulers be denied this privilege? This was racism at its worst!

Nothing surprised an unsurprisable nation more than the case of Gajendra who came to be called Gateway to India by envious colleagues.

As a probationer at the National Academy of Administration he was a gangly youth with a preponderance of teeth that gave him the appearance of a lovable colt, especially when he smiled. He had a humorous if vitriolic tongue; his observations delighted his timid batchmates such as me, Raman. Despite my superior Tam-Brahm brain, I held Gajendra-Gateway in mortal dread as must have the numbskull Turco-Afghan invaders when they saw the propensities of this chameleon tribe. Gateway-Gajendra could charm the administrative birds or beasts out of their nests by his honeyed words.

His gestures were even more entrancing. During lectures at the academy we observed that Gateway became convulsed by laughter even before a staff member completed his joke if the staff member had a role in giving the final marks for the year-end assessment of the probationer. This assessment would determine the seniority of the officer for all times. Gateway would be the first to leap up when a staff member entered the lecture hall. During interactive sessions with senior officers, he laced his interjections with 'as you so brilliantly put it', or 'you have put into words our unformulated thoughts', or 'we have such high standards to live up to when we leave the academy. I hope we will not shame you, Sir.'

Now tell me, dear reader, which tired, disgruntled civil servant or academic could resist such homage from a bright IAS probationer? I learned a great deal from Gateway, lessons that would take me, if not to the dizzy heights to which Gateway clawed his way, but at least to reasonable success.

Gateway-Gajendra was a civil servant for all seasons. In our lean socialist days when names of Soviet politicians were known to us, our hero Subhash remarked to Gateway, 'You know, *yaar*, you are a bit like Mikoyan, the Russian foreign minister, who survived several dictatorial regimes.'

Gateway-Gajendra laughed indulgently. 'If you want to succeed, angel child, you had better be like Mikoyan.'

Success. That was the keyword, the motto that Gateway followed as if it was the pole star. And the motto never failed him. It took him from regime to regime with effortless ease. He deleted the words 'loyalty' and 'gratitude' from his lexicon except with the reservation that he was totally loyal to himself. It must be said in his favour that loyalty extended to his progeny, wife and varied relatives. Whether he helped them out of affection or because he wanted adherents is not known. Anyway he was a good family man; no man should be blamed for aiding kith and kin. But Gateway aided them beyond the limits of propriety; he promoted their interests at the cost of far more deserving people.

Gateway became a powerful secretary in the Union government, played his own games, planned the moves for his success and plotted against friends and foes alike. When he became chief adviser to a prime minister, he brought into his coterie dubious men. A notorious bureaucrat who earlier had been thrown out of the home ministry for grave misconduct was anointed home secretary of India!

Bewildered citizens asked – *Why*?

Perhaps his inner being could no longer differentiate between good and evil? He used his influence to distort the best traditions of the bureaucracy. Before Premier Sardonius's defeat in elections, he gave Gateway one of the highest Tuberose Awards of the country for 'upholding the best traditions of administration'. We all laughed.

Gateway made numerous pacts with Mephistopheles. I will not denigrate the grandeur of Goethe's dramatic poem *Faust* by comparing this colleague with the wonderful scientist-philosopher Faust who made his bargain with Mephistopheles for love and youth.

Gateway made it for gain and profit. He succeeded. Faust failed.

Subhash Chowdhury, the Don Quixote of our batch, raised a philosophical question about these civil service colleagues. Is there a fundamental difference between success and achievement? Success is when a person attains power and wealth. Achievement is when a person performs good deeds and, in the end, makes this contaminated planet a better place.

But, dear reader, achievements or goodness do not always guarantee entry into Shwindler's List.

New Talleyrands

Machiavelli gave a political nuance to his name. The Renaissance thinker has been unjustly maligned for his realistic advice to princes for attaining and preserving power. His advice was always followed though no politician would admit it.

Charles-Maurice de Talleyrand-Périgord imparted significance to his name. Talleyrand gave a new dimension to diplomacy. In a manner that would make the Florentine adviser Machiavelli quail, this French politician used all the weapons in the political arsenal to achieve his end.

Talleyrand was of aristocratic lineage but without the wealth that gives power to pride. And pride was certainly an important feature of this dynasty. The family coat of arms showed three rampant lions with the motto *Rien Que Dieu* – Nothing but God. This was a covert snub to the French monarchy.

The French Revolution opened opportunities of advancement to ambitious men and women. The French revolutionary government sent Talleyrand to London in 1792 to persuade the British to be neutral in a war between France and Austria. Britain agreed to do so. This was Talleyrand's first diplomatic victory. When Napoleon Bonaparte became consul for life, Talleyrand returned to France. Impressed both by his tact and mendacity Bonaparte appointed him foreign minister of France; he could not know that one day Talleyrand would use these very attributes against Napoleon. Even astute judges of character make mistakes.

Pleased by his brilliant negotiating skill, Napoleon, now emperor of France, appointed Talleyrand as Grand Chamberlain. Talleyrand accompanied Napoleon to conferences for formulating peace treaties and alliances. He betrayed his imperial master on numerous occasions by negotiating behind Napoleon's back. When Napoleon was defeated, Talleyrand became a trusted foreign minister of the restored French monarchy. When criticized for his many volte-faces Talleyrand defended himself by saying, 'I did not serve regimes and rulers. I served France and protected her interests.'

Our idealistic young republic was plunged into the international arena when she attained Independence. Until then Brittannia had guarded our coasts from European adventurers and kept potential invaders bottlenecked in the Hindu Kush ranges after receiving bloody noses in several Anglo-Afghan wars. China was too weak to encroach on our frontiers. Japan did not even try. The United States was too busy formulating her own foreign policy to bother about other countries. If only they had remained that way!

Jawaharlal Nehru realized that India must stand alone if the country was to avoid being a Russian or American satellite. While sagacious Russian policymakers accepted this policy, Americans like Dulles, brought up in the tradition of TV cowboy heroes, declared 'you either *fir* us or *agin'* us'. Since Nehru refused India to be drawn into other nations' cold-hot wars, it was perceived as *agin* America. To intimidate India, Dulles & co. drew a fiery ring of hostile nations around India. An unseasonably warm (and waiting) Russia held out welcoming arms to aid India in sunshine and storms.

So did China whose formidable leader Mao had liberated his country from a century of humiliation by Western powers. Communist China was a pariah not recognized by the West. Chiang Kai-shek's tiny Taiwan represented China in the Security Council of United Nations. Russia cautiously assisted China in economic and military matters. The Russian Bear knew the potential of the Chinese Dragon; the Mikhail Borodin affair of 1926 had left scars in the memory of both nations. Neither trusted the other but they had to unite against the common enemy – the West.

When Subhash and I joined government service we saw the rising tension between China and India over the status of Tibet. British Raj strategy was to protect Tibet from China. Numerous intelligence officers who doubled as Orientalists – Moorcroft, Younghusband, Aurel Stein, Czomo de Koros – brought back reports of Chinese troop movements around Lhasa. British departure left a dangerous vacuum here.

India entered this landmine with gusto. A brilliant scholar was sent to China as Indian ambassador; he ignored the threat potential and continued to romance the dragon. To assess and spy on the ambassador, Nehru sent his nephew, Kikki Taul, a former member of the Indian Civil Service. After Indian Independence this pragmatic species (devoid of loyalties) swiftly reinvented themselves as zealot Indians. Secure as a kinsman of Premier Nehru, Kikki Taul had violated many codes during his assignment in USA. These indiscretions were hushed up. Chinese intelligence however had information about his financial and erotic frailties.

Infatuated by his role as a prophet of non-alignment, Nehru brushed aside British intelligence reports. He patronized the Chinese and assured them of his support for entry into the United Nations – while the People's Liberation Army of China was building roads to Tibet and towards India's north east frontier. Junior military attaches and professional soldiers brought these developments to the notice of the ambassador and diplomat Kikki Taul.

Knowledge of Kikki Taul's susceptibilities prompted Chinese intelligence to plant an alluring woman agent on the diplomat's path. Counsellor Taul's residence vibrated with the presence of the Chinese siren and her handmaidens. Photographs were taken secretly, conversations and sounds were recorded. The historian-ambassador warned the prime minister of these happenings who angrily recalled the historian and sent another august diplomat of his tribe. Far from restraining Kikki, R.K. Pheru joined the bacchanalian feasts; once more secret devices photographed scenes and recorded sounds.

Intelligence agents in Central Asia, Ladakh and Tibet had kept the British government aware of developments there. In late 1958 British intelligence informed their Indian counterparts of the imminent Chinese march on Tibet. Ambassador Pheru and Counsellor Taul rushed to the Chinese foreign ministry to protest. Ministry officials informed them that Chinese intelligence had photos of their private lives which would be exposed if they informed the Indian government of what they had learnt.

In March 1959 the People's Liberation Army crushed a rebellion against Chinese rule in the Autonomous Region of Tibet, in violation of earlier treaties and international law. Dalai Lama, the Tibetan-Buddhist spiritual leader, fled to India where he lives as a revered exile.

I, Raman, knew nothing of diplomacy, but my diplomat friends later told us what no one dared voice while Nehru lived. Talleyrand would have been astounded by such betrayal of a nation's interest.

End of the Soviet era necessitated a reassessment of India's foreign policy. Dismayed by the sudden decline of Russian power, Premier Nedonius and his advisers rushed to court the West – believing that salvation lay with them. Gadonius, the humble farmer, became prime minister. He had no clue about foreign policy. Nuclear proliferation and non-alignment were incomprehensible concepts. Next came Vajonius who continued the pro-Western policy since his party drew strength from the merchant class which favoured relations with the West. His defence minister, hostile to the West, stunned the world by exploding the atom bomb, and made India a member of the nuclear club. India was now a power to be reckoned with and was drawn into this perilous partnership. As the spectre of Islamic fundamentalism darkened the world, there were interminable jabberwocky sessions on strategic partnerships, nuclear proliferation and economic cooperation.

Many predicaments lay before India. Was she to maintain neutrality or was she to become a satellite of the West? Was she to take into consideration the imperatives of geo-politics or plunge into an unrequited love affair with America and obey that country's dictats on whom India should befriend? Should India finally do what the founding fathers of the Indian republic abhorred – to be once more subjugated by the West? It was a time when the country required an expert on diplomacy and international affairs, and a patriot to safeguard Indian interests – like Talleyrand who served not regimes but his country.

Where was such a man to be found?

For Defence of the Mother Land

My tenure with the central government was drawing to a close. I, Raman, dreaded reverting to the state cadre. Not that I had achieved great things in the Union government but I was having a wonderful time. While I brooded on the future my wife articulated my thoughts: that I should be more aggressive, and secure a lucrative appointment, with all the perquisites of office. I had admonished her; why did I need a lucrative appointment? Did we not have enough?

No, Satyabhama had retorted. The money that her father had settled on us was half its value after twenty-nine years. We had to get our daughter married well, hopefully to an IAS officer. In today's schedule of rates for IAS bridegrooms, the dowry would run into crores. We wanted to send our son to study in a Western university. The house in Pallavur needed refurbishing. The cottage in the Nilgiri Hills had to be repaired. And then she burst into tears. 'I wear the same Kanchi saris given as trousseau. My diamonds look old next to the stuff that some of the IAS wives wear – Cartier and Van Cleef & Arpels!'

Angrily I told her that she was being vulgar. But she ranted and raved about her deprivations. 'You are such a *pavam*,' she taunted. 'You just sit in your office like a clerk! No enterprise, no glamour! My father paid a heavy dowry – for a drone!'

'Get yourself a new husband,' I taunted in response. 'It may cost your father twice the amount now – considering how you look!'

'Have you seen yourself in the mirror lately?' Satya asked. 'Balding, pot-bellied, jowls hanging! Nobody would pay a dowry for you now!'

I left the house, banging the door behind me, and went three houses down the lane in Ravindra Nagar, where Subhash lived.

Ravindra Nagar is a bureaucratic preserve with government quarters of different gradations – D-I, D-II and C-II bungalows and flats. It is enclosed by green shrubs, has a tract of green grass for walks, and is within easy reach of the famed Lodi Gardens as well as the costly Khan Market where the diplomatic corps and rich locals come shopping. We denizens cast glances at the exclusive two-storeyed C-I bungalows on Amrita Sher-Gil Road adjoining Lodi Gardens which are reserved for secretaries to government of India.

Wearing a faded salwar kameez Radha was tending the garden. She turned upon hearing the gate open. 'Welcome, Raman. Subhash was thinking of calling you for a drink. Why don't you go inside? I'll finish watering the lawn and join you. Will Satya will be joining us?'

She negotiated the hosepipe towards the six rose bushes which came with a C-II grade quarters and started spraying the plants.

'If she does, I'll go away,' I said angrily.

Radha laughed the silvery laugh which I remembered from our sub-division days. 'Had a lover's quarrel?'

'Do real lovers quarrel, Radha?' I asked quietly.

Alerted by my tone she turned to glance at me, and said, 'How would I know? I have never had a lover. Better ask someone who knows about these things.'

It was a pleasant Sunday afternoon. Satya joined us later; Radha negotiated peace between us. Our wives went to the kitchen to make dinner talking cheerfully as they worked. At dinner we talked about our offspring and our plans for them. Later Subhash and I discussed our future prospects in the capital.

I could not help envy Subhash. Everything seemed good for him. He had the competent and serene Radha. She was no longer the lissome girl with a single plait of hair following the path of her spine. Her slender figure had thickened, hair had thinned; now she wore it short. But she possessed an indefinable grace that drew one. No wonder, Subhash did not ask for a dowry when he married her. A woman like her cannot be assessed in money terms.

Radha brought back memories of Vidyavati who nudged my insomniac hours. The sound of her voice singing Thyagarajan's songs was a sad echo around me; her poignant smile haunted me. I had thrown away all that for property and wealth. Perhaps if I had loved Radha in my youth I would have cast her aside as well. But Subhash had adhered to his own code and seemed at peace with himself. No doubt he would become secretary of an important ministry, get post-retirement assignments, see his son well placed, daughter well married. He and Radha would enjoy a wonderful old age.

I did not see the dark shadows hovering over him.

Subhash was serving as additional secretary in the prestigious defence ministry where he worked in his usual efficient systematic manner. He rarely saw the secretary of the ministry who was so busy defending the nation's terrestrial and aerial frontiers that he was obliged to be out of the country most of the time, negotiating for better and bigger weaponry to arm the nation's armed forces.

This defence secretary knew all about the urgency of defence strategy. For centuries his clansmen had stood before the invading hordes from the north-west frontier. Instead of shedding a lot of useless blood like the numbskull warrior caste, his clansmen had guided the invaders to the granaries and watering holes and then took them home to be cared for by their women. In return the clan was unharmed and sometimes rewarded by the invaders. This clan cannot be extinguished even by nuclear holocaust.

Subhash had access to information that by virtue of being 'classified' came to be known sooner than later. Scrutinizing the files, Subhash saw that The Powers That

Be had initiated a project to purchase artillery equipments from a foreign nation. Before he joined the ministry, there had been an advertisement calling for international tenders. Though several nations submitted tenders at lower prices The Powers That Be (TPTB) decided to negotiate with the nation that quoted higher figures. The reason for this singular decision was not known though speculations were rife about motivations.

Fate takes a hand in our lives, especially when it wants to inflict misfortune. Had Subhash remained in the innocuous establishment desk of the ministry he would not have been drawn into the vortex of intrigues that derailed his career for years. Subhash began a close scrutiny of the files about the proposed purchase. His queries raised hackles from seniors and subordinates alike.

'The negotiations are almost over,' he was told brusquely by a colleague – at the behest of the defence secretary.

Then he was warned more menacingly by the defence secretary himself. 'What do you think we have been doing the last year, if not scrutinizing every aspect of the deal? Are you questioning our competence or our integrity?' The defence secretary permitted himself a dry laugh before saying, 'Is it a case of new brooms sweeping clean?'

Subhash's unsmiling silence was more damaging than words. It unsettled the habitually imperturbable defence secretary who had walked through impenetrable bureaucratic mazes all through his successful career without ever losing his direction. He saw in Subhash a dangerous adversary, the type of man who does not mind who gets hurt so long as the truth is established. Possessing the survivor genes of his clan, the defence secretary felt a flattering confabulation would be more productive than a confrontation with the 'maverick additional secretary'. So he invited Subhash for a cosy dinner where every courtesy was shown to him and Radha by the defence secretary and his remarkable spouse. It was whispered in the ministry corridors that she was the only person the defence secretary feared – apart from his perennial personal assistant who knew all his secrets.

I, Raman, would have drawn in my reins then. I would have realized that one cannot single-handedly oppose a system.

But Subhash was not to be deterred. He contacted an expert on artillery engineering and discussed the quality of the proposed weaponry. Guardedly and reluctantly the artillery engineer informed Subhash that the weaponry being considered for purchase was not superior to other ones even if they were said to be better and therefore costlier.

The expert studied the lines of his palms as if he was contemplating his destiny. Then he spoke slowly. 'In fact, I am not very sure if the proposed artillery are any better than the ones we produce in India, but the chairman of our principal artillery factory says that his organization cannot produce that kind of weaponry. So what can the defence ministry do but purchase the foreign ones?'

'It is a wide conspiracy, isn't it?' Subhash asked quietly.

'There are many definitions of such things,' the elderly artillery expert replied.

'What does one do – regardless of definitions?'

The engineer sighed. 'What men have done throughout the ages – make an ethical choice. You either ignore your conscience or face the consequences of obeying your conscience.'

'You make it sound very simple. Either or.'

The artillery expert smiled. 'The most difficult things in life can be reduced to simple mathematical formulas - the ones we use in artillery engineering.' He rose from the chair to indicate that the discussion was over. 'Think - and then act - because once you act you cannot afford the luxury of thought.' Subhash stood outside the engineer's apartment building as the mist of a winter night spread over the city, wondering what he should do.

Though the Republic of India was born amidst the massive carnage of the Partition, the founder fathers advocated non-violence. However, the latter-day parades on Republic Day became a display of India's military might. The parade begins in the cold of a Delhi January morning. Atop moving platforms tableaus from Indian states and various Union ministries depict their work. Colourful floats from various organizations follow. And then come the dancers and singers from different parts of India, demonstrating the perennial government theme of 'unity in diversity' - even when a thousand mutinies are brewing. The parade of armoured vehicles, missiles and aircrafts is a display of the nation's might and attracts wide attention. At the conclusion of the ceremonial parade fighter aircrafts speed overhead, their fuselages spewing plumes of orange, white and green smoke in homage to India's tricolour flag.

Thousands watch this impressive parade from the stands erected along Rajpath. At vantage points *achkaan* clad senior officers from ministries, armed forces personnel in uniforms and medals, sit with their wives wrapped in *pashmina* and *shatoosh* shawls.

On that Republic Day Subhash and Radha sat at the VIP enclosure and watched the parade. Since Subhash, unlike me, was not in the habit of confiding official matters to his wife,

Radha was bewildered by Subhash's visible turmoil. As the three aircrafts flew overhead, Subhash glanced up and stared grimly at their retreating wake long afterwards. A disquieted defence secretary sitting on the front row turned back to look at his intransigent additional secretary; catching the derision in the latter's eyes, he hastily looked away.

The grand Republic Day 'At Home' of the president in the former viceregal palace passed off without any untoward incidents. Subhash put on a smiling mask. He found amusement at seeing Radha shivering but looking pretty in a silk sari with a Kashmiri shawl thrown over one shoulder. Most of the women abstained from wearing woollens so that their opulent plumage could be seen along with goosebumps on their arms. Hundreds of guests milled around the lush lawns of the Rashtrapati Bhavan, picking up defence service, bureaucratic and political rumours. Some were content to watch the dazzling spectacle of power, status and influence. Subhash retreated to the rose-scented Moghul Gardens to contemplate his predicament. He had seen Radha do obeisance before Honey, wife of the cabinet secretary, as well as the spouse of the defence secretary. He wondered if Radha was visualizing herself as the wife of a future Union secretary. He would hate to disappoint her; she had always been content to bask in his little glories. Troubled by these thoughts, Subhash rose from the bench and returned to the presidential lawns.

As the sun slanted westwards and hid behind Raisina Hill the national anthem struck up once again and brought all movements to a halt. Defence personnel in resplendent uniforms stood ramrod straight, some slouching officers made attempts to stand erect as their spines were dysfunctional from disuse. Taking advantage of the sudden stillness, some women looked round to assess each other's sartorial assets. The military band played our stirring national anthem composed by the great poet Rabindranath Tagore forty years before India attained Independence where he cried out to the Almighty:

> *Slumbering India awakes*
> *To Thine clarion call,*
> *And sings Thy praise,*
> *Glory to Thee, glory to Thee,*
> *Arbiter of India's destiny.*
>
> (translation by author)

Subhash felt a lump in his throat. At moments like this he felt that he would happily die for his country. The president and his lady smiled, joined palms together in *namashkar* to the multitude, and returned to their palace. Ghosts of departed British viceroys must have whispered the Roman phrase *'sic transit gloria mundi' – so passes the glory of the world.* Unaware of such wisdom and believing their glory would never fade, the governing elite of the nation made their way to their chauffeur-driven official vehicles.

Three days after Republic Day comes Beating the Retreat ceremony enacted before the Lutyens' edifices and Vijay Chowk, the huge square fronting them. Myriad lights illumine outlines of the presidential palace and edifices of North and South Blocks. Camels and horses and their mounts stand in motionless dignity until the ritual begins. Regiments march to martial music as important people sit in the square to watch this resplendent spectacle.

It was while watching the ceremony of Beating the Retreat that Subhash came to a decision. He felt that beyond these spectacles of power and glory there was a grim reality – of soldiers, sailors, airmen laying down their lives for their country and compatriots. These men went into battle with absolute trust in their superior officers, and the cohorts of officials who selected weaponry to be used for the defence of the motherland. Never would these people imagine that the conglomeration of high-placed men would supply them with inadequate weapons. Trusting their seniors with their lives the fighters would go into battle never knowing that deals had been made within sacred portals of the Secretariat.

The ceremony concluded with the playing of the national anthem. As the drums, brass and trumpets intoned the anthem composed by the great poet who dreamt of free India, Subhash felt his throat constrict with emotions. Yes, he was prepared to suffer for his compatriots. And why not? When innocent unarmed people at Punjab's Jallianwalla Bagh had been mowed down by a British general, Rabindranath Tagore renounced his British knighthood. Tagore was fully aware that the gesture would cool the ardour of the British for his educational work at Visva-Bharati University but he did not mind. When the academic staff at Visva-Bharati cautioned him, the patriot-poet said, 'Indians are dearer to me than Visva-Bharati.' And now a few Indian politicians, bureaucrats and defence personnel were planning to buy inferior weaponry from a foreign power to make millions for their pockets and which would soon be sent to secret Swiss bank accounts.

Subhash decided to oppose the arms deal on the file with all his power. He had learnt all the technical details from the retired artillery expert he had met earlier. While scrutinizing the files he had acquired damning details. Subhash brought the files home before they were withdrawn from him; he typed out the notings and photocopied them because he would not endanger his stenographer with the burden of his defiance. A warning voice told him that he might have to pay a heavy price for his non-compliance, that colleagues would desert him when he fell from grace, that his adoring Radha might resent his defiance because she would not become the wife of a Union secretary, and that he might end his days in obscurity. And then the words of his parents echoed within him: *it is on the sacrifice of a few that civilizations are built.*

It was at the annual lunch party of the Indian Administrative Service Wives Association in the gardens of the secretary to the president that Subhash felt the first cold breath of his distancing colleagues. There is mandatory bonhomie among the colleagues on this occasion. Their wives are on display; cheerful, compliant, and eager to promote their husbands' careers.

The cabinet secretary is surrounded by officers whose empanelment for higher status is about to begin. If the cabinet secretary is not dour and has a moist eye for comely ladies, a few bold spouses saunter around him. If the cabinet secretary's spouse wields power the cleverer wives hover around *her*, bringing food, napkin, juice or whatever her ladyship requires. They compliment her on her sari if they cannot praise her figure and whisper to her what a lovely change she is from her predecessor who would have received the same homage in *her* halcyon days. The souls who have once been powerful come with considerable courage to this gathering; they are treated with condescension by juniors and seniors alike. It is like attending the wedding of a former spouse.

Subhash's ministry colleagues greeted him and then moved away. It would not do to be seen on friendly terms with an officer who was questioning the wisdom and integrity of exalted officers and ministers – because in an egalitarian society all spoils are shared. If Subhash wanted to be a maverick (the pejorative brush with which spirited officers are tarred) then it was not their concern. The defence secretary's wife studiously avoided Radha; when they met at the pudding table, the defence lady's baleful glare caused Radha to spill the gajar-halwa.

Some ministry wives took the cue and avoided Radha, especially the less attractive ones who must have once envied her beauty. Two lady officers who were our batchmates and had made matrimonial overtures to Subhash at the National Academy of Administration, now glanced at him with malicious delight. Before adipose fat had blurred the outlines of their bodies they had made their way upwards by virtue (wrong word really) of their soporific habits with powerful senior colleagues who repaid them with empanelment even if they had little else to recommend them. Stung by Subhash's indifference to their banal banter they went to Radha and said, 'So your husband didn't make it as secretary?' Shaken, Radha took refuge with the wife of a former civil servant who was past the stage of gainful occupation.

I, Raman, saw the tawdry drama enacted before me. My life-long envy of Subhash dissolved before the admiration I felt for this brave and solitary man. I felt an unknown rage swell within me when I saw Radha's flushed cheeks and tear-bright eyes. I wanted to stab the defence secretary's wife and my two women batchmates. It was then that I realized what I had never acknowledged before – that I loved Radha, with the dull ache of a coward. I wish I had the courage to rush and take her in my arms, kiss those anguished eyes, and abuse the people who had snubbed her all afternoon. But I,

Raman - denizen of a temple town on the banks of a sacred river, who as a toddler had heard of the righteousness of our avatars - stayed glued to my seat, trying to smother my pain in bureaucratic banter.

And then I saw a spectacle that I thought I would never see. My wife Satyabhama in her crimson Kanchivaram sari, diamonds on nose and ears, early jasmines in her hair, sauntered to where Subhash was standing with a distinguished retired bureaucrat. She joined her jewelled hands in *namashkar*, clasped his hands, and gave him a rich warm smile. Slightly bowing his head, he responded with a wry smile and held her hand. She quoted a Sanskrit mantra loudly so that others would hear. '*Veero bhagya vasundhara*' – *the earth belongs to the brave.*

If the realization of my enchantment for Radha astonished me, Satyabhama's conduct unnerved me. Why did she, always circumspect, always discreet, throw caution to the winds and openly display her support for Subhash? Was it respect or something more powerful that made a sensible woman reckless? Did Subhash evoke in her emotions I had failed to do for three decades? Bewildered, I watched her as she chatted with Subhash for a while, unconcerned that people were looking at them with considerable interest. Then grave-faced, she came to where I was sitting and said clearly in atrocious Hindi, 'I feel nausea. Is it the lunch? Let's go home and drink good coffee.'

I prayed no one was within earshot because this single remark could ruin my career. Radha had also witnessed the scene. Trembling visibly, she rose, bade goodbye to her elderly companion, and stumbled towards Satyabhama who stretched out a hand to steady Radha. She beckoned to Subhash who, both amused and touched, joined them. I had no alternative but to follow which I did - trailing behind the trio in order to inform onlookers that my heart was not with them.

That night, as the first spring breeze blew through the trees, I lay next to Satyabhama, seething with anger at her indiscretion and also for her open admiration for Subhash. So I spoke brusquely, 'You have committed hara-kiri on my behalf.'

Satyabhama sat up, her single thinning plait falling over a plump shoulder. Looking at me she said gravely, 'I am not stylish like the defence secretary's wife, nor smart like those two lady officers - but I am not a tart. This town has tarts - of both sexes.'

After she fell asleep I wondered whether she had called me a tart as well.

Before the matter of Subhash's defiance became public he was transferred from the defence ministry and kept on compulsory waiting. This is a bureaucratic device to provide opportunity to the rebel and heretic to ponder and reflect on his sins - like the solitary confinement given to Christian heretics in medieval times to repent their ways. The Spanish Inquisition believed that the ardour of heretics was cooled by harsh confinement which allowed them to reflect on their credo.

The customary farewell tea parties for Subhash were not arranged in the ministry though I learnt later that some junior officials had gone at lunchtime to take leave of their just and generous additional secretary. The secretary of the ministry had been extremely prompt in issuing orders to withdraw the official car and disconnect the official residential phone.

Days passed. Subhash neither repented nor confessed his sins as is expected of rebels and heretics. He spent time pottering around the *barsati*, terrace-garden, of his bungalow or read there in the mornings. Subhash went for long walks in the adjoining Lodi Gardens late in the evenings so that his erstwhile friends and walking companions would be spared the embarrassment of cutting him dead.

There, among the mausoleums of long-departed sultans, along flower-girt flagstone pathways, under lowering trees, twittering birds and frolicking squirrels, one is inclined to reflect on the past and future, on the transience of glory and possibly the futility of life itself. But when a violet dusk settles over the garden and stars appear, a mood of reconciliation with the universe takes possession of one's soul. Like Omar Khayyam one can look for 'Guests star-scattered on the grass.' Lodi Gardens is a balm for bruised minds and weary bodies at night, when the wind whistles through monuments, when imperial ghosts saunter past with the consoling mantra – *Grieve not for this too shall pass.*

Finding Subhash 'bloody but unbowed' and fearing he might wage a campaign through the Press, The Powers That Be decided to send him to an innocuous post in a ministry that had no allure of power or privilege. Having expected this he took it in his stride. This in itself is considered a punishment and demotion.

Worse was to follow.

Empanelment

When flowers begin to bloom in Delhi's numerous parks, the bureaucratic citadel commences the agony and ecstasy of the Empanelment process. In arcane times the process was dictated by considerations of merit of officers - their achievements and their integrity.

The El Dorado for Indian civil servants was appointment as Secretary to the Government of India. Formulating national programmes in important sectors, spelling out strategies for implementing these in the states, seeing one's ideas and vision take shape - are exhilarating experiences. Attending Union cabinet meetings to obtain approval for one's ministry's programmes, presenting the details before a gathering of the nation's prime minister and his cabinet colleagues, provide some excitement in the lives of sober bureaucrats.

There are international conferences where a secretary to Government of India represents and speaks on behalf of his/her country. There is great satisfaction in wresting benefits for the country at these gatherings. The larger and more important the ministry, the greater is the prestige for the secretary. Since events which shape the nation's destiny are planned in the grand Lutyens edifices, there is intimate involvement and participation in the life of the nation.

The atmosphere of the national capital is charged with power and prestige. The dream of every civil servant is to serve here and carve a niche for oneself in the highest echelons of the bureaucracy. There are more mundane benefits; spacious bungalows in the elite Lutyens' Delhi, free domestic help in return for servants' quarters, good educational prospects for the progeny, and opportunities at every stage for advancement and fulfilment for having served one's country.

There is also the pomp of ceremonials: Red Fort on Independence Day when secretaries sit on the ramparts and see the prime minister unfurl the flag; parades on Republic Day which are intended to intimidate our adversaries; garden parties at Rashtrapati Bhavan where ghosts of viceroys hover

over the Moghul Gardens; the breathtaking spectacle of Beating the Retreat. Finally there is the grandeur of Delhi of the Seven Cities, whose sand and stones are seared with glory, drama and tragedy. Perhaps it is the mystery and magnetism, allure and promise, which brings officers to Delhi, who are in quest of success and fame. For some civil servants it is just old-fashioned job satisfaction.

In comparison to the number of officers who wish to be secretaries, the number of secretary-grade posts is few. No wonder then, that there is such frenetic activity as the time for the crucial empanelment for secretary-ship begins. The quest for obtaining confidential reports which are graded *Outstanding* becomes an obsession, like searching for the Holy Grail.

To select the best officers for these sought-after posts and to preclude possibilities of arbitrariness and nepotism, Government of India, in the early premiership of Rajiv Gandhi, evolved the procedure for empanelment of secretaries in the Central Staffing Scheme of the ministry of personnel. This scheme formulated detailed guidelines regarding the eligibility criterion for selection to the post of secretaries, special secretaries and those of secretary's grade outside the ministries. These posts are equal and interchangeable.

The Central Staffing Scheme states that –

> *Selection for inclusion on the panel of officers adjudged suitable for appointment to the posts of Special Secretary/Secretary to the Government of India and for posts equivalent thereto will be approved by the ACC (Appointments Committee of the Cabinet) on the basis of the proposals submitted by the Cabinet Secretary. In this task the Cabinet Secretary is assisted by a Special Committee of Secretaries for drawing*

> *up proposals for the consideration of the ACC. The Special Committee of Secretaries comprises the Cabinet Secretary, the Union Home Secretary, the Union Personnel Secretary and the Principal Secretary to the Prime Minister.*

The composition of this committee is based on sound sense. As head of the nation's civil service the cabinet secretary is the chairman of the committee. The home secretary is a member of the committee since he is in a position to give his opinion on the suitability of an officer from the security point of view. An officer involved in anti-national, anti-social or political activities is not *normally* considered eligible for appointment to the highest echelons of the country's bureaucracy though there have been exceptions. The personnel secretary is the custodian of all rules and regulations governing selection and appointment, and is expected to ensure that all procedures are correct and in accordance with rules. The principal secretary to the prime minister represents the prime minister.

Should there be some serious problems about an officer the principal secretary will voice these concerns. The principal secretary alone may have confidential information about an officer of which the other members of the special committee may not be aware. It is then the responsibility of the principal secretary to the prime minister to bring such matters to the attention of the other members of the special committee.

> *Inclusion in such panels is to be through the process of strict selection and evaluation of such qualities as merit, competence, leadership and a flair for participating in policy making process. The needs of the Central Government would*

> *be of paramount consideration. While due regard would be given to seniority, filling up of any specific post would be based on merit, competence and specific suitability of the officer for a particular vacancy in the Central Government.*

The five confidential reports in the run-up to the empanelment are particularly crucial. The merit of an officer is judged by the Annual Confidential Reports, established reputation and the achievements during his/her service.

The citadel of the Union government has its own hierarchy and power centres. There has been a qualitative change in the power structure of the citadel from the days of Nehru, Shastri, Indira Gandhi and Desai.

Both the cabinet secretary and the principal secretary work under the prime minister. In theory, the cabinet secretary is at the apex of the country's vast civil service. In earlier decades there were cabinet secretaries who made their writ run. Recent political ecology has led to the disappearance of that breed. They are in fact now *rara avis,* rare birds. The selection of cabinet secretaries is not always based entirely on seniority, reputation or excellence. It can be a gladiatorial contest. It is not unusual for the roughest customer to win. There are, even now, a few who have become cabinet secretary on merit and bureaucratic miracle.

The principal secretary to the prime minister worked as adviser to the prime minister. They were discreet and unobtrusive with no personal agenda of their own. Their work was more political than administrative. They seldom sacrificed the nation's interest for political or personal gains. They offered objective and disinterested service, and were in some ways the final corrective figure in the bureaucracy. A few of them, when they could no longer agree with the views of the prime minister, relinquished their position of power and authority.

However, when there were prime ministers who had little experience of administration, and others who had little inclination to look at files, the principal secretaries played a more 'pro-active role'. In other words they meddled and used their position to further their own interests.

The cabinet secretary is expected to act on the basis of rules, norms and precedents. The prime minister's office acts on political wavelengths. In matters such as the selection of secretaries to the Union government, prime ministers such as Nehru, Shastri, Indira Gandhi and Desai went by the advice of their cabinet secretaries. The cabinet secretaries of those times were men of legendary ability. They did not permit principal secretary to the prime minister to stray into their bailiwicks. In the course of time and in response to changing ecology, cabinet secretaries became environmentally acclimatized men. They realized that toeing the PMO line can ensure a smooth tenure, possibly an extension of service, and definitely an attractive post-retirement berth.

As a result the cabinet secretariat became subservient to the prime minister's office in decisions like appointment of Union secretaries. In this power nexus, the officers who want to 'make it' in the empanelment must therefore be 'acceptable' to the PMO. The political neutrality of the civil service thereby became a casualty.

The Special Committee of Secretaries is required to assess the suitability of the officers under consideration and, having arrived at some consensus on this, they send their considered opinion to the Appointments Committee of the Cabinet comprising the home minister and the prime minister. When the lists are approved at this level they are sent down to the cabinet secretary, who, assisted by his colleagues, starts the appointment process.

It is a process of waiting, hoping and praying (and in later times, conspiring and manipulating) for the deserving, aspiring and desperate alike. In traditional times the verdict was accepted without demur because no one doubted the fairness of the system or the correctness of the selection process.

Once the era of Nefaralization began these criteria appeared outmoded; the citadel began to look for other and more useful aptitudes – adjustability and tolerance. Nefaralization brought in a new dynamism. No more the outmoded process of selection on merit. Now officers had to 'enjoy the confidence' of The Powers That Be. The nation's citadel took on the atmosphere of a Turkish seraglio where odalisques vied for the sultan's favour. While in the seraglio the criteria were for wasp-like waists, deep bosoms, swan-like necks, not to mention rosebud lips that smiled bewitchingly, in the citadel it was all about 'enjoying confidence'.

There were officers who did not enjoy the confidence of The Powers That Be (TPTB). My batchmate Subhash was one of these. I do not know if it was his intensity, his obstinacy and inflexible beliefs that caused TPTB to distance themselves from him. Perhaps it was a residue of his background; his brave and rebellious father, a member of Subhash Bose's Indian National Army, who taught him to be proud and stubborn in the face of death. Such extremism was bound to be an impediment to professional success in our liberated times.

The Four Horsemen of the Apocalypse – the premier's principal secretary, cabinet secretary, home secretary and secretary personnel – meet to scrutinize the performance data of the officers under consideration for appointment as secretaries, additional secretaries and joint secretaries. Meetings are held from spring until the onset of summer when longlists become shortlists and then the final list.

The Special Committee of Secretaries held their first meeting in April that year for empanelment of IAS officers of Subhash's and my year of allotment for the posts of secretary in the Government of India. Subhash's name was unanimously recommended by the Special Committee of Secretaries. He had been graded as *Outstanding* in the five annual reports by various seniors. His personal and professional integrity had been impeccable for thirty years in the Indian Administrative Service.

While some of our powerful batchmates were 'lurking in the arras' or haunting the hallowed precincts of the Rashtrapati Bhavan Annexe which houses the Cabinet Secretariat, to glean any information that can be obtained about The List, Subhash worked at his desk, went on tours of inspection and sent brilliant reports. The cabinet secretary sent a panel of names of twenty-two officers of our IAS batch who had been selected by the Special Committee of Secretaries for appointment as secretary for approval of the Appointments Committee of the Cabinet (ACC). Both Subhash's and my name were in that panel. The home minister approved the list. What remained was the approval of the prime minister. After that we would be appointed as secretary to Government of India.

Subhash felt as if his luck had turned after the ordeal of humiliation. He went up to the *barsati* of his official residence and gazed at the sky. The hot silent night suddenly felt like spring.

The Arsenal

One monsoon morning, a well-dressed, smooth-talking man came to Subhash's office. He introduced himself as an artillery engineer and proceeded to enlighten Subhash about the superiority of certain weaponry. Seeing Subhash stiffen, his tone became more dulcet.

'I am not trying to influence you. I just wanted you to know the other side of the matter. The weapons that you consider inferior are not so. It is of first-class category and can put the enemy to flight.'

'The matter is closed as far as I am concerned. I am no longer in that ministry,' Subhash replied curtly.

'You could give your reconsidered views on the concerned file.'

'I recorded my views when I was in that ministry. There is no question of my writing anything now,' Subhash replied.

'The file can be brought to you for recording your reconsidered views and pre-dated. It would help the purchase,' the visitor suggested.

Subhash lost his temper. 'What you are saying is not only improper but illegal. How dare you suggest such a thing!'

Subhash rang the bell to inform the visitor that the meeting was over. The emissary went away, visibly angry.

Nishi Sting, then a powerful officer in the PMO, telephoned him a few days later suggesting that Subhash could record his 'reconsidered views' on the file. New sheets of paper would be introduced so that there would be no discrepancies.

Subhash was furious at the suggestion. 'I do not indulge in forgery,' he said coldly.

Nishi Sting enunciated menacingly, 'I suppose you know that the file regarding your appointment as Union secretary is now in the PMO?'

Having close contacts with subordinate officials, especially if they are of one's caste-tribe, is a boon. That is how I, Raman, came to hear of the fate that had befallen Subhash.

The empanelment file of our batch was approved by the prime minister. Only Subhash's name was not approved. No reasons were given. The joint secretary in the PMO, Nishi Sting, recorded, 'All names recommended by the Special Committee of Secretaries have been approved except that of Subhash Chowdhury.'

The cabinet secretary was appalled when he saw Nishi Sting's noting. He was not a man for crusades - far from it - but even he acknowledged the illegality of the PMO. More so because the prime minister's principal secretary Anastas Virus had been a member of the Special Committee of Secretaries and had approved Subhash's name on the proceedings file. Surprised and dismayed, because he liked Subhash, the cabinet secretary summoned him to his office which is located in the annexe of the Rashtrapati Bhavan. Subhash went to meet him there. He waited in the visitors' room.

The room is usually a reflection of the personality of the cabinet secretary. In the days of sober chiefs the room was neat and austere with newspapers on the glass-topped table. As levity increased, silk cushions and stylish lamps appeared, purchased either by wives or lady friends who wanted their presence to be felt. A chaise longue would have made it a scene from Jacques Louis David's famous painting *The Seraglio*.

As he sat in the visitors' room, Subhash glanced at the names of previous cabinet secretaries of India who were respected for integrity, high competence and impartial conduct. There was a fiercely independent one who sifted the chaff from the grain with an unerring touch. When officers performed beyond the call of duty he accorded recognition to them. Most performed their duties according to rules. Others let things drift and enjoyed the pleasures of life.

People have often speculated on the procedure for selection of the cabinet secretary. The principal secretary to the prime minister is usually asked to shortlist the candidates; some previous eminent cabinet secretaries are invited to give their views. The final decision is the prime minister's. Seniority has not always been the criterion. There are numerous instances when the 'topper in the batch' has been overlooked for someone way down in the list - for various reasons - both valid and extraneous.

The stakes are high and no holds are barred. Till the selection is made, it is a free-for-all; long-dead departmental enquiries are brought to life by rival factions, newspapers become active about the merits of different candidates (while rooting for their favourites) and various types of slander are practised. Finally the victor is installed in the stately office.

Cabinet Secretary Birendra Blink was astonished that after the principal secretary to the prime minister, Anastas Virus, had approved Subhash's name, how could the prime minister veto it.

Subhash told him all that had transpired.

Subhash observed that the cabinet secretary paled a little. He stared at the stormy monsoon sky for sometime. Outside in the Rashtrapati Bhavan forecourt a band was playing a march to honour an arriving foreign dignitary. Then he turned to Subhash and said, 'Give me a detailed résumé of your solid achievements up to date. I will meet the prime minister and get his approval.'

Subhash thanked the cabinet secretary. He was going out of his way to redress injustice. Though he smiled, Subhash saw that the cabinet secretary was more troubled now because he realized that Subhash had taken on a powerful cabal.

Subhash prepared his representation to the cabinet secretary enumerating his achievements, especially in the last five years that are considered a run-up to empanelment. His achievements were impressive. Subhash enclosed letters of appreciation for his work that he had received in the course of his career.

Weeks passed. Nothing happened. Subhash's juniors were promoted. Subhash bore this stoically.

Without informing Subhash, a distraught Radha went to meet the formidable consort of the cabinet secretary to seek her intercession. The consort, Honey (of Wimbledon fame in an earlier chapter), served Radha weak tea and stale biscuits. Then her eyes fell on Radha's earrings.

'How unusual!' the cabinet secretary's consort trilled. 'Where did you buy them?'

'These stones are called the seven sapphires of Sri Lanka,' Radha replied.

'Let me see them,' Honey purred.

Taking off the earrings Radha placed them in the pale outstretched hands of the consort who promptly put them on, went to the gilded mirror on the wall and admired herself. 'How lovely!' she cooed rapturously and turned to Radha. 'Could I buy them off you?'

'They are … a gift … from …' Radha faltered in apprehension.

The consort tweaked Radha's nose. 'Oh, a lover's gift, huh?'

Radha shook her head, tears of vexation threatening her eyes. 'No, they are from my husband on our silver wedding anniversary. He bought them when he went to organize that relief mission in Sri Lanka.'

The consort's eyes hardened. 'Hmm,' she murmured, and began taking off the earrings. 'I see you are devoted to Subhash. What a pity he hasn't made it to the secretary's post.' Honey spoke in a sinister tone.

Radha bowed her head. 'That is why I came here ... to ask for your help.' She looked imploringly at Honey, the powerful consort, who was gazing lovingly at the sparkling cluster of the seven-hued stones on the palm of her hand. Honey wanted to possess them. Possessions gave her a pleasure that numerous lovers failed to give.

'What can I do? It is an official matter.' The consort's bird-like trill began to sound now like a crow's cawing. She handed the earrings to Radha who wanted to scream 'everyone knows of your interference in official matters – for a consideration.' Instead she rose and handed the earrings to Honey who giggled. 'Oh, you stupid darling,' she trilled again in a manner that had vanquished many men. 'I wish you would visit me more often.'

'I am at your disposal, Ma'am,' Radha murmured, rage and pain warring in her heart.

The consort rose and said, 'Let me see what I can do.'

Leaving the designated residence of the cabinet secretary on 32 Prithviraj Road, Radha felt hopeful about Subhash's appointment. If she felt sad about the seven sapphires, she consoled herself by saying that women had sometimes surrendered their honour for their husband's advancement. Subhash had never asked her to compromise her dignity for anything; he would be furious if he came to know of her visit to Honey.

In the months that followed Subhash found the cabinet secretary's enthusiasm wane perceptibly. Whereas before he used to take Subhash's phone calls, the chief bureaucrat now stopped taking Subhash's phone calls and refused to grant him an audience. The chief's change of heart sprang from concern for his own future; he was retiring shortly. He had already received an extension of service that no cabinet secretary, not even the outstanding ones, had received until then.

His wife-cum-campaign manager had ensured that through means of her own. Honey was now looking around for other possibilities. Summoning her contacts she told them to put pressure on the prime minister to give her husband a prestigious assignment abroad. She met Anastas Virus, the principal secretary to the prime minister, and struck a deal. She told him that if he supported her husband's appointment abroad, the misdeeds committed by Anastas and his cohorts in the name of Nedonius the Nefaralizer would be buried by her husband, the cabinet secretary, who had shown her the damaging dossiers.

Subhash's central tenure ended. This is what the Sting cousins had been waiting for. The cabinet secretary refused to lift a finger to help Subhash. Why should he? He was on the road to a paradise-on-earth as Indian representative at the Cosmopolitan Bank in Washington. Subhash returned to his state cadre, rage swelling within him. He left Radha and their daughter in Delhi where the girl was studying law. Inwardly he hoped to be back in the capital, victorious. Now he had a trump card in his hand. He would file an application before the Central Administrative Tribunal.

Kangaroo Court

Lasciate ogni speranza voi ch'entrate
(Abandon all hope you who enter here)
– *Inferno of Divine Comedy* by Dante

Nowhere is the truth of the saying 'the road to hell is paved with good intentions' more poignantly demonstrated than the attempt made by our republican emperor Rajiv to establish tribunals where the humblest official could seek redress against the illegalities of powerful mandarins. Within a year of his mother's assassination, Rajiv saw the machinations and manipulations of powerful mandarins. Perturbed by their immense and arbitrary power, Rajiv decided to ensure the interests of the lesser mandarins. After protracted consultations, Rajiv's advisers mooted the idea of tribunals where judges and bureaucrats would deliver swift judgments in defence of the wronged. Every state of the republic was endowed with such tribunals of justice so that honest and humble officials need not run from pillar to post to fight injustice. Fees too were modestly fixed so that the noble practitioners of law did not drain the poor and the wronged.

These tribunals were established with the full panoply of legal niceties – with the intention of delivering justice, and speedy justice at that. Rules and sections of the tribunals decreed that all cases must be disposed of in six months, that an applicant could argue the case himself. If he engaged a legal practitioner the fees would be strictly regulated. No one need again suffer what Shakespeare had called 'the law's delay' or 'the insolence of office'. A strict time limit was fixed, defying the Hindu philosophy of time as a cycle of eternity.

Honest bureaucrats rejoiced at this administrative innovation because no one knew when they would have to seek relief in these tribunals.

It became clear early in the proceedings that the administrative tribunals were checking the arbitrariness of powerful bureaucrats. Minor officials rushed to the tribunals with their grievances and challenged the might of the mighty. Arbitrariness, nepotism and vindictive decisions now came under scrutiny; the wrongdoers were exposed.

Laws however good do not change the defects of a system. The very purpose for which the young prime minister had established the tribunals was shortly to be sabotaged by circumventing the independence of the tribunals.

Like most people who lead sedate lives, Subhash never contemplated going to a tribunal to seek administrative justice. These Kafkaesque nightmares were preserved for others, for denizens of a bizarre literary world. It is a sad irony of fate that those who live by an ethical code are sometimes drawn in the cobwebs of unethical conspiracy just as peaceful spectators are caught in violent crossfires during riots. Subhash was not particularly ambitious; he took professional reverses and rises with a nonchalance that his seniors found puzzling. But even he was compelled to fight when a cabal of corrupt bureaucrats decided to block his deserved promotion.

He felt a sense of exhilaration when he took on the Establishment and challenged its caprice in a court of law. It was like David fighting Goliath, with the same anticipation of victory. David had right on his side and Subhash thought he would wrest victory by upholding dharma.

On the first day at the tribunal of Sandalore branch, Subhash felt a sense of power. In one document he had challenged the prevailing nefarious system whereby the Prime Minister's Office could delete names of senior bureaucrats from a panel prepared by the duly empowered selection committee. This Special Committee of Secretaries had been structured to ensure fair play and justice in the selection process. Officers in the PMO had subverted fair selection for their own ends.

Subhash had no doubts that he would be vindicated. What all those months of representations and entreaties before the cabinet secretary could not achieve, would now be done by one day of argument! Subhash had prepared his brief meticulously, and then entrusted the matter of filing it to a senior counsel.

On the first day of hearing the tribunal members came into court. Subhash was reassured by their sombre mien as they took their seats on the dais.

Subhash believed that with a newly elected Union government there would be no problems in conducting the case. He assumed that with the departure of Premier Nedonius, his infamous coterie of Anastas Virus and the Sting-Blink group would also depart. He did not realize that such fraternities do not die nor do they fade away. Their tentacles spread into every regime.

The new chief bureaucrat of India sent its counsel to defend the indefensible. With dyed red hair plastered over a charcoal face, teeth bared into an intimidating grin, the counsel for the Union government promised to provide entertainment. He provided much more; he offered stiff resistance to the progress of the case. Since the PMO's officers had no case, their strategy lay in delaying the denouement. The government counsel asked for adjournments for three consecutive months. The chief member of the tribunal finally objected and ordered that the connected records of the case should be produced or orders would be passed ex parte.

Mr Dribble-acharya, the advocate for Subhash, felt a frisson of unease. It would not do to finish the case so early. While he was exploring means of delaying the hearings, the leftover bureaucrats of the previous regime advised the new premier Gadonius to appoint Dribble-acharya as his advocate for a minor case so that Dribble would not argue properly for Subhash.

'But why?' the bewildered Gadonius asked. 'I have nothing against Subhash Chowdhury!'

Nishi Sting said, 'This insolent, insubordinate officer has questioned the divine right of prime ministers to do what they wish. Such insolence and defiance has to be crushed ruthlessly if the office of the prime minister is not to be turned into an empty shell.' Terrified that their skullduggery would be revealed, Anastas Virus, the Sting cousins and the new chief bureaucrat T.S.R. Subrammy formulated a plan to subvert Subhash's case in the Sandalore bench of the tribunal.

The new chief bureaucrat tempted Dribble-acharya with offers of arguing for the Union government. In return he had to sabotage Subhash's case. Dribble-acharya subverted the proceedings by making twenty officers as respondents. By the time a furious Subhash got their names removed a month was lost.

Another curious episode took place. One of the members of the tribunal, the only one who was not to be 'influenced' by the citadel, was hurriedly promoted as chief member and transferred to another tribunal. Another member of the tribunal heard Subhash's case along with the chief member. He was enthusiastic about Subhash's case. The chief member had pronounced that the case would be heard early. The case had been simplified once more to the pivotal question – did the prime minister have the authority to arbitrarily delete the name of an officer duly recommended by the nation's highest selection committee for empanelment as secretary? By the attitude of the administrative and judicial members it seemed as if they would decide in Subhash's favour.

Three weeks later Subhash flew on winged feet up the long flight of stairs leading to the Sandalore tribunal. 'I will be vindicated today,' he exulted. 'And I will be in the capital as a secretary in a few weeks.'

Chief bureaucrat T.S.R. Subrammy told a member at the tribunal that he must pass an adverse order on Subhash's case. This high-minded member told Subrammy that Subhash's case was cast iron and that the Supreme Court of India would pass strictures if such illegal orders were passed. Subrammy thundered, 'We have to protect officers of Premier Nedonius's regime! They are our allies! So what is it to be – a tribunal in a remote north east state or chief at the Sandalore tribunal?' The high-minded member now agreed 'to do the needful'. Subhash's case was falsely adjourned on the ground that all the courts were fully booked for hearings for three months.

Seeing the injustice done to Subhash the chief member decided to expedite the case and announced that he had constituted a special bench for final hearing.

Subhash emitted a long sigh of relief. He thanked the chief member who nodded in acknowledgement and walked slowly towards his chambers. He had worries of his own. In a month's time, he mused, my tenure as chief member will end and I will finally retire. What shall I do after forty-two years of active life?

Reaching home he indulged in some introspection on his contribution to jurisprudence. He had a sudden craving to deliver justice before leaving the tribunal. He would help Subhash to attain justice. A phone rang insistently in the bedroom. Frowning, the chief member took the call. He did not know the caller who proceeded with T.S.R. Subrammy's message. 'Yes, I understand,' he said before hanging up. 'I am very grateful.'

Chief member struggled to suppress the guilt that surged within him. He had made a bargain. It was not a new experience; he had transacted such bargains before but there was something demeaning in this one because it involved acquiescence in a diabolical plot to destroy an honourable officer's career. Chief member emitted a long sigh. There was no alternative. The post of chairman of Consumers' Forum was not to be scorned … not at this stage of life anyway. A strange metamorphosis took place; the honourable chief member began to resemble a kangaroo.

Several hours before the special bench was to hear Subhash's case, the tribunal clerk announced that Subhash's case would not be heard by chief member of the special bench. It would be taken up by a new bench after the summer vacation. Subhash felt anger surge within him. It was now abundantly clear that a conspiracy was afoot to deny him justice. It seemed as if the Sandalore tribunal was now transformed into Franz Kafka's kangaroo court.

When the kangaroo court opened six weeks later Subhash went there with stubborn hope. He had tutored his advocate Dribble-acharya on all points of the case, and typed out clear, cogent aide memoirs for the advocate's oral presentation. Dressed in sponge-bag trousers and crisp white bib, Dribble-acharya began to fumble and mumble his way through the arguments. He forgot a few points here and there but Subhash promptly sent brief notes which Dribble-acharya read aloud. The entire case was finally presented. The respondent's counsel also argued their case with incompetence.

Franz Kafka would have been interested to see the performance of the kangaroo court that sultry monsoon morning. The two kangaroos who heard the case grinned displaying rotting teeth. Kangaroo Ramamurthy was black and bald, kangaroo Ramakrishna was yellow and hirsute. The former had rhodentine cunning, the latter had an assinine aura. Both were united by a desire to repay debts of loyalty to the dubious officers in the regime of Nedonius the Nefaralizer who had appointed them as kangaroos.

The hearing was over. The two member-kangaroos on the dais ordered the records of the case to be opened in court. Subhash's claim was verified and found correct; his name had been categorically recommended for appointment to the rank of secretary. He asked for the court's writ of mandamus to Premier Gadonius to implement the unequivocal recommendation of the selection committee.

That evening Subhash stood under the stars and thanked his Maker for His kindness. Subhash did not hear his Maker laugh.

The date for passing orders was fixed. Legal luminaries in Delhi had assured Subhash that his case was cast iron. No one could pass adverse orders on his petition. As Subhash ascended the sixty-nine steps to the court hall, he thought: *It is over; the long waiting, the representation, the round of lawyers, the interminable court hearings, disappointments and anger, resulting sometimes in the onslaught of despair. Now, my stand would be vindicated. Not only shall I benefit but all others who come after me shall be protected from the arbitrary power and malice of those who are absolutely corrupted by absolute power.*

This very aspect of the case troubled the citadel. Passing of a favourable judgment would expose the grave irregularities committed by Anastas Virus and the Sting cousins in the appointment of secretaries. This brazen cabal was now afraid of courts and tribunals. If the Sandalore kangaroos passed an order against Subhash the cabal knew the higher courts of appeal would pass strictures against them. The Virus-Sting cabal consulted the chief bureaucrat who used his vast experience in administrative skullduggery to guide the Sandalore kangaroos.

Subhash went to the kangaroo court expecting vindication on that rain-washed morning. He watched the two kangaroos climb the dais and sit on the plush red chairs designed like thrones. Then kangaroo Ramamurthy spoke. 'Case of Subhash Chowdhury stands transferred to the principal bench of the tribunal in New Delhi. We will not pass orders.'

Subhash was speechless. It took several minutes for him to recover from this astounding announcement. Composing himself with effort he asked: 'But the hearings on merit are over! The government's counsel had also completed his argument. How can you transfer the case at this stage?'

The two kangaroos grinned in reply.

'This is an utter miscarriage of justice!' Subhash's voice now rose. 'It is fifteen months since I filed my application. In spite of every harassment and discourtesy I have encountered here, I have not ever protested against your misconduct. But this is beyond endurance! How can you transfer a case without my request or my consent! You are engaged in subversion of justice! This move is designed to deny me justice by delay!'

The two kangaroos were unmoved. They had obeyed orders of chief bureaucrat Subrammy. Now Subhash would have to go through the agony of getting his case heard again. It would take another fifteen months. Time was slipping away. Subhash had everything on his side - law, justice and dharma. The only thing he lacked was time. He would retire in two years. But the die was cast. The kangaroo court of Sandalore bench had connived with T.S.R. Subrammy to have the case transferred to the capital where the hearing would be postponed - until Subhash retired.

Time. It was slipping away.

Principal Bench of the Administrative Tribunal

A former maharaja's palace now houses the Delhi tribunal.

The sandstone building of pillared porticoes, tall doors and mullioned windows recall the British Raj. The large rooms that were scenes of receptions and banquets now house legal sections. The old ballroom with gilt-framed wall-mirrors is now the domain of the chief member of the principal bench of the tribunal. The wide curved staircase stemming from the central vestibule leads upstairs to rooms where rajas and ranis, courtiers and courtesans, lived out days of indolent debauchery. Now these are partitioned off as court rooms where hearings for the hapless take place. The *jeunesse dorée* of the past has been replaced by black-coated lawyers scurrying around, giving short shrift to bewildered petitioners. Occasionally a member appears and there is greater scurrying around to make way for those who are held in dread and fear.

On my wife's insistence, I, Raman, gathered courage to accompany Subhash to the principal bench in Delhi. Gloom pervaded the place. Subhash had filed an application for early hearing at the principal bench. The chief member of the principal bench of the tribunal, who was part of the conspiracy to deny justice to Subhash, snarled at him. 'Who are you to give me ultimatums? Behave yourself or else I shall slap a contempt case on you!'

'On what grounds will you slap a contempt notice on me?' Subhash asked loudly. Anger gaining upper hand he said, 'This high-handedness has impelled the celebrated Chief Justice Rama Jois to petition the supreme court to abolish tribunals, saying that these had become the den of corrupt favourites of the government.'

There was stunned silence in the crowded court.

Subhash continued, 'The new regime has initiated moves to dismantle the tribunals where justice is denied by delay. You are all trying to deny me justice by delay. You all know that a former prime minister's officers have done something illegal. Yet you are shielding the guilty. Is this why these tribunals were established? Unless I get a hearing in a month I will go to the supreme court and present to them the chronicle of events of how instead of six months stipulated for disposal of a petition, it is two years since I filed my petition. It is a year since my case was heard in entirety. Instead of passing orders the worshipful kangaroos in Sandalore illegally transferred the case to the principal bench. I will make all this public shortly and then let me see what the worshipful kangaroos do!'

There was another shocked silence in the little court. Faced with a man who seemed determined to do his worst, the chief kangaroo finally decided to allot Subhash's case to a court where both the denizens were regarded as 'docile'.

In other words they could be 'made to see reason'.

I accompanied Subhash again. He went wearily up the curved staircase and stood before the allotted court. He recited the great poet Dante: *Lasciate ogni speranza voi ch'entrate* – abandon all hope you who enter here. Shall I abandon hope?' Subhash asked.

'No, we are almost there,' I said, unconvinced. 'This is the time to gather hope.'

Subhash was somewhat reassured when he saw the two figures sitting on the dais. Against all odds, the two members had maintained their homo sapien character despite the blandishment of kangaroo-hood.

The judicial and administrative members had heard of Subhash – of his candour, courage, his unswerving integrity that inevitably embroiled him in battles with law breakers. They had expected to see what he was called by his detractors – a maverick, a misfit and any other name necessary to snuff out a determined spirit. What they saw was a man of pride and dignity.

When destiny takes a hand improbable things start happening. A celebrated lawyer of the Supreme Court of India, Ram Jethmalani, who had heard of Subhash's battles and who was now a member of the Union cabinet, requested another brilliant lawyer friend to argue Subhash's case at the central tribunal.

Arun Jaitley was indignant when his guru first made the request. 'I don't argue before tribunals!' he had retorted. 'You know that!'

Mr Jethmalani smiled and coaxed him. 'But *you are* going to argue before the tribunal, my son, because I request this of you. No, I entreat you to do this – as an act of dharma.'

The younger lawyer had reservations about the matter. Ram had a habit of foisting difficult cases on him. Arun had seen many seedy bureaucrats who did not always abide by dharma. When Subhash went to meet Arun, he was brusque and made his scepticism clear. With a sinking heart Subhash left the brief he had prepared on Arun's table.

Three days later the brilliant supreme court lawyer telephoned Subhash and said, 'We have to discuss your case. I hear the tribunal has fixed a date.'

'So you are taking my case?' Subhash asked gravely.

'It looks as if I have no choice,' Arun said dryly. 'As our mutual friend Ram said, it is going to be a battle for dharma.'

A few weeks later the battle began in earnest at the assigned tribunal court where the two sombre-faced members sat on the dais. Judge Bhatt, the judicial member, was grey haired, sharp featured and wore spectacles. He asked a few questions, listened intently and made notes as the advocates spoke. His stern countenance and inscrutable eyes revealed little. As judge of a state high court his experience was wide. Mr Biswas, the administrative member, had served in several central ministries. He too asked questions, and made notes as the advocates argued. They went through the cause list in a business-like manner.

The light of the winter day was fading as Subhash waited tensely for Arun Jaitley to arrive in the court hall for the afternoon hearing. He appeared shortly, in elegant legal attire, accompanied by two junior colleagues, who brought a few law volumes in a bag.

Everyone in the tribunal court hall looked at the supreme court lawyer. He was one of the young luminaries of the party whose government was in power. The bush telegraph of the court corridors spread the message of his presence and the tribunal court hall filled up, even though Subhash's case was the last on the list. Arun sat next to Subhash.

The two judges gave Subhash a swift glance of concern; they wondered how Subhash's lawyers would ever contend with such a formidable opponent. The judicial member leaned forward to ask the supreme court advocate, 'I take it you, Mr Jaitley, are appearing for the Union government?'

'No, your honour,' Arun Jaitley replied quietly, 'I am appearing for the applicant, Subhash Chowdhury.'

Both the judges were surprised. Was this brilliant lawyer, a leading member of the ruling party, going to argue against the government? After moments of throbbing stillness, the judicial member said, 'Please proceed, Mr Jaitley.'

As Arun Jaitley opened the leather folder before him, a commotion erupted. The standing counsel for the Union government stared in terror at Arun Jaitley. 'Your lordships,' he began in a choked voice, 'I was not aware that the applicant had appointed a senior advocate … he never told me this … I seek some more time.'

Despite the terrible tension of the moment Subhash burst into laughter when he saw the respondents' standing counsel slumped over a chair, ashen faced, eyes bulging out. Could this be the man who had sneered at him that morning and predicted certain defeat?

'You will speak when your turn comes,' the judicial member rebuked the respondents' counsel.

Then looking at Arun, he said, 'The learned counsel for the applicant may commence his arguments.'

Arun Jaitley rose, his head bent for a brief moment, as if marshalling his arguments. Or did he say a brief prayer for Subhash's salvation? Then he raised his head and began to speak. The court hall fell into a deep silence. Arun Jaitley had never before argued in the administrative tribunal. His presence seemed to elevate the status of the tribunal.

Arun mentioned the facts of the case, of how the petitioner, an IAS officer, had been selected and recommended by the duly authorized Special Committee of Secretaries. They had scrutinized Subhash's entire service records which praised his impeccable integrity and his achievements in the thirty years of his service with the Union and state governments. They had seen the five consecutive confidential reports, all graded *Outstanding*, by different superiors, which are the relevant confidential reports in the run-up to empanelment. These reports had described his integrity, ability, achievements, qualities of leadership, and his unswerving loyalty to his country. According to the Central Staffing Scheme these are the qualities required for empanelment to the highest position in the bureaucracy.

The court hall filled up with advocates from other court halls who had dropped in to hear Arun Jaitley speak. The benches on the left side were occupied by people who were neither advocates nor petitioners. They were the anxious and uneasy emissaries of the respondents. They had much to fear from the disclosures and by the fact that the formidable Arun Jaitley was arguing for Subhash.

Arun Jaitley continued. 'The home minister, who is one of the two members of the Appointments Committee of the Cabinet, gave his unqualified approval to the panel prepared by the Special Committee of Secretaries, which contained Subhash Chowdhury's name.' Then he paused, a long pause, and drew in a deep breath. 'And then what happened? The panel was sent to the prime minister who is the other member of the Appointments Committee of the Cabinet. The panel was approved except the name of Subhash Chowdhury.' Arun paused and looked grimly around the tribunal hall.

'It appears that the note from the PMO was written by the joint secretary Nishi Sting, without the knowledge of the prime minister.'

The judicial member and administrative member exchanged shocked glances. The onlookers exclaimed astonishment.

Arun Jaitley then swung into the main thrust of his argument. 'The decision-making process at the level of the honourable prime minister has been vitiated. Such a decision is not only unfair and arbitrary but appears to have been based on extraneous considerations.'

The stillness of the court hall was now broken by exclamations and murmurs. The judges and Arun Jaitley waited for the ripple of noises to subside. With logic and clarity, and exhaustive citations of constitutional law, Arun Jaitley proceeded to tear into irretrievable shreds the ludicrous arguments and rejoinders proffered by the cabinet secretary and other respondents. Arun Jaitley cited the supreme court judgments where it was laid down that it was *incumbent upon the ACC to state the reasons why the applicant's name was rejected.*

Arun Jaitley placed the papers before him and looked at the judges. He said, 'Let me submit a point to your lordships. If the prime minister did indeed have reasons to disagree with the unanimous recommendations of the cabinet secretary, the Union home secretary, the Union personnel secretary, his own principal secretary, and the approval of his senior-most cabinet colleague, the home minister, then the reasons must be known only to him and must be of a serious and secret nature. These are not reflected in the applicant's service records, or in the confidential reports in the run-up to empanelment in which he has been graded as *Outstanding*. Let us speculate what could be the other considerations for non-approval by the prime minister. A foreign bank account where large sums of money have been kept? Secret activities as the agent of a foreign government? Unbecoming conduct of any other type, alcoholism, drug addiction, incriminating correspondence, illicit relationships?'

Arun Jaitley did not speak for a few moments. 'Even now, your honours, let the learned senior counsel for the government inform us what were the grave drawbacks in the petitioner which made the prime minister or his officers decide against Subhash Chowdhury. If the reasons are valid, even now, I will ask Mr Chowdhury to withdraw his petition before this court and pay for the costs to the Union government.'

There was a deafening stillness in the courtroom.

Arun Jaitley continued, 'In that case, your honours, we have to accept the ruling of the Supreme Court of India which supports Subhash's fundamental contention, that *no authority, not even the prime minister – has the privilege to act in an arbitrary, unjust and capricious manner.*'

Spectators and participants sat motionless and silent. Never in the administrative tribunals had the arbitrary act of a prime minister been challenged.

Arun bowed slightly. 'I thank your lordships. My argument rests.'

He glanced at Subhash who murmured 'thank you' in a choked voice.

All eyes were on the judicial member and administrative member as they exchanged a few words. Then the judicial member spoke.

'We have a question to ask the learned senior counsel for the petitioner.'

Arun Jaitley stood up.

The judicial member spoke grimly. 'We have heard in these last few days the arguments on behalf of both the petitioner and the respondents. The learned counsel for the petitioner has informed us how the petitioner has been selected by the Special Committee of Secretaries. Have you any idea, Mr Jaitley, why the then prime minister did this?'

Arun Jaitley glanced briefly at Subhash. Intuition had impelled Arun to ask Subhash the same question on their first meeting. Grim-faced, he looked at the judges and said, 'Perhaps, your honours, the applicant was asked by the prime minister's secretary and joint secretary to do something highly irregular in the course of his duties. Perhaps he refused. Perhaps he believes in upholding rules and regulations.' Arun paused and added, 'Perhaps he believes in a moral order.'

There was a deep hush in the courtroom.

Tears came unbidden to Subhash's eyes, tears held back so long through harassment and humiliation, through anguish and anger.

The two judges were silent for long moments. Then they rose. The court clerk announced: 'Reserved for orders.'

Glittering sunlight glanced off trees and danced among the leaves in the compound of the court building. Arun, his junior colleagues, Subhash and I, Raman, walked together in silence until we came to the place where our cars were parked. Subhash thanked Arun Jaitley profusely and told him that the terrible tension of the court proceedings was worthwhile because he could see and hear him speak. 'It was an experience in itself – hearing you.'

Arun smiled now, a happy boyish smile. 'That's all right.'

'My wife and I would like to call on you after you return from tour.'

'Please do,' Arun said pleasantly.

Several days later Subhash and Radha went to meet Arun Jaitley at his well-appointed office where a dozen young lawyers were working. Arun escorted them to his consulting room. They thanked Arun effusively for his concentrated attention to his case and for his formidable arguments before the tribunal, for doing everything with grace and courtesy, for combining brilliance of mind with warm humanity.

'That's all right,' Arun said with his boyish smile. 'All for a good cause.'

It was awkward but Subhash took a deep breath and said, 'We have come to give your fees.'

Arun Jaitley shook his head. 'There is no fee,' he said quietly. 'I did what I did because of Ram Jethmalani. He is my guru and a dear friend. He wanted you to be represented properly.'

Subhash could barely speak from emotion. 'We know you took up my case because of Mr Jethmalani but *we owe* you a great deal. You have done something very important for us.'

Arun looked pensively at them. 'We lawyers do not always get a chance to fight for a moral cause. You have shown courage and honesty. If all civil servants had your integrity and courage this country would be different. I am glad to assist the cause of justice. I wish you all the best in your career.'

Finally Subhash went to see the incandescent, courageous and generous Ram Jethmalani. He was sitting in his garden surrounded by sunlight, winter flowers, and many visitors. Subhash sat with them, looking at the garden in bloom until the visitors left. Ram Jethmalani was eager and anxious to know all about the hearings at the tribunal. 'Arun has told me over the phone all that has transpired,' he said.

'Mr Jaitley said that he did it for you. That he owed it to you.' Subhash paused before saying, 'I am deeply grateful to you, Sir. I will never be able to return your kindness.'

'Subhash,' Ram Jethmalani said quietly, 'between friends there are no "debts", no "owing" and no "gratitude". We wanted to help you because we saw a grave miscarriage of justice.' He smiled and his grey eyes twinkled. 'Good lawyers fight for just causes. Bad lawyers fight for money.'

'I have seen both types,' Subhash said.

'For those of us who are in a position of power,' Ram Jethmalani said gravely, 'we have a responsibility to ensure that the bureaucracy is strengthened by excellent civil servants and not the dubious ones who get power and position through manipulation and immorality.'

Ram Jethmalani accompanied Subhash to the arched gate which separated the garden from the courtyard where many cars were parked and where a fresh cluster of visitors, powerful and famous, humble and anxious, waited to see the great lawyer.

'Do you think I will win, Sir?' Subhash asked.

The great jurist looked up at the cerulean sky. 'Pray to Him,' he said quietly. 'I am sure He will answer your prayers. Justice will in the end prevail.'

Two months later the two judges of the administrative tribunal of Delhi delivered a thirty-five-page landmark judgment in Subhash's favour, indicting the Union government for failing to give him appointment as secretary, for arbitrariness, for selecting secretaries on whims and fancies. No officer had ever won a case in court challenging the arbitrariness of the then prime minister and his officers. Subhash had done just that.

The divine right of the prime minister and his officers to do wrong had been declared illegal.

Does Justice in the end prevail?

Sic Transit Gloria Mundi – So Passes the Glory of the World

I, Raman, never imagined that such a terrible day would finally come; the day of retirement.

When we are born, we never imagine that we will die. We push that knowledge beyond our conscious being. But death comes nevertheless. So, when we enter the heaven-born administrative service (or any service for that matter) we never imagine that we will retire one day. Retirement, like death and disaster, we deceive ourselves, happens to other people.

To most people retirement from government service is a sort of death. On that day we realize that all men are born equal and die equal but in between some are raised to power and glory. The road to power is not always through achievements; it can come through manipulations and intrigues. Sometimes it requires closing ears and eyes to what is happening around one and forging ahead with one's own plans and ambitions. Acquisition of power sometimes requires renunciation of moral codes. A seeker of power may have to betray friends, ideals and principles hitherto held with fervour and passion.

And glory? What are the constituents of this phenomenon? Does it lie in great achievements? Does it lie in courage? Or in fame wrested through extraordinary deeds?

On the morning after retirement we are faced with an aching emptiness. The spacious government house fronted by manicured lawns and encircled by barbed wire fencing has ceased to be home. The retired officer has a limited time to find alternate dwelling place. The servitors in the servant quarters have already begun investigating which senior officer will claim the C-I or AB bungalow so that they can ingratiate themselves with the new exalted tenant and stay on in the SQ or servants' quarters. Since occupation of the servant's quarter is no longer dependent on the benevolence of the current madam-ji, they become insouciant and impertinent. They refuse to answer summons and neglect their tasks. Since we are on notice to leave the exalted government bungalow, we cannot give notice to others.

The official car has been withdrawn instantly. The official car-driver who appeared promptly at eight thirty in the morning regardless of winter blizzards or summer blasts is absent. There is no one to take madam-ji shopping or gallivanting or for lugging heavy bags after purchasing sprees. There is no one to fetch the '*baba-loks*' (youngsters) from their places of education or (more likely) entertainment. There is no one to chauffeur one to a party or evening outing. After many decades one must learn to negotiate through urban traffic and watch the speedy depletion of the fuel gauge which no one ever had cause to notice before. One cannot afford to imbibe excessive alcohol on these outings because a cop may pull one up for a debasing inhaler test or one may simply crash into another car or run over a stupid pedestrian. There is no possibility whatsoever of hushing up the manslaughter with a peremptory call to the assistant commissioner of police. In any case opportunities of imbibing excessive alcohol are few since free alcohol is not on offer from favour-seekers. The wine bearers have taken their favours and vanished from one's universe.

To add insult to injury the former obsequious personal assistant sends cheeky reminders of amounts to be paid for 'non-official use of government vehicles by madam-ji'. Then come the bank statements indicating the pension, a truncated amount of the substantial salary once automatically credited to the bank. This is followed by a frantic exercise in calculating the amount that has to be made over to the income tax authorities. Earlier the income tax would be automatically deducted by the government after the personal assistant and an accounts clerk have found loopholes to pay less.

Junior colleagues who fawned over you, showered you with compliments on your brilliant noting and your dynamism, now smirk and give you the wounding cursory nod when they encounter you. They do not even wait for your falsely genial response. There was a time when they stood by your portals on cold Diwali evenings laden with baskets of goodies, with an expensive piece of jewellery for your 'lady wife' (as if a wife can be a gentleman!) tucked in the midst of dried fruits and a bottle of Glenfiddich or Moet champagne. This was to facilitate you to record an *Outstanding* graded Annual Confidential Report (ACR). And when the all-important empanelment process for joint secretary, additional secretary, and secretary began in April, these same officers would be braving fierce dusty winds to 'pay our respects' with substantial inducements to receive your goodwill. Now those juniors risen to high ranks look through you because you have become what a distinguished bureaucrat once humorously called 'a recycled cadaver'.

Worse is to follow. The progeny who flaunted your name and position for their advancement look upon with youthful derision. They have learnt terms that you once used for official seniors when they retired. They secretly call you 'a has been'. Since expenditure on filial profligacy has now to be curtailed, they cease to show you respect.

The wife who smarmed over you, and assured you of your genius in anticipation of costly clothes, jewels and accompaniment on free foreign trips has begun to display the impertinence that the servants' quarters occupants have displayed to her. The husband is no longer the centre of her universe. In fact, he has begun to be a bit of an albatross around her neck - especially if she still is in possession of carnal allurements. The wife who waited eagerly for your return home from office (especially if a five-star hotel party was in the offing), now complains that you are in the way. She suggests that you get yourself another job. If you have managed a post-retirement assignment, she continues to be obliging, though not with the same ardour as before. But if you are unemployed, woe be to you. She will recite the names of officers who were smart enough to be re-employed. She does not beautify herself at bedtime to entice you because a man stripped of power is not attractive - unlike a woman who stripped of virtue becomes more attractive. Once the recipient of conjugal ardour you are now treated like a supplicant.

Finally, the question has to be asked - what have I achieved through this bureaucratic journey? Are these worthwhile achievements not enough: prestige of office while it lasted, comfortable life, security of tenure, benefits and perquisites, illicit wealth for those daring enough to acquire it?

That is the moment of Truth. The ineluctable truth from which there is no escape. When Truth came to demand our explanation for violation of the moral order, we banished Truth.

It seems as if all things eventually fade into the past and become shrouded in oblivion. And yet during the days of our glory it was so important to be acknowledged, praised and pursued by rich and poor, the humble and the exalted. We remember them but they have consigned our images to the morgue. We have ceased to matter to them. How fickle was the homage of these favour-seekers! How hollow seems the sounds of applause! What does it matter since they have all vanished? What does anything matter?

We, the retired, are as good as dead, with no hope or promise for immortality.

Wounded Dreams

I, Subhash Chowdhury, must complete the chronicle that Raman and his father Elangovan began – because Raman has lost his mind through boredom.

Delhi is the city of imperial phantoms. I remember that day when we young men and women newly recruited to the administrative service stood before the grand edifices with empty pockets and dream-filled eyes. The pockets are now heavy with possessions but the eyes are blurred by wounded dreams. I now stand before the city whose splendour seems elusive.

No, do not fear, no rogue terrorist has nuked our capital whose origins lie in misty antiquity. The grand edifices are still there. But what about their message? Do you remember what was wished for at the commencement of this chronicle? We hoped that this capital would be a new Augustine's *Civitate Dei* or City of God, a new republic that was ancient with anguish. It had begun to take shape like some celestial dream. Humble folk came from remote parts of the vast republic, trudging across dusty highways and unquiet waters to see their *Civitate Dei*, where diverse heroes of a unique revolution had left the imprimatur of their ideals and sacrifices, when unsung heroes had resurrected a dying people and stirred them to stubborn rebellion. This City of God became a curio for the world, product of human fantasy, assembled by the hopes and tears of a people who believed in goodness even when they were being plundered and massacred.

Casting my mind back over half a century, through the first faltering steps our country made to attain freedom, dignity, adequate food and shelter for the millions living in crushing poverty, I feel the burden of remorse. Indians have always revered their rulers even when they were unworthy of that reverence. Myths and legends had invested rulers with a mystical quality that gave them security. Long before Augustine's exhortation to build divine cities reached our shores, a ruler like Rama was regarded as a particle of that divinity, the Avatar, who descends from the heavens to guide and protect the humble.

This reverence has been our undoing; we have never been able to depose our oppressors. Without a cleansing carnage – as happened during the English, the French and the Russian Revolutions – only the branches of the infected tree were lopped off but the poisoned roots went deeper into the soil – and the soul.

Perhaps the veneration for rulers sprang from the fact that India had great dynasties in the past. Chandragupta

Maurya evicted Alexander the Greek from India. While expanding territories the rulers spread the grandeur of Hindu and Buddhist civilization across Asia. The imperial Mauryas, Guptas, Palas, Cholas and Vijaynagaris ushered in efflorescence of art and sculpture. One of the greatest rulers of India, the Moghul Akbar, was an eclectic humanist and visionary. To protect India from religious strife, this descendant of Timur and Gengiz Khan married a Hindu princess whose faith he honoured because it was the faith of Hindustan - the land he loved and ruled. He towered over his contemporaries - Elizabeth of England, Henry IV of France, Tsar Ivan IV, Philip of Spain, and Shah Abbas of Persia. Indian products accounted for one seventh of world trade. In these eras there was no plunder by the state. Tax was collected, merchants paid their rightful dues, and peasants had food security and safety.

When the powerful Moghul Empire disintegrated, invaders from India's north-west frontiers plundered, and then retreated to their homelands with fabulous booty, leaving behind scenes of desolation. The East India Company carried on more systematic plunder. Charles Rawlinson, a renowned British historian, observed that the condition of India in the eighteenth century was 'perhaps the unhappiest in the checkered history of the country'.

In contrast to these white brigands there were great Englishmen dedicated to the welfare of Indians. Thomas Munro, governor of Madras Presidency, believed that the ruler must govern by ethical principles. While personally organizing medical relief for a cholera epidemic, this great humanist caught the contagion and died.

Paradoxically, a renaissance or reawakening of India began in the early days of British rule. What unleashed the forces of Enlightenment was the dedication of brilliant British scholars such as Sir William Jones, Nathaniel Halhed, Charles Wilkins and Henry Colebrooke who studied and translated ancient metaphysical and literary works, codified Hindu and Muslim laws and established the Asiatic Society in Calcutta in 1784. They made Indian civilization known to the world once more.

In the diatribe against British rulers it would be worthwhile to remember the dedicated men who established a system of law amidst the chaos and violence following the disintegration of the Moghul Empire. India is still governed by the Indian Penal Code, Code of Criminal Procedure and the Indian Evidence Act. Inadvertently they brought India into the mainstream of the modern world.

Exposure to the ideas of European Enlightenment stirred Indian minds. Why should India not have the benefits of these ideals? And so the movement for freedom began. The First World War halted the freedom struggle and agitation for self rule led to incidents like the massacre of Jallianwalla Bagh in 1919. Indians began the agitation in right earnest. The Second World War ruined Europe and paved the way for the dismantling of empires – European and Asian. Sovereign nations were born.

Soon after joining the administrative service we probationers were taken on a grand tour of India called Bharat Darshan so that we could glimpse the places and people whom we were expected to administer with wisdom and compassion. After retiring from the exalted service I, Subhash Chowdhury, embarked on another such journey to re-discover the wellspring of my identity and ideals. People who are ignorant of their culture are like trees without roots. They wither.

My travels took me to the source of the sacred river Ganga at Rudraprayag where the glacial stream rushes down mountains and on to dusty plains to moisten the earth which yields food. The roaring water, the formidable hills, the azure skies, the tinkle of temple bells and chanting of *Om Namah Shiva* do indeed evoke awe and veneration for the Creator. I was inspired; I also realized my insignificance before the universe.

From the snow-covered hills I went to Sarnath where Lord Buddha gave sermons on the Eight-fold Path of Righteousness. I was awakened at dawn by the chanting of prayers by pilgrims who had come from far lands to find solace in Him, to carry the message of peace to their once-strife-torn lands. We Indians pay homage to India's greatest son, Gautam Buddha, a prince who forsook love, power and glory in search of Truth but do we follow his example of austerity and compassion?

My journey ends in my home state which a century ago became the centre of both rebellion and resurgence. Near a dusty town in Bengal, the greatest Indian of our age, Rabindranath Tagore, built Visva-Bharati or world-university. Here the great poet of India nurtured dreams of a resurgent India, where poverty, ignorance, oppression and injustice would be removed, where his compatriots would be led by heroic men. Wistfully he wrote,

> 'Thy seat is empty today,
> Oh brave one, assume thy place.'

We wait for that hero.
We wait for that great dream to be realized.

Acknowledgements

Many people have contributed to this book.

After spending an idyllic youth in Washington, New York, Rome and London, I came to India to join the IAS. The transition was not easy. Between horse-riding accident, near fatal jaundice, and snoopy seniors in an alien world, I often felt like escaping to my alma mater University College, London.

Living in faraway Rome, my parents Leela and Moni Moulik told me to accept these misadventures and to record the profiles of people, sights and sounds of my new world. That was perhaps when this book began.

I shared these episodes with my sister Aloka, who had a flair for literary criticism and gave sage advice on these stories.

My husband Mohan read the first draft and gave his valuable editorial comments and deleted passages having potentials for undue controversy.

I express my gratitude to my publisher friends - the late C.M. Chawla of UBS Publishers and Distributors and Ashok Chopra of Hay House - who encouraged me in this enterprise, and to Nirmal Kanti Bhattacharjee who readily accepted the script.

I thank the colleague-friends who shared their experiences with me and those colleagues who unwittingly provided grist to the mill.